STUART (
writes occasionally
the door by dabbling in business ventures,
the latest of which is providing material for
a new book.

He divides his time between Gibraltar
and Devon.

Stuart Chesterfield

LAST HIT

The Thriller Club
T.002

Aspire Publishing

An Aspire Publication

First published in Great Britain 1998

Copyright © Stuart Chesterfield 1998

The right of Stuart Chesterfield to be identified as author of this work has been asserted by him in accordance with Sections 77 and 78 of the Copyright, Designs and Patents Act 1988.

All rights reserved.
No part of this publication may be reproduced, stored in a retrieval system, or transmitted in any form or by any means without the prior permission in writing of the publisher, nor be otherwise circulated in any form of binding or cover than that in which it is published and without a similar condition, including this condition, being imposed on the subsequent purchaser.

ISBN 1 902035 05 4

Printed and bound in Great Britain by
Mackays of Chatham Plc, Chatham, Kent.

Typeset in Palatino by Kestrel Data, Exeter, Devon.

Aspire Publishing – a division of XcentreX Ltd.

This publication is a work of fiction. All characters therein are fictitious and any resemblance to real persons, living or dead, is wholly coincidental.

RE-BIRTH

Chapter One

The warbling noise dredged me from a too-deep afternoon nap. Disorientated, my defensive instincts swinging into action, I rolled off the bed and plunged a hand into the holdall, groping for a gun that wasn't there.

Then the bubble of panic popped and the walls of the bland hotel room snapped into focus. With a sheepish headshake I reached for the chirping, flashing telephone in the bedside table.

'Yes?' I had stipulated no calls, so was mildly put out.

'Sorry to trouble you, sir. There is an urgent call for you.' No chance to protest. The line made the usual electronic noises and the now-familiar, tight lipped tones of my current employer hit my ear.

'Townsend?' My psuedonym. Thank God he'd remembered.

I grunted an affirmative.

'You have collected the . . . package?' The French accent was pronounced, overlaid with tension.

'Yes.' The bulky envelope containing $50,000 American in used, large denomination bills reposed in my Swiss numbered account. Safest place on this planet, bar none.

'Tomorrow then? As agreed?'

He seemed reluctant to break the connection.

'Okay?' I said. 'That's all, Mr Dauphin?'

'Well . . . yes.' He still wasn't sure. A natural born worrier. 'Just . . . well . . . good luck.'

Luck? He had to be joking.

'So long, Mr Dauphin.' I put the phone down on his protesting squawk. As an afterthought, I unhooked it again, placing the receiver on the table.

I stared up at the ceiling and reviewed the arrangements for tomorrow. It was going to be a tricky one. Not the trickiest I'd ever tackled, but high on the list. For a start the subject's mistress would be there. Messy. It meant an unnecessary disposal. Professional anathema. *Personal* anathema: it transgressed a private code of conduct. In this instance though, the location – their secret love nest – was so made-to-measure for my purpose, and alternatives at such a premium, that I quashed my reservations and whipped my scruples into line. Planning a hit was all very well; it was the part I enjoyed most. The actual execution was entirely a different matter – villains though my victims invariably were. The prospect of killing an innocent party out of mere expediency was stretching me out on a rack of morality.

Another, lesser, worry was the identity of the mistress: wife of a prominent West German politician and businessman. The stink would make a Paris *pissoir* seem sweet-smelling by comparison. With luck . . . I stopped the thought in mid-formation. Luck was out . . . remember?

Then there was the escape route: a long, twisting track with no turn-offs, to get back to the Bundestrasse. A good three minutes in which to meet another vehicle. The risk was slight, but I'd lived to the ripe middle-age of thirty-eight years, two months, three weeks and something, by keeping risks to an irreducible minimum.

I was thoroughly awake now, so I got off the bed. Outside it was grey, damp and dismal. November in Bavaria. It didn't ring of sunshine and flowers; rather of saturnine skies, of incessant rain varying only in its intensity, and of mist that hung motionless in cobwebs. Which is exactly how it had been ever since I arrived in Oberpframmern, on the outskirts of Munich, two days ago.

From the window of my functional, plastic-veneered cubicle of a hotel room, I looked out over the Höhenkirchen Forest – Forest of High Churches – all ups and downs, every slope with its black stubble of conifers. Here and there a farm. And on the other side of those hills, all unsuspecting, a man with twenty-six hours and thirty minutes left to live.

I met Günther at the Olympic Stadium. On the observation platform of the Olympiatürm from where you can see clear across to the Bavarian Alps. In the opposite direction, looking down, you have a bomber pilot's view of the Bayerische Motorenwerke plant, dominated by a twenty-storey clover-leaf building and next to it a cup-shaped edifice topped by an enormous black white and blue BMW motif.

It was wet and windy up there, and consequently deserted. Which suited me, as the business I was about to transact was not for public viewing.

Günther was ill at ease, which was unlike him. We shook hands routinely. His was sweaty.

'*Grüss Gott*, Günther.' Statutory Bavarian greeting.

He bobbed his head like a nervous hen. He was a small, slim man with thick black hair. Very un-master race. His coat was beautifully tailored, pure wool for sure, with an expanse of astrakhan collar.

'How are things with you?' I said, the same as I always did.

'Okay.' He was still twitchy, avoiding my eyes. Something was up all right.

'Got the merchandise?'

'*Ja* . . . yes . . . but there is a . . . difficulty.'

'Uh-huh.' I wasn't uptight. Yet. The ball was in his court. When he got around to patting it over the net, I would decide how to pat it back. Slow and easy, or a forehand smash with all my weight behind it.

'It is not the model you request. The short barrel model was not available. I have only the long barrel model for you obtained.'

I leaned on the parapet and gazed out over the rooftops of Munich, ancient seat of the Kings of Bavaria. Apart from the twin domed towers of the 15th-century Frauenkirche, hemmed in by the spires of lesser churches, it was not inspiring. Too many blocks and cubes deforming the skyline, effacing the city's character. The rain didn't do a lot for it either.

I was still calm, marginally able to keep my hands off him.

'Okay,' I said. I even grinned disarmingly, to put him at ease and dry the sweat on his brow. 'If that's the way it has to be. I can live with it, just this once. Don't let it happen again – all right?'

If my plans jelled as they should, I wouldn't need his services again, but he wasn't to know that.

'Here in Germany, it is very difficult for the arms business. There are many new laws, new controls. Since the East came back to us we have much more crime. It makes business difficult for all of us.' He looked dejected. I almost offered him my handkerchief. 'Prices increase every day.'

A-ha. Here comes the punch line, I thought.

'You know how much I must charge for this one – yours?'

'No, but I guess you're going to tell me.' My voice was dry.

He leaned towards me, rocking on his heels. *'Drei tausend drei hundert mark.'*

I whistled. That was expensive, all right.

'Hey, Günther, you can't kid me. Inflation in Germany was only two per cent last year. And here you are trying to stick me with a price hike of fifty.'

'Inflation, schminflation.' He dismissed the retail price index with a flicking of his fingers. 'This has nothing to do with inflation, I tell you. It is the importers – they are putting on the big squeeze.' He drew the last word out, dramatising it. I noticed he had lost his nervousness. Maybe I had let him off too lightly. I decided to let my displeasure show, otherwise the word might get around that Jack Henley was a sucker for a hard-luck story.

I crowded him back against the parapet. From there the outlook was straight down the windowless side of the tower.

'Listen to me, my good wurst-eating friend,' I said gently. 'When I order a gun from you I expect to get what I order, at the agreed price. I do not expect an extra couple of inches of barrel, nor do I expect to be ripped off. Do I make myself clear?'

'Ja, ja.' His head jiggled like a marionette's. 'I have done my best. I always do my best.' He breathed, schnapps fumes over me.

An elderly couple meandered past, sliding curious glances in our direction, he in Tyrolean feathered hat, she in blue mink with a matching rinse. I stepped away from Günther, patted him lightly on the cheek. He tried for a grin but it didn't come off.

'The merchandise,' I said.

'Ja.' His face was the colour of putty, and shiny with sweat. He edged a furtive hand inside his coat and drew out a rectangular package measuring about nine inches by six inches, wrapped in multi-hued gift paper. This was standard camouflage.

It just fitted the pocket of my quilted waterproof, projecting a couple of inches over the top. The two unwanted inches of barrel, so generously supplied by Günther. To be truthful, from the technical aspect, it mattered hardly at all that the gun was that big longer; it made it somewhat more awkward to handle and in an emergency it might slow me down a fraction. I could live with these handicaps. The increased range and accuracy that go with a longer barrel were not, sadly, attributes I could capitalise on, since this particular contract called for point-blank work. What really riled me about the substitution was the principle and its portents. I depended on the likes of Günther for the tools of my trade – not only firearms, but false papers, transport, inside information. The underworld bush telegraph travels fast; let just one of the clan short-change you, and the rest would think it was open season on Jack Henley. It was, I decided, lucky for him that this was to be my last hit.

'Don't forget what I told you,' I said, spacing my words so there should be no misunderstanding. 'Any more cock-ups like today and it's *your* scalp I'll be after.'

'Scalp? I don't . . . '

'Head,' I said shortly, and he understood then.

Again the jittery nod. 'It will not happen again, Mr Henley.'

'So, how much do I owe you, Günther?'

As usual he put on a deprecating air, as if the

subject of money was distasteful to him.

'Already you have paid one thousand marks. Normally I would only five hundred more ask, but as I explain, it is two thousand two hundred for the gun, plus the ammunition and my services. Altogether . . .' He pretended to do a complicated mental calculation, but it was all show. He would know the total to the exact pfennig. Rounded up, of course. 'You must pay two thousand nine hundred and twenty-two marks.'

No wonder he swallowed hard as he said it.

'Balls. That's nearly a thousand more than I paid in January. Don't expect me to subsidise your expensive tastes.' I rubbed the astrakhan collar between finger and thumb. 'Your fancy clothes and your new Merc – yes, I saw you trying to park it out of sight.'

'Mr Henley.' He drew himself up, but since there wasn't much of him to draw, he still had to bend his neck to look me in the eye. 'I have always been correct with you. My profit on this job is very small . . .'

'Bullshit!' I opened my wallet, drew out an envelope containing ten one-hundred mark notes, handed it to him. 'There's another thousand. That's all you get, Günther, and this . . .' I broke off, glancing around to make sure we were alone.

He had been peering inside the envelope; now he looked up.

'*Ja?*'

I socked him hard as I could in the guts. Just the one punch, but for him, doll-sized except for his paunch, it was more than enough. He jack-knifed at the waist and knees, coughing and retching over my shoes.

I crouched beside him, my mouth to his ear, which was also doll-sized. He was still clutching the envelope, venal instincts unimpaired.

'Don't ever try to sucker me again, Günther, because it makes me mad.'

I left him on his knees, head bowed, gurgling and gasping, and rode the free-falling lift down with only the attendant for company.

The light was fading when I pulled the VW Golf – that most ubiquitous and therefore unremarkable form of transportation – off the Bundestrasse into the secondary road that ran down into the village of Güntering.

The rain had eased off. It was now a fine but persistent drizzle through which ragged clouds could be seen clinging to the hillsides in dirty-looking clumps, like grey candyfloss. A Porsche swished past, throwing arcs of spray from its ultra-wide wheels. I held my 50 kph. Confrontation with the police, notorious in Germany for enforcement of urban speed limits, was to be avoided. Today I was a model motorist.

The radio was on. A female singer was belting out a rendering of the old Dietrich number. 'Falling in Love Again.' In German, naturally. I sang along with her, in English, naturally. I was as cool and relaxed as any nine-to-five commuter on his way to work. Cooler. No rush hour traffic to contend with.

I was through Güntering, the houses and other buildings just . . . houses and buildings. Likewise the next hamlet, Wasach. From there it was open road, country lane, rather. No other vehicles at all.

The turn-off was just ahead. A rough track with a shiny-bright metal signpost: Schloss Thomashoff. Thomashoff Castle indeed! It had amused me yesterday, seeing it for the first time. Admittedly, it occupied an elevated site with views out over a large lake – the Ammersee. Admittedly, too, it was made of stone, a grey granite-like stone, coarse grained; but the resemblance went no further. It was essentially a single-storey building, with a small dormer window in the steeply-angled roof, a porticoed entrance, and a cupola at one corner. Cute. Pretentious. And worth about two million marks on the open market.

The surface of the track had been made treacherous by the rain. Even with front-wheel drive I had to go easy on the accelerator. Between the trees, the light was poor and I flicked the headlights onto full beam, driving a white shaft through the gloom. A pair of yellow eyes sparkled momentarily, fox probably. Then they were gone and I was slithering on, holding the car in third, the trees seeming to press in on me now, looming up in the headlights, then whipping past as if whisked away by a giant hand.

The road was climbing, a succession of increasingly acute bends. Raindrops dripped from the trees making little explosions on the windscreen. I slowed, dropped down into second. I could no more afford an accident than I could a run-in with the law.

The dashboard digital clock showed 15.26 and already night was spreading its mantle across the land. Darkness was fine by me. The best natural protection going. Unless I was using a rifle, and thus remote from my victim, I generally avoided making a hit in daylight. Nosey neighbours and inconvenient passers-by posed much less of a threat after nightfall.

I had other codes of conduct, other axioms, whose observance helped me stay in business. Enabled me to cross borders anywhere in the world without let or hindrance, just as Her Britannic Majesty requests and requires. Not so much as an unpaid parking fine besmirched my name. I was what is known in underworld vernacular as 'clean'.

The Ammersee was coming into sight on my right, a dull gunmetal glint below the cliffs. There was no wind, no eddies or currents, to ruffle its surface.

The car skated on a patch of mud, the front end slewing towards the verge which was only spitting distance from a sheer hundred-foot drop. My grip on the wheel instinctively tightened as I lifted my foot off the accelerator, slowing to a walking pace. At this point, too, I dispensed with the head-lights. A hundred yards or so further on, a broad rectangle of light showed through the trees at ground floor level; above it was a smaller rectangle. The exterior light, mounted above the front entrance, cast a yellow pool over the gravel-covered parking area where usually reposed a Mercedes and a Maserati: hers and his in that order.

I rolled to a standstill short of the house, reversing into a space between the trees and killing the side-lights. It was a spot I had already selected for this role. With its dark green paint-work, the car would be all but invisible from the track. As an extra precaution, however, I draped a drably-coloured ground-sheet, purchased earlier in the day, over windscreen, bonnet, and that indiscreet, reflective number plate, weighting it with a dead branch. Now the car was indistinguishable from its surroundings.

It was a few minutes to four. Here under the trees it was quite, quite dark. The lake was a flat monochrome through the pencil-straight trunks; no moon to reflect, only dark grey clouds, their underbellies sagging with more unshed rain.

I zipped my waterproof jacket up to my chin, pulled the hood over my head. I listened to the irregular tattoo of raindrops on the car; it was the only sound in that cathedral stillness . . . except . . . yes, faintly, from the house, music. So muffled and indistinct I couldn't even piece together a tune. I was still straining my ears when the dormer light was extinguished and the darkness became darker still.

I stood there a while, beginning to get chilled, the dampness climbing my legs and permeating my body. I stamped my feet but the pine needles offered no resistance – it was like stamping on a rice pudding. How the minutes crawled by when you had nothing to do but wait. But wait I must. My arrival had been timed to ensure I was off the road during the evening rush, when the country-dwellers streamed out of Munich to their neat, synthetic, dormitory towns; and when I made my getaway, all but the tail-end workaholics would be tucked up in front of their TV sets. More precautions Henley-style. Every motorist was a potential witness to my presence in the neighbourhood.

None of this prevented me from walking in this very minute and making the hit. Get it done with. It had its attractions, to be sure. Yet to do so would be to compromise other elements of my schedule and this was simply not on. Not this contract, nor any of the thirty-nine that preceded it. The Plan was sacred. The Plan was all. Wasn't I the living proof of it?

The drizzle had petered out, so I strolled across the track to stand on the bare cliff top, gazing out over the lake. The far shore was black and shapeless, only relieved by sprinklings of lights around the towns of Diessen and Utting. In the daytime it was quite a panorama, and explained why Thomashoff had built his 'castle' here.

From the woods behind me came the fast chatter of a bird, a magpie, I guessed. Another joined it and the pair of them carried on in chorus for a while, working up to a crescendo then cutting off so abruptly that the ensuing silence was like an explosion.

At the foot of the cliffs far below, headlights appeared. There was a little-used track by the water's edge, leading to a fishing chalet, a lonely spot. The car slowed, performed a complicated manoeuvre, ending up pointing back down the track. Then the lights were extinguished and all that remained was the spectrum on my retina. A courting couple, most likely. Lucky them. A back seat bunk-up beat slowly freezing to death.

In this deadly boring fashion I whiled away the next two hours. Sauntering aimlessly about, I left plenty of footprints, which would excite the police beyond measure. So much the better; let them go chasing will-o-the-wisps. I had bought the shoes from a market trader in Tehran in the days when Khomenei still ruled. Along with the waterproof and the gun, they would be disposed of when I left. So, too, would the mid-brown hairpiece, the phoney, gingerish moustache, and the grey-flecked-with-brown contact lenses, appurtenances I had already discarded. I had no need to hide my yellow-blond hair and my too-brilliantly blue eyes from the hit and his mistress. They would hardly be making up photo-fit pictures for the police afterwards. Roger Townsend was of the past. Non-existent. Just one of a string of dead false identities. I would leave Germany under my own name.

At half-past six I got ready to move. I pulled on a pair of thin leather driving gloves and loaded six .357 magnum rounds into the Colt Python. I made sure the safety catch was on and stowed the gun away in my side coat pocket. The six inches of barrel made it too long for the pocket but I had poked a hole in the lining to accommodate the barrel, binding insulating tape around the shallow, triangular sight to smooth out the profile and stop it snagging on the material.

My tactics were never the same from one hit to the next. No use going up to the front door and ringing the bell here at Schloss Thomashoff. The hefty door chain was not an ornament and, considering their need for secrecy, I would expect them to use it. Entry, therefore, was to be via the back door, the same as yesterday, when I had carried out my final reconnaissance. The lock was of the mortice variety and I had a skeleton key to fit it. The only complication was the bolt, thick as a man's thumb, at the top of the door. I had neutralized it by sawing three-quarters of the way through, masking the cut with dirt. All it would take to snap it was a gentle nudge on the door.

Silent as a wind-blown snowflake, I crossed the open ground between the wood and the knee-high hedge that bordered the garden. I prowled past the cupola and gave the lighted rectangular window of the sitting-room a wide berth, for the curtains were not drawn. The TV set, a big Grundig in a rosewood cabinet, flickered in a corner of the room. A dark head was visible over the back of an armchair. That would be him; she was blonde. No sign of her. Then the dormer window lit up again: she was back in her natural environment – the bedroom. Getting ready for more erotic games, I bet. The stuff I'd come across up there had startled even me, which is saying a lot. Crotchless knickers and peephole bras galore; leather corsets, thigh boots with spindly heels, dildoes, including the two-pronged kind designed for anal as well as vaginal orifices. When it came to sex I was all for variety and experimentation, and was as close to unshockable as mortal man is likely to get. But photos of her, in glorious colour and glorious close-up, performing certain perfectly natural functions not usually performed in the presence of a camera, were real eye-openers. I had heard the Germans got a kick out of what they term *toiletten-sex* and here was the confirmation. I wondered who took the snaps – husband, lover, or lavatory attendant.

The kitchen was in darkness, which suited me. The door was locked, as expected, and the key had been left in the lock. This is not unusual and I had foreseen it; with the aid of my pencil torch and some long-nosed pliers of a pattern you won't find in any tool shop, that obstacle was soon removed. The key made no sound when it hit the floor, thanks to a bristly doormat.

I was putting torch and pliers away when the kitchen light came on.

Although I had no automatic pre-set responses to the unexpected, I never panicked. Somewhere along the line between start and finish of a contract the odd crisis was bound to occur. Keep cool – that was my only rule.

The light itself didn't cause me any embarrassment. It bathed the lush green lawn in light, picking out the drops of moisture on the grass, but I was flat against the wall and in shadow. My only worry was the key, lying there on the doormat. If spotted, it might arouse suspicion, though more likely it would be assumed it had simply fallen out of the lock.

The person in the kitchen was whistling tunelessly. Cupboard doors were slamming, something fell with a metallic clatter. A muttered '*Merde!*' – it was him, the Frenchman. More doors banged, then a triumphant 'Ah . . . *vous voila.*' Seconds later, the pop of a cork. Footsteps came to the door and I stepped away from the wall, ready to run for cover. The footsteps receded, the light went out.

It was raining again, with renewed vigour. I glowered at the heavens but to no effect. I gave the Frenchman a minute or so to settle down with his bottle of plonk, then leaned my shoulder against the door depressing the handle slowly. My modification of the bolt had not, after all, been necessary; the door opened smoothly and I was inside, in the palatial kitchen, all glossy tiles, stainless steel, and enough mechanical aids to equip a dozen average homes.

The mutter of voices filtered through the open door between the kitchen and the inner hall. Had they got company? I remained motionless, my head cocked towards the doorway. A police siren, brakes squealing, the ripple of gunfire. I remembered the flickering TV screen and grinned to myself.

I had the Colt out now. Hammer cocked, safety off. I moved diagonally across the kitchen and wedged into the corner behind the door.

'*Liebling*?' the Frenchman called, in his accented German. He was in the hall, just a few feet away.

'*Bist du noch nicht fertig*?' His voice was edged with impatience.

'*Ich komme sofort*.' The answer was barely audible. She was still upstairs.

A grunt from him, then silence. Water dripped from my hair, running in rivulets over my face. I didn't dare wipe it away, not with him so close.

Presently, I took a cautious peep around the edge of the door. All clear. I emerged from the kitchen into the carpeted hall. The pile was thick and I waded through it soundlessly, the jabber from the TV removing any need for caution.

The sitting room door stood ajar. I widened the gap with my toe and went in.

The Frenchman – his name was Fabrice Tillou – was back in his armchair, which was sideways on to the door. He didn't see me right away, so, raising my voice above the grating dialogue from the TV, I said, '*Bonsoir*, Monsieur Tillou.'

His self-control was impressive. The glass of white wine that was halfway to his mouth hesitated only momentarily before continuing its journey. He drank, in generous gulps that you could see travelling down his throat, then his head slowly turned towards me.

He was just under thirty years of age according to the dossier I had been given. Handsome; with dark hair, not too long, dark eyes, slightly hooded, and thinnish lips. Well-groomed: dark blue trousers and waistcoat, shirt whiter than white. I knew him to be tallish, an inch over six feet, which was about my own height. He was married, no children.

The sitting room at Schloss Thomashoff was as plush as a millionaire politician's fortune could make it. The cornfield-deep carpet, the furniture all in rosewood to match the TV, the walls panelled in contrasting pale pine with plenty of knots. Not forgetting the hi-fi with its library of CDs you could have played non-stop for a month without hearing the same one twice. Shelves behind the mini-bar sagged under a profusion of designer label booze.

The curtains, tasteful brown velvet, were now drawn, which made one less precaution for me to take.

'*Qui êtes vous?*' Tillou asked finally, reverting to his native tongue. He was still composed, disdainful even.

It's funny how they always want to know who I am. As if it mattered.

'*Aucune importance*,' I snapped. I could speak French too – fluently. I told him, as I had been instructed to, who had sent me.

His control slipped, face darkening, lips twisting in a snarl. 'So . . . he finally declares himself,' he hissed. 'And you . . . you are English? American?'

'English, if it matters.'

He continued to smile, still more angry than afraid. 'Have you come to kill me?'

I just nodded.

'How much is he paying?'

I waved the question away as an irrelevancy. In this business you don't negotiate with your victim.

'He just asked me to wish you a nice stay in Hell.'

He went white. His jaw tightened and his eyes flashed and burned like live coals. In this job you have to learn to recognise warning signs; the twitches and jerks that often presage some rash act. The signals from this guy were about as subtle as a tart's wink.

For me the actual kill, while representing a perverse form of thrill, had always been a psychological fence of Grand National eminence; a hurdle to be run at and cleared before the final, irrevocable taking of life. I was bracing myself for the leap when there came the clack-clack of high heels on wooden stairs. Still cool, still in control, I sidestepped to get clear of the doorway and was backed up against the wall by the time she came in, a whirling flurry of pale flesh and black accessories – a lot of one and a little of the other. The sight startled me into inertia.

Tillou, to whom this vision would be commonplace, was not slow to exploit my divided attentions.

The gun he whipped from inside his waistcoat was a slim automatic (its slimness explaining why I hadn't spotted it) and his actions were smooth and snappy.

Not quite smooth and snappy enough, though.

'*Was machen Sie*!' the woman screamed at both of us, and that was when I shot him. Three slugs as always, squeezed off two-handed and fast, tearing holes in his chest so close together that the blood burst out in a single scarlet geyser and slamming him against the back of the armchair. His dying grip tightened on the automatic and pumped out a single shot – a shot that passed me at arm's length, finding a home instead in his mistress, entering and leaving her throat, travelling on and out through the doorway to be brought to a splintering halt by unseen woodwork. She collapsed without a whimper, and hit the carpet on her back. Twitched once or twice, but otherwise lay still. Blood bubbled around the bullet hole. I had encountered enough gunshot wounds to diagnose the outcome of this one. Without immediate and skilled treatment she was a goner.

Her name was Ingeborg Thomashoff, wife of Erich Thomashoff, chemicals magnate and junior minister in the Christian Democrat Government of the day. She was thirty-four, lots of fluffy blonde hair, tarty make-up, a mouth designed for oral sex – sort of permanently parted in an 'O'. Tall, with a goodish figure, she had notably generous breasts that hung low and swung wide – or they had when she was upright. Her skin was pale, almost white, which made for a dramatic contrast with the black thigh-length boots and black suspender belt. The finishing touch came from what appeared to be a pair of black nipple covers, like miniature shields, extending over the areolae. As I bent over her, I saw that the 'shields' were in fact black lipstick, and that her breasts were completely bare.

She was past my help; past any help, probably. I was glad it hadn't been my doing, that my code and conscience could rest in peace. If merely *planning* to kill her had caused me such heartache, how could I ever have gone through with it, face to face, and with her done up like that? I couldn't, was the short answer. And now I had been spared that moment of truth and self-discovery.

The Frenchman was unquestionably dead. But, perfectionist that I was, I checked him out just the same. He had come to rest, sprawling sideways over the chair arm, eyes still open, mouth agape. No longer a suave and handsome fellow. Just another corpse. Just another dead villain – and a particularly nasty villain at that.

The job was done. Contrast executed. $250,000 of death supplied according to my client's wishes. No evidence to implicate him – he was many hundreds of kilometres away and would have reliable witnesses to testify to it – and no evidence to implicate me. My tracks would be covered as consummately as a sand-storm wipes footprints from the desert.

Tillou's gun lay on the floor beneath his limp hand. I retrieved and inspected it: a Walther PP Super, an updated, up-market version of the original 'Polizei Pistole.' 9-mm calibre, and double-action as expected – he had fired that shot without cocking the slide. The grip plates had been removed to further slim it down; it must have measured less than two centimetres across. I stuck it in my spare pocket. Unlike dead men, guns have a habit of telling tales. Let the police scratch their heads over the different calibres of cartridge they would dig out of body and wall. Let them try and figure out who killed whom and with what. It would all add to the confusion.

Leaving, I had to step over the Thomashoff woman. Her eyes were shut tight, her breathing rapid and shallow. The purple-fringed hole in her throat still leaked blood in little dribbles that meandered down towards her armpit, staining that white, white skin. I shuddered, suppressed an impulse to reach down and touch her, to caress that soft white body. Necrophilia was not for me.

Then it hit me. Nausea, sudden and sapping, a whole tidal wave crashing over me, siphoning off my strength. Gagging, doubled-up, I swayed against the wall; without it I would have been down on the floor with the woman. My breath came in gasps as I fought the revulsion that was wringing out my guts.

I won. That is to say I didn't throw up. The spasm slowly loosened its grip, leaving me clammy and cold. When at last I felt capable of moving again I went at a superannuated shuffle, bent as a fishing-rod with a fat pike on the hook.

Switching off all the lights, I left the way I came. I locked the door, tossed the key into some bushes. Before the bodies were discovered I would be long gone, back home in Geneva, the evening's work no more than a memory among memories.

The rain was still doing its thing, descending in vertical stripes from a uniformly matt black sky. Recovering fast now from my nausea, I made haste back to the car. There I changed my shoes, put the discarded pair together with my waterproof jacket, my gun and the Walther – both guns wiped clean of prints – into a tough polythene bag which already contained several chunks of rock for added weight. The bag was destined for the muddy bottom of the

Starnbergersee, the Ammersee's neighbouring lake.

I tore the indentication pages from my beautifully forged American passport, later to be flushed down the lavatory at Munich airport. The rest of the passport joined the stuff in the bag. I ran a comb through my dripping bedraggled hair, stripped the groundsheet from the car, and drove out of the forest and back down that slimy, slippery track without meeting a soul.

Two hours later, all tools of my trade disposed of, I was sipping champagne and chatting up a suntanned stewardess on a Lufthansa Airbus bound for Paris.

And retirement.

Chapter Two

The evening after returning to Geneva, my home of these past seven years, I dined out on *filets de perche meunière* at Le Bateau, a boat restaurant moored alongside the Promenade du Lac. During the course of the meal, my thoughts went a-wandering of their own volition, down the corridors of the past, back to what I privately referred to as the Marion era.

Marion was my first wife. I was twenty-three when we married, she not quite twenty-one, with a fragile, porcelain prettiness and an IQ that went off the scale. I had just come out of the army and had joined Defence International, the arms trading organization, as a well-paid export sales consultant. She was fresh from Brasenose College, Oxford, with a double first and an inclination to spend a year globetrotting. Which fitted in nicely with my new career. Her family were well-heeled – her father was a QC with a number of lucrative directorships in the City – and were willing to subsidise her so that she could accompany me on my business trips.

We travelled far and wide: Cairo, Jeddah, Tel Aviv, New Delhi, Brasilia; anywhere weapons were in demand. I worked hard, and in between times we played hard. Temperamentally, we were well-matched, Marion and I, and our relationship was a happy and loving one. Until . . .

Even now, after all this time, I can still picture her coming out of the shower in that hotel in Ankara – the Büyük – the droplets of water on her naked body catching the light; towelling her long, fluffy blonde hair, the enormous azure-blue eyes laughing, always laughing . . . Then her mouth writhing with sudden pain, her body hunching, clutching her stomach, crying out, 'Jack, Jack, help me!'

Haemorrhagic Pancreatitis, the doctor pronounced later in his educated English, after consulting a Turkish-English medical dictionary. Death from massive internal bleeding. Too late for surgery. He was visibly upset, taking it almost as hard as me. 'So sorry, Mr Henley . . . so very, very sorry . . .'

And then running, running, anywhere just to get away from there. Running into the night, desolate with the injustice of it, the sheet unbearable agony of it. Collapsing, finally, exhausted, on the south bank of the river and falling asleep there among the beggars and other down-and-outs. I suppose I was lucky not to have had my throat cut while I slept.

Later, back in the UK, I learned that pancreatitis was inflammation of the pancreas brought on by an obstruction. It could have a variety of causes, from alcoholism to pregnancy. In Marion's case pregnancy was the culprit. So in a single throw I had lost wife and progeny.

I got over it, of course, after a fashion. One does. But I lost all heart for my work, in spite of a promotion to Export Area Manager or some such. I dropped out, drifted around, odd-jobbing in Spain and, later, North Africa. Which was where, two days after my twenty-fifth birthday, I met up with Frank Farrar – Canadian, middle-aged, and a hired assassin.

It was one night in early July at the Matmata Bar in

Tunis, typical of the low-grade Arab dives endemic in that city: crumbling, white stucco walls outside and in, except that inside they were now smoke-grimed and stained (some of the stains even overlapped). Flimsy wooden bar with a top polished by a million elbows and bearing the scars of disputes settled with knife or broken bottle. Shoddy furniture: chairs that were prone to disintegrate if sat on, tables that were never wiped but rather scraped clean when the build-up of gunge could no longer be ignored.

Above all, there was Habib, the bartender. The Matmata's *pièce de résistance*. It was rumoured that he slept with a family of goats, a rumour fuelled by the smell that hung about him like a cloud of poison gas.

It was an appropriate setting for me. I was on the fringe of destitution. Funds were at an all-time low. Yet, there I was, living it up like a man with a bottomless bank account, the Matmata version of a whisky sour – which is a lot more sour than whisky – on the table before me. Semi-sloshed. I was often semi-sloshed in those days. When I wasn't totally sloshed, that is.

Farrar was chatting up the club belly dancer at the bar. One of yer actual dusky maidens: sensuous black hair, eyes like deep pools and plastered with eye-liner and other sundry sludge. Narrow waist, buxom hips, and an arse on her that wouldn't have disgraced a hippo.

Then Farrar caught me watching him. He gave a friendly nod, which I reciprocated, and aimed a thumb at the girl, winking lecherously. I rose to the occasion with a correspondingly lewd raised forearm, and he beckoned me over. I was surprised; he was obviously making a play for the girl and my presence would hardly enhance his prospects. But I went over anyway, hoping he was generous enough to stand me a drink. I emptied my glass and took it with me to jog his wallet.

'Hello there,' I said, banging the empty glass ostentatiously on the counter.

'Hi, fella,' he grinned, showing a small fortune in gold-capped molars. The girl looked a bit startled at my impromptu arrival. Her eyebrows wriggled angrily at Farrar.

'It's all right, Morita,' he said soothingly. 'This guy's an old friend of mine, ain'cha . . . er . . .'

'Jack,' I supplied, entering into the spirit of things. 'Henley. How's your wife?'

He roared, slapped me on the back. He was a big man, well over six feet with shoulders to match, and it was like having Nelson's Column fall on you.

'Well, hi, Jack.' He wrung my hand as if he were trying to squeeze pips from it. 'I'm Frank Farrar. Just got in from Vancouver. Via Montreal, via London, via fuck knows where.'

'Canadian?'

'Can't you tell a mile off?' He roared again, tossed the contents of his glass down his throat. 'What'll it be?'

I thought he'd never ask. 'Whisky sour.'

'And I will have champagne,' Morita snapped. She wasn't amused by our pantomime.

'No, you won't, you little vixen, you'll have a beer.' He leered at me. 'Beer makes 'em fart – I like to hear women fart, don't you?' Another bout of hilarity. He was already becoming a bit of a strain.

The drinks came. We drank, Morita finishing ahead of us. She didn't fart, not audibly at any rate. Another round was ordered. And another. And another. Farrar and I got to talking about places we both knew, and there were quite a lot of them. Evidently, he was a much-travelled man. I asked him what he did for a living.

His thin, bony face closed up. He didn't look friendly any more. 'It's kinda . . . confidential,' he said, after a longish hiatus.

Interesting. As much as I found anything interesting these days, outside of the amount of booze left in my glass. I didn't probe. As long as he kept setting up the sours, his credentials were okay by me.

It was about then that Saadoun strolled in with his convoy of hangers-on. Saadoun was the owner of the club and if there was a meaner bastard this side of the South Pole, I hoped I never got to meet him. He was an enormous blimp of a man, perfectly spherical in shape, tapering at top and bottom to a pointed bald dome and a pair of dainty, gleaming shoes, respectively. Around his waist a blood-red cummerbund; above it a white silk shirt and a cream suit that looked as if it had been fed through a mangle. The hangers-on, bees around the honey-pot, were, without exception, undersized, scrawny runts. I never did figure out their precise function. Ego-boosters, probably.

It was singularly unfortunate that Farrar chose that moment to shove a hairy mit down the back of Morita's pants. Saadoun, advancing ponderously upon the bar, took one long, disbelieving look, and let out a squeal of fury, not unlike a whistling kettle. Farrar didn't appear to notice, he was too absorbed in kneading Morita's rear end. Now, I had no idea what proprietary rights Saadoun claimed over Morita; she could even have been his wife or one of them. Anyway, whatever the connection, he clearly was not best pleased by Farrar's familiarity with her person. He came thundering across the tiled floor, flicking aside some reeling drunk who happened to obstruct his path. I moved forward with some vague notion of heading him off before he ploughed into Farrar and pulped him against the bar. I made the mistake of supposing Saadoun was amenable to reason. In fact, I only got as far as opening my mouth, and that earned me a smack in the teeth that almost took my head off.

Up to that point, Farrar had been unaware of the developing drama. My abrupt change of stance – from vertical to horizontal, in company with several chairs, a table, and two customers, alerted him to Saadoun's descending wrath. As I sank to the floor in the debris, he turned, letting go of Morita, to collect a punch in the mush that made mine look like a fond caress.

He went over the bar, whisky glass flying from his hand, and the crash of his landing set the bottles tinkling on the shelves. I heaved aside a thin, hook-nosed cove who had somehow got his foot in my mouth, and went to Farrar's aid. Not by tackling Saadoun – I wasn't *that* tired of living – but just to make sure the poor bugger was still alive. By this time Saadoun had transferred his attention to Morita; the poor kid had fallen to her knees, petrified, and was tugging plaintively at the cummerbund that held that gross belly in check.

Saadoun wasn't having any truck with forgiveness or compassion. Nor was he worried about the wife-beating laws, if there were any. The cuff he dealt her was enough to send her cartwheeling, arms and legs flailing disjointedly, and she screamed as she went. I picked up a chair, shook it at him threateningly; Sir Galahad to the rescue. He looked at me as if I were mad.

As if the odds weren't lousy enough already, the

hangers-on had formed a circle around me and their hands had grown knives: long, thin-bladed *shivs*, designed, so I understand, for penetrating between the rib bones. How the hell did I get into this mess? I asked myself. More to the point – how to get out of it?

The club had emptied. Only Saadoun and his mob, Morita, Farrar, and Sir Galahad remained. The rest had folded their tents and stolen away, as Arabs are wont to do.

Maybe if I explained I was just an innocent bystander. 'Look, Saadoun . . .'

He made a short, sharp jetting sound through clenched teeth, accompanied by a sideways slashing motion with the edge of his hand. This didn't augur well. The hangers-on closed in, knives extended hungrily. Manouevering room was becoming very restricted.

It was Farrar who baled me out. It was the least he could do, since I was in this jam on account of his wenching with Morita. He rose up behind the bar, his right arm dangling uselessly by his side, clearly broken, his left arm bent back, poised to launch a litre bottle of what looked like quality Scotch. I could think of better uses for it but there was no stopping him. The bottle took flight and struck Saadoun on the ear with a velocity that would have killed most men. Saadoun, being Saadoun, just shook his head, emitted a two hundred decibel roar, and, moving faster than I would have believed possible for someone the size of a hot-air balloon, went for Farrar.

Farrar didn't run away. He pulled out a gun.

It wasn't a big gun, as guns go. Having spent several years in the arms business, I was acquainted with most marketable models: his was a Browning GP35 auto, the lightweight Canadian version with the fluted slide, 9-mm Parabellum, 13-round magazine. Thirteen slugs would put a strain on any digestive system – even Saadoun's.

Farrar's action had brought everyone to a standstill, including Saadoun.

'Right, fatboy,' Farrar said. He was grinning now, lips drawn wolfishly back over his rather prominent, gold-capped teeth. 'You wanna play games?'

'Farrar . . .' I began, but he silenced me with a hard glance.

'You've busted my arm, you overgrown pumpkin. Now I'm gonna bust something of yours, so's you won't forget me in a hurry.'

'Farrar . . . no!' I said, my voice shooting up. 'This guy's a big cheese around here. He'll have you boiled in oil or buried alive in the desert or something.'

He stared at me, the gun still locked unwaveringly on Saadoun's great gut. It made a lovely target. 'You keep outa this, you . . . what's your name?'

'Jack. I'm on your side.' There was a groan behind me: Morita was on the mend.

'You would be well-advised to listen to this gentleman,' Saadoun said to Farrar in that deep voice of his that sounded as if it were coming up a mine shaft. 'You will never leave this town alive if any harm comes to me.'

Farrar sniggered nervously. The fixed stare vanished and he nodded jerkily. 'Okay, blimp, you win. But you and your playmates,' his eyes roved meaningly over Saadoun's entourage, 'better keep outa my way. Next time, I won't be so forgiving.'

Saadoun said nothing, but his eyes were twin pebbles of hate.

'Come on, Farrar,' I said urgently. Even with a gun

I didn't rate his chances of holding Saadoun in check for long.

The hangers-on fell back, opening up like the petals of a flower as Farrar and I made our retreat, back to back, him with his gun, me flourishing my chair. His arm hung straight from the shoulder and he kept giving out little grunts of pain.

At the door I unloaded the chair, and we ran down the three semi-circular steps into the street, Farrar supporting his injured arm. He had no transport, but my VW Beetle, a battered, Seville-registered wreck, was not far away. Without ceremony or explanation, I grabbed Farrar and dragged him along the dusty pavement to the corner of the block, where the VW was parked, illegally straddling the kerb. The streets were almost empty of pedestrian traffic, though the old blind beggar was there outside the central post office. He rattled the coins in his tin-can as I fumbled with the door lock. Sorry, chum, not tonight. The state my finances were in, I'd soon be joining him.

Nobody had followed us out of the club. Farrar's gun must have really frightened them. I thumbed the starter button: it took three goes to fire, which was better than average, and the engine ran with a bumbling growl, accompanied by the clatter of worn big ends, worn small ends, and worn every other mechanical part under the sun. Somehow I got into gear – synchromesh was just a distant memory – and we hiccupped away, squeezing into a gap between a finned Dodge pick-up and a Mini containing at least six people. The motorists of Tunis believe in living dangerously.

'Where to?' Farrar asked. His face was tight with pain. The springs of the VW were about twenty years overdue for renewal and they let you know it.

'Hospital. It's only about a kilometre from here.'

'No way, brother. No hospital. No doctors.'

'Why not, for Christ's sake? You've got to get that arm seen to.'

'I just gotta steer clear of hospitals – let's leave it at that.' He turned his head towards me. 'Take me to your place. You have *got* a place, I suppose?'

'Yeah,' I said, a bit sourly. My place was a grubby, greasy room at the Hotel Sidi Mahrez, named after the adjacent mosque. I shared it with itinerant lizards and cockroaches as big as mice. All it had to commend it was the price – three dinars a night. The music and singing from the boozer next door was a bit of a drag if you had notions of sleeping at night, but so what? I would tell myself, lying awake and listening to the raucous chanting and the shrilling of the pipes, you can sleep all you want when you're dead.

'Look, Farrar,' I said heavily. 'It's not on.' It wasn't as though I even liked the guy all that much. I needed him as a house guest-cum-patient like I needed two heads.

'Goddam it, Jack, or whatever your name is, do I have to shove a gun up *your* nose now?'

'Okay, okay.' I didn't want any trouble. I swung right, off Rue Gamel Abdul Nasser into Rue el Djazira, and, against my better judgment, took him to the hotel.

Over breakfast, bought at the mobile sandwich shop and shared with my personal retinue of bluebottles, I got to know a lot more about my unwanted guest.

I had set and splinted his arm to the best of my limited ability with two handy lengths of wood filched from my so-called wardrobe, and he spent a restful enough night on the bed while I, charitable to the last, made do with the floor. In terms of comfort, floor and bed were indistinguishable, I discovered, and the floor, if anything, was cleaner.

'Don't you think you owe me an explanation, Farrar?' I said, breaking off another unappetising piece of stale roll and spreading honey on it.

He looked blankly at me. 'Explanation? What for? Nobody asked you to stick your snout in last night. I didn't need your help.'

'Not at the club, I agree. But if I hadn't stuck my snout in, as you so delicately put it, you would have spent the night in a police cell, having your other arm broken – and your legs as well, maybe. Apart from that, who else would have given you overnight lodgings and fixed your arm?'

'All right, all *right*,' he growled, waving away a persistent bluebottle. 'You've made your point. What do you want me to do? Grovel? Pay? I don't mind paying, just tell me the going rate for a bed and medical treatment.' He reached inside his jacket, awkwardly left-handed, and drew out a roll of bank-notes fat enough to stuff a turkey.

I could certainly have used the money but I let the opportunity pass. 'I'd just like to know why you wouldn't let me take you to hospital. What are you doing here in Tunis?'

He tilted back on his chair and broke wind noisily, his close-set eyes boring into me like a pair of diamond-tipped drills. He made me feel as if he could see inside my skull.

Through the open window came the bleating of a herd of goats on their way to the *souks*. A babble of voices, raised in argument, suddenly rose up from the streets below. Somebody called somebody else the equivalent of a mother-fucking pervert. It was the only Mahgreb Arabic expression I had so far learned, which goes to show what low circles I moved in.

'I guess I gotta tell you anyway,' Farrar said at last. 'This busted wing is gonna give me a king-size problem.'

I sipped coffee, home-made on my portable camping stove. It tasted vile, which was the norm.

'What do *you* do, Jack?' The sun was on his face now, highlighting deep rifts and creases around his eyes and mouth. Daylight had put ten years on him. I revised my estimate of his age; I doubted he'd see fifty again.

'Me?' I was unprepared for the question. I'd thought *I* was doing all the asking. 'Nothing much. I just sort of . . . well, look out for . . . opportunities.'

He raised a cynical eyebrow. 'Opportunities? Here in Tunis? I could name you a million or so better places to make money.'

'I like it,' I said defensively. I didn't add, 'because it's cheap and I haven't got the wherewithal to move on.'

'It takes all kinds.' He gazed around, noting the spartan grubbiness of the room. He was not impressed; I could tell by the sneer and the wrinkling nose. 'How'd you like to earn ten grand?'

'Ten grand?' I repeated stupidly. 'You mean ten thousand dollars?'

He gave a snorting laugh. 'What else? That's dollars US, too, not dollars Canadian.'

The row in the street was still raging. From the sound of it, half the population of Tunis was in on the act. I would have closed the window if there had been a window to close.

'Ten thousand dollars,' I said again, tasting the words. They were succulent, all right.

'In cash.'

Even better.

'Ten thousand in cash.'

He frowned then. 'Look, quit saying it over and over, will you? I'm offering you ten thousand US dollars in cash, for maybe a couple of hours' work. Now, are you interested or not?'

Having adjusted to the idea of ten thousand dollars, I became wary. 'What do I have to do for this te . . .' I almost said it again, 'for the money?' I amended.

'Kill somebody.' He said it quickly but matter-of-factly. 'A man.'

'Kill a man.' There I went again. 'Only one?' Now I was being facetious.

Farrar got up and walked to the window. The empty right sleeve of his jacket flapped in the breeze. He stood there for quite a while, stirring restlessly at intervals. I didn't speak. Half of me hoped he would let the matter drop. The other half of me was already hooked. But to kill a man? Me? It was preposterous.

Farrar breathed out hard through his nose, and came back into the centre of the room.

'I'm here to fulfil a . . . contract,' he said. 'You'll know what that means, I reckon.'

'A contract? I think so. You're here to kill someone on behalf of a third party. And being paid for it.' It explained his confident, practised handling of the gun at the Matmata Club; also his refusal to go to hospital. A professional killer needed to remain incognito.

'That's exactly right.' He ran agitated fingers through his grey-flecked hair. 'Hell, I wish I was sure you could be trusted. You might be a stoolie for all I know.'

'Come off it. If you really believed that, you wouldn't have told me in the first place.'

'Yeah. Yeah, I guess you're right.' He sat down, tugged a pack of Lucky Strike Export out of his top pocket, held it out to me.

'I don't, thanks,' I said. He grunted and lit up with an old-fashioned lighter that smelled of petrol.

'What about it then?' he said. 'Will you do it? I can't.' He gestured towards the strapped-up arm. 'It's a rifle job; long distance. Otherwise I'd chance it with my left hand.'

I laughed. 'You're round the twist! What makes you think I can even use a gun? I might not know a rifle from a pick-axe.'

His face fell then, as if it hadn't occurred to him, and he asked, '*Can't* you shoot?'

'As it happens, I can.' It was a fateful admission. He pounced on it.

'Great! I had a feeling there was more to you than meets the eye.' He leaned across the table towards me, drawing hard on his cigarette. 'Now listen . . . this is the deal. I'm here to knock off this Tunisian – it doesn't matter who he is – and the job is set for tomorrow at 3.00 p.m. It won't be face-to-face: the range will be anout four hundred yards. And if it will ease your conscience, the hit has personally caused the deaths of over a hundred innocent people. Women and children included. If he wasn't a real bad 'un I wouldn't have taken the contract. I'm choosy. I like to have a cause.'

It helped that the prospective victim was deserving of death, though my conscience troubled me less than the risks.

'Everything is set up: the hit will be on the road in an open jeep.' Farrar was talking fast now, like a racing commentator. Trying to sell me the idea while I was still punch-drunk. 'There'll be just one other person, the driver. The rifle has a scope sight, even a rank amateur couldn't miss with it.'

He was already talking as if I'd agreed to do it.

'What model?'

'The rifle? A Weatherby. Mark V, magnum.'

An interesting choice of weapon; it was a hunting rifle. American. That was the extent of my knowledge.

'Where is it? How did you get it into the country?'

'It was already here when I arrived; I have . . . er, contacts here. As to where it is . . . let's just say it's in a safe place.' His grin was lop-sided. 'I can collect it any time. No problem at all.'

'I've never killed anyone,' I said absently. I got up and prowled around, thinking hard. About the implications, about the getaway, about ten thousand dollars. Especially about ten thousand dollars.

'Well, whaddaya say, Jack? The job's gotta be done. I don't welch: if I did, I'd be finished in this game. You're only as good as your last job and the word soon gets around if you fall down. The hit's gotta be tomorrow. My principals won't wait.' He pounded the table with a balled fist. 'It's gotta be tomorrow!'

I was staring out of the window, over the flat, white rooftops that resembled nothing so much as a jumble of children's bricks. From here, halfway up the hill on which the old Arab quarter of Tunis is built, you can see the port and, beyond it, a bit of the lagoon, sparkling in the sun. Blue skies, white buildings, relieved by the green of the city's parks and cemeteries. The only eyesore, an enormous orange crane at the lagoon's edge, where a new office block was slowly growing, a concrete and steel toadstool.

The dispute under my window had withered away

and the street was empty apart from a trio of hooded Bedouins ambling to market, and a ragged urchin sitting in a doorway, nursing a puppy.

'I'll make it twelve grand,' Farrar offered, construing my silence as a probable 'no'.

'How long have you been doing this?' I said. I had supposed hired killers to be a rare breed. I was fascinated to know what made them tick. 'Killing for money, I mean.'

'What's wrong with killing for money? Soldiers do it all the time.' He lit another cigarette. Smoke drifted past me through the window. Then he said, grudgingly: 'About fifteen years, I guess.'

'How did you get into it?'

He shrugged loosely. 'A guy I knew wanted another guy wasted: he'd been screwing his wife, or something. He knew I was handy with a rod, so . . .' He shrugged again, his mouth turning down at the edges. 'I made five hundred bucks on that job. Since then, I've upped the ante a mite.'

'How many . . . er . . . contracts have you done?'

He moved uneasily. You could tell he wasn't happy with this line of questioning. 'Twenty-eight, I guess. This one will make twenty-nine. Just enough to make me a reasonable living. Hell! I don't *enjoy* it, you know. Killing people don't turn me on. It ain't like a drug, something that gives you a kick, if that's what you think.'

'I wasn't thinking anything. I'm just curious.'

'Well, I ain't taking any more of your goddamn curiosity. Just tell me "yes" or "no". If it's "no". then I'll beat it and find me somebody with some guts.'

He was bluffing and we both knew it. You don't find a pro killer by sticking a notice in the Sits Vac column of the International Herald Tribune. Much as it must have galled him, I was his only hope.

'Make it twenty thousand and I'll do it,' I said it half-jokingly.

Perhaps, subconsciously, I hoped to discourage him; equally, it might have been nothing more than avarice. I was a far from violent person, notwithstanding my abbreviated career in the arms business, yet here I was, volunteering to *kill* a man, someone who had done me no harm and who might be a thoroughly decent bloke with a wife and kids. And not for any high-flown motives, like Queen and Country. I was intending to commit murder in the first degree for no more noble a cause than twenty thousand United States dollars.

And it didn't trouble me at all. I scarcely recognized myself.

Farrar was slow to recover from the hyper-inflationary increase in my fee. He wasn't amused; his expression hardened, became thoughtful. Then, to my surprise, he exploded into laughter.

'If you ain't the bees-knees! Pretending butter wouldn't melt in your mouth, and all you was doing was hyping up the ante. What a chiseller!' He shook his head wonderingly, chuckling and gurgling. 'All right, Jack,' he said, between splutters. 'Twenty grand it is.' He stuck out a big, square paw and we sealed the bargain with a sweaty handclasp.

'Half now, half later – in cash,' I said firmly.

He hooted like a ship's siren at that. 'Now you're really kidding. I'll give you a grand now, the rest after the death's announced over the radio.'

'Not on your life! Tell you what – I'll settle for eight now, twelve after.'

'Four and sixteen,' he countered.

'Bollocks. Six and fourteen, or the deal's off.'

'Watch it, Jack. Nobody welches on me. 'Five and fifteen.'

I could see it was the most I would squeeze out of him. 'Done.'

He resurrected his bankroll, started to peel off hundred-dollar bills. 'First thing we do – five hundred, six hundred, seven hundred – is pick up the hardware; then we take a ride outa town – twelve hundred, thirteen hundred – so's you can get in some target practice. After that – nineteen hundred, two Gs – we go case the spot – twenty-four hundred, twenty-five – the place where you make the hit. And we ain't got a lotta time.' He tapped the pile of bills. 'You wanna check it?'

'Yes.'

'Trusting bastard, ain'cha?'

The rocks were hot, which was fine for the lizard community; me, I could have used some shade. I was finding out how a fried egg must feel, except I didn't even have the luxury of a pool of fat to sizzle in. It was a slow, dry burn.

Ultra-high temperatures were, of course, normal for Tunisia in July. I just wasn't in the habit of exposing myself to them. It was too hot even to sweat; moisture just evaporated. Fortunately, my hide has the consistency of leather and was already fairly well-baked from my wanderings in North Africa. Even so, shorts, T-shirt, and a battered straw hat, were not the most practical form of dress, as I should have realised.

It was 2.50: ten minutes to go if the hit – I still didn't know his name – was punctual. Don't count on it, Farrar had said. I rolled on to my side, to give the backs of my legs some relief from the sun's rays, and cursed my pack of preparation, my amateurism. All I had to counter the heat was a hip flask filled with lemonade, and what remained of that was already close to boiling point.

I took up the rifle. It was not new, not by a long chalk, but it had been well-cared for. The walnut stock was oiled and gleaming, the metal parts free of rust. The words 'Weatherby Mark V' were etched into the top of the barrel, beyond the Weaver V8 telescopic sight with its neat De Vissing hinged covers. It was a bolt-action weapon, five-round magazine, .300 calibre. An odd choice for an assassination. My own preference would have been a Belgian FN 7.62mm, or an M.14; both semi-automatics and with them you could get off three or four shots while you were still working the bolt of the Weatherby. It was accurate enough though. During a practice session in the lonely Zaghouan valley, south of Tunis, I had placed all five rounds in a one-inch group at a hundred yards.

All was quiet, the road evidently seldom used, especially at siesta time. Even the flies dozed. On a large, flat stone, just out of arm's reach, a sand-coloured lizard, about a foot long from nose to the tip of its tail, regarded me with an unconcerned stare. It was motionless, prostrated by the heat, which made two of us. I changed my position and in a blur of movement it was gone.

A puff of dust rose from the road, out by the junction with Route Régionale 3, the Tunis to Kairouan highway; it grew into a long brown pennant streaming out with a boxy, vehicle at its head. Land Rover or jeep. My watch said 3.02; this must be my man. The vehicle was about a mile-and-a-half away and travelling fast. Two minutes at the outside, and it would be here, making the hairpin turn at the end of the escarpment, slowing to a crawl, offering a perfect sniper's target. Two minutes to reflect, to have a change of heart, to pack up and scuttle off to my rendezvous with Farrar at the hotel . . .

To hand back those five thousand dollars . . .

Sod that for an idea! Determinedly, I lifted the Weatherby, cuddled the rubber recoil-pad into my shoulder, lined up the cross-hairs of the scope on a heap of boulders by the hairpin. Made a last-minute adjustment to the focus. Worked the action, a series of satisfying, metallic clunks, ramming bullet into firing chamber.

The dust trail was much closer now, less than half-a-mile. I couldn't see the vehicle; it was temporarily hidden behind some low dunes alongside the road. It came back into view: a jeep, a Willys by the look of it. Brown and well-worn. Two occupants: driver in short-sleeved beige tunic and peaked cap, passenger similarly attired but with epaulettes. Through the scope I could make out his features: swarthy, moustache like a hairy caterpillar on his top lip, hooked nose; aged about forty, I would say.

The cross-hairs were centred on his chest but still I held my fire. They were doing about fifty, though the driver was coming down through the gears now as they went into the long, looping curve before the hairpin itself. Where I would kill my man.

All emotion had left me. I was now no more than a machine: press the starter button and off I would go like a clockwork toy. Nothing existed outside me, the gun, and the target. It was not necessary to think, only to act. To follow a sequence of prescribed functions. It was just a job. Employment. It was . . . business. No room for sentiment.

In a way, that afternoon, lying there on the blistering rocks above the Kairouan road, I discovered my true self.

The rifle barrel was as steady as if mounted on a tripod. The sun was flailing the skin off the backs of my legs, and off my arms, but I scarcely noticed it. All that registered was the hard outline of the edge of the escarpment, coming down to meet the tarmac surface of the road, the air above it trembling in the heat, the dead tree-less backdrop, the painfully blue sky . . .

The jeep ground around the hairpin, filling the scope, and I fired. Twice in quick succession, working the action smoothly and unhurriedly.

The first bullet smashed through the windscreen and hit the officer in the chest, plumb centre, bending him backwards over the seat. The second struck high and to the left, my aim disturbed by the jeep's sudden swerve. Twin red smudges had appeared on the front of the officer's tunic. He crumpled up tiredly, arms dangling, then sagged sideways towards the driver, who was doing his best to crawl under the scuttle while bringing the jeep to a standstill.

I fired twice more. At the front and rear nearside tyres. Farrar had urged me to eliminate the driver, for my own safety. Faced with the decision, I copped out; two flat tyres would slow him down long enough to see me back in Tunis and off the streets.

Before the jeep came to rest I was up and sliding down the hillside to where I had left the Beetle, parked in the shade of an overhanging crag at the next bend in the road, and I reckon I broke a few world records getting to it. I shoved the Weatherby in the front boot, and with a muttered prayer turned the ignition key. The engine spun, faltered, died. Don't let me down now, you bitch! Not today of all days. I repeated the process – whirr, burp, whirr, cough, then a lovely, lusty *vroom* and she fired in traditional Beetle fashion, a sort of controlled explosion, settling down to a hesitant beat.

I pulled out from under the crag as if I were at the wheel of a Formula One racer instead of a very weary banger, bumped across the rock-strewn ground that lay between me and the road. Nothing in sight in either direction. I turned right, away from the hairpin, and made that Beetle perform miracles of acceleration that in theory it had never been capable of, even when new.

I glanced in the mirror. Saw only a ribbon of empty road, tapering to nothingness. My nerves stopped fluttering and I began to believe I might actually have got away with it. That, in the space of a few hours and for minuscule effort, I had earned a sum of money that would keep me off skid row for a whole twelve months.

The assassination was announced over the radio that evening and I learned that my victim was the Tunisian Chief of Police. At the time of the broadcast I was in my hotel room with Farrar, the two of us making short work of a bottle of *boukha*, the schnapps-like local firewater. To give Farrar his due, he handed over the rest of the cash without any prompting.

'Well?' he said, staring at me whan I had finished counting those crisp, crackly dollar bills.

'Well what?'

'How does it feel?'

I riffled the wad before tucking it in my hip pocket. 'What feel? The money?'

'To kill somebody,' Farrar said in exasperation. 'Don't tell me it's an everyday event for you.'

That made me laugh. 'Not quite. But . . . it's not such a big deal, is it, Farrar? You of all people ought to know that. I mean, he wasn't *God*, was he? Only a man. He might have been run over by a bus tomorrow. Or electrocuted himself. Or fallen downstairs.'

Farrar had been perched on the edge of a chair; now he rocked back on it, his expression disbelieving. 'I'll be goddamned! You really don't feel a fucking thing, do you?' He lit a Lucky Strike, pulling hard on it. 'You know, I've met some amoral bastards in my time but you sure take the prize.'

'Flatterer,' I murmured and helped myself to an olive. Farrar had bought a bagful at the market; he ate them like sweets.

He roared, slapping his thigh, and sparks flew from the tip of cigarette. 'You'll go far, kiddo. My profession needs people like you.'

We said our goodbyes. I settled my hotel bill and left town, my possessions crammed into the grey fibre-glass Antler suitcase I had had since I left the army and, driving through the night, arrived at the Tunisia-Algeria border before dawn. It had seemed prudent to avoid any contact with officialdom in the aftermath of the killing; foreigners were bound to be suspect and those with twenty thousand dollars in cash hidden in the roof lining doubly so. Consequently I crossed into Algeria south of Highway 6, using a dirt road that had no permanent customs post.

As a weak diversionary tactic, in case of interception, I had two cases of St Joseph de Thila liqueurs stowed in the boot, a minor smuggling offence that would be overlooked in return for a 50-dinar consideration. A hired assassin was hardly likely to go in for petty bootlegging, I reasoned.

It was an example of the ability to anticipate that was to keep me out of trouble in the years to come.

In the event, I made it without incident. Linked up with Route Nationale 20 in Algeria, and clattered into Constantine around 10 am. Bought a newspaper from a French-style road-side kiosk. Read about the latest developments in the slaying of the Tunisian Chief of Police; read that a certain Canadian by the name of Frank Farrar had been arrested at Carthage Airport late last night, attempting to board an Alitalia flight to Rome, and was now being held for questioning on suspicion of having committed the crime.

Poor Farrar. The irony of it.

I chucked the newspaper on the back seat and drove on. To a new profession, taking over, you might say, where Frank Farrar involuntarily left off.

I never did get to hear what happened to him.

Casablanca became my new base. At the Kas-bar, a fly-blown replica of Saadoun's flophouse, I put it judiciously around that I was in the pest-control business. There followed a four-month famine during which I lived quite comfortably off the fat of the Farrar pay-off; the famine ended when I was hired by a consortium of whores to do away with their pimp-protector, a vicious little sewer rat with sadistic leanings. My clients had raised five thousand dollars in various mongrel currencies; a meagre enough sum considering the risks. Murder carried the death penalty in Morocco. To be honest I only accepted the contract out of charity: I really felt sorry for the silly, pathetic bitches. Like Farrar, I had my virtuous side and it demanded a cause.

Word of mouth is an effective form of advertising. Soon, other more remunerative commissions came along and my reputation travelled further afield. So did I. I set up house and shop in Andorra where I was to spend five years.

From the outset I was selective, a code to which I remained ever faithful. My victims were invariably criminals, often of the vilest kind. I dispensed just desserts. Exterminated vermin. Eliminated lice. Once I even killed a woman – the leader of a pornography ring, responsible for the corruption and suicide of a titled Frenchman's fourteen-year-old-daughter. I didn't feel a thing.

Just before the definitive move to Geneva I married again – when I was thirty-two and she was twenty-seven. Rebecca. As Jewish as the name implies. Black curly hair, masses of it, dark deep-set eyes; tall, big bosomed, athletic; also hot-tempered and stubborn.

From the honeymoon onwards, we quarrelled incessantly and, ultimately, violently, though not about my profession. I managed to keep that under very secure wraps. As a grand finale she took a meat cleaver to me and I was lucky not to lose an arm – I still carry the scar, a thin white crescent below the inner elbow. We split up after that and the divorce was a formality on the grounds of 'irreconcilable differences'. Since then, apart from periodic bunk-ups of varying longevity, I had been alone and now, with thirty-eight years on the clock, all I had to look back and congratulate myself on were the murders of forty human beings and the financial fruits of my work, namely an apartment in Geneva, a thirty-four-foot sailing yacht berthed at Monaco, a Jaguar XK8 coupe, and, according to the latest statements from the Schweitzerische Kreditanstaltbank in Zürich, the Crédit Lyonnais in Monaco, and a little known, very private bank in Luxembourg whose name I couldn't pronounce let alone spell, cash deposite totalling two million and forty eight thousand or so US dollars.

My meal was finished, all five courses of it, and I hadn't tasted a morsel. I paid with my AmEx card, left a generous tip for Sergio, the Italian waiter, and went back to my apartment on foot.

The apartment. On the fifth and top floor of a small, exclusive block on the Route de Frontenex, across from the Parc la Grange and with a fine prospect out over the lake, taking in the Jet d'Eau – nowadays more often than not switched off.

Nobody was waiting for me at the apartment. Only my possessions, all of good quality, genuine antiques in some cases; Bengal tiger-skin rug, gaping jaws and all, occupying pride of place before the imposing *faux cheminée* with its gas-fired ceramic logs. Real oak beams across the ceiling; shelf upon shelf of books – some rare first-editions. Lots of dark woodwork, relieved by the cream hessian-covered walls and pale green ceiling, and a carefully chosen collection of paintings, all originals and all, apart from a Manet, bright modern watercolours by little-known and usually struggling artists. I collected paintings, not names.

So much for the living-room. The kitchen, where I strove to whip up wholesome, nourishing meals, creating heaps of detritus like shale tips, was also clean and sparkling, thanks to the rather dignified Swiss widow who 'did' for me twice a week to supplement her state pension.

As for the rest: two bedrooms, one rarely slept in; two bathrooms; a tiny entrance hall just big enough to take a coat-stand and for visitors to pass through in single file; and finally the balcony where, in summer, I often breakfasted.

It was home. And it was about as cosy and cheerful as a high-security cell in Durham Prison.

At the international newsagency in Place Neuve I bought copies of three leading German newspapers: *Die Welt, Allgemeine Zeitung*, and the *Bavarian Suddeutsche Zeitung*, and stood under the broad canopy at the front of the shop, out of the rain, whipping through their pages for an account of the Tillou-Thomashoff killings, while a flood-tide of grey-faced Swiss swirled past and around me.

Nothing. Eight days now and still no mention. It was inconceivable that the bodies still lay undiscovered. Apart from the certainty that Thomashoff would have instituted enquiries into his wife's whereabouts, a charlady visited the house every Friday and it was now Monday.

Conclusion: the story was being suppressed, possibly because of the involvement of a government minister's wife. The police might even believe *she* was the target, not Tillou, and that the killing was politically inspired. So much the better. It would be a useful red herring, tending to divert suspicion away from hired assassins and towards terrorist factions.

A passing trolley bus deposited a quantity of dirty rainwater on my feet. I glared after it and set off for more congenial surroundings at a brisk walk.

Chapter Three

As a rule, in Geneva, the month of May signals the advent of summer, a fairly abrupt transition from freezing squalls straight off the Alps interspersed with snowfalls of diverse intensity, to days of warm sunshine, of chestnut trees in blossom. The cafés and *brasseries* and restaurants bring their weathered chairs and tables out of storage and arrange them on the pavements and in the squares, and often as not it's warm enough to take morning coffee outside.

Not this year. This was the year of the never-ending winter. If there had been less snow than usual, the rain more than compensated. Some said it was the wettest winter in living memory. What was more, it showed no inclination to change for the better. The sun continued to skulk behind clouds that ranged in hue from battleship grey to purplish-black; flowers and foliage obstinately and sensibly observed a non-existent profile.

Gloomy weather reflecting my gloomy spirits. Quite apart from the incessant rain, I was generally brassed off. In the almost six months since my retirement I had played the playboy role to the hilt: sex, sex, and still more sex (mostly the paid variety; it's instant and devoid of commitment); frantic parties where animal behaviour was not merely tolerated but expected; gambling to the point of recklessness; a fortnight's solo holiday in Venice, even damper and more depressing than Geneva; a week in Marbella, in southern Spain, still seeking the sun and still failing. Then, thoroughly disillusioned, taking an oft-deferred trip to the UK to visit my sole surviving relative, my sister June. Sickeningly content at thirty-six, with a hard-working, successful husband and two quite likeable kids. There, at least, when it rained, I could take it philosophically.

Otherwise . . . otherwise, day after day of increasing monotony and, worse still, no improvement in prospect.

Or so it appeared, sitting in the lavatory with my trousers around my ankles, during which ceremony I habitually planned the day ahead. More and more often now, I would rise from my throne with those plans still unmade, the day a yawning void, empty as a churchyard at midnight.

In short, retirement was not proving to be the panacea I had expected, and I was beginning to hanker after the dangers and excitement of the hit business. This, I recognized, would be insanity. That phase of my life was closed. Dead. My determination to return to it was undiminished. Which meant I had to find some other means of filling the empty hollows.

I got no further than that in my deep ponderings. I needed inspiration, and in that area I was bankrupt. Mooching around the apartment was not likely to generate original ideas either, so I went out for a coffee. Hopefully to find the answer in the dregs at the bottom of the cup.

It was only a few minutes walk to the Comédie, my local *brasserie* on the Quai Gustave Ador; come fair weather or foul, I always walked. I stepped out between the automatic sliding doors of the apartment block, umbrella held aloft like the regimental colours. Most other pedestrians were similarly armed, the street a forest of bobbing brollies. Traffic swished past, wipers sweeping, headlights on. Rain descended in vertical lines and the cloud base hooded the top of the tallest tower blocks. You could develop a complex about rain if it went on long enough, I mused. So why not head south, to Monaco and the yacht? It was early in the season, even for the Med, but what did that matter?

Customers were thin on the ground at the Comédie, and I was able to secure a seat by the window, where I sat, staring across the wind-swept, rain-swept lake until the *patron* came to serve me in person.

We shook hands.

'*Comment allez-vous*, Monsieur 'Enley?' He asked formally. He was a Parisian and his name, believe it or not, was Bolloque, with the emphasis on the second syllable. The English community in Geneva were fond of taking the mickey; he was widely referred to, and not always behind his back, as 'All-balls'.

I said I was '*Ça va*,' and left it at that. I ordered a coffee and he whisked away, smooth and efficient. Nobody ever had to wait long for service at the Comédie.

Rain rattled against the plate-glass window, a fusillade driven by wind that came off the lake with the keenness of a cut-throat razor. An old man, with a brolly big enough to cover a football pitch, scuttled past, weaving a zig-zag course, the wind slamming him this way and that. Whenever a gust caught him he became momentarily airborne.

The coffee came and I sweetened it with a rock of brown sugar. Bolloque's coffee was consistently good.

I downed it in a few appreciative gulps and right away he was there with a top-up. After my seven years of patronage, he had learned to anticipate my needs.

Somebody came in through the squeaky swing door and, for want of other diversions, I glanced up. The new arrival was my next-door-but-one neighbour, a shortish, balding man in his sixties, carrying more paunch than was good for him. He had moved in just a few weeks ago and I only knew him by sight.

He recognized me, nodded, and after a moment's indecision came over to my table.

'Good morning,' he said in English, with the guttural intonation of a German-speaking Swiss. 'May I join you?'

'Please.' I waved my hand at the vacant chair opposite. 'It's time we got acquainted.'

He sat down heavily, slightly out of breath. His narrow face was at odds with his overweight condition, and his blotchy complexion hinted at some internal disorder. I hadn't noticed before, but his eyes were ice-blue, almost colourless; once he had probably been as blond as I was, and indeed there was still the odd yellow streak in what remained of his white hair. His clothes were well-tailored: dark blue blazer, light blue slacks; pity about the sickly mustard-coloured waistcoat though.

'My name is Schnurrpfeil,' he said, as I took his proffered hand. 'Carl Schnurrpfeil.'

'Schnurr-pfeil.' I repeated it slowly; it was quite a tongue-twister. 'I'm Jack Henley.'

'Mr Henley.' A stiff, sitting-down bow. 'It is pleasant to meet you properly at last. You are in Number 52, are you not?'

I inclined my head. 'Will you join me in a coffee?'

'Yes . . . please. You are most kind.'

I flagged Bolloque and he came prancing across like an aged ballet dancer. Schnurrpfeil ordered *café au lait* in mutilated French that made Bolloque cringe visibly.

'How do you like it here?' I asked, just making polite conversation.

'Geneva? It is very acceptable but the weather has not been too good, eh?'

'You can say that again. I've been here seven years and I've never known rain like it.'

'I, too, have been many years in Switzerland; since 1969, in fact, when I left Germany. But until I came here, in march, I always lived in the east – first in Zürich, later in Winterthur.'

I stirred my coffee, sampled it. I never pried into people's backgrounds other than for professional reasons; just as I was close-mouthed about my own. But Herr Schnurrpfeil seemed willing, even eager, to be forthcoming, so I said: 'You're German?'

'Yes.' He said it proudly, and something akin to a beam lit up his unhealthy pallor.

'I suppose you're retired now.'

'For many years.' His coffee arrived. '*Merci,*' he said to Bolloque. Well, that what I *thought* he said.

'I haven't worked since I came to Switzerland, although I dabble in this and that.' In contrast to his dreadful French he had a good grasp of idiomatic English. 'My family is quite wealthy, you see. My father died just before I was rel . . .' He stopped, axing the word with a forced cough, and fiddled with his coffee spoon.

I was mildly intrigued, no more than that. I guessed the word he had baulked at was 'released', which suggested either a prison or a mental institution. If he didn't want to talk about it, it wasn't for me to press him. I had plenty of secrets of my own: a cupboard full to bursting with skeletons. If it was the same with him, who was I to disapprove?

'And you, Mr Henley, an Englishman living in Geneva,' he said, after a longish and rather uncomfortable silence. 'What is the nature of your business?'

I was tempted to say, 'I mind my own,' but that would have been churlish after his own candour. 'Like you, I'm retired,' I said instead. I didn't elaborate.

'You are young to be retired.'

We eyed each other over our coffee cups, a tentative appraisal, like sparring boxers.

'You remind me of a man I knew during the war – the second world war. One of my officers.'

'You were in the army?' I asked, showing polite interest.

'Not exactly; not the *Wehrmacht*, at any rate.' He was toying with his spoon again, not looking at me. 'You are not Jewish, are you?'

The question was so unexpected, so apparently out of context, that I gaped at him.

'Jewish? No, I'm not Jewish.' Admittedly my nose had a very slight concavity, but then so do the noses of many other gentiles.

'Good . . . then you will not be disturbed when I tell you I was with the SS. A *Sturmführer*.'

'*Sturmführer?*' I wasn't familiar with the SS pecking order.

'Equal to an army rank of Leiutenant. That was at the end of the war, of course. I joined, as a recruit, in 1944.'

'You climbed the ladder quickly, Mr Schnurrpfeil;

recruit to Lieutenant in one year is some achievement.'

I wasn't at all shocked by his revelation. The SS were just common criminals; no different from me, except I didn't advertise it by wearing a black uniform.

'In times of war, promotion is always rapid,' he said modestly. 'More so in Germany than any other country because of our many casualties. But as I was saying . . . you bear a certain likeness to a *Stürmbannführer* who was with my *Untergruppe*, though he was younger than you. He was killed late in 1944, during the Russian winter offensive.'

'I didn't think the SS did any fighting. Weren't they promarily a security force?'

'That is correct, apart from the Waffen SS, which was the special military division; they fought on all fronts, and very bravely.' He was gazing at me fixedly. 'I was with the *Einsatzgruppen*.'

The *Einsatzgruppen*. Yes, I'd heard of them: the special extermination squads whose job was to wipe out any nationality or creed that offended the Führer's concept of racial purity – women and children included. Jews, Russians, Slavs, and other *Untermenschen* were all legitimate targets.

But it all happened long ago. It was nothing to do with me.

'You have heard of them? The *Einsatzgruppen*?' A note of anxiety had entered his voice. Possibly he interpreted my lack of response as censure.

'I have read of them, yes. Indiscriminate killing was their function, wasn't it? Murder on a grand scale.'

His laugh was harsh. 'Killing – yes; indiscriminate – no! Absolutely not. We killed Jews, Slavs, and other sub-human species. We killed to preserve the integrity of the human race. We killed to make a better, purer world . . .'

'Keep your voice down!' I hissed, aware of the frowns being directed at us by the scattering of customers. 'Do you want all Geneva to know you were in the SS? There are plenty of Jews living here. I'm sure they'd love to know about you.'

'*Ach!*' He clicked his tongue in self-reproach. 'You are right. I must be careful. But I still believe in what we did. I hope . . . I believe that, one day, there will be a Fourth Reich and that the SS will be re-formed to finish its work.'

God forbid.

'I don't know enough about the subject to comment on the rights and wrongs,' I said, with tact. 'It seems to be generally accepted though, that the SS was an illegal organization and that it performed countless atrocities for which there appears to have been no military or political justification.'

'Hah! That shows how naive you are, my friend. What you do not understand is that the word of Adolf Hitler was the word of God in Germany at that time. We all trusted him, absolutely and totally, and we would have followed him into the flames of hell.'

Which was more or less what the German nation ultimately did, I reflected.

'You know, we of the SS all had to swear an oath of loyalty to Hitler personally?'

'I seem to recollect hearing that,' I said, with a nod.

'It is an oath we, the *Ehemaligen SS-Angehörigen* – former members of the SS – have never renounced.' Again the glow of pride. '*Ich schwöre Dir, Adolf Hitler, als Führer und . . .*'

'I think I can guess the rest,' I cut in.

He finally took the hint and another silence

descended while I finished my third cup of coffee and drummed up refills for both of us. Schnurrpfeil produced a flat tin of small cigars, and held it out. I took one. Although a non-smoker, I enjoyed the occasional cigar with a drink.

Outside, the clouds were breaking up, a dirty white peeping through the cracks. A boy on a bike went past, swerving to avoid two doddery old ladies crossing the road where they shouldn't, hanging on to each other for support. His shouted abuse went unheeded.

Across the wet street, people waited in a glum line for a tram; sober Swiss faces, sober Swiss clothing. A dour, unexcitable race, the Swiss. Preoccupied with numbered bank accounts, gold, and keeping out of world wars. You had to go back to William Tell for a Swiss of international prestige.

'Well, Mr Henley. I have told you about my past. I will also tell you I spent fifteen years in prison for my so-called crimes. I have nothing to fear from the police any longer. But what of you? Is *your* past so pure and white?' He sat back, smiling now through a film of tobacco smoke, a thumb hooked in the armhole of that yukky waistcoat. 'Have you been a good boy all your life? Hey?'

When I refused to rise to this bait, he chuckled. 'Don't be so . . . how do you say? Reticent? You know, Mr Henley, you have the look of a man who could be ruthless.'

'Really,' I said, with wide-eyed innocence. On such short acquaintance this was a little too personal.

'Yes.' He studied me. 'Yes, I should say you could be *very* ruthless. Tell me—', conspiratorially, '—have you ever killed a man?'

'In war, you mean?' I said quickly. 'No. I was in the

army for three years but didn't see combat.' Herr Schnurrpfeil was beginning to irritate me.

'Have you visited Germany?' he said, abruptly switching subjects.

This was safer ground.

'Several times.'

'You know München – Munich – perhaps?'

Alarm bells began jangling again. I managed a stiff 'Yes.'

'I was born near there. I often go back, although my family are all dead now.' He blew smoke at the window. 'It is most beautiful there in the autumn, in my opinion. It is often warm and sunny even in November.'

Munich. November. A place and a time. Separately, meaningless. Together, they rang of a certain contract, memorable only in that it was my last.

I used to play poker. It helps one exercise facial control. Right now I needed it.

'I'm sure,' I said distantly. I made signs to Bolloque to bring the bill.

'Have you ever been there in November?' Schnurrpfeil persisted. 'In Munich?'

'Er . . . no.' My cigar had gone out. I mashed it in the ashtray. 'I must go, Mr Schnurrpfeil. I have an appointment.'

Bolloque loomed up. I took the bill, winced, parted with a hefty bank note. 'Thanks, Bolloque.' I punched him lightly on the arm. '*A bientôt.*'

'*J'espère. Bonne journée,* Monsieur 'Enley.'

'Thanks for the chat,' I said to Schnurrpfeil. 'It's been . . . educational.'

I walked to the door, standing aside for a young couple, sodden hair plastered flat to their scalps, escaping the latest downpour. In the doorway, I put up my brolly, cast a final glance at Schnurrpfeil. He was watching me, unblinking, with a gloating expression that did nothing at all to allay my fears.

Listening to classical music was, for me, a potent form of relaxation. Returning home, a little after 10 p.m., from a meal at the Parc des Eaux Vives, lauded by some as Geneva's premier restaurant, I settled in my reclining armchair, a Bourbon and soda at my elbow, soaking up the second movement of Dvorák's New World Symphony. On such occasions, I usually emptied my mind of all distractions, content to wallow in the swirl of the strings, the mournful bleat of bass clarinet, the furious leap of massed brass. But this evening I was still gnawing away at my strange conversation with Schnurrpfeil of some twelve hours earlier. I had set aside my initial disquiet; why should I worry about some old codger playing guessing games? Munich in November. A coincidence? Why not?

Yet whenever I dismissed his maddening presence from my mind, it boomeranged straight back, unwanted, unsummoned, but there; a black spot dirtying my untroubled, if somewhat colourless, skies. He was an itch I couldn't scratch away.

As the second movement entered its closing phase, solitary French horn leading into a string finale, my thoughts travelled south again, to Monaco. The summer season was still weeks away, but, if nothing else, I wuld be able to potter about on the boat, and drink the rough, red *vin du pays* with Jean-Pierre of an evening; even run down to Corsica, or along the coast to Toulon or Marseilles. What was there to keep me in rain-soaked Geneva? I was a free agent now. Instead of a two-month summer layoff, I had twelve months, year-in, year-out to choose from. More chance, too, of decent weather down there on the Côte d'Azur than here among the mountains, whose peaks were still crowned with white.

Fired, at last, with a sense of purpose, I stopped biting my nails over Schnurrpfeil, and went into the bedroom to sort out my luggage. Now bedrooms have a curious effect on me, and it's nothing to do with sleep. I stood at the foot of the bed, letting those age-old primitive urges roll over me. The packing was postponed. I sat down by the phone, skimmed through my personal subscriber index, dialled a number. No answer. A second number was more fruitful.

''Allo, oui?' Her high, almost childlike voice called forth visions of longer-than-long, slimmer-than-slim legs, dark velvety skin, and nipples the size of cherries.

'C'est moi – Jack,' I announced.

'Jack, *mon cher*!' she squealed, with what I supposed was delight. Then, in English: ''Ow are you?'

'Fine, Evelyne, fine. But I'll be even better when you get here. Are you available?'

'For you, *chéri*, always. But first I have to tell you, I have had to make a leetle increase . . .'

'Bugger that, Evelyne, you get over here. We'll discuss inflation afterwards.'

She giggled, a delicious, schoolgirlish sound. 'I shall be there in thirty minutes. You can warm the bed while you are waiting.'

We said our *'A tout à l'heure'*, and cut the connection.

Evelyne was expensive, even without the increase. Her skill, her enthusiasm and inventiveness, and perhaps most of all, her cleanliness, entitled her to demand the sort of fees that most prostitutes only aspire to in moments of wild fantasy. She also ran her own company: exotic lingerie by mail order, which enabled me to pay for my pleasure with my AmEx card: a little refinement that somehow made the whole business so much less sordid.

Chapter Four

The Jaguar was drawn up at the kerbside, fresh from the high-priced ministrations of the local concessionaire, its black coachwork polished to the brilliance of patent leather. As always, the senior mechanic had returned it to me in person, and as I came out of the apartment block he was flicking residual specks of dust from the long, drooping bonnet.

I slipped him the customary ten Swiss franc-note, which he pocketed with an appreciative grin.

'Merci, patron. Bonnes vacances là-bas, et . . .' he patted the bonnet, *'bonne route. Attention la vitesse, hein?'*

He took off back to the garage on foot, and I chucked my two large suitcases, my canvas holdall, and my camera bag in the boot. I reached inside the boot, under the section between its front lip and the rear window, into the narrow padded compartment that didn't figure on the manufacturer's blueprint, and made sure the .38 Police Special revolver, with the two-inch barrel, was securely held in place by its spring clips.

Transporting arms, even a modest pistol, across the border into another country, was a risk; slight, but still a risk. I took it because I had grown accustomed to going everywhere with a gun, unless one happened to be waiting for me at my destination. It was a habit that would die hard, for I had many potential enemies.

Because of the gun, I intended to cross into France at Ambilly, where the customs officials are sloppy and their checks half-hearted at best, especially in the early afternoon.

I glanced up at the apartment before getting in the car; I don't know why – I wasn't sentimental about my home. Two balconies along, a movement caught my attention. Leaning on the steel rail, staring down at me was Schnurrpfeil. He waved, a slow-motion raising of the forearm. I nodded brusquely in return, and got behind the wheel. I wouldn't pine for *him* while I was away.

I eased into the hip-hugging seat. Only the thickness of my hair separated my head from the low coupe roof. I surveyed the maze of dials and switches and felt like a fighter pilot. In the six months I had owned the car I had covered less than five thousand kilometres, and almost all of that was long-range, top gear motoring. None of your pottering down to the shops for this piece of iron.

The sun was trying hard to shine, patches of blue here and there in the sullen skies. I fitted a pair of Polaroid sunglasses over my nose to give it some encouragement. Pulled on leather driving gloves. My Michelin route maps were to hand, in a map holder between the seats. I was always well-prepared.

I twisted the key. The engine broke into an indolent rumble, the twin tailpipes thrumming, the tacho needle steady on 400 rpm; Eight cylinders and 290 bhp of raw power literally at my fingertips.

A feather light touch on the accelerator and I pulled away from the kerb behind a milk tanker. Another tap of the toe and I was half way down the street. Wishing Herr Schnurrpfeil a fast ride to the ground floor without the lift.

The first stage of my journey, to Grenoble, was fast: *autoroute* nearly all the way, only slowing down for those infernal toll booths, blights on the otherwise superb French motorways. The weather conditions remained good for high-speed driving. I cruised at a lazy 150 kph, with the occasional faster burst on straight stretches where the police couldn't sneak up on me unseen.

I was in Grenoble before five o'clock and booked in at a modest hotel on the north side of the river, under the ramparts of the Fort de la Bastille.

The next day I left early. It was sunny, just the odd cottonwool ball of cumulus perambulating over the mountains. I likewise perambulated, taking the slow but pretty route south, via the Col de Croix Haute, one thousand, one hundred and seventy-six metres above sea-level, and often closed by snow in the winter. To Digne, my next staging post, was a leisurely one hundred and eighty kilometres.

I dawdled through the curves, let her off the leash on the infrequent straights, generally taking it easy and making halts whenever the panorama merited it. At these high atitudes, snow still lay picturesquely in the fields on either side of the road, and in the folds and creases of the mountainsides.

The mountains stayed with me, now only a blue-brown smear away to the east, now closing in; sometimes, dependent upon the twists and turns of the road, lying directly ahead. I lunched at a quaint, terraced *auberge* with a sweeping Périgordian roof rather like a witch's hat, just beyond Asprès.

As the miles unwound beneath the Jag's bloated

wheels and Geneva receded into the past, so my worries over Schnurrpfeil receded. I even began to toy with the idea of quitting Geneva altogether and moving to sunnier climes: Sardinia, perhaps, or southern Spain. After all, my residence in Switzerland had been governed by professional criteria which were no longer relevant.

Two girl hitch-hikers in faded jeans and halter tops, and laden with rucksacks, stuck out hopeful thumbs on the far side of the old stone bridge coming into the village of Montrand. I was tempted; I was always tempted by the opposite sex, but somehow I just wasn't in the mood; they were a bit on the young side, too. Further on, I did take pity on a woebegone motorist, standing by a old Peugeot with a collapsed front suspension. He was, I learned, a schoolmaster at Sisteron, a town along my route. I took him as far as the next village, which boasted a small motor repair outfit. And then I was alone again, in my instrument-laden cockpit, hands at a quarter-to-three, eyes swivelling to the mirror. Catching a glimpse of a dark blue BMW 3-series that rounded each bend behind me. How many dark blue BMW 3's in the whole of France? A thousand? Five thousand? Not so many as that, surely. And what were the odds against seeing a car of that description purely by chance on no less than four separate occasions within two days of driving? And always travelling in my direction, always pacing me no matter what my speed, never overtaking.

My survival antennae were bleeping ten-to-the-dozen. If . . . *if* I was being shadowed, by whom, and why? Not the police; they wouldn't tag along after me, halfway across France – they'd haul me in for a cosy grilling. So – a private enterprise operation. Then again, who? Schnurrpfeil immediately sprang to mind, for no obvious reason. Was he private fuzz?

It behove me to consider another, far more serious aspect: the BMW only appeared at intervals; it had not followed me constantly, I was sure of that. This pointed to a team of cars, working in relays, which, in turn pointed to a major operation. To maintain a tail of such sophistication for two days, using two or more vehicles, takes money and organisation. Which conclusion still led nowhere. It didn't tell me who or why.

At Chateau Arnoux the road forks, the N.96 going south-west to Aix, the N.85 south-east and later east, to Digne. There I passed under the railway, the sudden gloom inside the short tunnel bringing a curtain down over my vision, and searched again in the mirror for the BMW. The road was empty, and it stayed like that for several miles, until a motorcyclist came out of a side turning, exercising his *priorité à droite*, and nearly became another accident victim in the process. He rode ahead of me, rarely out of sight on this relatively bend-free section, and in due course I began to entertain suspicions about *him* too.

In a fit of annoyance, I wrenched the wheel over, pulling off the road on to a flat piece of ground serving as an unofficial lay-by. Dust spewed up in a thick, choking storm, rolling over the car. Geneva's monsoon weather obviously hadn't reached this corner of France.

I switched off the engine, cursing blue BMWs, motorcyclists, and my own paranoia. As I got out, an ancient truck clattered past, spilling gravel. I cursed it too, for good measure.

I took a can of beer from the pack behind the passenger seat, and sat on the bonnet, sipping the lukewarm brew, and watching all the cars go by. The two girl hitch-hikers passed in the back of an estate car, and one of them poked her tongue out at me. I grinned back to show there were no hard feelings. The motorcyclist didn't come back to look for me, and after a while I felt slightly foolish.

There had been a longish interval between vehicles and I was enjoying the solitude, when *she* went by, travelling at a sedate 70 kph or so, her face turning towards me: almost-blonde hair, shoulder length plus a bit, and tousled by the air-stream. I had only seconds in which to assimilate her features, but what I saw I liked: striking rather than classically beautiful, she had large eyes, colour uncertain, a generous mouth, a shade too much make-up for my taste. Then her concentration was back on the road, and I had a fleeting impression of a long but straight nose and a firm jaw.

That was all. Just a girl coasting along in a nondescript car – a Peugeot 306 to be exact. A fanciable, beddable girl, but just a girl for all that. There were thousands more of her breed down on the Côte d'Azur, just panting for wealthy, eligible males. I speak from experience.

So I didn't hare off after Miss Almost-Blonde. I polished off my beer and resumed my journey at the same unhurried pace, the engine barely ticking over. It was almost hot now, even up here in the foot-hills, yet I still drove with window open, rather than sealed up with the air-conditioning. I liked the play of wind on my face, the contact with the elements.

The railway ran parallel to the road for part of the way on the last lap before Digne, and an orange-and-silver SNCF express drummed by, decelerating for the station. I trailed after it into town, pulling up for a red light by the first of the two bridges spanning the River Bléone.

I glanced in my offside mirror, and my heart give a tiny skip. Sitting squarely in the centre of the mirror, just off the rear quarter of the Jag, was a motorcyclist. Nothing unusual in that, except that in my paranoid state I was ready to suspect all and sundry. It was impossible to say whether this motorcyclist and the one I almost ran down back along the route, were the same; the bike was the right colour, white, but beyond that my recollections were vague. I studied the rider: his head was mostly helmet, but the visor was raised and I took note of the flowing moustache with curly extremities, and the prominent Gallic hooter. I also noted the expensive motorcycle gear: black, one-piece leather suit, standard attire for all discerning bikers. No use at all though for future identification – too easily discarded. Clothes maketh not man.

The lights went to green and the crocodile of vehicles jerked away. I said goodbye to the *route nationale*, and went around the roundabout into Boulevard Thiers, past the park and the Municipal Swimming Pool, the motorcycle clinging on to me like a sticky bud all along the boulevard. Until I swung left into the pillared gateway of the courtyard of the Hotel Grand Paris, Digne's biggest and finest, when he accelerated away, continuing on down the road.

I was in an evil mood when I strode into the hotel reception, carrying the smaller of my two suitcases, convinced now that I was under some form of surveillance. I was short with the charming lady receptionist who managed to rise above my boorishness and smiled endlessly, no doubt regarding me as typical of my race. I also forgot to tip the flunkey who hauled my suitcase up to my room – a double (just in case) on the second floor, with running this, that and the other. Even a TV, still something of a luxury in traditional French hotels.

After a shower and a nap my humour improved, and I went for a walk around the town, pausing ostensibly to window-shop every few minutes, checking behind, ahead, and opposite, for persons of hostile intent. Silly really. All they had to do was keep a watch on the hotel.

Out of my walkabout came a resolve to bite back. To provoke a showdown on the road tomorrow. To extract a few answers by the tried and tested gun-barrel-in-the-teeth method.

It was warm enough to eat out of doors that evening and, in anticipation, several tables had been set on the terrace at the rear of the hotel. I declined the unspoken invitation; I enjoyed lingering over a meal and it would be ten o'clock or later before I finished. Digne is about two thousand feet above sea level and in May, even this far south, the nights were still nippy.

I was three quarters of the way through my dinner, carving into a triangular slab of Bleu d'Auvergne cheese when she came in. By 'she', I mean the girl in the Peugeot 306, the almost-blonde. She was dressed in a cool lemon shirt with a matching skirt that swirled about her knees, and she looked a treat. She didn't toss so much as a sideways glance my way as the waiter showed her to a table at the far side of the restaurant, and then rubbed salt in the wound by sitting down with her back to me. I resumed my attack on the cheese, but meditatively now, my mind elsewhere – specifically snuggling up to the almost-blonde. How to break the ice was the problem I now had to tackle, for broken it must be. A girl as luscious as this couldn't be left to her own devices for an entire evening. Or even an entire minute.

My techniques for ensnaring lovely ladies ranged from pre-emptive strike to subtle wooing. It all depended on my assessment of the subject and how much time I had to work on her. This one had all the outward self-confidence of a bra-burner and, since I was leaving in the morning, subtlety would have to be sacrificed for speed. Unfortunately, she was about to dine and it would have been bad form to barge in while she was eating. Patience, my boy, patience. We would see soon enough whether she was as delicious without her clothes as she was within them.

I was nothing if not self-confident.

I eked out the interminable wait with cognac-laced coffee. The restaurant, with its Napoleonic decor, contained little to divert. In human interest terms the girl was further removed from the other diners than the Taj Mahal from a council house: two sun-tanned elderly couples sharing a table by the tall window; a young sales representative-type demolishing an emperor-sized steak as though he'd just ended a year's fast; a middle-aged man and woman speaking German or Dutch – I was too far away to tell which; and, occupying a circular table near the double doors, a family of six: harassed-looking father with a mop of unruly hair, mother pretty and plump and laughing a lot, their brood, age range about three years old to early teens. Full of squeals and chatter. The way it might have been if Marion . . .

I elbowed the oncoming melancholia aside, concentrated on the girl's back since it was all she had given me to concentrate on. She didn't eat much: just the main course and fruit, with only mineral water to drink. Possibly a health fanatic. I waited until she was on her coffee before making my play.

There was a wide expanse of floor to cover and I felt a mite self-conscious as I homed in on her left flank.

'Bonsoir, mademoiselle . . . j'espère que je ne vous dérange pas.' You couldn't get politer than that.

She looked up, no surprise registering at the sight of me standing there instead of the waiter; maybe she couldn't tell us apart. Her un-plucked eyebrows climbed enquiringly.

'Please speak English,' she said, to the tinkling of icicles. She had no accent to speak of and was therefore probably English, whereas I had naturally assumed her to be French.

Whatever her nationality, she was, as I had judged from afar, stunning beyond my ability to describe. The most arresting feature was her lazy-lidded, slanting green eyes; there was a catlike quality about them and they were disturbingly worldly-wise, sizing me up almost cynically. Nose and mouth were both on the large side, but not ugly, and her hair was the near-blonde I've already mentioned; in pure trichological terms possibly only a step removed from mousey. Be that as it may, it was attractively styled in soft waves with a centre parting and fell across her shoulders thick and glossy. I put her age at twenty-five but I was often embarrassingly wide of the mark in such matters. Of her figure, not much was on show – her breasts were smallish, about the size of oranges, but jutted satisfactorily enough. The other bits would have to await inspection.

'I was apoligizing for the intrusion,' I said, fixing her with an ingratiating smile. 'May I introduce myself? My name is Henley . . . as in Regatta . . .' I got no further. The green eyes gave off a shower of sparks.

'How do you do, Mr Henley-as-in-Regatta? I'm sure you're aware you're a good-looking man. I expect lots of silly, empty-headed girls have told you so. As far as *I'm* concerned, however, you're just someone forcing his attentions on me. I am not, emphatically not, interested in talking to you, drinking with you, or going to bed with you; not tonight, tomorrow night, or any other night. So will you kindly piss off and find some other girl to pester.'

All this, I am thankful to relate, was delivered in an undertone and I was therefore able to retain some external semblance of dignity. I didn't take amiss – you can't win them all. Nor did I persist in my overtures. She was an attractive girl, more than attractive, and I would have given a great deal for an hour in her company. But when a girl gives me the cold shoulder, I accept it with a shrug and move on to the next in line. Regrettably, there was no visible next-in-line dossing at the Hotel Grand Paris this night.

I managed a stiff nod at Miss Iceberg and murmured an apology. I always tried to behave like a gentleman, even in adversity.

I signed the bill and went up to my room, where I switched on the TV. I was bored stiff within minutes and wandered into the palatial Louis XIV bathroom with its exposed pipes and cranky plumbing, there to release the evening's intake of liquid into the appropriate receptacle. Afterwards I examined my physiognomy critically in the mirror. It had been nice of her to say I was good-looking: I suppose I was – in the mould of a matinée idol of the thirties era. My hair was that cornfield yellow with a few kinks that looked artificial but weren't. Maybe she had reckoned I was too old for her. Now *there* was a thought to make you shudder. But, at thirty-eight, my jaw was still lean, no jowls or extra chins developing; teeth all my own, slightly crooked but still in good shape. I was tall, slim, no hint of a pot belly. I could easily have passed for a well-preserved thirty-seven.

I gave up regretting Miss Iceberg and this resurrected my dormant worries about blue BMWs and moustached motorbikers. Damn it, what with this mysterious gang tailing me through France and now the girl slapping me down harder than I've ever been slapped, my sabbatical was off to an inauspicious start.

To a ringing '*Bonne route, Monsieur*!' from the ever-smiling lady receptionist, I toddled across the vestibule and down the stone steps, out into the morning sunlight.

The Jag was half-in, half-out of a patch of shade thrown by the line of mature beech trees in the hotel courtyard. The boot lid was already warm to the touch. I stowed my suitcase away, discreetly removed the .38 from its place of concealment and transplanted it in another, less secret, but more accessible compartment under the glove box. In readiness for the planned confrontation.

My preparations complete, I was poised with one leg in the footwell when a voice hailed me from several cars down.

'I say.' It was female and slightly breathless. 'I say . . . could you help me?'

It was her – the almost-blonde with a nice line in brush-offs. Dressed in a white cheesecloth shirt with short sleeves, and skin-tight designer jeans. I was tempted to pay her in her own coin and drive off, leaving her to choke in my exhaust smoke. I didn't, because I can't say no to a pretty face.

'Are you speaking to me?' I said, as though the courtyard was full of people.

'Of course I am. There's no one else here!'

'Oh . . . well, since you ask so nicely . . .' I shut the door of the Jag and walked over to her Peugeot. She was standing in front of it, hands resting languidly on slim hips.

I braked in front of her. 'Well?'

'It's my car. I can't seem to get it in gear although the clutch feels all right.'

'I see.' If she had described the symptoms accurately, I didn't have to be a mechanical wizard to diagnose the problem. Solving it was another matter.

'Don't just stand there saying "I see",' she said tartly.

'All right.' I turned to go.

She grabbed my arm, her cool fingers encircling my elbow. Her grip was surprisingly strong.

'Look . . . about last night.' She looked down at her sandalled feet, presenting the top of her neatly-parted mane to me. 'I'm sorry. I was rather . . .'

'Rude?' I prompted. 'Yes, you were. But now your car's broken down, you're prepared to forgive and forget. Have I got it right?'

Her mouth formed an 'O'.

'Because, if so,' I ground on remorselessly, 'I insist that we talk, have a drink, and go to bed together, before I take a look at it.'

The 'O' grew bigger and rounder, and the eyes were lazy-lidded no more. Until I gave the game away by laughing. Then she laughed too, a sudden whoop, and there we were, two complete strangers, convulsed with mirth in the courtyard of the Hotel Grand Paris. The German-Dutch couple strolled past, trying unsuccessfully not to stare, and this restored a degree of sanity. It wasn't all *that* funny, anyway; I'd been more than half serious if she but knew it.

'I'm Georgina Gregg.' She stuck out a hand. A peace offering. 'And you're Mr . . . Henley. Have I got it right? As in Regatta?'

'So part of me made an impression at least. Jack Henley at your service, Miss Gregg. Now let's have a shuftee at this clutch of yours.'

The clutch pedal proved to have plenty of resistance, so the hydraulics were okay. But when I ran the engine and tried to engage gear, the lever wouldn't go through the gate, and horrible grating noises issued forth.

'It's an internal fault in the clutch unit,' I said from the driver's seat. She was leaning on the open door, her arms resting along the top edge, the cheesecloth pulled taut against her breasts. One notices these small details.

My diagnosis brought her out in a rash of anxiety.

'Is it serious? I've no mechanical knowledge whatsoever.'

'Serious enough to keep you in Digne for a day or more. The clutch will have to come out for repair or, more probably, replacement.'

'Oh, lord. I can't wait a day. I have to be in Monaco this evening.'

How about that for a lucky break? Opportunity was knocking again, much louder now. In a purposely flat voice I mentioned that Monaco was also my destination. It worked like a dream.

'I don't suppose you could give me a lift?' she said, and if I'd been writing her script I couldn't have done it better. 'I simply *must* be there by this evening. It's absolutely imperative, it really is.'

'You could always hire a car,' I suggested. I didn't want to appear over-eager for her company.

'There isn't time. You know how long the formalities take in France.' She directed those heat-rays eyes on me then, boosting them to maximum wattage. 'Please. I'd be so grateful.'

How grateful was that? wondered the bestial side of my nature.

I made a big show of relenting. 'Okay – why not? Two's company.'

'Oh, thanks. I really am grateful.' Her hand was resting on my forearm. I kind of liked it. 'I'll just pop into the hotel and get them to phone for a breakdown truck.'

'Do you want any help?'

'With the language, you mean?' She shook her very attractive head. 'I'm half-French; I've lived here all my life. My father's in the Diplomatic Service – rather, he used to be: he retired last year.'

This explained the tiniest nasal inflection in her otherwise Queen's English.

'But last night you said . . .'

'Speak in English?' She smiled, arching a coquettish eyebrow. 'That was to put you off. I thought *you* were French.' She skipped off, up the steps. I went around to the back of the Peugeot, opened the boot, and emptied it of her luggage: two pigskin suitcases and a large shoulder bag.

I mulled over the turn of events, the remarkable change in my fortunes, romantically-speaking. No chance of an overnight halt en route to Monaco, more was the pity, since she had to be there this evening, and even I wasn't such a heel as to engineer a breakdown. No, far better to strike up an *entente cordiale* during the seven hours' drive, which would naturally take in lunch, in the hope of an eventual night of bliss on board my boat. I wasn't greedy. I didn't seek a long-lasting, meaningful relationship, not even with this humdinger of a girl. Just a few hours in a double bed would do fine. Then we could kiss goodbye and forget each other's existence.

She emerged from the swing door, ran down the steps. She moved with the flowing ease of an athlete.

'Your three pieces of luggage are in my car,' I told her. 'Are there any odds and ends you want to take?'

'No thank you.' She was looking quite pleased with herself. I didn't ask why. It sufficed that she was in good humour.

We took our leave of the Hotel Grand Paris, Digne, and trundled out of town.

'Lovely car,' she remarked, caressing the leather upholstery. 'I'd love a Jaguar. Unfortunately, secretaries don't earn that kind of money.'

'Secretaries? Is that what you are?' I slowed down for the always-red lights by the bridge, accelerating when they changed unexpectedly.

'Mmm. For a company called Sud-Marine. They make diesel motors and marine equipment.'

I was stuck behind a horse box, the oncoming traffic inconveniently spaced so as to rule out overtaking. During this enforced crawl I did a rapid scan of all three mirrors for unwanted adherents. Several cars were queueing up behind me, but none of them stood out. The planned showdown was cancelled, of course: I could hardly produce a gun in front of the lovely Miss Gregg. Instead, I meant to use the Jag's speed and acceleration to shake them off. Also to impress her with my driving skill.

The road cleared. Darting past the horse box and a garbage truck, I gave the Jag the gun, blasting through the gears to 150 kph in the space of half a kilometre. The first bend spoiled that bit of fun, though I still negotiated it fast enough to make the tyres howl in anguish.

'Wow!' Miss Gregg gasped. 'I thought we were going to take off.'

I tucked in behind an Alfa with Torino plates, waiting for an opening. 'That was just to whet your appetite,' I said, and booted past the Italian. A white saloon followed through after me, but he couldn't keep up, was soon a diminishing dot in the mirror.

'Speed doesn't frighten you, does it, Miss Gregg?' I asked.

'Not in the slightest.' She didn't add, 'It makes me amorous,' which was something of a let-down.

After maybe a minute's silence, she said, 'By the way, my friends call me Gina.'

'Not George?'

'Gina,' she said firmly. 'You've been reading too many "Famous Five" books.'

I laughed. 'Not guilty. So Gina it is. I'm Jack.'

'Hello, again. And what do you do, Jack, when you're not using the highways of France as a race track?'

We were bowling into a set of bends and I was obliged to reduce speed to a 100 kph crawl. I had my answer ready; in fact, I had answers ready for a whole set of routine questions. She wasn't the first inquisitive young lady to sail into my harbour.

'Essentially I'm retired,' I said. No lie that. 'I made a pile in currency speculation. I still dabble from time to time but the opportunities aren't there any more. This single currency business will certainly take the fun out of it.'

She made no comment, just stared pensively

ahead. I had my work cut out holding a respectable speed on these bends, so I was content to let the dialogue lapse.

We drove on like that for some distance, making desultory conversation, remarking on this gorge, or that mountain. My mind was still partly on blue BMWs and suchlike; in that respect, my racing tactics seemed to have paid off. Towns and villages came and went: Châteauredon, Barrême, La Tuilière; then the murderous bends before Castlellane, loop after loop after loop.

We were through to La Garde before she renewed her not-so-subtle probing.

'You live in Switzerland, in Geneva.' It wasn't framed as an enquiry; she would have read the number plate.

'With the gnomes.'

'Well, it does have that image – or rather Zürich does. Genera is a rather un-Swiss town, I think.'

'If it wasn't, I wouldn't live there.' I whipped past a dawdling mail vain, illegally crossing a continuous white line.

'Naughty, naughty,' Gina chided. 'Just because you've got Swiss plates, don't think you can get away with murder.'

I agreed that was my philosophy. I'd been doing literally that for thirteen years.

We lunched at an *auberge* converted from an old water mill, somewhere north of Grasse, hemmed in by the mountains with their evergreen-clad slopes and grey notched summits. Peering at the hand-written menu together, our hands came into accidental contact and when she didn't pull away I experienced a tingle of pleasure, like a teenager on his first date.

'I'm going to have the *truite meunière*,' she decided, after a perusal of the *à la carte* section. 'But no starter.'

'I'll join you.'

We had *pastis* for aperitifs and, over them, I was tempted to fire a ranging shot across her bows, to test her reaction to an innuendo or two. But I held back, with what was, for me, commendable restraint.

'You must have thought me an awful bitch last night,' she said at some point during the meal. 'I was so cross with myself afterwards.'

'Were you?' I speared a juicy morsel of fish flesh. 'I deserved it. I was only trying to chat you up, and you were quite right to put me in my place.'

I could afford to be magnanimous now.

She left off munching and regarded me with a frown. 'I ought to tell you. I was married until . . . until recently. I've been rather . . . off other men.'

I expected her to elaborate. She didn't, so, as a gentle prompt, I said, 'Divorced?' Once my curiosity is aroused it has to be satiated. Like my lust.

She didn't respond, just chewed at her lip. I drew my own conclusions.

I tried to catch her eye, without success. 'I'm sorry . . . for you, that is.' For *me*, it was good news.

'Oh. I'm getting over it.' A quick, on-off smile. 'You're helping too, in a small way. Do you know, you're the first man I've been alone with like this since . . . since it happened.' She sniffed, and covered up her embarrassment by rummaging in the depths of her handbag from where, with a triumphant 'Ah!' she produced a crumpled handkerchief.

I pretended not to notice, concentrating on my food.

'My, this trout *is* good,' she said presently. 'How's yours?'

'Delicious.'

'I must come here again.' She wiped round her plate, French-style, with a hunk of bread. 'How old are you, Jack?'

'Thirty-eight.' I didn't like admitting to it publicly.

'And married?'

'Was. My wife died.' I didn't mention my second attempt, it was best forgotten.

'Oh.'

'It was a long time ago.'

She nodded jerkily. 'Since then?'

'You want me to bare my soul?' I joked. 'I'm hoping to sell my memoirs to the News of the World.'

'If they're *that* down-market, it might be better for you to keep them to yourself,' she agreed. 'Anyway, for a ripe old thirty-eight you've kept in good shape. I would have put you at around thirty-five.'

'Kind of you to say so. You don't look so bad yourself; what are you – twenty-five?'

She fluttered her eyelashes in mock-humility. 'My, my, the compliments shoh are flyin'', she said, in a parodied southern belle accent. Then she tittered self-consciously into her hand. 'Actually, I was twenty-nine last month.'

'I would say you're remarkably well-preserved, madam.'

This bit of badinage led her to talk about her life in France: educated at an exclusive and expensive school just outside Paris, courtesy of HM Government – a standard perk for diplomats' children; grew up bi-lingual, also fluent in Spanish and Italian; was accepted for the Sorbonne University – modern languages, naturally – which was about when she met and fell in love with her husband. That killed off all aspirations to a degree. She was eighteen, he twenty-one, and they got married within a month of meeting, much to the disapproval of both families.

She managed to spin the yarn without an emotional relapse, sticking to the bones and leaving out the meat. I didn't ask for more. It was enough that she was available. I didn't care whether she climbed into my bed on the rebound from her ex-husband, or because she genuinely fancied me. That's the beauty of pure, untrammelled lust; it's entirely physical and makes no demands at all on the soul.

This girl was giving me the biggest ache in my loins since I didn't know when. I was boiling up inside for her, and keeping off subjects sexual was a sore trial. I had a major challenge on my hands, and no mistake. An easy lay she was not.

'When you get to Monaco, what are your plans?' This, I felt, was an innocuous enough enquiry. It didn't smack of ulterior motives; I could be very devious when motivated.

She drained the last dregs of Fouilly Puissé from her glass before replying. 'My appointment is at six pm, at the Hermitage Hotel. I should be through there by eight. I'll probably stay there overnight and drive home in the morning in a hire car.'

Home being Marseilles.

Our waitress chose that delicate moment to come and clear away our dishes. Had we *bien mangé*? she asked, rather anxiously. We assured her that we had.

'Have you any commitment for dinner?' I said to Gina when we were alone again. This was a crucial question, and my heart, of its own accord, was thudding away fit to burst.

She didn't reply at once. She subjected me to a scrutiny that was almost hostile, before finally admitting she had no commitment for dinner.

'Your cue to make one for me, I presume,' she added dryly.

I made a moue. 'Don't be so cynical. But you're right, of course. I was going to ask you to join me. I always eat at the Hotel de Paris my first night in Monaco.' I didn't, but I hoped to impress her by name-dropping the most exclusive of Monegasque establishments. '*Will* you join me?'

She appeared to consider the proposition, her head tilted sideways. 'No strings?'

A whole ball of them, my love.

'No strings,' I said, in my best upright tone. 'Just eat and talk. Afterwards, you go to your bed, and I go to mine.' And if that's how the evening really ended, I'd give up chasing girls and take a vow of celibacy.

'I think perhaps not.'

'Why ever not?' I said lightly, hiding my irritation. 'Think of it as further therapy.'

'Therapy? With somebody like you, I rather suspect the reverse would be true.'

'Somebody like me?' I repeated blankly.

She hedged. 'I mean . . . oh, damn . . . Jack, you're a nice man. I like you and I've enjoyed your company during the drive. I don't want to offend you but . . . I think you know what I'm getting at.'

'Look, Gina, all I'm doing is inviting you to have dinner with me. It doesn't have to lead to anything – it takes two, and I'm no rape artist, believe me.'

'I do believe you, but it's still no thanks.'

With that I decided to let it drop for now. Our coffees arrived then, and between sips Gina asked where I would be staying in Monaco.

'On my boat.'

She frowned. 'You've got a boat? You didn't mention it before.' She made it sound like an accusation.

'I thought I had,' I said lamely. 'She's a thirty-four foot yacht named *Spindrift*. She's the reason for this trip.'

'Spindrift.' She said it slowly, as if savouring the word. 'What a romantic name. Spindrift is the spray that comes off the tops of waves, isn't it?'

'Something like that. Do you like boats?'

'Love them. I've a little dinghy of my own, only a modest three-and-a-half metres, nowhere near so grand as yours. Where have you sailed her?'

'Oh, most places in the Med: Corsica, Sicily, Malta, North Africa, the Greek Islands. The Canaries, too, and Oporto in Portugal.'

'You don't sail alone, do you? She'd be quite a handful, that size of boat.'

I poured more coffee for us both. 'No. A Frenchman, name of Pradelou, crews for me and takes care of the boat while I'm away. A first-class seaman: in his teens he crewed for Barrault, and more recently for the Jeanthiau brothers, so his credentials are excellent.'

'I'd love to see her – your boat.'

'You're welcome aboard any time.' I didn't make it any more specific than that – I didn't want another brush-off. I had my pride to consider.

After the coffee came the bill which was unbelievably modest, especially in comparison with Geneva restaurant prices.

'Bet you can't get me to Monaco before five,' Gina dared as we walked to the car.

It was 3.40 pm and Monaco about ninety minutes safe driving away. But the male ego, once stimulated, is a powerful force.

'Hang on to your nerves,' I grinned.

'Fighting words, sir. Now let's see fighting deeds!'

*   *   *

We crossed the non-existent frontier of the three-kilometre-by-three hundred-metre piece of real estate called Monaco, with five minutes in hand, but owing to a combination of road-works in the Boulevard de Suisse and a dithering Belgian tourist, I failed in the end to make good my boast. It was three minutes past the hour when we rolled up before the Hermitage's grandiose entrance, the blue-uniformed doorman snapping as smartly to attention as any Buckingham Palace sentry.

'Nice try,' Gina consoled.

I didn't trot out any excuses. 'Good thing for me we didn't lay bets.'

We both got out and the doorman came to unload Gina's luggage. All that remained now were the adieus.

'So . . .' Gina smiled brightly. 'Goodbye, Jack.'

'Au revoir is better,' I said, my lascivious hopes crumbling faster than a sandcastle at high tide. 'You know where to find me if you ever need another lift.'

She flushed at that barb. 'Thank you, Jack. It's been very pleasant. Good luck.' She turned and click-clacked on her stiletto-heeled sandals in the wake of her luggage. Leaving me out there in the hard sunlight, feeling foolish and frustrated.

That was to be the last I saw of her for six weeks.

Chapter Five

I drove down into the Port de Monaco, and parked the Jag opposite the automobile club offices. *Spindrift* was moored three-quarters of the way along the Quai des Etats-Unis, where most of the English and American-owned craft lie, and even from up here on the promenade I could pick her out by her distinctive royal-blue hull.

She looked good – sleek and racy, and the silver-anodised mast sparkled as though dipped in frost. I had bought her three years ago and she was still as new, thanks mostly to Jean-Pierre Pradelou who, for a yearly hundred thousand francs retainer, plus an extra thousand a week when he crewed for me, did all that was necessary and more, to keep her in trim. I was fastidious to excess: I even had her dry-docked once a year which, in Monaco, is as expensive an operation as ever conceived by mankind.

I passed the Bar-Restaurant du Port, tossing a greeting to Victor Jammais who ran the place and was on the edge of his terrace, peering about anxiously for hungry customers. With June still a week away he would be pressed to meet his overheads.

'I'll be along later,' I called over my shoulder to cheer him up.

'Merci, Jack! *A toute à l'heure.'*

I plodded on along the *quai,* glancing down at each

boat in turn, out of professional interest. I was still several berths short of *Spindrift* when, with a squeal of delight, a slight, jeans-clad figure exploded from her cockpit on to the quayside and was all over me while my hands were still full of suitcase.

Pascal was ten years old and the only son of Jean-Pierre. His mother had died giving birth to him, and Jean-Pierre had raised the boy alone. The result was a credit to him.

Although the French hugs-and-kisses greeting is alien to most Englishmen, I had long since grown accustomed to it and unselfconsciously gave Pascal the full treatment.

'Did you have a pleasant journey, Jack?' he asked, with solemn politeness, and I laughed, well aware that his father drilled him mercilessly in protocol, in advance of my arrival.

'Excellent, Pascal, thank you.'

We spoke in French, the *lingua franca* on board *Spindrift*, though Jean-Pierre and I were inculcating into the boy everyday English phrases such as 'Where is the nearest brothel?' and 'I am admitting nothing until I speak to my lawyer.'

'How's your father?' I asked him, as we covered the last few yards to the boat; he struggling manfully at his own insistence with the smaller of my two suitcases. 'I hope you've been looking after him properly.'

This was a standing joke between us. Jean-Pierre was that comparative rarity among Frenchmen: he couldn't cook. Even so straightforward a culinary process as heating up a tin of soup usually ended in disaster. Conversely, Pascal showed signs of becoming a true *cordon-bleu*, and during his holidays catered for both of them.

'Yes. Last night I did *moules marinières* and *veau escalope*.'

'I hope he appreciated it,' I said gravely.

He flashed me an engaging grin. 'But of course.'

He was a fine-looking boy, typically Mediterranean with straight dark hair, olive complexion, and huge brown eyes. Tall for his age and bright, his ambition was to be a merchant seaman, ultimately to captain his own vessel. He was already making progress towards that goal, helping out on *Spindrift*.

As we stepped down from the gangplank into the cockpit with its slatted teak seats, Jean-Pierre came out through the companionway, massaging oily hands around a no-less oily rag. He was clad in a pair of blue overalls open to the waist, his barrel-shaped chest a V of black curls.

Our handclasp was warm, born of real mutual affection.

'*Comment vas-tu, Jack?*' His grin was as broad as the horizon, teeth flashing in a bronze visage, an adult replica of Pascal. He was shorter than me, but more than made up for it in other directions. Stripped, he was all bulges and rippling flesh; alongside him, I was skinny. His pugilistic frame fortunately contained a mild manner.

'Very well, Jean-Pierre. And you?'

'Also. The boat is fine too,' he added, anticipating the enquiry.

I made a noise to indicate satisfaction. 'You can take me over her tomorrow. Meanwhile, I could use a shower.'

Pascal's voice floated up the companionway: my suitcases were installed in the so-called master suite, and would I like a beer. I told him to bring one for his father, too.

We killed an hour, and more than just the one beer apiece, Jean-Pierre and I; sitting in the cockpit, updating each other on our respective doings since the end of last season. From there we could see right across the harbour with its surrounding crescent of buildings, dominated by the Rock and the Royal Palace, to the sheer, wrinkled wall of the Tête de Chien *massif* frowning down on the concrete and glass towers clustered in pastel-coloured steps on its lower slopes. The orange parasols that lined the Boulevard Albert during the summer months were not yet in evidence and the harbour looked curiously stark without them; the tall slab of the triple high-diving board at the Nautical Stadium made a lonely landmark.

'It is early for you to come here,' Jean-Pierre commented, levering the cap off yet another beer. 'I was surprised when you telephoned me on Friday.'

'It was a spur-of-the-moment decision. The weather has been lousy in Geneva – nothing but rain, rain, and more bloody rain.'

'Here, also, until ten days ago. Now I think the sun is here to stay.' He drank thirstily in great swallows, emptying the bottle. 'So, Jack . . . where shall we sail this year? I have some new charts for Corsica and Sardinia.'

I gave a small chuckle. 'That's an unsubtle hint that you'd like to visit your brother.'

'Well . . .' He looked sheepish. 'If you decide to go to Corsica, it is true that I would like to visit him. But, of course, the decision is entirely yours.'

He knew damn well we would be going to Corsica. I was a soft touch.

Pascal came aft; he had been operating the radio-controlled model yacht I had brought for him. Now it was tucked possessively under his arm, and his face was lit up brighter than Monaco at night.

'It goes very well, Jack,' he announced. 'I can control it from more than a hundred metres. Thank you very much.'

I ruffled his hair. There were times when I wished I had a son like Pascal. He evoked pleasure and regret in equal proportions: the pleasure I derived from his presence; the regret for a son that never was and never likely to be.

'You can give me a demonstration in the morning,' I said. 'Right now I'm going to shower and then we'll go and eat.' I glanced at Jean-Pierre who was eyeing his son fondly. A lucky man: uncomplicated, undemanding, content with his lot. All he lacked was a wife, but then, like me, he preferred to play the field. He didn't go short of those special comforts only womankind can supply.

True to my promise, we dined at the Restaurant du Port, washing oysters, king-sized *langoustines*, and other sundry sea creatures down with a magnum of Möet '89. Our first and last meals of the season were always in the nature of a celebration; in between the two occasions we made do with wine.

I slept badly on board *Spindrift* that night, as was invariably the case until I grew used to the gentle undulation of the deck and the slap-slap of water against the hull, inches away from my pillow. On top of this I had to contend with the encroaching image of a certain Georgina Gregg and what might-have-been. The sense of frustration was strong. At my age, every night spent alone was a night wasted.

So it was that I rose next morning, sometime after nine, in below-par humour. Jean-Pierre and Pascal took my grumpiness in good part, and after a breakfast of black coffee and a mountain of hot croissants, we did our customary inspection tour.

Spindrift was an Evasion 34 Bermuda-rigged yacht, built by Beneteau in France, and partially customised internally with a single master bedroom forward instead of the two rather crampled doubles provided as standard. She was a fin-keeler, with wheel steering in the cockpit and a second position in the wheelhouse-cum-saloon for control in bad weather. The standing rigging was of stainless steel and she carried three sails: main, stay, and a furling Yankee jib. Auxiliary power came from a Perkins 50 hp diesel inboard.

Her equipment included an inflatable tender, Antohelm steering, echo sounder and repeater, transceiver, gas detector, radar reflector, and beaching legs to keep her upright when stranded at low tide. We were a sail-anywhere outfit.

That afternoon we made ready for sea. We were going to sail across to Bastia, in Corsica, spend a day or two in port for Jean-Pierre's annual brotherly reunion, then on down the western side of the island to take advantage of the nor'westerly airflow, to neighbouring Sardinia – it would be my first visit to that island.

From Sardinia we would head for north Sicily, then back up the boot of Italy, stopping off at Naples, Rome, and possibly Genoa, returning to Monaco at the end of June. Just the three of us. No girls on board. But it would be a rare voyage indeed when, at our ports of call, Jean-Pierre and I went short of nubile partners.

There was only a warm, light breeze to help us along when we cast off in the early evening, and I used a short burst of the motor to kick us clear of our berth, past our immediate neighbour, the American catamaran *Sailaway*. An Offshorer speedboat dribbled past our bows, heading, like us, for open water. Its only occupant, a bearded man in a peaked yachting cap, waved to Jean-Pierre who broke off from unfurling the mainsail to return the greeting.

Once past the harbour mouth, the swell caught us and a stiff breeze arrived from nowhere. I brought *Spindrift*'s head round to the wind and held her on a low throttle to reduce the pitch and roll, while Jean-Pierre sorted out the canvas.

Pascal stayed in the cockpit with me, practising with the helm. As yet he was too young to be entrusted with it unsupervised, but he was a fast learner and, equally important, he was strong.

'Next year,' I promised, 'we'll promote you to relief helmsman.'

His eyes sparkled like firecrackers, and we grinned at each other in easy companionship.

Jean-Pierre was winding up the halyard, the sail climbing steadily up the tall mast, rustling and flapping as the breeze caught it. Having secured the vang, the strap that holds the boom in place and reduces mainsail twist, he came aft. The sail began to fill as I bore away to leeward; a sharp gust hit us while we were still on the turn, and *Spindrift* heeled over, sails crackling, a small bow wave forming. Jean-Pierre switched off the engine and now there was only the creak of the boom, the hum of the rigging, and the rush and chuckle of water under the hull.

'Next stop Bastia,' I said to Jean-Pierre.

He winked. It wasn't only his brother he intended to look up over there. In a recent letter, his brother had spoken of a blonde divorcee, awash with generous alimony payments and ripe for plucking.

Good for Jean-Pierre. Good for me, too: the blonde

divorcee had a younger sister, also blonde, also divorced, also ripe.

Thirty-eight eventful days later we sailed back into Monaco harbour under a molten sunset.

Thirty-eight days in which we had battled with force ten gales, been intercepted by an Italian Coast Guard cutter on suspicion of smuggling heroin, and run aground off Naples – to mention but a few of the trials that had beset us. We had fought battles of another kind, too: my most memorable concluded with a drainpipe descent at dawn from the boudoir of a voluptuous Italian *contessa*, whose husband, renowned for his violent temper and the pearl-handled pistol he carried, returned home unexpectedly at the disgustingly early hour of 9.30 a.m.

As for Jean-Pierre: his tangle with the private property of an over-protective Sicilian pimp was resolved satisfactorily, and the unsavoury little gentleman was last seen suspended upside down by his fancy braces over the pan in the evil-smelling Men's Room at the 2000 Club in Palermo.

Having screwed and whored our way around the western half of the Mediterranean, we were coming back, dissipated and weathered, to recover from our excesses and our escapades. As we tied up at the *quai* I noticed that *Sailaway* had sailed away.

Jean-Pierre and Pascal were going home to the neighbouring town of Roquebrune for a few days. All I wanted to do was get my head down for the next century which, having seen them off, I promptly did.

The next day, a Saturday, was the last day of June and I was restored enough to do a dozen press-ups on deck before breakfast. A modern motor yacht had entered harbour overnight, and was riding at anchor, her white thoroughbred profile mirrored in the still surface of the water. Elsewhere the usual hustle and bustle; a tiny cabin cruiser was being lifted on to the opposite quay, her bottom festooned with streamers of weeds and great clumps of barnacles.

I breakfasted off day-old rolls and afterwards went to see the Harbourmaster. I was crossing the road by the police station when my eardrums were smitten by a squeal of brakes, punctuated by the crunch of metal and the dainty tinkle of glass breaking. Like everyone else within earshot, I swung round, seeking the source of the accident. A scruffy, once-yellow VW tourer had rammed the rear of a black limousine with dark-tinted windows, and the drivers of both vehicles were getting out for ritual remonstrations. I clicked my tongue sympathetically and was about to resume my walk when the car behind the VW made me do a double-take: it was a dark blue BMW 3-series.

The weeks of high seas and low dives had exorcised my BMW phobia and I almost thought nothing of it. Even the driver's curly black moustache, which ought to have recalled a certain motorcyclist in Digne, didn't set the alarms ringing. It was the man occupying the passenger seat who raised the hairs on the back of my neck: *Herr Sturmführer* Carl Schnurrpfeil.

He was looking towards me with some anxiety, as well he might, and while I was still doing my imitation of a waxwork, his nerve broke. The BMW reversed, too hastily, and crunched into the car behind. They didn't hang about to exchange insurance details. To enraged horn blasts from the damaged car, they U-turned out of the line, bringing traffic travelling in the opposite direction to a screeching halt, and tore off up the hill towards Monte Carlo.

Their panicky departure confirmed that, whatever

lay behind their interest in me, it wasn't benign. Schnurrpfeil's references to Munich and November, that morning at the Comédie, had not been throw-away remarks. They were part of . . . what? What *was* their game? This perpetual surveillance that seemed so purposeless. I was back to square one, back to where I had been in Digne. Puzzled and angry.

Then, my solution had been to force a showdown. So be it. Though if there were two (or more?) of them, I would need an equalizer – my .38, now secreted away on *Spindrift*.

After my meeting with the Harbourmaster, a minor matter of new mooring regulations, I returned to the boat and removed the gun from behind the false back of the wardrobe in my cabin. As I tossed the weapon in my hand I was forced into a reappraisal: to fire it in Monaco was to court disaster. The city has no open spaces, apart from the Palace grounds; from east to west it is solid concrete, and a gunshot would be heard across half the principality. What use is a gun you can't fire?

I put it back behind the panel. I had just remembered the switch-blade knife in the locker above my bed.

It was a brute of a weapon, with a single-edged six-inch blade and a fast savage action. I thumbed the cutting edge: it was well-honed but flecked with rust, and I decided to give it a few licks with a file. Perhaps a drop of oil in the mechanism too.

After my maintenance work on the knife, I spent the rest of the day on deck, restless and heavily disguised under a multi-hued baseball cap with a peak big enough to land a helicopter on, and a pair of sunglasses. Only removing the latter to sweep the harbour and the adjacent streets with my binoculars, like an army commander surveying enemy trenches.

These particular enemies were keeping their heads well down.

When darkness began to close in, the lights along the quay springing into life, I called it a day, changed into a lightweight dove-grey suit and went at an easy stroll for a session at the baccarat tables of Monte Carlo's casino.

Midnight-plus found me comfortably settled at the table by the main door of the *salon privé*, plaques to the value of fifteen thousand francs stacked before me, a profit of five thousand francs on my original stake.

A rotund Italian with the jowls of a bloodhound and a neck that had more folds than a concertina, held the bank, and he was making sweat the way a squeezed lemon makes juice. With good reason: his bank was showing a loss of fifty thousand or more, mostly because of his own inept play, brinkmanship alternating with over-caution.

There were two *tableaux*. I was in the left with seven others, of which more were winners than losers. The most successful player of the evening was opposite me, a woman in her middle-thirties, ravishing and ravishable, with raven hair drawn severely off her high, smooth forehead into a serpentine coil that hung down her back. Her eyebrows were thick black commas over her blue eyes, and she didn't shave her armpits either. Her figure was all good old-fashioned curves: when she walked in she had set the *salon* alight with her mobile behind. The slinky black dress, which had the sheen of silk but wasn't – it didn't crease – clung to her like a skin diver's outfit. She spoke French, but execrably and with a North American twang.

Glances had passed between us now and again as the game progressed. Mostly she looked away quickly, hiding behind another long cigarette, carefully fitted into a slim black holder. She smoked incessantly.

'Un banco de cinquante mille,' the croupier was chanting, and I realised with a start that the player on my left had passed and it was my shout.

I gave a small nod. *'Banco.'*

The Italian perspired anew. Good. Anxiety makes for bad judgement.

The dimpled hand that delivered my two cards was trembling. I hid my contempt, frowned at the pair of deuces making four points. On a count of less than five, one always draws a third card. Which I did and received an ace, bringing me up to five points. Big deal.

The Italian flipped his cards over, smiled down at an eight and a queen. At bacarrat court cards have no value, therefore his total was eight. He won. His mouth formed a crescent of jumbled yellow molars as the croupier shovelled five of my plaques across the table into no man's land.

The dark-haired treasure cast a sympathetic eye in my direction. I responded with a wry smile and a shrug to match. Contact established.

On the green baize in the centre of the table there now reposed a hundred thousand francs. A useful pot.

'Un banco de cent mille,' the croupier droned.

At this point I could either pass or commit the rest of my plaques. The greasy Italian was watching me closely under lowered eyelids, the wide, flabby shoulders hunched with tension. Smoke from the cigarette in the ashtray by his arm rose in a spiral towards the hooded shades illuminating the table. Around us the murmur of voices from other tables, the imperious cry of a croupier, *'Rien ne va plus.'*

'Suivi.' The word tripped spontaneously off my tongue. I couldn't back down before the delicious North American lady on whom I was now having certain designs. Even losing my stake was better than losing face.

Again the cards, skimming over the baize. They lay there, pieces of pasteboard, inoffensive yet deadly. Men have paid with their lives on a show of cards. I picked them up slowly, fanned them behind my hand. Four and three made seven. A respectable enough tally.

Fatso Italiano revealed his hand: six and an ace, also seven. A draw. Unlike *vingt-et-un*, a draw at baccarat does not result in a win for the bank, so I could let it ride; the other players would expect it.

Normally I would have done just that.

The lady across the table was smoothing a tendril of hair back over her ear. Her gaze was on me and there was no flinching now when I held it. Then, as I was about to lay my cards face down on the baize, settling for what I had, her lips puckered ever so slightly in a blown kiss.

In a sudden rush of madness, incited by that tiny gesture, I went for broke.

'A card,' I said top the Italian. He shot one out, unhesitatingly, flicking it across. I faced the card: a two! Now I had nine, the maximum count; unbeatable. The Italian would likewise have to draw a deuce to save himself and the stake.

His card slid out of the shoe and it was a nine, giving him sixteen, less the ten, since only the final digit counts at baccarat: thus a final total of six.

My heart nearly went out to the fat slob. Sweat had soaked his jet-black hair and he looked like a fat wet cat. He regarded me stonily and without warmth. I hoped he wasn't a big wheel in the Cosa Nostra – you never could be sure with Italians.

The huge mound of plaques was bulldozed across to me. I tossed five hundred francs to the croupier, who signalled a *huissier* to wheel my small fortune off to the *caisse*. For me the game was over, *this* game at any rate. Other games were about to commence.

'Bonsoir, monsieur,' the croupier said effusively. *'Merci et à bientôt.'*

'Je vous en prie,' I responded.

The dark-haired dish was on her feet too, murmuring in the ear of a *huissier*. He glanced sharply at me, and spoke to her in an undertone. I circled the table as she vacated her place and left the *huissier* in charge of her quite respectable pile of plaques.

'Mr Henley, I presume?' she said, beating me to it. At close quarters I still couldn't fault her looks, though the make-up had been laid on with a trowel. Her breasts were middling size and drooped rather sensuously. No artificial uplift there.

'And you'll be Dr Livingstone,' I rejoined, taking her arm. She let me lead her across the sea of red carpet, to the nearest bar. As we walked, past walls adorned with tapestries and paintings, symbolising the splendour of a bygone era, I tried to peek down the front of her dress, but all was in shadow, mysterious and exciting.

'What do I really call you?' I enquired, once we were installed on the high padded bar stools.

'Mrs Folkov,' She spelt it out for me. 'That's V-o-l-k-o-w.' She had used the correct German pronunciation.

I wagged my finger censoriously. 'Mrs is a title I don't recognize.'

'All right.' She gave in without a song and dance, which was a good omen. 'Drucilla, then – or Dru, if you prefer.'

'Hello, Dru – I'm Jack.' The dry Martinis I had ordered appeared and we raised our glasses, eyes exchanging signals over the rims.

'Where's Mr Volkow?' I said, not really caring a hoot – unless he happened to be right behind me.

'On the yacht.'

'The yacht? Would that be the big diesel job that sailed in last night?'

She nodded.

'So-o-o,' I said thoughtfully. 'You're not short of a dollar or two. Which means I don't have to offer you any to get you where I want you.'

Some woman might have been insulted. Not this one.

'Where might that be?'

'I'd prefer to show rather than tell.' I downed the rest of my drink. 'Your place or mine?'

'I have a room at the Hotel de Paris across the road.'

How convenient. 'Don't you sleep on the yacht then?' I said innocently.

She gurgled delightfully. 'Sure – I *sleep* on the yacht.'

The penny dropped. 'Oh . . . and I thought *I* was being forward.'

She took my hand, squeezed it. 'You know, you're the best looking man I've met . . .'

'Thank you.'

'. . . this evening,' she finished, tongue visibly in cheek.

I pretended to be stung. 'For that, Mrs Volkow, you're going to get your nipples nibbled.'

'Ooh . . . yes, please,' she breathed and she wasn't fooling around any more. A pink arrowhead of a tongue wormed around the outside of her lips, a come-on of such blatancy it gave me an instant hard-on.

'We'd better go,' she murmured. 'You're making me all wet.'

I blinked. 'What do you think you're doing to me?'

'Er . . . mmm.' She had suddenly acquired a puzzled air. 'Do you know that man?' She was staring towards the wide corridor that led to the *salon privé*.

'What man?' Right then I wasn't interested in men, but I dutifully half-turned for a look-see.

'He's been watching us ever since we came in the bar.'

Had my mind not been full of other matters I might have reacted a bit faster. The man in question, lurking by the square pillar in the centre of the corridor, was Curly Moustache, motorcyclist and, latterly, chauffeur to Schnurrpfeil. While recognition was still dawning on me, he took off like he was jet-propelled.

'Wait for me in the hotel lobby,' I snapped at Dru, and fairly shot across the bar, careless of the milling multitudes, using my elbows to clear the path. Abuse flared in my wake.

I passed the startled commissionaire and burst out of the main entrance into the cool night air. I spotted CM straightaway: he was the only person doing a hundred metres sprint across the Place du Casino with its serried ranks of Rolls-Royces, Ferraris, and Mercs gleaming expensively under the street lights.

In physical terms I was undeniably past my peak and though still good for a short, high-speed dash I wouldn't have stood an earthly of catching CM – if he hadn't tried to cross the road just as a procession of three taxis came sweeping around the island in the centre of the square. He wallowed uncertainly at the kerbside, like a becalmed sailing boat, while I ran down the casino steps and belted across the square. Late-night promenaders goggled at the unusual spectacle of a man in a lounge suit running full pelt through the tranquil streets of Monte Carlo.

Discarding the idea of crossing the road, CM accelerated away towards the Café de Paris, via the island. But he had left it a fraction of a second too late and, with a flying rugby tackle that would have won me a standing ovation at Twickenham, I brought him down.

We rolled over in the lush grass of the island, hidden from view by the shrubs and bushes that grew there in such profusion, and came up against the bole of a dumpy palm. I tried to put an arm-lock on chummy and made a hash of it: he was slippery as a bar of wet soap and no sooner had I got a firm grip on a wrist when it dissolved and left me clutching at the night. Fortunately, he was slight of build and I had weight and strength very much on my side. Henley's big battalions would inevitably prevail.

I ought to have remembered the adage about famous last words.

'Now, you bastard,' I said, using French, when I finally had him pinned to the grass, his neck under my arm. 'What's the idea? Why are you following me? Who's paying you?'

His teeth were bared like the fangs of a rabid dog. He renewed his struggles, arching his back to throw me off. That earned him a sock in the ribs and he grunted with pain, which was some sort of progress.

So I did it again, only harder. It made a satisfying thump. I felt better.

'Spill it,' I snarled at him. 'Come on, you little shit-heap – give!'

He was tough all right. He suffered my punches in jaw-clenched silence; our scuffle had so far passed unseen and he would be as anxious as I was to keep it that way.

'Who's your boss?' I demanded, shaking the little rat like a cocktail, banging his head on the ground, a procedure which probably did more harm to the turf than to him. His teeth rattled but no other sounds came forth.

While I was concentrating on his head I had let go of his body. Next thing I knew he executed a tricky manoeuvre with his legs that had me hunching up to protect my privates. He pulled free of my clutches and staggered to his feet.

And that wasn't the only device in his repertoire.

A slim-bladed stiletto came between us, leaping into his hand, as neat a conjuring trick as you ever saw. A grin of malicious delight illuminated his features. The slick, smooth way he'd summoned up that foot of steel, now flashing and winking at me as it caught the casino lights, unnerved me.

'I think you are not so brave now, *hein*?' he said, in the thick accent of the Midi with its flattened vowels. He was right. I wasn't eager to rush in and mix it with that overgrown knitting-needle. Until I remembered the switch-blade in my inside pocket. If I wasn't quite so fast on the draw as chummy, I was fast enough to wipe away his smirk. The blade came out with a businesslike smack.

'You were saying?' I crooned, with a confidence I didn't really feel.

He didn't retreat. His stance merely became more wary, more alert, and his knife arm extended, the needle-sharp tip of the blade aimed at my throat. It occurred to me I might have picked the wrong man to cross blades with: he handled that sticker as if he was born to it.

At my back, traffic was still moving, hissing around the tight bend of the Avenue de Monte Carlo; I could even hear the voices of passers-by only feet away. I suppose I could have bolted, throwing pride to the winds. There was a strong inducement to do just that waiting for me at the Hotel de Paris. I didn't though: above all, I still wanted to make the guy talk. I might never get another opportunity.

At arm's length we described a watchful circle, each searching for a weak spot in the other's defences.

'*Allons-y, mon brave,*' he taunted. 'I am going to cut you into little pieces and feed you to the fish in the harbour.' Which didn't at all fit in with my plans to exit the world at a ripe seventy-plus, with a troupe of mourners and a carved headstone to mark my last resting place.

He feinted, lunged, missed my rib cage by no more than half-a-centimetre, feinted and lunged again, proving that he knew his stuff depressingly well. At the third lunge I deflected his blade with a crude but vicious sideways slash, turning the weapon aside and almost disarming him in the process. His eyes glinted, with fury rather than fear. He came at me again, and I made the only evasive move open to me – a backward hop to get out of range of that darting point. He swore as I slashed defensively, a series of rapid swipes, no finesse at all.

He had me on the run. Lunge followed lunge, while I twirled and pirouetted, giving ground until my back thudded against that fat palm tree and I could give no more.

'Enfin . . .' he said, a whisper of triumph.

The thin blade lanced towards me, a savage stab that would have gone clean through me had it connected. I saved myself by sidestepping, lifting my knife to counter his thrust. The stiletto went through my jacket under the armpit, missing my sacred flesh and pinning me to the tree by my sleeve. My knife was still descending and it didn't stop until it cleaved through his right bicep, up as far as the hilt.

He forgot all about the need for reticence. His yodel of pain was truly a prodigious fortissimo. He wrenched free, taking the switch-blade with him, lashed out wildly with his good arm, doing more mischief with that uncoordinated blow than all his previous efforts put together: it caught me under the chin and knocked me backwards into a small and extremely prickly bush.

Then he was gone, abandoning his stiletto which stuck out at right angles from the tree, a good third of the blade embedded. I didn't pursue him. I was still groggy from his lucky punch. I was also impaled on multitudinous thorns. In any case, of more pressing concern was the attention chummy's noisy exit had attracted. A buzz of excited voices close by spurred me on and, much as I would have preferred to disengage my hindquarters a thorn at a time, I concentrated instead on escaping undetected. Heading away from the rising hubbub, I emerged on the far side of the island into a deserted part of the square. The stiletto I left in the tree; I wasn't sure I was physically capable of plucking it out. Anyway, it bore no incriminating evidence: no Henley dabs, and – thank God – no Henley blood.

I brushed loose dirt and other nameless adhesions from my once-immaculate suit, now multi-hued, and made off towards the Hotel de Paris where hopefully Mrs Drucilla Volkow still awaited me.

At the hotel entrance the *de rigueur* commissionaire in his smart beige outfit, bedecked with braid and brass buttons, was pacing back and forth. He gaped at my dishevelled appearance, stuttered a belated '*Bonsoir, monsieur.*'

'*J'ai eu un accident,*' I muttered by way of explanation. '*Je visite* Madame Volkow.'

I swept royally past him, nose elevated as befits a frequenter of the Hotel de Paris, and on through to the reception lobby. There I came to a dead stop: no Dru. My delightful de-lovely wanton had run out on me.

A rotund, uniformed figure rolled up at a tangent: the night porter.

'Monsieur 'Enley?'

'*Oui!*' I barked and he took a backward step in alarm.

'Er . . . Mrs Volkow asks that you join her in Room 202,' he said, round-eyed.

So the hussy hadn't deserted me after all. I gave the porter a bank note without even looking at it; if his incredulous reaction was anything to go by it must have been a big one. That's me – all heart.

I spurned the lift and went up the wide, curving staircase as if it were a downhill piste.

Room 202 had a mahogany-stained door with a large buzzer set in the centre. I thumbed it.

'Come in,' she called immediately.

I did as I was bid, going through a short entrance hall into the day room. And there she was at last, disappointingly still clothed in the black dress, though her hair was uncoiled and hung to her narrow waist, a shimmering, lustrous cascade.

'You took your time,' she accused, her eyes roving over my suit. 'Have you been in the wars, or what?'

'In a way. The guy I went after has been tailing me and I wanted to know why.'

'Understandable.' She had a glass half-full of green liquid: *crème de menthe.* 'You want something to put some zest and zing back into you?'

'Don't mind if I do. Scotch and soda, if you've got it.'

'What happened?' she said as she poured a snorter the QE2 would happily have floated in. 'Did he get away?'

'Yes, but he was leaking.'

'You don't say. Better not tell me any more. I don't want to be an accessory after the fact, or whatever.'

'Maybe we ought to do other things instead.'

The suggestion seemed to find favour with her. She crooked a finger and went through an open door on my left: the bedroom, what else? I tagged along obediently and the immediate impression was of light. Lots and lots of it, including some free-standing spotlights placed strategically around guess-what. So it was to be *that* kind of session. I didn't mind. I would much rather see the goods on offer – in particular as picturesque a package as Mrs Drucilla Volkow.

She had set her drink down on a small table at the head of the football-pitch-size, four-poster bed. Now she faced me.

With a knife in her slim, white hand.

I had had my fill of knives for this evening. I didn't even stay to ask why, but went full astern.

'Don't be stupid,' she snapped. 'I want you to cut it off!'

That showed me. 'What?' I said weakly.

'My dress, dummy.' She reversed the knife; the black plastic haft now pointed towards me. 'Cut it off!'

A-*ha*. Now she was talking my language. I didn't protest about ruining an expensive dress: that was her business. Mr Volkow, with his luxury yacht and all could surely afford to have them run up by the dozen.

I deposited my glass next to hers so it wouldn't feel lonely, and took the proffered knife.

We lay on our backs, Dru smoking, me just recovering. All was quiet except for the rasp of our breath and the muffled throb of the city's night-time pulse, drowned by the occasional passing car.

It had been an experience to end all experiences. A pinnacle of sexual fulfilment from which, realistically, the only route lay downwards, a long spiral of decline to ultimate, inevitable impotence. Not an enticing prospect.

Twenty minutes, no more, had gone by when she raised her beautiful head, the raven hair now in disorder, the make-up smeared, yet still hotly desirable.

'Well?' she said, propping herself up on one elbow. Her finger traced a line down the centre of my forehead, over my nose and down my chin.

'What?'

'Is that *all* you're going to do, lover?'

Bloody hell! I puffed out my cheeks. 'Give me half-an-hour to get up steam.'

'The fuck I will!' She got busy with mouth and fingers, and in no time at all I was multiplying and being fruitful again. To my utter astonishment.

'This time . . . I want it up my ass. Okay?' She fixed

me with a challenging stare, expecting objections.

In matters of sex, I never said no. The more arcane pleasures of the flesh were no stranger to me.

'Let's go,' I said, and she resumed an action-stations posture.

It was a tight fit, but with liberal applications of extraneous lubricant we managed it. Marvellous stuff Ambré Solaire – so versatile.

I breakfasted with Dru at a window table from where you could see out over the lavishly-tended casino gardens across the Point Focignana to the sparkling blue vista of the Med. Except it wasn't sparkling this particular morning; a rare sea-mist had cast a clammy shroud over it and all was damp and dismal.

I was, perforce, dressed casually, in shirt sleeves and the trousers of my suit, restored to not quite their former glory by the hotel's damage-control service; the jacket was still under intensive care.

Dru was as bright and merry as the weather was dull and gloomy. In a jersey dress of blue and white diagonal bands, her hair tied loosely back with a matching ribbon. She had confessed to thirty-three summers, but could have passed for a lot less this morning.

'What will Mr Volkow say?' I asked, as I partook of fresh lemon juice, sucking my teeth at its raw sharpness.

'About?'

'Your all-night absence.'

Her eyes flared wickedly as she leaned forward so that I could see down the loose front of her dress. 'He won't care. He spent all night at the tables.'

I spluttered over a mouthful of lemon juice. 'You mean . . . he was in the casino all night? Just across the road?' I glanced round furtively. 'He isn't *here*, is he?'

Dru clapped her hands together delightedly. 'Oh, you're a *peach*! Of course he isn't here. He went back to the yacht at about six. He'll be sound asleep right now, don't you worry.'

'How do you know all this?'

'I have my sources,' she said with a wink.

I selected a croissant, tore off a chunk. 'Pass the jam, will you?'

She obliged, smilingly, and I was spooning out a generous helping when a group of people – three women, two men – entered the breakfast room, talking rather loudly. I had only glanced casually in their direction, but instantly it was as if I had touched a live cable; a tingling sensation ran through my body.

Lovely as she was, Drucilla Volkow paled into insipid insignificance alongside Georgina Gregg, one of the three women in the group, and the cause of my temporary paralysis. The sight of her instantly put the clock back six weeks.

She was seated now, her profile darkly silhouetted against the big bay window, the firm jaw, straight nose and high forehead all splendidly outlined for my appreciation. As yet, she wasn't aware of me, but my moonstruck gaze brought an acid laugh from Dru.

'I've a rival already, I see,' she said. 'Somebody you know, or just another flight of fancy.'

The jam spoon was still poised above my plate; the jam itself had slid off, missing the plate, and lay like a red jelly-fish on the tablecloth. I scooped it up.

'Somebody I know,' I replied, dabbing my lips with my napkin. I'll just say hello, Dru – shan't be a sec.'

She waved her croissant airily. 'Don't mind me, lover.'

Gina didn't exactly shout for joy when, tendering apologies to her party, I greeted her in the manner of a long-lost school chum. I asked for a word with her alone, and her friends, all French and all middle-aged, excused us. Conscious of Dru's basilisk glare, I hustled her away, out of the breakfast room.

'What fantastic luck!' I gushed. 'I thought I'd never see you again.

'Really?' She was cool, neutrally polite. But I was determined not to be fobbed off again.

'Come sailing with me tomorrow. Just for the day. We'll leave early, be back before dark and then you can decide whether you want to put yourself in mortal peril by dining with me.' All this came out as a gabbled sales pitch.

The green eyes with their slumberous lids were weighing me up, and there was a knowing light in them that unsettled me. It was like being under a hospital scanner.

'The son of a friend will be coming along too,' I said. This was a snap inspiration. Just for you, madam, we are making this unique offer of a chaperone. I only hoped Jean-Pierre didn't have other plans for Pascal. 'He's only ten, in case you're wondering about gang-bangs.'

She smiled then, and set off a fireworks display inside me. 'You certainly don't give up easily – and you do a good selling job, Mr . . . Henley.'

'Jack . . . remember?'

'Jack.' She still had me under scrutiny, coolly assessing my motives.

'I don't know . . .'

Talk about playing hard to get!

'Please,' I said, in my most earnest voice.

'No strings?'

She'd remembered then. The iron curtain was melting.

'No strings – like before,' I assured her.

'All right,' she capitulated. 'You've sold me. Tomorrow then. The *Spindrift*, I believe you said your boat was called.'

'Yes. She's moored on the Quai des Etats-Unis.'

'Expect me at nine.'

She breezed off, flaunting her cheeky little *derrière*, and I hurried back to make my peace with Dru. I wasn't quite ready to burn that particular boat just yet.

Chapter Six

Jean-Pierre brought Pascal aboard shortly after the sun climbed over the top of the harbour wall, and all was chatter and laughter as he helped make *Spindrift* ready for sea.

I put on a carefree show for his benefit, though truthfully I was not in the best of spirits. My night with Dru – now restored to her obliging spouse – had brought me to a spiritual crossroads, representing as it did a low-water mark in my relationship with the female species.

When it came to finer feelings such as affection, tenderness, and yes . . . love, I had long lived in arid country. In an emotional desert irrigated only by plethoric copulation. And far from showing signs of flagging as I grew older, I was driven by a calculated form of lust to pile depravity on debauchery, collecting bizarre sexual exploits like medals.

What had made me pause now, for such profound reflection, was the tiny star that had crept over my dark horizon, twinkling so feebly that it surely could not survive. It went by the name of Georgina Gregg, and it served less as a symbol of hope than to highlight my secular wallow in carnal pigsties. To bring me to examine and deplore my code of behaviour. Seeing her again at the Hotel de Paris I had also come to realise that she had rarely been far from my thoughts. Only a vague shadow in the background, it was true, yet ever-present and evidently only lying dormant, waiting to be triggered off. Now the shadow had firmed out, acquired shape and colour and substance. With this girl, even I could recapture lost emotions; I hadn't always been a creature of the flesh.

'Don't be so bloody sentimental,' I said aloud, giving an extra-hard turn to the rigging screw I was tightening.

Pascal, coiling a warp nearby, glanced up. '*Comment*?'

'Nothing,' I said, with a twisted grin. 'I was talking to myself, Pascal. It's a very bad habit.'

'Why? I do it all the time. Especially when I want something very much.'

Yeah. That's how it was with me right now.

My watch told me Gina was due any minute, and sure enough, when I next raised my head, there was a familiar figure coming past the ticky-tacky front of the Hotel MiraMar, looking for a gap in the traffic. My heart gave a hop, skip, and a jump. The effect she was having on me was without precedent.

I hitched up my shorts, pulled on my striped matelot's T-shirt, and went to help her aboard. She was all in white: biker shorts, T-shirt that stuck to her torso like wallpaper, and practical gym shoes. She carried a red-and-white duffel bag slung over her shoulder. She had good carriage, I noticed: her back was straight and she took long, elegant strides that tautened the lightly-tanned skin over her thighs, causing the muscles to ripple slightly.

Then she saw me and waved. I waved back but was looking beyond her, a swift, uneasy survey of the promenade. Are you out there, Schnurrpfeil? I was suddenly afraid for Gina. If my enemies got the idea she was something special to me, what better way to apply pressure than through her? Like any unsuspecting member of the public, she was so vulnerable. I was used to having only my own skin to worry about: worrying about someone else's was a whole new ball game.

She arrived at the gangplank, teeth flashing in that wide mouth – an absolute dream. A couple of guys on a launch next to *Sailaway*'s empty berth were blatantly ogling her. You chase your own crumpet, fellas.

My helping hand was politely spurned. I relieved her of her duffel bag, then stood there, feeling as awkward as a country bumpkin at a high-society ball.

Pascal saved me, skating along the coaming, nimble as a grasshopper, and accosting Gina with a cheerful '*Bonjour, madame*!'

She responded with such a radiant smile that Pascal was immediately captivated.

'What's your name?' she asked him in his own language, from which point on all conversation was in French.

'Pascal Pradelou,' he said. 'I live with my father in Roquebrune.'

I hadn't primed Gina about Pascal's family circumstances; fortunately, she was enough of a diplomat not to ask about his mother. They exchanged a few more pleasantries, getting acquainted, while I checked the rest of the rigging screws.

'You did say you've done some sailing,' I said to Gina when, presently, she came over to me.

'Yes. Smaller boats than this – dinghies realy, but the principles are the same. Dinghies are harder to sail, not easier. Everything happens so much faster; you need the reflexes of a fighter pilot.'

'You'll be able to pay your way then.' I twanged the shroud whose tension I was adjusting, gave the screw another quarter-turn. 'Have you breakfasted? There's coffee in the galley; it just needs heating up.'

'Thanks but I'm fine.'

'I couldn't agree more.'

She absorbed the compliment without visible reaction.

'Let's get the show on the road then.' I slipped into my brisk, competent skipper's role. 'I thought we'd go along the coast to Villefranche, have lunch there, and come back early evening. For dinner.'

'Sounds lovely.' She moved aside to let me pass. I went across the cockpit to where Pascal was inspecting the life-lines for wear or damage.

'All okay, *chef*?' I asked him, resting a hand on his shoulder.

He made a circle of forefinger and thumb, and I punched the starter button. The Perkins grumbled awake, settling quickly into the customary diesel clank. Gina was standing by to cast off the two stern mooring-ropes; Pascal had grabbed a boat hook and was heading for the bow to fend off in case I bungled the operation; a not-unknown occurrence.

'Let go aft,' I called out, and Gina unhitched the two lines, her movements economical and assured. I injected some throttle and we eased forward, straight out, well clear of the yacht moored to port, and Pascal's boathook happily surplus to requirements. Gina plonked down on the teak cockpit seat next to me, her cheeks flushed, hair swirling in the breeze that hit us as we cleared the line of boats.

'Handy, your being a sailor-girl,' I remarked.

She just nodded, gazing ahead towards the harbour entrance. We were passing the bows of the Volkow motor yacht, close to the harbour mouth. Even close-up the yacht was immaculate. No rust streaks below the anchor hawse-hole or the various water outlets.

Since the wind was blowing from the north-east, we would be running before it along the coast until we reached the Cap Ferrat peninsula. Rounding the peninsula would call for several directional changes, gybing from a run to a reach, from downwind to wind abeam, and we would have to either tack into Villefranche harbour, or use the engine. I would decide which later.

As we motored out of harbour, *Spindrift*, even with no canvas set, heeled slightly before the stiff breeze. Gina took the helm while Pascal and I, safety lines attached, raised the mainsail, the boat responding immediately as the canvas whipped and cracked and filled.

'Cut the engine,' I shouted to Gina as I trimmed the sheets, and *Spindrift*, while in fact losing way, gave the impression of surging forward, the motor no longer drowning the rush of the hull through the water and the strum of the wind. The head-sail was already on deck in its bag and, with Pascal helping, I hanked it on to the forestay, attached the sheets and halyards to the mast, and up she went, fluttering like a bird with a broken wing, then hardening, the canvas becoming a smooth, taut curve. The increase in speed was at once apparent: she was doing six or seven knots now, I estimated, and would do better still if the breeze continued to stiffen.

I could now afford to relax, drink in the unique sensation of wind-powered motion. It had a therapeutic quality, soothing and yet sensual. Almost a love act.

Pascal, released from his crewing duties, went to fetch his fishing tackle. I added a notch of tension to the sheets, then found a space in the cockpit beside Gina, careful to leave a few virtuous inches between us.

'Your boat's lovely,' she said; one hand rested lightly on the wheel, the other on her bare thigh. Lucky hand. 'You enjoy the good things in life, don't you, Jack? Boat, expensive sports car. What else have you got tucked away – a private jet?'

'That's all.' I had detected a note of censure. 'Nothing else up my sleeve. Possessions for their own sake don't interest me if that's what you're thinking. I only want things that give pleasure.'

'Spoken like a true lotus-eater.' Still the reproving tone, the lips unsmiling.

I didn't speak. I was a mite miffed.

She sensed it, tried to make amends. 'I didn't mean to be personal, Jack. I like you. I wouldn't be here if I didn't. It's just how I feel about the general trend towards more and more possessions. Believe me, I'm as guilty in that respect as you are, probably more so. I just don't have the money to indulge my tastes.'

I wasn't entirely mollified, but I let the discussion atrophy. We talked banalities for a while.

The breeze was freshening. I went into the wheelhouse and bent an ear to the radio for the latest weather information. No deterioration was forecast, although a *mistral* was building and was expected to hit the area by mid-afternoon. This would swing the wind round from north-east to north-west; very convenient, since we would then be able to run before it on the homeward leg.

'If you'd like to take over,' Gina said, when I got back to my seat, 'I'll brew up some coffee.'

'Great. I think Pascal would as soon have orange juice or a Pepsi though.'

'Leave it to me.' She relinquished the helm and went forward, ducking under the hatch and presenting her rounded bottom. The biker shorts did it justice and more.

Already the wind was shifting, veering degree by degree towards the north, forcing me to ease the sheets. It wasn't yet inhibiting our progress, which so far had been rapid – so much so that by 11.30 we were rounding Cap Ferrat, and then it was all hands on deck ready to gybe. Gina took the helm again, leaving Pascal and me free to deal with the sails. We commenced our turn to leeward, the canvas flapping, the sheets snaking with the uncertain movement of the boom. Pascal had unhitched the headsail from the starboard cleat, and it whipped away like a wild thing, almost wrenching the sheet from his grasp. Tempted as I was to take over, I let him battle on alone; he wouldn't have thanked me for intervening. The crisis quickly passed, with Pascal keeping his cool throughout. Jean-Pierre would have been proud of him.

The Cap Ferrat peninsula, with its toytown holiday homes, slid by to starboard, the rugged shoreline white under the sun, sailboards zig-zagging in the foreground, splashing the scene with colour. Within half-an-hour we were tying up at a mooring buoy in Villefranche's tiny port, squeezing between two cabin cruisers. Pascal wanted to stay on board for lunch so I chucked the tender over the side and rowed ashore to fetch him a take-away meal – hamburgers and chips with lashings of tomato sauce. He doted on this diet.

Gina and I left him wolfing the unappetising mess and I did a second stint at the oars. We strolled along the cobbled quayside to the Mère Germain restaurant, securing the last vacant outdoor table; from there you could just see the port around the edge of the Chapelle St Pierre, the walls of the Citadelle frowning over it.

An orange-and-white gingham tablecloth was spread over our table and places speedily set. Menu, wine, and starters came in quick succession, and we ate hungrily, and soaked up the sun, the scenery, and the French chatter around us.

'When it comes to cuisine, the French leave the rest standing,' Gina observed, draining the butter sauce from a mussel shell. 'I couldn't imagine living anywhere else – certainly not in England.'

'Harsh words.'

'You disagree?'

'About putting it so bluntly, yes. But let's not get drawn into taking partisan stances. I meant to ask you: what are you doing in Monaco right now – if it's not indiscreet to enquire?'

'Not at all. I'm with my boss. We have a branch office there, and he visits it once a month. Now and again he brings me along.'

I squinted askance at that. She correctly interpreted my expression and giggled.

'You couldn't be more wrong, I assure you. His wife accompanies him too, more often than not. You saw her at the hotel yesterday morning – the tall woman with auburn hair. Anyway, he's not interested in me in that way.'

'Looked in a mirror lately?' It was meant as a quip, but the tenor of my voice said different.

She gave me a fast, funny look. 'Jack . . .' She stopped, concentrating very hard on splitting open a stubborn mussel shell, fumbling with it, all fingers and thumbs. To put her at ease, I changed the subject, telling her about my first and last participation in the Fastnet race a few years back when a storm blew up. I was crewing for Jacques Lalanne on *Le Vainqueur*, and we had battened down the hatches and hove to with bare poles and a sea anchor. It made a dramatic tale and she listened enraptured, her mussels forgotten.

'But what heppened to the missing crew member? Wasn't he ever found?'

'No. Only a plimsoll and a packet of French letters. They were picked up by an Irish trawler off The Lizard.'

'A packet of French letters? How did you know they were his?'

'We didn't, not for sure. But he used to be a boy scout, so it was a reasonable assumption.'

She was slow on the uptake. 'A boy scout?' Then her face cleared, and she laughed with me.

After that I made a point of avoiding personal comments. We ranged over topics as diverse as my love for classical music to her escapades at the *lycée* where, so she claimed, the concierge was bribed to let the *filles-de-nuit*, as the more adventurous young ladies were called, back into the building in the early hours in return for a quick grope. Until one day his control slipped, and the quick grope became a quick rape, followed by a quick ten-year stretch in the Château d'If prison. A salutory experience.

'You steered well clear of all that, of course,' I said.

Her eyebrows wriggled indignantly. 'Are you implying I'm a prude?'

I had wondered.

'No. Only that I think I'm beginning to know you better and I don't see you letting some greasy concierge stick his fingers up. Am I wrong?'

'I wouldn't have put it so crudely, but . . . no, you're not wrong. As a matter of fact . . .' she hesitated.

I kept quiet.

'What I was going to say was, that I've only ever . . . you know . . . done it . . . with my husband.'

A shrewd hands-off-I'm-not-a-pushover artifice. Superfluous. I'd already received that particular message weeks ago.

Just then the main course arrived and we tucked into *bouillabaisse à la Provençale* of such succulence that conversation was suspended for the duration. As I chewed, however, I mulled over her professed fidelity in admiration, and it fuelled the fires she had already lit inside me. Sure, I still wanted the clothes off that slender body, still wanted to bed her, only somehow the sexual yen had lessened; or perhaps it was the same and other, different, priorities had assumed greater importance. For instance, I badly wanted to earn her respect, her esteem – call it what you will: this would clearly not be achieved by dragging her off to the bushes caveman-style.

Towards the end of the meal, I happened to glance up at the sky and noticed a build-up of clouds over the Mount Gros observatory which sits atop the mountains behind Nice – great clumps with fleecy edges, like tattered flags of truce. The wind was blowing from the north-west, quite strongly, force four at least. The sea was thrashing against the harbour mouth and the masts of the moored yachts oscillated in the swell.

'Something brewing up there,' I said casually.

She looked up. 'I see what you mean. We're in for a storm.'

'Afraid so. Question is: do we sit it out here or head back home in the hope of outrunning it?'

'I've been at sea in a storm before,' she said slowly, considering it. 'And in a smaller boat than yours.'

A gust lifted the edge of the tablecloth at the next table, recently vacated, and sent an empty wine glass crashing to the floor, splinters exploding everywhere.

I called for the bill. 'Glad to hear you've been blooded. Okay. We'll try and run ahead of it.'

'Aye, aye, skipper.'

Maybe it was the wine, maybe she was beginning to loosen up; whatever, she swayed against me as she spoke, her hair touching my cheek, the smell of it entering my nostrils. It smelled clean and healthy, with just a hint of lightly-perfumed shampoo. It smelled also of woman – it excited me. I ached to make some small, intimate gesture, it was an ache so potent, it was almost a physical hurt. Then she was sitting upright once more and the psychological moment had slipped away.

The Harbourmaster's office gave me the latest weather report: wind in the north-west, rising to force five, gusts to force six or seven; squalls, possibly heavy, dying out before nightfall. The good news was that the heart of the storm was expected to pass over Nice, and the coastline between Villefranche and Monaco should therefore escape the brunt of it.

I rowed us back to *Spindrift* through the choppy green waters of the harbour, and we made ready for sea. Pascal and I lashed the tender extra securely to the cabin top, then we all donned life-jackets and harnesses before upping anchor and going astern to get clear of the two bucketing cabin cruisers beside us.

Immediately we cleared the harbour mouth, up went main and head sails. We were running before the wind again, south-by-south west, down the side of the peninsula towards Cap Ferrat point. It pushed us along like a train and in no time at all we were abeam the Cap lighthouse and preparing to gybe.

Then the sun disappeared. It was as if a light had been switched off: one minute blazing sunshine on our backs, the sails so brilliantly white it hurt to look at them, the spray from our leaping bows a sparkling rainbow; the next minute a great shadow was cast over everything. We all looked up together and I gasped involuntarily. Unseen, an enormous purple-black mass, extending as far as the eye could see, had rushed up behind us and was now blotting out half the sky, gobbling up more blue even as we watched in horrified fascination. The wind speed had increased too, howling through the rigging, the sails ballooning, the mast flexing whip-like.

'My God!' Gina said at last, and she spoke for all of us.

The shore towards Villefranche was already lost behind a wall of rain, which meant the storm was no more than five kilometres away. Since low-pressure systems travel at twenty to twenty-five knots, we had only minutes before it hit us.

Lowering the sails became a matter of urgency. With the wind behind, this would be a difficult and potentially dangerous undertaking, so I went ahead with the gybe and brought *Spindrift* round head-to-wind. Then, with the autohelm engaged and the motor at low revs, it was all hands to get the canvas off her. The deck was lurching and rolling crazily now and our task was not easy. As the headsail was freed from the restraint of the sheets, the wind took hold of it. We all stood to windward – less chance of becoming entangled in the flailing canvas – and by weight of numbers muzzled it. Even so, I collected a nasty clout from a wayward headsail-shackle before the job was finished. The mainsail proved easier; it was down and lashed in half the time taken for the headsail, the boom made secure by hitching the sheet around the block.

The sea was no longer blue, but slate-coloured and angry, with crests that curled and flattened, flinging spray over us. The hump that was Cap Ferrat was fading, losing shape. It disappeared altogether as the deluge reached it – our last visual contact with land. All that remained now was us and the heaving, writhing seas. Only one thing was in our favour: the shore lay to windward, so I had no immediate worries about sea-room. The storm would push us south-east and the next piece of land was Corsica, more than a hundred miles distant.

'Pascal, get below,' I ordered, taking over from the autohelm.

He objected to this banishment. 'But, Jack, I have my safety line.'

'Get below, Pascal,' I repeated, and signalled to Gina, who was clipping her safety line to a stanchion. Observing the stubborn set of Pascal's jaw, she took firm hold of his skinny brown arm and pulled him towards the companionway.

He grumbled something, a last token protest, and unhitched his safety line.

Then the storm proper burst upon us: darkness, wind, and rain, acting in concert – except that the rain was hail and so cold it made me catch my breath. Pascal slipped, and went sprawling on the cockpit grating, and while all three of us were thus momentarily distracted, a rogue wave smacked into *Spindrift*'s port bow. It was not gigantic as waves go, maybe twenty feet from trough to crest; just big enough and vicious enough to push the bow sharply round to starboard, presenting our beam to the wind. We took a roll that sent the starboard rail under and tipped Pascal effortlessly out of the cockpit and into the water. He didn't even have a chance to shout.

For a few vital seconds Gina and I didn't move, immobilised by the suddenness of it; then with one accord we rushed to the side. Pascal was close under the lee of the boat, bobbing in his life-jacket. I wrenched a lifebuoy from its seating, and tossed it in the water. My throw was hasty; I made no provision for the wind and it landed well out of reach. To add to our difficulties, *Spindrift*, her wheel unmanned, was spinning round through 180 degrees and the seas were now breaking astern. She was pitching like a see-saw, waves crashing aboard and swamping the cockpit, the hull shuddering under the impact. If I didn't quickly get her bows back into the wind we would all be swimming in the Med.

'Take the wheel!' I yelled to Gina. 'Bring her into the wind.'

Her reactions were fast and positive, and I thanked my stars she knew boats. A novice would have been useless, a liability even. As it was, I could devote my energies to retrieving Pascal and that in itself would be no mean feat. He was already drifting away with frightening swiftness. I didn't even stop to think. Jean-Pierre had entrusted his only son to me and I had placed his life in danger. Now I had to save him, no matter what it cost me.

I unhitched my safety line – it wasn't long enough to reach Pascal – and dived in.

It was not the smartest way to recover a man overboard, but I was worried that he would be lost from sight before I could get a line to him as the visibility was down to about fifty yards and worsening. I also feared that, if I tried to pick him up from *Spindrift*, I might run him down. Going in after him like this was the best of a lousy bunch of alternatives.

Spindrift's hull offered some temporary protection from the sea's turbulence, and I made the most of it. I swam as I'd never swum before, and to blazes with conserving my strength. Every second stroke I shouted encouragement to Pascal, though I doubt he heard me. He was doggy-paddling to meet me, his arm movements made awkward by the life-jacket.

We linked up and clung together, grinning in mixed relief and anxiety. I glanced back at *Spindrift*; she was almost stern on to us now, a rolling cockle-shell, the naked pole of her mast describing a quadrant against that awful, boiling sky. Gina's face was a pale blur in the murk, watching us, doing her best to maintain position. No, damn it, she was doing a whole lot better than that: she was allowing the boat to be pushed steadily stern first towards us while keeping her bow into the wind. What a girl!

Now I had Pascal safely in tow, I determined to save my strength for getting us both back on board. I would need it; it is notoriously difficult to climb over the gunwale of even a small boat from sea level. Pascal would be easy enough, with Gina pulling and me pushing. The danger was that, by then, I would be too weakened to save myself.

Spindrift was continuing to slide backwards. I could distinguish Gina's features, her hair plastered flat to her scalp like a balaclava helmet, and her eyes huge. But she was keeping her head, sideslipping under minimal power so as to pass us to port.

The bucking hull came up close, shutting out the

dark sky with its own royal blue darkness. The lower lifeline was already uncoupled to facilitate our recovery. A safety line came over the side. Gina appeared and hung both arms down the topsides for Pascal to grasp; back on autohelm *Spindriftf* was cranky, her stern crabbing to port. I worked fast: hooked the line to Pascal's harness, breathed in deeply, and boosted him up as hard and far as I could. Having nothing solid under my feet to provide leverage, it was a feeble effort. Nonetheless, it just sufficed to launch Pascal into Gina's arms – also, less happily, to immerse me in the green depths.

When I emerged from my ducking, Pascal's feet were passing from sight over the gunwale. I let out a sigh of relief. Up until then, Pascal had been my only concern. Now that he was safe, my own survival became paramount. I had nothing to hang on to, and staying close to the hull was not easy in such circumstances.

'Gina!' I bawled. 'Don't forget me!'

In the howling and crashing of the storm my shouts sounded puny. *Spindrift* was still on autohelm, I guessed, and still pointing into the wind, climbing the steep, white-capped rollers with ease and swooping into the long troughs with a kind of disdainful glee. I wished I could share it. What was Gina doing up there?

I paddled closer under the hull, careful to stay well clear of the spinning propellor that could chop slices out of my hide without missing a beat. A wave came and lifted me and I made a grab for the pulpit rail, my left hand locking around a stanchion. And there I swung, my legs only inches from the propellor, unable to lift myself any higher. My stamina was dribbling away like sand through an egg-timer.

Waves were bursting over me almost continuously, salt water filling my nose and mouth.

'Gina!' I yelled again, almost a scream. I was near the end of my endurance, my grip on the stanchion weakening. I was inflating my lungs for a last mighty holler, when I saw the safety line, dangling over the side not half-a-dozen strokes away. It wouldn't restore me to the boat, but it would keep me in umbilical contact while I got my second wind. Somehow, enervated though I was, I had to swim for it. Either that or go under. Either that or die.

I swam. I drew on reserves I would not have believed existed after the battering I had taken, and splashed ponderously through that cauldron of a sea, in the driving hail and the wind. And made it to that line.

Even clipping it on was a herculanean task. Under the lee of the boat I was protected from the worst of the elements, but my fingers were numb, barely able to respond to the signals sent by my brain. I succeeded finally; at the very instant the clip snapped into place, the line was reeled in from the cockpit. As it pulled taut, there was a flurry of impatient tugs, a manifestation of annoyance rather than a serious attempt to raise me. Then Gina's head came over the gunwale, peeting down at me. Her mouth fell open, and before I could speak she was gone again, only to return with another safety line which, wordlessly, she lowered to me. I attached it. Now I was doubly secure, if still no nearer to climbing aboard.

'Can you haul me part of the way up the side?' I called.

'I'll try,' she shouted back, through the strands of hair smeared across her mouth.

'Wait until she rolls to port.' Hardly were the words

out of my mouth when *Spindrift* did just that, and pulled me clear of the water. For perhaps a second the topsides were at an angle of forty-five degrees, with me plastered on them, limbs splayed, incapable of movement. Gina, with precision timing, hauled on the two safety lines, and I crashed into the cockpit just as the boat flipped back, rolling on to her starboard side. If I hadn't hung onto the wheel I would have been tossed smartly back into the sea, probably for good.

When she rolled back again to port I rolled with her, into the safety of the narrow space on the cockpit floor, between the binnacle and the seat. I lay there, utterly done, an untidy, squelching heap. Even speech was beyond me.

Presently, the corkscrew motion of the hull moderated, the hail eased off, then abruptly ceased altogether. Pascal's voice came to me through a fog of exhaustion. More presently, the sun peeked out, warming me, beating against my closed eyelids, a fierce, cynical heat, as if it had never been away and the storm had only happened in my imagination.

I sat up, groaning, and there was Gina, sitting coolly behind the wheel, her hair almost dry and fluffing out again. And Pascal, naked but for his underpants, cross-legged on the cockpit floor.

He was the first to speak.

'The storm's over, Jack. Are you all right now?'

'I think so, Pascal.' I dredged up a shaky grin to reassure him. Then remembered his own frightening experience. 'How about you?'

'Okay.' He waved away his near-drowning as of no consequence. 'Thank you for saving me.' He looked down, wouldn't meet my eyes. Aware of his own culpability.

'Don't be silly. You'd do the same for me.'

Gina said, 'I was sure you'd drowned. I . . . I . . .' Her free hand covered her face.

'What happened?' I asked. 'After you pulled Pascal on board, I expected you to throw me a line at least.'

'Yes . . . yes, I'm sorry,' she said miserably. 'First I wanted to get Pascal inside . . . out of danger. Then I . . . I . . . fell – I must have stunned myself. The next thing I knew I was lying on top of a safety line, and someone was tugging it. That's when I saw you.'

She burst into tears, and I got up to sit by her side, gently prising her fingers away from the wheel.

'Don't cry, love,' I said, holding her against me. Sobs wracked her body, the tears making tracks down her salt-stained cheeks. 'It wasn't your fault. I should never have put to sea in such conditions and with a storm forecast. I'm the one who should feel guilty.'

The sky overhead was back to standard Côte d'Azur azure, the black band of cloud receding to the south. The sea was still choppy though, and the wind shrilled through the rigging.

Pascal had taken up a position on Gina's right flank, and was making consoling noises which, ultimately, brought her out in a tearful smile.

'You're very sweet, Pascal,' she said. 'You're both very sweet, and I'm very silly and stupid to get upset about it.'

'I think you were very brave to handle the boat all alone,' Pascal said, some of his father's charm rising to the fore. 'It's not easy for a lady – they are not so strong as we men.' Overlooking the fact that it was Gina who had hauled him to safety.

'You were bloody marvellous, Gina,' I agreed. 'And you, Pascal, were brave too for not panicking when you went overboard.'

His chest puffed out with pride. 'Oh, it was nothing special.' His innate modesty would last only until he related the story to his friends when he would, of course, assume the role of hero and saviour.

'While we're all being so complimentary to each other,' Gina cut in, wiping her nose with the back of her wrist, '*you* were the bravest of all. When you dived in like that without your safety line, knowing how difficult it is to get back on board a boat this size, it . . . it . . .' She gulped, and the crying restarted. 'It was the most courageous, most unselfish act I've ever seen.' She finished through a cataract of tears, slumping against my shoulder.

'Make some coffee, will you, Pascal?' I said gruffly. 'Then we'll get some canvas on her and capitalise on this wind.'

I had brought *Spindrift* back on course, north by north-east, running parallel to the shore. Gina still rested against me, and our two bodies swayed in harmony with the roll of the deck. Except for the steady beat of the diesel beneath us, and the cries of a pair of gulls trailing us at masthead height, all was at peace in my world.

It was a strictly temporary situation.

Under full sail we made it back to Monaco by six and, by prior arrangement, motored over to Roquebrune to restore Pascal to his father.

Jean-Pierre had spent the day with one of his local 'steadies', a fiery gypsy of a girl with coffee-hued skin and a red gash of a mouth, who was knocking up a light five-course snack when we trooped in.

Over the meal an account was given of the day's events and although I deliberately played down the violence of the storm, Jean-Pierre paled noticeably when I told of Pascal's loss overboard, and afterwards his appetite was not what it had been.

Later, he took me unobtrusively aside. 'I am more grateful than you will ever know for what you did, Jack,' he said and his face was hard. 'I think that storm was worse than you say.'

I was silent. I knew what was coming and, employee or not, he had the right to say it.

'You know you should not have left Villefranche in the conditions you have described.' He wasn't asking me, he was telling.

I just nodded. I felt lower than a snake's belly.

'I only want to say I think you made a very serious mistake; also that you learned a lot today and you will not make this mistake again. So if you ever wish to take Pascal sailing again in the future—' his grin was the Jean-Pierre of old, '—it will be okay by me.'

I was too moved to speak, so I gave him a good old man-to-man French hug. He understood that far, far better than anything I might have said.

We rejoined the party to drink a toast to friendship. Various other toasts followed until I lost count. But we didn't stay late. Jean-Pierre clearly had plans for his gypsy rose, and though he protested as a matter of form when I announced our departure, he couldn't hide an anticipatory smirk.

I wasn't drunk, but my alcohol intake was certainly over the prescribed limit. So I piloted the Jag back through the winding streets as if it were a hearse. Gina sat with head back and eyes closed.

'A nightcap before we part?' I ventured, expecting a refusal. 'It's not yet eleven.'

'Okay.'

So I was wrong again. I didn't mind.

I parked on the Quai Albert and we mingled with a

handful of late-night drinkers at Victor Jammais' bar. Victor was there, yarning with a couple of regulars, and didn't see us right away. We ordered cognac and nibbled nuts and raisins from a dish on the counter.

'It's been quite a day,' I observed.

'Not short on excitement,' Gina agreed. She was contemplating the pink reflective tiles with which Victor, in his wisdom and bad taste, had covered selected areas of wall.

'I know,' I said. 'Ugh. Everybody says it.'

Victor chose that moment to gatecrash, inserting his long, svelte figure into the space between our stools.

'*Salut*, Jack,' he said, smothering me in whisky fumes. 'How goes it?'

'Could be worse. Have you met Mademoiselle Gregg?'

Instant charm spilled out of Victor like water over a weir. 'I don't believe I've had the pleasure. *Enchanté, mademoiselle*.' He bent his lips to Gina's hand. She accepted the gesture gracefully.

'May I offer you both a drink?'

We prudently declined. He ordered a cognac for himself, then said, 'Someone came here today looking for you, Jack.'

'Oh yes?'

He swivelled enquiring eyes towards Gina.

'You can speak freely in front of *mademoiselle*,' I said.

'As you wish. This man would not give his name. He asked where you were, and I told him you were probably sailing.' He knocked back his cognac in one go, running his tongue over his thin, rather reptilian lips.

'He didn't say who he was, or what he wanted me for?' A suspicion was growing.

'He told me nothing. He was quite old, at least seventy. Rather fat, and with not much hair. Also he had a German accent.'

Schnurrpfeil. I was no longer surprised, nor even put out.

'He was asking where you stay in Monaco. Where you eat; who are your friends. naturally, I answered none of his questions.'

'Do you know this man, Jack?' Gina butted in.

'Vaguely.' I gripped Victor's shoulder. 'Thanks, my friend. Let me know if he shows up again.'

'Certainly. Now . . . if you will excuse me . . . *mademoiselle,* Jack.' He drifted off, apparently aimlessly, yet when next I looked he was chatting up a redhead at a table.

'You may find this hard to believe,' I said to Gina, 'but the guy Victor just described has been trailing me ever since I left Geneva, him and others. I'm getting just a little bit teed off with it, and by God I'm going to get to the bottom of it.'

'Why should anyone want to follow you? Are you in trouble?'

'Not as far as I'm aware.'

'Do you know . . . ?'

I cut across her. 'Hush a minute, love. I need to think.' She fell quiet, though I sensed she was miffed by my brusqueness. How was I to put a stop to this nonsense? These guys were as slippery as a river full of eels. How to confront them, waylay one of their number – Schnurrpfeil for preference? Of course! Wherever I went, so would he. Including back home to Geneva. Where we *both* had apartments. It was a long shot. There was no certainty he would come after me or that, if he did, he would visit his apartment. I might have a wasted journey, and just when my relationship with Gina was getting airborne.

But what else was there? I had to do something, for Christ's sake.

'I have to go back to Geneva,' I said decisively. 'Tomorrow.'

There was a moment's silence, then, 'Is it to do with this mystery man?'

'Sort of.' I slopped cognac around in my glass. 'I'll probably fly – that'll knock a couple of days off the trip.'

'How long will you be away?'

Did she care? Or was it just politeness that made her ask.

'A week maybe, no more. I'll be back as soon as I can.'

'I doubt I shall be here when you do. We're returning to Marseilles at the weekend.'

'That's a pity.' I pushed a vacant beermat across to her. 'Jot down your phone number. I'll buzz you from Geneva.'

She looked dubious. 'I shall be away a lot over the next week or two. Better if you give me your Geneva number, or a number where I can contact you here in Monaco.'

'Suit yourself.' She produced a notebook and pen from her handbag, and I reeled off my home number and that of Victor's bar. 'He'll pass on any messages.'

'I'll probably call you over the weekend.' She glanced meaningly at her watch.

'I'll run you back to the hotel,' I said.

More funereal driving up the hill to the Hermitage. I parked near, but not in front of, the hotel entrance whose blazing opulence was not designed for parting lovers.

'I'll say goodbye then,' she said. 'I had only just applied the handbrake.

I drew her to me. Surely I rated a kiss. She didn't resist, but her body was stiff and unresponsive. I sighed, pecked her on the cheek.

'Don't expect too much . . . too soon,' she said softly, not looking at me. 'I'm not ready . . . to think of anyone else in that way.'

'I understand. Believe me, I do.' And I did too. For months after Marion's death I hadn't given other women a thought. It had taken a drunken bar crawl around the 9th *arondissement* of Paris and an extraordinarily accomplished tart to remind me of what I was missing.

Our farewells, then, were warm but platonic. She went off into the hotel. I drove down to the port.

And spent the night alone on *Spindrift*. In bed, but not asleep.

And next morning travelled openly, indeed ostentatiously, to Nice Airport and flew Air Inter to Geneva.

Chapter Seven

Surprise, surprise, it was raining when we touched down at Geneva airport, the runway awash, the uninspiring terminal cowering under the downpour. It might have been yesterday when I left. Then the cheerful taxi driver informed me that today's rain was the first in five weeks.

I might have been tailed from the airport. Then again, I might not. I ignored all other inhabitants of the planet. For once, I didn't mind if Schnurrpfeil, Curly Moustache, and the whole lousy crew were tagging along in my wake. Rather, I was counting on it.

The apartment was neat and tidy – and as welcoming as Dracula's tomb. I fed Rachmaninoff's Piano Concerto Number 2 to the CD player, and prowled about, only half-listening. By and by, I discovered I was hungry. I went out to the Italian Bar-Restaurant, where I made short work of a *canneloni* lunch, then sauntered back to the apartment in the pale sunshine that the rain had resentfully surrendered to.

The afternoon dragged by. I played seven classical albums, read a book, and consumed coffee by the litre. Came early evening I went forth to engage the enemy. Stuffed the SIG P.210 automatic, my 'house gun', inside the back of waistband of my trousers, and put on a jacket to hide it. Poked my head outside my front door to check for loiterers; I wanted no witnesses to my call on Schnurrpfeil. Then, like Sylvester the Cat stalking Tweetie Pie, I scuttled past apartment 53, home of a middle aged bank executive, and leaned heavily on the bell-push of number 54. Nobody came. I leaned harder and longer. The door remained solidly shut. Seething, I crept back to my apartment.

So much for stoking up the adrenalin. I plonked the SIG on the coffee table, glared at it. What now? The telephone at the other end of the table sparked off an idea, just in case Schnurrpfeil was in his apartment but lying doggo. He might be more inclined to answer the phone than he would to answer the door. The Geneva directory was not helpful: no Schnurrpfeils listed at all. So, on to the Information Service. The girl who answered was charming and courteous. How was the name spelled, *monsieur*? Over the line, a rustle of paper. Presently, 'I am sorry. There is no Schnurrpfeil listed in Geneva.'

'Try again,' I pleaded. 'He moved in in April, about the third week.' A tiny sigh, just audible. 'Please, *mademoiselle*,' I said, injecting a wheedle into my voice.

'Just a minute, please.' A staccato clacking and everything went quiet. I waited, poured lukewarm coffee, drank. The line stayed dead for so long I was beginning to think she had abandoned me and when her ''Allo, 'allo' erupted in my ear, I almost dropped the receiver.

'I'm still here,' I said, with teeth-clenching civility.

'We have a record of Mr Schnurrpfeil's application to take over the line formerly allocated to Mr Spinelli.' Spinelli was the previous occupier of number 54. 'This was in . . . April – the 20th to be exact.'

'So I can look him up under Spinelli,' I said. Why hadn't it occurred to me to do so before going through all this rigmarole?

'Ye-e-s.' She sounded doubtful. Then, 'It seems that Mr Schnurrpfeil cancelled his application on 22nd May. He didn't stay very long,' she remarked, as an afterthought.

Too right, he didn't: he'd packed his bags just two days after my own departure for Monaco.

'Monsieur?'

I thanked the girl and hung up. I released a few expletives into the atmosphere. If Schnurrpfeil had cancelled his telephone, it was safe to assume he'd likewise cancelled his tenancy. My journey to Geneva was already a wash-out.

I was pacing the room in simmering frustration with the doorbell rang.

My pacings were abruptly curtailed as I spun round to stare at the door. Personal callers were a rarity. Officially I was out of town and my friends and acquaintances, who were not that numerous, all knew it. That made it a professional visit. I dithered briefly over whether to let it ring until the caller got fed up, but curiosity won the day. I consigned the SIG to a shelf under the cocktail bar where, under the pretext of pouring a drink, I could get at it.

My caller was tall, thin, with a chin like Punch of Punch and Judy, and sparse brown hair brushed severely sideways and flat to his head.

'Mr Henley?' he said in English.

I confessed I was he.

'Police.' He flapped an ID card at me. I surprised him by relieving him of it, and scrutinising the mug shot and the physical description of the holder who, it proclaimed, was Inspector Klaus Diethard

Wittwitz. A music hall sort of name.

When I handed the card back, he snatched it from me with undisguised petulance, as if unaccustomed to having his credentials checked. Then the second cop, the back-up squad, came into view, sliding out of the recess between my door and number 53; a big man, wearing a pork-pie hat and an ill-fitting brown suit. He acknowledged me with a dip of his head.

'This is Sergeant Dumas.' Wittwitz smiled, exposing the whitest set of teeth – too symmetrical to be natural – I had ever been dazzled by.

I blocked the doorway. 'What can I do for you gentlemen?' I wasn't yet convinced these guys weren't with the Schnurrpfeil crowd. Police ID cards can be forged the same as passports.

'We'd like to ask you a few questions, Mr Henley.' Wittwitz flashed his chompers again. This guy wouldn't need any bright lights for conducting an interrogation—his were all built in.

'If it's about that parking ticket in March . . .' I began, but he silenced me with a karate-type slash of the hand.

'This is nothing to do with traffic misdemeanours. May we come in?'

Still I hesitated.

'Or would you prefer to continue the discussion at Police Headquarters?' He said it with a disarming blandness.

'I thought they only talked like that in the movies,' I grunted and retreated before him. Now I needed to get close to the SIG. If these flatfeet were here to slap the cuffs on me, it wasn't going to be a walk-over.

'Drink?' I offered, walking over to the bar.

'Why not?' Wittwitz said. Very civilised, the Swiss

police. None of this anti-social nonsense about not drinking on duty. 'Have you any Scotch whisky?'

I took a bottle of Glenlivet double-malt down from the shelf. 'Water? Soda?'

'That would be sacrilege, would it not?'

'What about you, Sergeant?' I said, as I tipped a liberal slug into a heavy-bottomed tumbler.

'The same,' Dumas growled, in Romansch-accented French. An economical man, our Sergeant Dumas. No wasted words like 'please' and 'thank you'.

I distributed the drinks, and invited them to sit down. I returned to the bar, remained standing behind it, tending a modest finger of Scotch.

'Well, gentlemen,' I switched on my clean-living, eager-to-help smile. 'What exactly can I do for you?'

Wittwitz folded one long leg over the other. Despite his self-assured exterior, I had the impression he was slightly uneasy. In my experience, police forces in democratic states are wary of foreign nationals. A wariness that I, as a foreign national, approved of most heartily.

'We are co-operating with the German police, the *Kriminalpolizei*, in their investigation into a certain . . . ah . . . incident.'

I maintained an expression of polite enquiry. Inwardly I was churning, doing a fast memory scan of all the hits I had ever made in the Federal Republic. It was a longish list.

'It is, in fact, a matter of murder,' Wittwitz said, and paused for maximum impact. I feigned a puzzled frown. His announcement caused no shock waves – murder was the only serious crime I had ever committed and I had thus been mentally prepared for the worst.

'Do you know a Mr . . .' Wittwitz pulled a note book from his pocket, shook it open. 'Roger Townsend?'

'Roger Townsend?' I held on to my composure – just. Townsend was my bogus identity from the Tilou contract in Munich; the grand finale. First Schnurrpfeil, now the police. Somewhere along the line my cover had been blown open.

Wittwitz was still wearing an enquiring stare. I had to give some kind of answer.

'I knew a *Bob* Townsend in England,' I said, converting the frown to pursed-lips rumination. 'But Roger Townsend? No, I'm sure I've never met anyone by that name.'

'No matter,' Wittwitz said, with deceptive indifference. 'What about a Mr Smith?'

'Smith? There must be a million or more Smiths in England, Inspector.'

'*Sebastian* Smith?'

Now it was really serious. Sebastian Smith was my 'trade name', supposedly known only to selected contacts. I dosed myself liberally with Scotch. For medicinal purposes – and I'm not joking. Wittwitz, if he did but realise it, was wandering into a minefield.

I waggled my head. 'Ask me another.'

'I will, Mr Henley, I will.'

My fingers rested lightly on the SIG. I was confident I could take both of them out if need be. And the shots wouldn't carry far; these top people's apartments had walls as thick as the Bastille.

'Let's try another name and a different nationality.' Wittwitz focused on me the way a hungry hound focuses on its food dish at mealtime. 'Günther Röschinger?'

My network of contacts and false identities was disintegrating around me. How had they got on to

Günther? Unless . . . I recalled that last encounter, at the top of the Olympiatürm, when I had given the little louse a pain in the breadbasket. Surely he hadn't grassed on me because of that?

'Mr Henley?' Wittwitz nudged gently.

I made a show of snapping back to attention. 'I was remembering a friend who died recently,' I improvised piously. 'He was also called Günther.'

'Then you don't know Herr Röschinger?' If Wittwitz was moved by my imaginary friend's death, he covered up well.

'Sorry. I don't seem to be much help to you, Inspector.'

'On the contrary. You will understand that crime detection involves a great deal of routine enquiry work. Many questions must be asked and most of the answers are only useful from the point of view of elimination. It's a negative concept.' He picked up his empty glass, examining it against the light.

'Well then, gentlemen . . . if that's all . . .' I was sure it wasn't all; I was simply maintaining my innocent act.

'Where were you in November last year?' Wittwitz rode roughshod over my attempt to conclude the interview. He continued squinting through the glass – was he angling for a refill?

'Hard to say. Here most of the time, as I recall.'

'Not in West Germany? Not at the Hotel Zum Goldenen Adler, in the village of Oberpframmern, near München, by chance? Wearing a brown hair piece and a false moustache.'

Up until now the news had been merely bad, but this was calamity. Soon he would come right out in the open and specify the crime in detail. Not that he needed to – not for my benefit.

The sky was darkening outside and the room with it. I switched on the light above the bar and a warm yellow glow was thrown outwards, spot-lighting my unwelcome guests.

'No, Inspector,' I said heavily. 'I was not in Germany; nor was I in France, or Mexico, or on a desert island. With or without hairpieces, false moustaches, and wooden legs.' My fingers were wrapped around the grip of the SIG, my thumb on the safety catch. 'Suppose you tell me a bit more about this . . . this murder you are investigating. And explain why you've come to question *me* about it.'

'You are quite right, Mr Henley.' Wittwitz glanced at his colleague. 'Don't you agree, Dumas? We owe him a full explanation.'

Dumas cracked his knuckles and said nothing. His function was primarily decorative with intimidatory undertones. He represented brute force, a counter-weight to Wittwitz's relaxed psychology.

'On 17th November last year, two people – a man and a woman – were staying at a private holiday residence known as Schloss Thomashoff, near the village of Breitbrunn, on the shore of Lake Ammersee; about forty kilometres west of München.' He was relating this in a bored tone, as if he had decided I was guilty, therefore must be more familiar with all this detail than he was. 'Between six p.m. and eight p.m., a person or persons unknown entered Schloss Thomashoff and shot the man three times, probably killing him instantly, and the woman once, through the throat, leaving her to die. Nothing was disturbed or damaged apart from a bolt on the back door which had been partly sawn through, suggesting the killer had entered the house on a previous occasion.'

'Amazing.' My sarcasm made Dumas scowl.

'The killing appears to have been the work of a professional. The male victim was Fabrice Tillou, a Frenchman, thirty-one years old and the only son of a certain Bernard Tillou. You have heard of him perhaps: I am informed by the French police that he is a notorious racketeer.'

'France is swarming with . . . er . . . racketeers.' The term sounded quaint and outmoded, smacking of Chicago bootleggers and G-men.

'Possibly. However, this Tillou, the father, controls most of the organized vice and illegal immigration on the Mediterranean coast, from Cannes to the Spanish border.'

'Sounds profitable.'

'This is not a matter for flippancy, Mr Henley.' He was right. But it helped conceal my dismay. 'In any case it is not the son who interests the German police: it may be there is a gang war between Tillou and a rival organization. If so – I believe you English have an expression – good riddance to bad rubbish? No, the fate of this French gangster does not concern them; it is the *woman,* Ingeborg Thomashoff.' He looked at his notes. 'Thirty-four, beautiful, sexually very active and addicted to certain . . . ah . . . perversions. She was the mistress of Tillou, the son. Also the wife of Erich Thomashoff, the German minister. The name will be familiar to you, I am sure.

I professed ignorance.

'Really?' Wittwitz said, registering polite disbelief. 'Even so, you can visualise the implications. If the intended victim was Frau Thomashoff and Tillou was eliminated only because he happened to be there, the matter assumes a different hue, does it not?'

What a sick joke: to be suspected of the killing I *hadn't* committed.

Wittwitz smoothed his already super-smooth hair. 'The shooting of a minister's wife might be the work of a terrorist faction. Perhaps part of a scheme to put pressure on the Government.' He shrugged. 'Who knows what these fiends will try next?

'Consequently, we have been asked by the *Kriminalpolizei* to follow up information received from an apparently reliable source, which . . . implicates . . .' he had chosen the word with extreme care, 'a certain Roger Townsend who, in turn, has been linked to a Sebastian Smith, and thence to a John, or Jack, Henley.'

Now at last I could let the outraged indignation flow.

'Me?' I said in a stunned voice. 'You mean *I* am suspected of being involved in this . . . this filthy business?' That was rather good, I thought. 'This is preposterous! Are you suggesting I'm a terrorist, or what?'

'We're not quite sure what you are,' Wittwitz said silkily. 'All we know about you is that you hold a British passport; that you have a Swiss residence permit with three years still to run; that you have no record with Interpol, and apparently have considerable wealth. Perhaps you would care to . . . ah . . . fill in the gaps.'

He flashed the phoney searchlight smile on and off. If it was meant to be reassuring, it failed.

'Tell me what you want to know.'

He proceeded, with skill, to extract from me the best part of my life history to date, duly modified to account for my affluence and lack of gainful pursuits. It was all straightforward stuff: no loaded questions, no chicanery. Dumas made copious notes but otherwise did not contribute.

This ritual occupied an hour or more and in the

course of it my guests' glasses were twice generously replenished. Regrettably, soaking the bastards in expensive hooch had no noticeable effect, except that Wittwitz's complexion gradually assumed a rosy tint. Dumas was unchanged. He would always be unchanged: he was hewn out of granite.

Wittwitz finally seemed satisfied that he had the full picture, down to the dimple on my backside and how often I changed my socks.

'If you've finished the cross-examination, Inspector,' I said, with a show of asperity, 'perhaps you would be so kind as to fill in one or two gaps for me.'

'I'll do my best. What would you like to know?'

'For a start . . . this Roger Townsend person. What led you to connect him with me in the first place?'

Glances were exchanged between Wittwitz and Dumas. They were clearly unhappy about parting with information.

'Come *on*, Inspector. Whatever you might think, this is just a great big bloody mystery to me. I've a right to know how you came to tie me in with this Townsend character.' Not bad, not bad. The degree of outrage was just right.

Wittwitz was tugging at his lower lip and looking uncertain. Then he spread his hands wide, as if to wash them of possible consequences.

'I would not normally reveal my sources at the enquiry stage. However, being an alien you are something of a special case, so I will break my rule for once.' A grunt of disapproval from Dumas darkened Wittwitz's brow but didn't stop him. 'The *Kriminalpolizei* were tipped off by an anonymous caller whom they succeeded in tracing – the man Röschinger I mentioned to you.'

So the little cocksucker had turned stool pigeon. I cursed him silently, regretted I hadn't chucked him off the Olympiatürm when I'd had the chance.

'Well, I don't know your Mr Röschinger, so I can only assume it's a case of mistaken identity. Honestly, Inspector, do I look like a murderer? Why . . . I don't even like swatting flies. To suggest I could have killed these people, especially a *woman* . . .' I dried up, implying incredulity.

Wittwitz looked surprised. 'You must have misunderstood me, Mr Henley. I said the man was killed, not the woman. She was shot, yes, but thanks to an unexpected caller, *she* survived!'

Far into the night, long after the departure of Wittwitz and Dumas, whose less-than-fond farewells included a warning not to leave Geneva without their say-so, I stayed up nursing glass after glass of Glenlivet. Wondering, wondering, wondering how to dig myself out of the dung-heap that friend Günther had landed me in.

The extent of the *Kriminalpolizei*'s evidence against me could be gauged on the assumption of Günther's unqualified co-operation – voluntary or otherwise. He would have told them about the gun and maybe, if they gave him a thorough going-over, about the other guns he had supplied me with. They would know about the car, since Günther had hired it for me. The Townsend alias must have been ferreted out from the hotel. Singly, none of these pointers led to Jack Henley, respectable resident of Geneva. The gun was lost forever to mankind and police alike, therefore Günther's allegations could not be substantiated, and the car hire on its own proved nothing. Even using a false name wasn't a crime, and my false papers, which *were* illegal, were as inaccessible as the weapon.

So far all was circumstantial. To make the charge stick, they had to place me at the scene of the killing. That was where the Thomashoff woman came in. Part of me was glad she was alive; however, not only could she provide the police with the requisite proof of my guilt, but, I gathered, she was also claiming *I* shot her, not Tillou. And about that I was not glad at all.

My nerves were jumping even before I arrived at this stage in my conjecturing. I went out onto the balcony to search for inspiration in the night air. The city gave off a restrained throb: traffic, people walking and talking, disco music, the cadence of metropolitan night-life. Lights still blazed in the tall blocks of the commercial sector; here and there neon signs pulsed their seductive messages.

All these familiar sights and sounds I had hitherto taken for granted, never dreaming they might one day be snatched away from me. That I might be doomed to drag out my years within the white, antiseptic walls of an eight-by-six prison cell. No more *Spindrift*, no more women, travel, gambling. Just a monotonous, colourless existence.

I shuddered. Sooner a bullet in the brain than it should come to that.

Should I go on the run? Get out of Switzerland to a country whose extradition laws were more benign? But such a move would be an admission of guilt. I would become another Ronnie Biggs, a fugitive, my movements restricted; almost as bad as prison, living in perpetual fear of a heavy hand on my shoulder, shaking with fright at every knock on the door, every clamour of the telephone.

No thanks. That route was not for me.

Defection, then, was to be the last resort. I must be ready to run, but only when all other options were exhausted. First, I must try and brazen my way out of this mess by every legal tactic at my disposal.

Legal tactics meant Jules Victor, my lawyer. I sat on the edge of an armchair and dialled his home number.

'You do know what time it is?' he growled, his voice blurred with sleep.

I hadn't, but I now saw it was after two a.m. I apologised, gave him a potted run-down on my troubles, arranged a lunchtime appointment for that day.

'Now go to bed,' was his churlish valediction.

I did. But not to sleep.

Five empty days dragged by, relieved only by my meeting with Jules who noted the particulars but felt disinclined to intervene until the police made contact with me again.

'We must play a waiting game for a little while,' he advised. 'It does not pay to over-react in a situation like this.'

So I drank coffees galore at the Comédie, lunched and dined out every day, gambled a bit. Unusually, I left the women alone: my appetite for sex was in limbo. With all this harassment going on, how could a fellow do justice to the likes of the ever-willing Evelyne, my favourite Genevoise? Consequently, when I wasn't eating, drinking, or gambling, I simply moped. Woe was me.

As well as fretting over my enforced confinement, I wrestled with various, mostly impractical schemes for getting off the hook, and the remaining gaps I plugged with thoughts of Gina.

The weekend had come and gone and she hadn't phoned as promised. If I'd had her number, I would have taken the initiative – I wasn't too proud. As it was, all I had was her name, and if she chose to drop me there wasn't a thing I could do about it.

And here I was, stuck in Geneva on the whim of a policeman called Wittwitz. I had just resolved, on the morning of the sixth day – a Monday morning of menacing skies that presaged more wet stuff – to go and create a stink in Wittwitz's office, when the telephone emitted its discreet whirr.

My charlady, Madam Segond, had just that minute shown up, so I took the call on the bedroom extension. It was Wittwitz. Well, well.

'I was going to pay you a visit today,' I said. 'I can't stay in Geneva forever. I have some business matters to attend to in France.'

'Naturally, we regret any inconvenience, Mr Henley,' he purred. 'Police investigations cannot be rushed, unfortunately. We have had to contact our counterparts in the *Bundesrepublik*, you understand.'

'Quite, quite. But you must understand that I have nothing to do with this shooting, and I am being prevented from leaving Geneva without justification.'

'Which is precisely my reason for telephoning.'

'You mean I'm now free to leave?'

Soft laughter came from the earpiece. I was glad *he* found it funny. 'Not quite, but if you would care to call here at police headquarters I am hopeful that the matter can be . . . ah . . . cleared up without further delay. You know where to find us?'

'Boulevard Carl-Vogt?' It was the only police station I knew of.

'Correct. No immediate hurry, but in the interests of . . . ah . . . justice, the sooner the better.'

I agreed and promised to be there that afternoon or the following morning. I couldn't be more specific, since I wasn't going without Jules and he might well be committed elsewhere.

I had only seconds to brood over the purport of my conversation with Wittwitz when the phone summoned me again.

'Monsieur Smith?' enquired my caller before I could open my mouth.

I went rigid with alarm, hearing that name used on an open line. It was all Wittwitz needed to put me on the next flight to Munich. Line taps aren't authorized willy-nilly in Switzerland, but the political implications of my case might just warrant such a measure.

'No one here of that name,' I snapped and banged the receiver down so hard the shock travelled up my arm. There was sweat on my forehead and on my palms.

The phone rang again. I lifted the receiver with an unsteady hand.

The same voice said, *'Rappelez-moi en France: cinquante, soixante-quinze, zéro-neuf, soixante-six. Jusqu'à midi.'*

Then I was listening to the hum of a dead line.

Through force of habit I had jotted down the number. In France, he had said, and I could reach him there until mid-day.

He was quick thinker, my caller. My initial reaction had warned him I wasn't free to speak and the number he had given me was almost certainly a pay-booth in a café or post office. All I had to do was get to a call box where we could talk without fear of eavesdroppers.

That is, if I wanted to talk to him, and about that I wasn't sure.

For my caller was no stranger: I had accepted a contract from him nine months before, to eliminate a certain Fabrice Tillou – a contract that was currently giving me more headaches than all its predecessors put together. He wouldn't have phoned just to say, 'Hello – how's tricks?' We weren't connected socially. No, it was a professional matter, either to do with the Tillou hit, or – the alternative struck me like a sonic boom – another contract. Such a possibility had been mentioned during our previous negotiations.

I hadn't consciously made a single move, but suddenly I was in the street, heading for the call box in the Place de Jargonnant. On the way, I bought a newspaper and acquired a pocketful of coins for my call.

He answered with a neutral ''Allo.'

'Smith,' I said tersely.

'Ah . . . thank you for calling back.' He was always civil this guy, I remembered. The name he had used last time was Dauphin, obviously a *nom de guerre*, though it contained a clue as to his motives if I'd been smart enough to figure it out. '*Ici* Dauphin.'

'I know. I recognized your voice.'

'I have been trying to contact you for several weeks. Have you been away?'

'Yes. I hope it wasn't urgent.'

'It is becoming so. When and where can we meet? I am only an hour's drive from Geneva.'

Meetings on Swiss soil were out as far as I was concerned. Switzerland was my home and my sanctuary, and only a cretin fouls his own back yard. Yet I couldn't cross the border until Wittwitz gave me the green light. I would just have to gamble on a happy outcome to the session at police headquarters.

'Tomorrow afternoon in Annemasse,' I proposed,

naming the popular ski-resort just across the border in France. 'There is a big square in the town centre. You know it?'

He didn't, but he would find it.

'Outside the BNP building. Three o'clock.'

'*Entendu*, Monsieur Smith.'

End of conversation. Whatever Dauphin wanted with me – and it had the smell of a contract – my compliance was by no means assured. To return to the assassination business while the prospect of being carted off to a Kraut slammer still loomed would, at the very least, be unwise. And yet, and yet, I often *did* regret quitting; I missed the planning, the preparation, the ultimate gut-tingling climax – the hit.

After seven months of free-wheeling, the prospect of action had the pull of a whirlpool. Meeting Dauphin wasn't a binding contract; it didn't commit me. I would see the guy, talk, and then . . . who knows?

I returned to the apartment block and, as was my custom, I ascended by the stairs, an uphill plod. I had reached the fifth floor landing and was fumbling for my keys when I saw her.

Perched on an upended suitcase by the door to my apartment. Dishevelled, hair any old-how, make-up hastily applied, blue slacks wrinkled. And her loveliness shining through it all.

Gina.

Chapter Eight

'I still can't quite take it in,' I confessed in wonderment.

'Join the club.' Gina's voice carried a hint of self-doubt. 'It took a lot of soul-searching before I could nerve myself to come here. I nearly turned back half-a-dozen times.'

A shower, a change of clothes, and lunch had transformed her. Relaxing on the long settee, one foot tucked under her bottom, she was a knock-out.

'Why didn't you phone? I'd have come to you.' Wittwitz permitting.

'Oh . . . I don't know.' She didn't meet my eyes. 'I wanted to. Honestly. But it wouldn't have meant anything. It's too easy to pick up a phone. I . . . I think perhaps I wanted to prove something to myself.' Some of her inner agitation broke through; she was clenching and unclenching her fists.

'When you left,' she went on, swallowing hard, 'I felt sort of . . . empty. Yet I was afraid of you. No . . . that's not right . . . I was afraid to commit myself to you.' She turned her head towards me, regarded me gravely. 'It was easier to just forget you – easier and *safer*. Then I could go on feeling sorry for myself, curled up in my shell like a snail; treating men with contempt.' She smiled, but not with joy. Instead, I saw only a sadness so profound that my heart turned over, and I longed to comfort her, to hold her tightly to me. It was not a sexual longing; for once I was thinking of a woman as a person rather than just meat on a plate.

I was tongue-tied. She was staring at me, eyes moist, lips slightly parted, waiting.

'I'm glad . . . I'm glad you came.' The words were stilted and conveyed about as much warmth of feeling as a polar ice-cap. I pressed on regardless, desperate to say things I hadn't said since Marion died. 'I'm more than glad. How shall I explain it? It's been so long since I formed a . . . well, a close relationship with a woman, I'm not sure I know how to behave any more. My emotions are rusted up. I meant to steer clear of love and marriage and all that stuff; I wanted freedom of choice. Then you come along and louse up all my fine intentions. Dammit, you've got me so I don't know whether I'm coming, going, or standing on my head!'

That produced sardonic amusement. 'It's comforting to know it's not just *my* life that's been turned upside down.'

I edged the dialogue away from these uncharted seas towards practical matters. 'Are you going to stay?' I asked flatly.

Her gaze was level. 'I've taken three weeks' holiday so I can do as I please. Do you want me to stay?'

'I want you to. Very much.'

'Then I'll stay.'

Just like that.

I didn't put forward any suggestions on the sleeping arrangements. I took her suitcase to the guest room and I determined that any alterations would have to arise naturally and not at my instigation. I was going to play it in low, low key. To test the strength of my feelings – and of hers. To make her want me, physically, as much as I wanted her.

My hopes and schemes might yet prove fanciful; I had the major hurdle of my meeting with Wittwitz to get over. Which reminded me I hadn't informed Jules. I excused myself and went into the bedroom to use the extension. He was about to go out, but expected to be free from four o'clock and, in consideration of my lack of transport, would call at the apartment for me at a quarter past.

I found Gina at the kitchen sink, washing the lunchtime dishes.

'Why don't you use the machine?' I indicated the expensive and under-utilised dishwasher at the end of the mile-long work top.

'Not worth it for a few plates and cups,' was her crisp response.

In addition to all her other more obvious attributes, she was economy-minded! I stood beside her, hands in pockets.

'It grieves me to say it, but I have to go out for a while,' I said.

She was scrubbing away at a stubborn mark on a plate. 'Will you be very long?'

'A couple of hours perhaps.' And perhaps for good. No profit in telling her that.

'Can I come with you?' Her face was hidden behind the curtain of hair that swung forward as she leaned over the sink.

'I'm afraid not. It's . . . it's a legal matter, sort of.' I sidled closer to her; our hips brushed; still she kept on scrubbing at that same blasted plate; she must have worn the glaze off by now. 'I'll be as quick as I can.'

'All right.' Inexplicably a barrier had sprung up between us. What had I said? Or was she just naturally touchy? Perhaps the scars from her divorce were still unhealed. I was unskilled in the kind of kid-glove handling she apparently needed, though I was game to try.

'What'll you do while I'm gone?' I wouldn't have put it past her to do a runner.

'Oh, browse through your CD collection – it looks magnificent. Watch TV, if there's anything worth watching. Don't worry,' she managed a fleeting smile, 'I'll while away the time somehow.'

'Promise me something.'

'If I can.' Small wrinkles of puzzlement etched her brow.

'You'll be here when I get back.'

She gave a little start, stepping back to study me. 'You're not just play-acting, are you, Jack? You're not just setting me up for a . . . a . . . oh, hell, for a quick *screw*?' She was blinking, fighting the tears. 'If you are, just say so and we'll go to bed right now and get it over with!'

I reached for her, but she backed off.

'It's not like that,' I protested. 'Not with you. With other women . . . yes, that's all it ever amounted to. With you it's something else. I tell you, love, you've got me so mixed up, I feel like sweet sixteen and never been kissed, all over again.'

She let out a long breath and some of the rigidity went from her body. I stood watching her, uncertain whether to offer comfort or shrug it off. It was hard to know what to do for the best. I would have liked to dig a bit into her past, to find out more about her husband and what went wrong between them, but I suspected she wouldn't take kindly to my raking up dying embers.

'I may be doing you an injustice,' she said at

last. 'If I am, I'm truly sorry.' She was under control, but quivering behind a veneer as thin as rice paper.

A car horn tooted down at street level.

'That's my lawyer,' I said, picking up my jacket from the back of a kitchen chair. 'I'll see you later.'

When I left she was still toiling away at the sink. Going down the stairs three at a time, it struck me I hadn't even kissed her goodbye.

Sergeant Dumas, predictably taciturn, showed Jules and me into Wittwitz's second-floor habitat, a cool and airy office with cream, emulsioned walls and steel filing-cabinets lining most of them. In the middle reposed Wittwitz's desk, also in steel, like an island fortress.

The man himself was in shirt sleeves. He looked distinctly down-at heel in comparison with Jules, who was suave and debonair as always in his pin-stripe lawyer's suit, not a straight black hair out of place. The rather disconcerting Hitler moustache bristled with aggressive efficiency and his small brown eyes were like gunsights behind the gold-framed spectacles.

'Thank you for coming, gentlemen.' If Wittwitz was bothered by Jules' presence, it didn't show. Hands were shaken all round. It was very amiable, very relaxed. Fangs as yet unbared.

At Wittwitz's invitation we sat in the two upright chairs arranged before the desk. Dumas went to a third chair, strategically positioned by a corner of the desk on Wittwitz's side. We were lined up like opposing armies.

Jules flipped open a broad, flat cigarette case that I knew to be solid gold and offered it around. Only

Dumas accepted and lit his and Jules's cigarettes from a book of matches.

'Now that we're all settled, Inspector,' Jules said in English, 'we are here at your insistence to clear up this misunderstanding over an incident in the Federal Republic. I demand that you now apologise to Mr Henley for this clear case of mistaken identity and lift the restriction on his movements with immediate effect.'

It was a nice try. Jules was a past-master in the game of bluff – his favourite form of relaxation was poker, at which he excelled and, moreover, usefully augmented his already considerable income.

Wittwitz gave a regretful smile. 'Alas,' he said, 'I cannot do what you ask. It is not a simple criminal matter; pressure is being exerted at a political level. As I have already explained to Mr Henley, the fact that the lady concerned was the wife of a member of the *Bundesregierung* has brought into play considerations other than who killed this Frenchman . . . this Tillou, and who shot Frau Thomashoff.'

Jules tapped ash into the ashtray on Wittwitz's desk. 'But my client was not in Germany at the time of the killing.'

'We have evidence to disprove that claim.' Wittwitz proceeded to give Jules a rundown of his evidence. It contained nothing I hadn't already heard.

'This is all circumstantial,' Jules said imperturbably. 'What evidence, what *proof* do you have that this person whom your Herr Röschinger allegedly supplied with a pistol was ever at the Thomashoff residence? That he ever used the pistol? That he used it on these two unfortunate people?' He checked these points off on his slender fingers.

Wittwitz's features drooped. 'None . . . as yet. The

police are still continuing their enquiries. They are confident that, given time, they will come up with definite proof.'

'Given *time*?' Jules was adept at seizing on key phrases. 'This crime took place last November, Inspector. How much more time will the German police require? For how long do they expect you to restrict my client's movements on their behalf? Eh?'

A shuffling of feet under the desk betrayed Wittwitz's uncertainty. I mentally congratulated Jules on herding the Inspector into a corner, though I didn't expect him to concede defeat. He was being squeezed from on high and wouldn't put his job at risk just because some smart-talking mouthpiece thumped the table.

'I have urgent business to attend to in France,' I said, adding a modest amount of fuel to Jules's inferno. 'I have to meet an associate there tomorrow. Failure to do so may cost me literally hundreds of thousands of dollars. Will you . . . will the Swiss government compensate me, Inspector?'

Out of the corner of my eye I saw Jules's satisfied nod.

Dumas, a non-participant until now, gave off a low rumble like a tractor starting up. 'These matters are not interesting us,' he began in his low-grade English, but Wittwitz silenced him with a sharp glance.

'I understand your difficulty, Mr Henley. However—' he turned to Jules, '—there is a new development: the Germans have asked us to send Mr Henley to München to either be identified or cleared, as the case may be. That will end all debate, will it not?'

It would. It would also be the end of me.

'You cannot extradite Mr Henley without incontestable proof of his guilt.' Jules spoke quietly and authoritatively, a no-nonsense tone. 'Not unless Switzerland has become a police state overnight.' He stubbed out his cigarette, looked at me. 'I think they will now ask you to go to Germany voluntarily, Jack.'

This was immediately confirmed by Wittwitz. 'Will you go?' he asked. His stare was disconcerting.

Jules was looking at me, too. 'You do not *have* to go, Jack. They cannot make you – no matter what Inspector Wittwitz says.'

'It is the only way to clear your name,' Wittwitz said sourly. 'Otherwise you will never be able to enter Germany again. Also, you may . . .' he shifted uncomfortably under Jules's glare, 'I say "may" be declared persona non grata in Switzerland.'

A scornful 'pah!' summed up Jules's view of that threat.

'*If* I do,' I said, having not the slightest intention of going, 'I cannot do so right away. As I explained, I have to be in France tomorrow without fail. Possibly I could go in a week or so.' I put on a dubious air. 'What do you advise, Jules? Should I go?'

Jules, in his ignorance of my former profession and presumably believing in my innocence, said, 'It is not necessary for you to go if you prefer not to.' He pursed his lips. 'On the other hand, I assume you will wish to clear your name and they will of course pay all expenses, plus perhaps a modest sum in compensation.' Here he fixed a legal-eagle eye on Wittwitz, who nodded vigorously.

'What would the Germans want with me?' I asked Wittwitz with sinking heart.

'The woman, Frau Thomashoff, can identify the person who shot her. She will simply say, yes, it was you, or no, it was not.'

'Why can't she come here?' Jules asked. 'Why inconvenience my client?'

'For reasons best known to themselves, the German police prefer that Mr Henley goes to München,' Wittwitz said unhelpfully.

Easy to guess why. If she identified me here in Geneva, the police would still have all the extradition rigmarole to go through, a procedure which can take months and whose outcome is never certain.

The cards Wittwitz was holding were all face up on the table now. Either I agreed to go to Germany and thereby commit *harakiri*, or I refused, which refusal would be interpreted by Wittwitz, and possibly Jules too, as an admission of guilt. I opted for the third alternative – prevarication.

'I'm willing to go on the basis of all expenses paid – but not at once.' The initial blatant surprise shown by Wittwitz faded when I added my rider, to be replaced by an equally blatant sneer.

'How long before you would . . . ah . . . consent to go?' he enquired in a civil tone that belied the curled lip.

'A month or so. As soon as I've concluded my negotiations in France.' I kinked an eyebrow at Jules. 'Does that sound unreasonable?'

'Not at all, not at all,' he said briskly, feeding another cigarette into his mouth. 'In fact I think you have been exceptionally tolerant throughout.' The unlit cigarette waggled as he talked. Dumas took the hint and lit it for him. 'I am sure the Inspector appreciates your co-operation.'

A door slammed outside in the corridor and somebody shouted, a torrent of vernacular French. The answer was indistinct but equally expressive. Another door slammed and the wall shuddered in sympathy before an uneasy peace was restored.

Wittwitz had borne this disturbance with an ill-grace and a frown was still in place when he said, 'If we could set a specific time limit it would be . . . er . . . appreciated. I have to say though, *Maître*, I am not sure whether Mr Henley should be allowed to leave the country. What is to prevent him from breaking his promise?'

'If Mr Henley so chooses,' Jules measured his words, his voice low and even, 'that is his prerogative, Inspector. He has no obligation either to the Swiss police or more especially to the German police, other than his own voluntary agreement to travel to Germany at some future date, possibly in about one month. If he chooses to remain in France, or go to England, or wherever his whim takes him, that is entirely his affair. Unless . . . ' He fixed a baleful eye on Wittwitz, whose displeasure was unconcealed.

'Yes, unless?' Wittwitz said impatiently.

'Unless you wish to prefer charges against my client.'

Christ, Jules, don't push him into a corner! was my immediate reaction to this, though I understood it was a stratagem to force Wittwitz to acknowledge the weakness of his case. Indeed, the form of open arrest already imposed was probably illegal given the lack of hard evidence and that the crime had been committed in another country; given also my nationality. For all I knew, Wittwitz was just as big a bluffer as Jules.

'Well?' Jules to Wittwitz. The Inspector had seemed to recoil from the suggestion of arrest and was now rolling a badly-chewed pencil in his fingers, his lips drawn in a tight line.

'We . . . we do not wish to arrest Mr Henley,' he

admitted at last, a piece of news that made me sigh inwardly with relief. 'He is free to come and go as he pleases, and to report here for the arrangements to be made with the German authorities as and when he pleases.'

'And . . .' Jules prompted.

Now Wittwitz was doing the sighing. 'And . . . if he does not please, then he does not need to report.'

'Ever,' Jules rounded off, his natural lawyer's pedantry dotting all 'i's' and crossing all 't's'.

'Ever,' Wittwitz conceded heavily. Then he looked straight at me and his face was bleak as a winter's morn. 'That, Mr Henley, is the official position I am instructed to advise you of. But before you go I should like to clarify my *personal* position.'

'Careful, Inspector,' Jules warned, as if he had an inkling of what was coming.

'I *personally* am not convinced of your innocence, Mr Henley,' Wittwitz went on without so much as a glance at Jules. 'With your legal representative present, I will not go so far as to say I believe you are guilty; I will only say that, in conjunction with the *Bundespolizei* who, I assure you, are determined to locate the killer, I intend to devote a great deal of time and resource to obtaining the necessary proof.' He tilted back in his chair, nodding in self-satisfaction. 'Do I make myself clear?'

I was about to say 'You do,' when Jules leapt in. 'I shall complain to your superiors about your conduct,' he said. 'Conduct which, I might add, I consider unbecoming to a senior police officer and an abuse of his powers.' He stood up so sharply that his chair rocked and almost tipped over. 'I trust I have made *myself* equally clear?'

Wittwitz blinked a bit, but otherwise wasn't

noticeably upset by Jules's counter-threat; he would dismiss it as obligatory legal rhetoric. Which was about the size of it.

The interview was clearly over, so I got up. Nobody said *au revoir* and nobody escorted us out. We just went, or rather stalked, Jules in front opening doors and flinging them back with a crash, me keeping step like an obsequious family retainer, and closing them quietly in mute apology. I didn't want to get clobbered for disturbing the peace or wanton damage to police property.

Driving me back to the apartment through another cloudburst that the wipers of his Merc were barely able to cope with, Jules was full of reassurance.

'Legally they can't touch you, don't worry. I know Wittwitz. He'll soon get tired of chasing a . . . what do you say . . . a mare's nest?'

'Will o' the wisp,' I smilingly corrected.

'Always the government here is eager to curry favour with the Germans. There is a great deal of German money invested in Switzerland, you know, and I don't just mean in the banks. And the Germans haven't changed, they like to flex their muscles with their smaller neighbours. There are those who joke about another *Anschluss*, only this time with Switzerland in the role of Austria. Of course, Wittwitz is a Zürich man and therefore pro-German by nature and language.' He patted my knee. 'Be assured, my friend, you are in the clear.'

'I'm relieved to hear it.'

Then, becoming more serious, he said, 'On a personal level, I would like to ask you something and I hope you won't be offended by it.'

I lifted my hand to indicate indifference.

'Did you actually do this thing? This shooting?'

Jules' bluntness was legendary and I should have foreseen the question. It was his legal right to ask it.

I resorted to more prevarication. 'What do you think?'

He chuckled softly. 'When in doubt answer a question with another question. But I will tell you: we have known each other for five, no, six years. I know you are quite wealthy. We have never discussed how you came by your wealth, and unless there is a legal reason why I need to know, I don't insist that you tell me.' We had pulled up at the junction by the Exhibition Centre and he took his eyes off the road to beam them in my direction. 'I think you are involved in this affair. And if you are involved, then I think maybe you did it.'

The road was clear. I pointed this out to Jules. 'Drive on, Jules – I'll find myself a new lawyer.'

He spun the wheel and we turned left up the Route des Arcacias. The rain was as bad as ever but Jules drove serenely, keeping his distance from the vehicle in front.

'You are too sensitive,' he admonished, a minute or so later. 'You are not merely a client – you are my friend. Friends do not desert each other in times of difficulty. Is that not so in England?'

I grinned at him. 'Thanks, Jules. Thanks, friend.'

'We will speak no more of this matter unless *you* say so. I am quite certain you will not be troubled again by Wittwitz.'

I wished I shared his confidence.

Thunder crackled overhead as we arrived outside the apartment. Jules tucked the Merc tidily into a slot between two lesser conveyances and, leaving the engine running, he twisted sideways to face me, an elbow resting languidly on the back of his seat. 'So . . . nothing is changed, Jack, *hein*?'

'Agreed. Come up for a drink. There's someone I'd like you to meet.'

He shook his head regretfully. 'I am sorry, I cannot. I have an appointment in fifteen minutes.' He took off his glasses and polished the lenses vigorously with a tissue. 'Nellie was asking about you the other day.' Nellie was Jules's second wife, a vivacious thirty to his nudging-fifty. As frivolous and mercurial as Jules was staid and sober, an amazing contrast in personalities. I liked her a lot; so much so that another time, another place . . .

'Come and have dinner tomorrow night.' Jules's invitation washed away a mildly-lascivious mirage. 'Bring your new . . . er . . . friend.'

'Okay, thanks. I'll look forward to it. About eight?'

'*Parfait*.'

The rain had abated, was now no more than a light drizzle, the thunder a resentful mutter backing away across the lake. I got out.

'Until tomorrow,' I said and watched him go, swishing off city-wards in a fountain of spray.

In the basement restaurant of the P'tit Vegas Club on the north side of the Rhône, one invariably dined well, albeit at extortionate prices. The cost of a magnum of vintage Dom Perignon was calculated to provoke heartburn in the most benign of constitutions.

It wasn't the sort of place where you dined alone, nor yet where you would expect to pick up some cruising floozie. The P'tit Vegas catered for the rich and influential, the upper strata of Geneva society. The service was faultless, the atmosphere intimate, and there was a discreet gaming room for those with money to burn – hence the P'tit *Vegas*.

I took Gina there that evening. She was in good form: she displayed a healthy appetite and talked animatedly, dominating the conversation. With three-quarters of that magnum inside us we were both relaxed and deriving the pleasure from each other's company that a mutually attracted man and woman should. I treated her more like my sister, hoping to put her at ease, and it worked.

Throughout the meal the nine-piece band maintained a flow of background music, subtle and unobtrusive, which is how I prefer it; all too often over-amplification kills the conversation. Now, with the majority of diners sitting back over coffee and *digestifs*, the band pepped up its output and the floor soon filled with dancing couples, their movements convulsive under the coloured strobe lights.

'Would you like to?' I said to Gina.

'Dance?' She looked out across the floor, nodded. 'I'd love to. It's ages since I did.'

I pushed my chair back, went around to take her hand as she rose. She smiled at me and I saw only happiness there now. Sheathed in an ankle-length, simple green dress that rippled as she walked, she knocked not only spots off the other women there, but stars and stripes too. Her hair was loose, caressing her bare back, shimmering with the rainbow colours of the lights. And I sensed that, beneath those heavy, sensuous eyelids, behind that often diffident exterior, lurked a roaring furnace just waiting to be let out. All it would take was the right combination; get it wrong and the works would just jam up solid and stay that way, like a badly-blown safe.

She danced well, much better than me, and I felt

like a clodhopping yokel as we waltzed and tangoed, bossa novaed and jived. And always her body, that slender form with its curves and hollows and legs that went on forever, was close . . . close . . . It was more than flesh and blood could bear. Yet I bore it: I stiffened my upper lip, stuck out my jaw and held my baser instincts in check.

During a slow, smoochy waltz she let me draw her closer than ever and with the moulding of our bodies, thigh to thigh, chest to chest, I became aroused, quite rabidly so. What was more, I sensed a similar arousal in her. It took the form of a deep, inner pulsation, a metronome beat, steady and regular, and her skin was afire under my touch.

'Feeling good?' I said.

'Very, very good.' We smooched on a bit longer, then she said in that taunting sing-song children often use, 'I-know-some-thing-you-don't.'

I laughed and sing-songed back, 'I-don't-be-lieve-you.'

She stopped, right there in the middle of the dance floor, those extraordinary eyes flickering over the contours of my face as if she were seeing it clearly for the first time.

'What's the matter?' I asked. She was tense and still. Around us the other dancers slithered, subjecting us to openly curious stares.

She bit her lip, started to speak, checked herself, then finally it came out in a rush. 'I'm falling in love with you.'

For once my repertoire failed me. I was caught wrong-footed, automatically rejecting all the usual slick responses. She had bared her emotions before me – sincerity was the least I owed her.

'Let's sit down, shall we?' I took her elbow and we

weaved through the shuffling couples to our table. There I poured the last of the champagne.

'To us,' I proposed. Then, 'To . . . our love.'

She gave me an uncertain look. 'Do you feel the same? Truly?'

I was like a man on a ledge at the top of a tall building, bent on suicide but shrinking from the irrevocable, terminal plunge.

'I won't kid you with an outright yes . . . but I think so . . . I really think so. I may even have been in love with you since the day we met, at the hotel in Digne. I didn't want to admit it; I'd had a bellyful of love – so-called love.' I was thinking particularly of Rebecca, my second wife. 'But you . . . you're something else. You're . . .' I fished around in my storehouse of superlatives for one that conveyed what I felt about her. 'You're . . . breathtaking.' I held both her hands and leaned across the table to kiss her.

As kisses go, it was not earth-shattering; just a simple meeting of lips, a tentative tasting, as with a vintage wine. But it was no less special for that; it marked the end of a beginning and, although neither of us could have foreseen it, the beginning of an end.

'I love you,' I said softly, and it was as near true as made no difference.

'I love you . . . my darling,' she whispered back, with a touch of shyness.

We clinked glasses. I drank the champagne but didn't taste it. I tasted only an elation so heady it made me dizzy and lightheaded. She was mine. *Mine!* This magnificent creature sitting before me, brimming with happiness, the lights picking out the planes and angles of her beauty, casting shadows along her jaw-line, emphasising the smooth texture of her skin. All mine.

We talked. About what, I can't recall. Endearing phrases, avowals of love repeated over and over; the exchanges, often trite but no less sincere, that pass between lovers the world over. I wasn't self-conscious and neither, any longer, was she; we trampled the barriers into the dust. From here on we could only go forward, building on the foundations of our feelings, tightening the knot that already held us in bondage.

I swore to make her happy.

'You have . . . you do. My only regret is that I didn't give in sooner, that I fought against my feelings.' She cupped a hand under her chin, gazed at me with an intensity that was disturbing. 'I've been so stupid. So blind.'

I stroked her lips, tracing their outline with my forefinger. She kissed my fingertip, a gesture so simple yet somehow so moving. I cast my mind back: was this how it had been with Marion? I couldn't be sure, it was so long ago now; a waning memory in a distant pigeon-hole of my mind. A fallen leaf, brown and curling at the edges, disintegrating slowly but necessarily to make way for new life, for a new love.

Presently we danced again, touching everywhere now, oblivious of all around. We were floating in a fifth dimension, a make-believe world, where no one else existed and nothing else mattered except that we were together.

And for a while, I imagined it would be like a fairy tale with a happy ending. That we would walk off into the sunset, hand-in-hand, the path straight and true, without pitfall or danger to threaten us. Hero (admittedly tarnished) and heroine.

Inevitably, sanity returned. To remind me of the quicksand foundations on which my immediate future rested. That afternoon's session with Wittwitz nagged at me still; the Schnurrpfeil affair remained a festering abscess. Then, too, I was committed to meet Dauphin, though I wasn't in the market for a contract any more: Gina had changed all that.

A more prosaic and compulsive need subjugated these worries. I escorted Gina back to the table.

'Nature calls,' I said and kissed her lightly on the forehead, before chugging off towards the discreetly-signposted *toilettes* in the darkest corner of the restaurant.

Like the rest of the place, the washroom was immaculate apart from a scattering of cigarette butts on the orange-tiled floor, the row of three urinals looking forlorn and unwanted. I gave the middle one a drink and was shaking off the drips when the door opened on what I naturally took to be another bursting bladder. As I glanced sideways, a pair of dark-suited characters entered and at once some instinct warned me they were bad news. My instinct was not wrong: they came straight at me. I had time enough to zip up, no more, before they pounced – and they pounced hard. Both my arms were seized, above and below the elbow, and I was flung against the wide mirror built into the opposite wall, my breast bone making violent contact with the glass. For a moment the three of us were poised, staring at our reflections, mine twisted with pain, theirs grim and uncompromising. It was like a scene from a cheap gangster movie, with me as the poor mug who gets beaten to a pulp and dumped in the river, wearing concrete boots.

The bigger of my two assailants sported a snazzy yellow tie to set off his loose-fitting dark blue suit; he had big Bambi eyes, at odds with his general appearance. The other had the blue jowls that go with heavy facial growth, the archetypal comic-strip hoodlum.

Bambi Eyes let go with his right hand to fumble inside his jacket. I didn't wait to see what goodies he kept there, but kicked out backwards, connecting with his shin. It was some shin; I've kicked tree trunks with less resistance. And the bastard didn't even grunt, though his grip on my arm loosened fractionally and I consolidated my flimsy gain by crashing into him, dragging the other gorilla, Blue Jowls, along with me. We all hit the tiles together and Blue Jowls came off worst: he cracked his neanderthal skull on the rim of a urinal. Hard to say which stood the shock better – bone or ceramic. No matter, the result was his immediate withdrawal from the contest, leaving me to concentrate on Bambi, admittedly the more formidable adversary.

We picked ourselves up, dusted ourselves down, and started all over again. Bambi's hirsute fist had acquired an extension: a big, butch automatic of indeterminable type. I gave him no chance to use it; I kicked out again, going for his balls. He was a mile ahead of me, his own foot intercepting mine in mid-flight, catching me on the calf and knocking me off-balance. I went backwards, tripped over the comatose form of Blue Jowls, to finish up sprawled on the tiles in my almost new mohair suit – my almost new *cream* mohair suit.

While I was still rolling about in the cigarette butts, Bambi got his cannon lined up. '*Ca suffit!*' he barked in a voice reminiscent of crunching gravel.

The muzzle was ogling me and it didn't look friendly.

'*Levez-vous!*' The crunched gravel was crunchier, more menacing. I obeyed, groaning as pain stabbed at me from several angles. Bambi pushed me up against the mirror, prodding impatiently with the gun. I was half-concussed from my fall and in no condition to argue.

Bambi's frisking was swift and practised. I wasn't packing iron; I didn't have as much as a razor blade on my person, but if I had he would have found it, he was that thorough.

'What's this all about?' I demanded, feigning indignation, my arms and legs still spread against the wall.

'You don't know?' Bambi's tone was disbelieving.

'Would I ask if I did? You've got the wrong guy.'

'You've been fingered, *mon pote*. No question – it's you we want.'

I switched quickly to a different approach. 'Who's "we"? Schnurrpfeil?'

'Who?' Bambi snarled.

Noises of revival were issuing forth from Blue Jowls. Bambi ripped off a terse command which roughly translated as 'Stop fucking about'. Moans rose from the floor.

'Are you going to kill me?' I asked, reasonably sure he wasn't.

He displayed a crowded mouthful of teeth in varying stages of decay. 'Kill you, *mon pote*? You should be so lucky. You're going on a little trip to the seaside. I got strict orders about you.'

Thanks, mug, for giving me the all-clear to tackle you without fear of fatal consequences.

Blue Jowls was up as far as his knees now, shaking himself like a dog after a swim. If I was going to move, I had to do it before he rejoined the party. Yet still I wavered. Going for an armed man takes a lot of nerve and I wasn't sure I had that much.

I went ahead just the same – what choice had I? I let my legs buckle, as if in abject terror, flopping against Bambi. He wasn't ready for that. He grabbed a lapel of my much-abused suit and hauled me upright. Strong as he was, my twelve-and-half stone was a lot to lift; balance and concentration were both upset, the gun wandered, and I rose up underneath him like the prow of a surfacing submarine. My forehead fetched up with sledge-hammer force against his chin. His teeth came together with a clack and his head snapped backwards, taking the rest of him along with it, and he came down on Blue Jowls who was in the closing stages of his long climb back from the floor. This made-to-order collision neatly dealt with all my problems. Even the gun chose a different trajectory from its owner; it bounced off the mirror, shattering it, and ricocheted through the open door of the nearest cubicle.

A multitude of '*Merdes*' and worse also ricocheted about the place. I didn't stick around to listen; I was out of that convenience – which was when I discovered the door had been bolted from the inside to ensure against interruptions – double-quick, assuming a sedate stroll as soon as I hit the corridor. I brushed the miscellaneous clinging deposits from my once-immaculate suit, the second I had ruined in the last few days, thanks to this mob. Smoothing back my hair, I re-entered the restaurant.

At my debouchment from the corridor, Gina left the table and came hurrying across. Her expression was a mixture of relief and concern and she almost stumbled into my embrace, heedless of the cream of Geneva society on all sides.

'Where have you been?' she demanded, as I whisked her back to our table.

'Was I gone long?' I asked blandly.

'Over ten minutes.' Which was less than I'd

estimated. 'And look at the state you're in; you look as if you've been in a fight.'

'I have.' I picked up her bag, thrust it into her hand. 'Come on, we're leaving.'

As we headed for the *caisse* I gave her a brief explanation.

'You remember I told you about some mob that's been tailing me everywhere.' She nodded worriedly. 'Well, I've just bumped into more of the same in the loo – and "bumped" is exactly what I mean.'

I felt her grip tighten on my bicep. 'Are you all right? You're not hurt?'

'A bruise or two, no more than that. And an expensive suit that'll never be the same again.'

'Sod the suit!' she said crossly.

I had a credit account at the Vegas. A hasty scrawl on the bill, produced by a computer gone beserk to judge from the number of digits, and we were off. I banked on Bambi and Blue Jowls taking five minutes or more to re-group for another try: time enough for us to get clear away from the premises.

The doorman rustled up a cab right away and Gina and I huddled together on the back seat in a clinch that enabled me to keep an unobtrusive eye on following vehicles. Traffic was light and no one showed any interest in us. As we crossed the Rhône via the Pont du Mont Blanc the road behind was clear.

I unwound sufficiently to indulge in some routine necking with Gina, but my heart wasn't really in it. Moreover, I was so rattled by the incident at the Vegas that I gave almost no thought to the sybaritic delights that might lie in store when we got back to the apartment.

In the event, we slept in our own beds. At the outset. Sometime during the night Gina came to me, which was as I had wanted it to be: *her* decision, not merely submission to my advances.

I didn't hear the door open, nor her footfall; only when warm, bare flesh skimmed mine did I jerk into wakefulness, tensed for action, reaching for the SIG between the mattress and the base of the bed.

The touch of her fingers on my stomach was light as fantasy; my nerve ends tingled as I came fully awake and conscious of who and what. A breast was pressed against my arm and I put my hand on it, gently at first, then, when she didn't draw back, more firmly, fondling the nipple which responded emphatically, becoming pebble-hard.

I kissed her then and the sweetness of it swept away the debauchery of the past in a single, cyclonic blast, transporting me back to the days beyond my first love, when ideas and ideals shone bright as a polished trophy. It was a kiss that transcended all others before it, and left me weak with the wonder and the power of it.

'Darling . . . darling . . .' She kept repeating it, over and over, her voice unrecognizably hoarse.

I slid my mouth down on her breast, lingered over those pebble-hard nipples that hardened anew under my oral caress. Now she was moaning and squirming. I nibbled experimentally and her body heaved as in a spasm. Her hands were busy too, sliding tentatively over my prick, hovering there then, as if she had come to a difficult decision, grasping firmly and pumping away at my rigid flesh.

I moved, over the smooth midriff with its deep navel, towards that thatch of crispy curls, last defensive line before the ultimate zone of pleasure. My mouth rested there on her pubis, kissing lightly, tugging the hairs with my teeth before travelling on, further southwards. Her legs were locked together, but they yielded to my persuasive onslaught and unclenched slowly, the inner thighs trembling and dewed with sweat. Her vaginal lips parted, like foliage at the entrance to a secret cavern, to release a trickle of juices. To release too, that unforgettable smell of a woman on heat: piquant, slightly musky, inflammatory. I kissed the delicate folds of her labia and she cried out harshly, an alien sound.

'Do it, darling.' It was almost a sob. 'Now . . . now!'

I was ready. I went up on my elbows and entered her, a flowing, co-ordinated incursion. A few, savage thrusts had her panting, her breath coming in little screams, underscoring every stroke.

It was as violent a coming together as I had ever experienced. We loved up a mighty storm, a howling, shrieking whirlwind, and let its turbulence overwhelm us. It tossed us this way and that way, squeezing, pounding, pulverizing, until it whirled on and away, leaving us breathless and exhausted, and all that remained was dust, settling slowly, softly, silently.

By the end of our lovemaking I was a little boy lost. Committed totally, helplessly, unequivocally to this woman. As in love as anyone could ever be.

It was like being born again.

RE-DEATH

Chapter Nine

It was only natural that Gina should want to accompany me to Annemasse for my rendezvous with Dauphin – a rendezvous I still had to keep despite my change of heart. If I stood him up he would be on the blower, demanding to know why, and I couldn't risk another of those 'Mr Smith' calls.

'I'll shop for some undies and things while you have your meeting,' she said, when I hinted at making the journey alone. Since she plainly didn't expect to sit in on the discussion therefore, I gave in.

My disposition that day was not of the sunniest. All morning and through lunch the attack at the P'tit Vegas had occupied my mind and, as we filtered through customs in the clapped-out, hired Ford Scorpio and entered France, it continued to plague me.

What had I learned from this latest development, this undoubted escalation? Not a great deal. I had learned that somebody had a whopping grudge against me, and wanted me delivered to them alive. But as to the identity of my enemy, there I came up against a blank wall. I had no *known* enemies, but logically any close relative or friend of my forty professional victims must qualify as a potential enemy. Anonymity was my only protection: they would have to have identified me as the killer. So had

I slipped up somewhere? And if so, how and when? Last year? The year before? Ten years ago? Impossible to even guess. I was just groping in a dense black fog.

'Penny for them.' Gina snapped me out of my brooding absorption, which was just as well since I should have been concentrating on the road, and the turn-off to Annemasse town centre lay just ahead.

'Hang on,' I said, indicating left at the last minute and incurring an indignant blast from the driver behind, who was too close anyway. We angled across the road, the Scorpio wallowing on its worn springs and dampers like a rocking horse.

'Sorry, love,' I said, as the bouncing subsided. 'I've been bending my brain over last night's business at the Vegas club.'

'How do you account for it?' she asked. 'Oughtn't you to go to the police?'

'It's not that simple . . . shit!' I swerved to avoid a Simca of yesteryear that came at us on the wrong side of the road with the single-minded determination of a charging rhino, only to lunge aside when collision seemed inevitable.

I discoursed obscenely on French driving standards. 'Driving in this country is like playing dodgems.'

Gina's hand was still over her mouth, whither it had flown at the height of the crisis. Now she took it away and managed a nervous grin.

'Ah,' I said, spotting a vacant parking-meter. I nosed the Granada into the slot just ahead of another candidate. The driver saluted me impolitely as he roared off.

I lined up, nice and neat, and switched off.

'To return to what I was saying . . .' Gina began.

'Why don't I go to the police?' I concluded for her. 'Partly because I don't have a lot of faith in their competence, partly because I prefer to take care of it in my own special way. But mostly because I'm still bound by the UK Official Secrets Act.'

She turned to stare at me. 'Official Secrets Act?'

I nodded. 'It's a long story and I can't tell you all that much anyway because of the Act, but . . . well, I used to work for the British Government. In a certain, shall we say, hazardous capacity.'

I had cooked up this explanation for the P'tit Vegas dustup overnight, in case Gina's curiosity needed satisfying. I was rather pleased with it.

Gina continued to stare and her scepticism was plain to see.

'Although I retired some years ago, the opposition would still love to wire me up to a set of electrodes and suck me dry.'

It sounded melodramatic, yet entirely in context with recent events. Somehow, though, I'd struck a wrong note with Gina; could be she was a dedicated Communist or allergic to spies.

I tossed out such whimsical notions and snicked her under the chin.

'Hey! I love you.' Saying it already felt natural.

'Oh, darling, I love you too. So much.'

So that was alright then.

'Shall we go?' I said and opened my door. She slid out and, as usual, I couldn't help staring at her backside in those almost-indecent, sprayed-on jeans she had worn the day we travelled to Monaco together.

As French towns go, Annemasse is only averagely pretty. It has a few tree-lined streets, a tree-filled square in the centre, a sprinkling of interesting architecture, and God-alone-knows how much through-traffic – a cross it has to bear owing to its situation on the Franco-Swiss border.

Gina and I parted company with a kiss by the covered market, arranging to meet up an hour hence. I watched her go with a blend of possessive pride and genuine deep affection. No post-mortem had been held over our night together. When I awakened she was already up and dressed, percolating coffee in the kitchen. The dialogue over the breakfast table had been superficial, the tone light and bantering. I understood that for her our lovemaking had represented a giant stride, and that she had to come to terms with it at her own pace. That was okay by me. The covenant had been made. There was no going back.

I came to the square, the Place de la Libération, just as the nearby church clock struck three. Dauphin was there, a dapper figure, slim, greying, not a lot older than me; thin and hawkish of features, with a pointed chin and a mouth like a steep trap. There was a ruthlessness in him; a streak of cruelty too, I shouldn't wonder.

As I greeted him in front of the war monument that pays homage to the *Glorieux Enfants* of Annemasse, *Mort pour la patrie*, my private distaste stayed under wraps. After all, civility costs nothing.

'How are you, Mr Smith?' he said, in his precisely-enunciated French, that trap of a mouth barely opening. Above his left eyebrow was an angry red pimple; he was rubbing it with the tip of his finger as if trying to wear it away by friction.

We waded through an army of hopeful pigeons to an empty bench under a fir tree. Dauphin lit a cigarette, and let the smoke trickle down his nostrils. He had extremely hairy nostrils.

'You rendered an excellent service for me last year, Mr Smith,' he murmured, not looking at me but watching the passers-by, especially the young and pretty girls in their short summer dresses. I imagined him watching Gina, imagined his slimy, reptilian gaze tracking her along the street. It was not an agreeable vision.

'Kind of you to say so, Mr Dauphin.'

The steel trap flickered – the Dauphin equivalent of a smile.

'I am told the Thomashoff woman is not dead.' It was said flatly, as were most of his utterances. I could have stood to hear how he came by the information, but I didn't pursue it.

'It needn't concern you.' I was equally flat. I wasn't about to make excuses over my failure to finish the woman off. I was the one in jeopardy, not him.

'True. You eliminated Tillou; you did what you were paid to do. I have no complaints, Mr Smith.'

A pair of teenage beauties strolled by, in identical short white dresses, thin as tissue paper. I couldn't help admiring them. 'Glad to hear it, Mr Dauphin,' I said mechanically.

The sun went behind a cloud and the air became chill, the branches overhead rattling in a sudden flurry of wind. The two girls had trouble with their dresses: they wore identical tissue-paper knickers too.

'You implied you had urgent need of my services again,' I said, when he made no effort to get down to the real nitty-gritty. 'You realise I'm no longer working.'

'Yes, but there is more to this than a straightforward contract.' He slid along the seat towards me. 'First I think there is something you should know.' His voice had dropped to a furtive hiss.

'What's that?' Now he had me hissing too. I cleared my throat.

'Tillou, the father, seeks to avenge his son's death.'

'So? Let him seek.'

'But he knows it is you . . . you who killed him.'

Tillou. France's answer to the Godfather. A gang boss with plenty of manpower on tap. Manpower of the ilk of Curly Moustache and Bambi and Blue Jowls. Typical hired muscle. Suddenly I understood a great deal. Mysteries were unravelled, answers to questions clicked into place like the tumblers of a one-armed bandit.

I asked Dauphin about Schnurrpfeil.

'Yes, I know Carl Schnurrpfeil very well. He is in charge of the Cannes end of the organization. Why?'

'Never mind. What about a big fellow with calf eyes?' I described Bambi.

'Ah. His name is Malpont. He is just a strong-arm man – a persuader.' He eyed me, frowning. 'How do you know these people? Have you met them?'

'In a manner of speaking. They and others have been trailing me on and off for the last couple of months. Last night they tried to snatch me.'

The clouds directly above had thickened. A few spots of rain fell, dark blots on the pavement.

Dauphin was staring down at his elegantly-shod feet, his brow still corrugated. 'I see,' he said slowly. 'I was not aware the matter had progressed so far.' He was nodding pensively as he spoke and a wayward lock of hair sprang up on his crown. 'I have not myself been involved in this . . . vendetta.'

Vendetta. It had a chilling ring. Mafia, the kiss of death, and all that stuff.

'Since the death of Fabrice Tillou, I have been number two in the organization. Frankly, I had expected Tillou himself to be dead by now. He is old and he is also ill: two years ago he suffered a heart attack and now he cannot even walk. He is permanently confined to a wheelchair.'

'Let me get this straight. Tillou is on to me and he's going to kill me if he can. Have I got it right?'

'I'm very much afraid so,' Dauphin said, with as much regret as a man receiving news of a bumper win on the lottery. 'Tillou will not rest until family honour has been satisfied. This means he must kill you – personally. That is the way these things are done, you understand. And that is why he is trying to kidnap you rather than simply have you assassinated.'

The rain was coming down harder now, pattering against the leaves of the giant oaks which, for the time being, would keep us dry. People had dispersed, scurrying for shelter. We had the square almost to ourselves.

'Where do you stand in all this, Dauphin?'

'I? My position is rather ambiguous.' He was picking his words with the care of a French housewife choosing tomatoes from a market stall. 'I am number two and I wish to be number one. A simple ambition, *hein*? However, as long as the *patron* lives I must give him my allegiance – my ostensible allegiance. As I explained, I am not involved in this vendetta. I run the businesses and the *patron* does as he pleases. In an operational sense I am already the top man, but still I receive only a salary, a pittance, and one per cent . . .' His eyes blazed, well, smouldered; blazing was for more irascible temperaments than his. 'One per cent of the profits. After fifteen years of loyal service, fifteen years of kow-towing to him and that . . . son of his, all I get is a miserable one per cent.' His voice shook. His hands too, when he lit another cigarette, dragging hard on it and puffing the smoke out in quick bursts.

'So you've got a grudge. It still doesn't tell me where you stand in the matter of Tillou's vendetta against me.'

His answer, when it came, was oblique. 'For your problem there is only one solution.'

I didn't need to be told what it was. 'Kill Tillou.'

'Quite.' The trap undulated at the edges. 'You are not stupid, Mr Smith.'

Kind of him to say so.

'Let us assume then that you decide to kill him. Out of self-defence. It's a powerful incentive on its own, is it not? But just in case you need another, more material incentive, I can give you one. As well as a certain amount of practical assistance – inside information, for instance.'

I wondered how Dauphin came to be in such a sordid line of work. He spoke in the idiom of a well-educated man and was to your run-of-the-mill hoodlum as caviare is to frog-spawn. I didn't entirely trust smark crooks: they were too tricky. You had the feeling they would stab you in the back as a matter of principle rather than for reasons of security or economy. For the present though, it suited me to jolly him along.

'This other incentive. What is it exactly?'

He came closer. His hot thigh pressed against mine which, of its own free will, retreated crabwise. If Dauphin took offence, it didn't show; the deadpan stayed firmly in place.

'My proposition is this: five hundred thousand US dollars, twenty per cent now, the rest on completion, to kill Tillou. Big money, *hein*? And at the same time you will have done yourself a favour. When Tillou is dead, the vendetta will also die. There will still be Fabrice's widow, of course, and his sister, but they do not count.'

'What about the inside information?'

'You accept then?' He spoke with affected indifference. The inner agitation was betrayed by the tremble of his hand as he took several successive pulls at his cigarette.

'Where does he spend his time?' I said.

'At his villa, on the island of Porquerolles in the Mediterranean. Near Toulon.'

I had holidayed there once. A wooded, tranquil place, and still undiscovered by the main tourist stream. Pretty but deadly dull, a monasterial backwater.

'Does he ever leave it?'

'Seldom. Travel is not easy for him. Twice, perhaps three times a year he sees a heart specialist in Toulon. For a check-up, you know.'

'How does he travel to the mainland? By boat, I suppose.'

'He has a helicopter.'

'Hmm. I assume he's well-guarded, and being on an island makes it even more hazardous. There are only two ways off: by air, which would mean hiring my own helicopter plus pilot, or by sea . . .' I stopped in mid-sentence. By sea – of course. In *Spindrift*. The perfect escape route. Just sail away and get lost in the Mediterranean.

Tillou was regarding me, eyes narrowed to slits. 'You have an idea?'

'Maybe,' I said cagily. 'A lot depends on how much inside help you can give me.'

'Ah, well, I can supply details of the villa and its grounds, Tillou's daily routine, the number of bodyguards and their routine. And so on. I can also keep you informed of developments concerning his vendetta against you.'

A large spot of rain splashed on the back of my hand and rested there, a shimmering pearl. I shook it off absent-mindedly. My mind was ticking like a time bomb. If Tillou was out to kill me, sooner or later he would succeed. I couldn't dodge his army of hired thugs forever. So why not beat him at his own game? Turn up in his back yard where he would least expect to see me. It had a certain swashbuckling appeal to commend it, if nothing else.

'As a proposition, it has attractions,' I admitted. 'Though I wouldn't normally accept a contract on someone as well-protected as Tillou.'

'Which is why I am offering considerably more than the going rate.'

'Assuming that the fee you propose is about right apropos the risks involved, what I don't like are the terms of payment. My usual is half when the contract is made, the other half forty-eight hours before execution.' I gave him a meaningful look. 'Like last time.'

Dauphin sucked at his fast-diminishing cigarette as if it were an elixir of youth. 'I regret I cannot pay so much in advance. Afterwards, when I take over the organization, it will be different. This is why I offer only twenty per cent now.'

I pondered awhile. The money was a secondary consideration, though I wouldn't turn my nose up at it. Self-defence, as Dauphin had put it, that was the prime motivation. I wanted to live. As incentives go, you can't get more potent than that.

I came down off my fence. 'I'll do it. And I don't want a down payment, just the full fee on completion.'

He quit polluting the atmosphere to goggle at me like a startled fish. 'That's absolutely fantastic. How can I ever . . .'

'The full fee being,' I went on, cutting across him, 'one million dollars by irrevocable letter of credit, post-dated to, say, 1st September, to be held by a mutually approved *avocat. D'accord?*'

He gagged. The cigarette was back in action, the tip glowed furiously. He was so overwrought he missed a tall, coloured dolly with unfettered boobs as big and bouncy as a pair of beach balls. My popping eyes never left her as she crossed the road towards us at a trot.

'All right,' Dauphin said reluctantly. 'It is agreed. One million dollars on completion.'

I stowed my tongue away and cranked my mind back towards less stimulating matters than the laws of physics as applied to the female form.

'Get the letter of credit prepared, drawn on the Schweitzerische Kreditanstaltbank in Zürich. I'll let you know when I'm ready to see the lawyer; meanwhile do nothing in that respect. We choose from a telephone directory with a pin.'

Dauphin actually looked hurt, if you can imagine it. 'You do not trust me, Mr Smith.'

'Why do you specially want *me* for this job?' I asked him. 'Why not some other hit-man? There's no shortage amongst your own countrymen: Vigneron, Lopez, Dejean; I could name half-a-dozen, and they would come cheaper. There's the Italian fellow, too, from Naples . . . sounds like ravioli.'

'Rabaiolo, I think you mean.' He chain-lit yet another coffin-nail.

'That's him. So you know these people. So again, I ask – why me, Mr Dauphin?'

'You are supposed to be the best,' he said stiffly.

I nodded. 'Good. That's what I wanted to hear. You just go on believing that, Mr Dauphin: Sebastian Smith is the best. Believe it and remember it;

especially remember it when I've killed Tillou and you're the top dog, with all that money and all those muscle-men dancing to your tune.' I whipped the newly-lit cigarette from that steel-trap mouth, reversed and held the glowing tip up close against his eyeball, simultaneously pressing him against the back of the bench with my other arm.

'Remember it if ever you get to thinking about carrying on Tillou's vendetta and saving yourself a million bucks.'

He was as stiff as a suit of armour, cringing away from the cigarette. 'You can trust me, Mr Smith,' he said and his voice was a falsetto squeak. 'I won't try to cheat you. I'm a man of honour.' The suave exterior had been stripped away like paint under a blowlamp and the fear in his face was stark and ugly.

I was satisfied he was as frightened as I could make him in such a public place, so I jettisoned the cigarette, straightened his ruffled feathers. He rubbed at his seared eyeball, too scared to remonstrate.

'No offence, Mr Dauphin. One can't be too careful in my business.'

'No.' Still squeaking. 'I . . . yes . . .'

I pulled notebook and pencil from my shirt pocket. 'I'd like some information now, Mr Dauphin, if you wouldn't mind. The exact location of the villa for a start.'

He recovered some of his lost aplomb, tossed a small but bulky brown envelope into my lap. 'It's all there. Including a number where you can contact me.'

A tepid sun was peeping coyly through a break in the clouds when, a minute later, I started back to meet Gina, leaving Dauphin still smarting and not a little sulky over my demonstration.

If he ever did make it to the top of the organization,

I didn't give a flea's fart for his chances of keeping the job.

Lying in bed that night, replete from the dinner party *chez* Jules, and ever so slightly under the influence of a twenty-three year old Burgundy, Gina and I discussed the past and our future.

She was relaxed, effervescently happy, as indeed she had been all through the meal and afterwards. Flushed with colour, her green eyes glittering like emeralds, she had completely won over Jules, and even Nellie warmed to her as the evening progressed. Seeing us to the door, she had whispered, 'She is good for you, Jack. Take good care of her.' It was unusual for Nellie to be so generous about another woman; all too often she saw them as potential rivals. I was mildly touched.

'Are there really no dark secrets you want to confess?' Gina asked lightly, at one stage during our tête-à-tête between the sheets.

'Cross my heart,' I lied, because a big lie is no different from a little one, and how could I tell her my secrets were numberless, beyond reckoning? 'I'm in a lily-white vestal state.'

'How nice for you. I wish I could say the same.'

'Honey,' I played lightly with her breast, heard her breathing instantly quicken, 'if you ever feel like baring your soul . . . don't. As far as I'm concerned, your life started about eight weeks ago at an hotel in Digne. What came before is ancient history and nothing to do with me.'

She chuckled. 'I might be a murderess, or a drug addict.'

'Yeah, sure. You're a murdering drug addict and I'm Joe Stalin.'

She went quiet then and rolled over, away from me. I could just distinguish the line of her shoulder against the window's pale rectangle.

'Gina?'

'Mmm?'

'Anything on your mind?'

'No, nothing. You said no baring my soul . . . so, no baring my soul.' Her hand came scuttling across my stomach. 'I love you very much, you know. I can't tell you how much. Nothing must ever spoil it.' She gripped my hand fiercely; there was a lot of strength in those slim fingers.

'Gina,' I said.

'Yes?'

'Marry me.'

Was that me? Was that the Jack Henley I thought I knew so well actually proposing marriage? Incredible. And I wasn't even drunk – not legless drunk at any rate. Hang it all, I must really want to marry the girl!

If my own recklessness left me stunned, it was Gina who delivered the knock-out blow. With her unhesitating, unconditional yes!

Chapter Ten

The Monaco skyline had sprouted a few more gigantic cranes in my absence, rearing over the city like skeletal dinosaurs. I supposed progress would have its way, but it always depressed me to see it so glaringly displayed, as if the ugliness and the noise and the dust were a virtue for which we should all give humble thanks. To the Great God Property Developer.

Disembarking from the taxi on Quai des Etats-Unis that hot Saturday afternoon, I almost collided with Dru, your friendly, neighbourhood bedmate. Pleasing to behold as she was, I could have wished for a more propitious moment. That well-loved, well-kissed, scarlet mouth parted in a smile of real pleasure which I couldn't avoid returning.

By then Gina was coming round from the other side of the cab and I hastily lowered the temperature by shaking Dru's hand, a style of greeting that would be as foreign to her as ballet-dancing to an elephant.

'You haven't met Gina, have you, Dru?' I said, all sweet and innocent.

The two girls exchanged conventional platitudes. I felt like a boxing referee at the start of a world championship bout.

I smacked my hands together with an exaggerated briskness that kidded no one, certainly not Dru. 'Must be off now, Dru. We're in rather a hurry.' The cab driver dumped suitcases at my feet and I shovelled banknotes at him.

'Get me to the church on time?' Dru hazarded. I could have throttled her. Gina reddened, which didn't help much.

'So long, Dru,' I said with simulated firmness.

'Any time, lover,' was her parting bombshell, thankfully dropped in a lowered tone. '*Any* time.'

'An old school chum, darling?' Gina enquired, when Dru was out of earshot.

I grabbed the suitcases, planted a quick kiss on her cheek. 'One of those dark secrets we were talking about.'

'You're not getting away with that – the kiss, I mean.' She hooked an arm around my neck for a lesson in how grown-ups do it. For Dru's benefit, I suspected, cynic that I am. Establishing proprietorial rights.

'Let's get aboard,' I growled when she released me. By then my red corpuscles were whizzing round like the Paris traffic at rush hour.

'We got aboard. Swapped kisses and cuddles with Jean-Pierre and Pascal, and next day the four of us sailed *Spindrift* to the Ile de Porquerolles.

As far as the others were concerned it was to be a languid cruise westward along the coast, calling in at such ports as took our fancy. Porquerolles was destined to be the first such fancy, though only I was privy to that knowledge. It lay on our planned course, I made sure of that, and was a natural stop-over: the largest of a group of three islands, lying one-and-a-half nautical miles south of the Giens peninsula, not far from Toulon. Roughly crescent-shaped, it measures seven kilometres from east to west, and just over two kilometres at its widest point, and is nowhere higher than one hundred and thirty metres or thereabouts. Trees of all descriptions, from oak to bamboo, cover half its surface and most of the rest is given over to densely-packed gorse and other scrub, impassable on foot except where official footpaths exist. The climate is all you would expect from a Mediterranean island.

So much for the travelogue. My priorities lay elsewhere. While posing as a camera-toting tourist it was my intention to reconnoitre behind enemy lines.

When, in the late afternoon of the second day at sea, I proposed a sojourn on the island, it was not well received: not by Gina, who grumbled about the lack of shopping facilities, nor by Jean-Pierre, who grumbled about the lack of women. Only Pascal was in favour. As skipper and owner I had a casting vote, so to Porquerolles we went.

Since *Spindrift* was known to the opposition, I had decided in advance to steer clear of the marina adjacent to the town, and to anchor instead in a nearby bay, the Plage d'Argent. We approached the island from the east and while sailing parallel to its coastline fell foul of the wake of one of the fleet of small ferries that plies between island and mainland. Pascal laughed with delight at our porpoise motion while Jean-Pierre, for whom sail was all and steam was naught, glared poisoned darts after the receding vessel.

'To Jean-Pierre, motor-powered vessels are a blight on the oceans of the world,' I said aside to Gina.

She smiled faintly, but said nothing. She had retreated into her private shell. I raised my eyes to heaven.

'Cheer up,' I said, pulling her to me.

'Oh, I'm all right.' She touched my cheek, the green eyes under their slumbrous lids meeting mine, and what she felt for me was writ large there. 'I love you. Whatever happens, I'll always love you.'

'Whatever happens?' I echoed. 'Whatever should happen? Nothing is going to happen – only good things for you from now on, my girl. Believe me.'

She sighed and leaned back against me, looking towards the buildings of Porquerolles *ville* with their pale pink angled roofs, behind the irregular cordon of palm trees on the foreshore; the grey turret of the fort, the Tour St Agathe, was just visible above the huddle of greenery on the hill behind. It was a vista more in tune with the tropics than the south of France and the impressive heat still churned out by the sinking sun enhanced the illusion.

'I hope you're right,' she said. 'I do hope you're right.'

I couldn't understand her disquiet. From various dropped inferences, it was apparent that her previous marriage had been going wrong for years before the actual split. Yet I was reasonably sure she had loved her husband up until and even beyond the divorce. If the past had been unhappy for her, then it would have to be wiped out by creating new memories to efface the old, overlaying bad with good, sorrow with joy. Whether I was capable of such delicate reconstruction was a moot point.

At the Plage d'Argent, where an assortment of small craft bobbed and tugged at their mooring ropes, we found a suitable anchorage next to a down-at-heel sloop with a high, square wheelhouse, and a crew consisting mainly of noisy kids.

I had to get to a phone. Before I started trampling all over Tillou territory I needed a progress report from Dauphin. To the best of my recollection the only public call-box was in the centre of town.

Gina came too. It was only a short walk to the hub of the town, an open square named Place de l'Armes. Here, olive trees with sun-bleached bark grew in the hard, packed earth, their slender leaves wilting. The heat and dust of the dying day cloaked the place in a dense nebula, deadening the chatter of the promenaders, even the children's squeals had a curious muffled quality.

Just as we entered the square, the street lights sprang on, the lengthening shadows shrinking back before their fuzzy haloes. The public telephone was in use so we wandered over to where a game of *petanque* was in progress, the players, mostly bereted veterans of World War II, lobbing the heavy, steel balls like mortar shells.

In due course I returned to the call-box and got through to Dauphin at once. Without preamble, he confirmed that Tillou's spies had lost my trail, though they were aware *Spindrift* had put to sea. A watch was being mounted at all the main ports along the coast, an operation which must have stretched even Tillou's octopoidal resources to the limit. And he was no fool: he must realise how slim were his chances of spotting me. What a hoot that I was parked in his backyard. I was gambling on it being the last place he would look.

Dauphin briefed me on the strength of the garrison at the villa: five armed men, two of whom were always on duty, plus a guard dog 'big enough to ride on.' Tillou's daughter and her husband and a small number of non-combatant house guests were also in residence. Dauphin tried to pump me as to my whereabouts and my next move. I deliberately misled him, implying I wouldn't be going to Porquerolles for a while. With that I hung up.

As I left the kiosk Gina joined me.

'Everything in order?' she asked, coupling my arm to hers.

'Hunky-dory.' I concocted a story about a precarious shareholding that required nursing, and we set off back along the road to the Plage d'Argent.

'After being cooped up in *Spindrift* with J-P and Pascal, it's kind of nice to have you to myself,' I said.

Her head snapped round. She scrutinised me for a long moment, then said, 'I wish I knew you better, Jack.' The wistful note was not lost on me. 'I can't always tell whether you're being sincere or flippant.'

'Flippant!' My astonishment was real.

We had reached the point where the tarmac surface fades away and the dirt track, concrete-hard and lying under a thick coating of dust, takes over. Most of the pedestrian and cycle traffic was going in the opposite direction, into town: families loaded up with cool-boxes, beach bags, and buckets and spades. On our left, a forest of bamboo chattered in the breeze; on our right, villas skulked behind high, creeper-garnished walls.

'Listen to me,' I said, stopping and placing my hands on Gina's shoulders. 'You must stop doubting me. I admit that, when we first met, you were no more than a beautiful face with a beautiful body – a desirable object to be laid, then discarded. Despicable, I know. But I can say it without embarrassment because I fell in love with you and everything changed. Especially me. *I* changed. It was like . . . how shall I describe it? . . . like coming out of a room full of smoke into the fresh air. Do you understand that? Now you're all that matters.' She had continued her scrutiny as I spoke and I felt as if I were under a microscope. 'I'm making no promises, love, and I'm giving no guarantees, except one. As soon as this jaunt is over we'll put a legal stamp on it.'

'And live happily ever after,' she agreed.

We kissed, and it was a kiss that inspired other desires.

'Better go,' I said, breaking away with an effort that tested my will-power.

She was similarly carried away, but made no demur. We went on and came to the bay where *Spindrift* rode at anchor, the silver anodising on her mast glowing red in the sunset's dying embers.

The noise was a shattering, rippling blast; it penetrated my mind with the shock of an explosive-tipped harpoon, catapulting me into wakefulness, instant and total.

I was on my feet, heart pounding like a dinner gong, staring wildly into a solid wall of darkness, sweat streaming into my eyes and down my cheeks. Still it went on, a discordant salvo, a crashing bombardment, as if the earth, the sky, the universe were ripping apart in a great cataclysmic finale.

I was vaguely aware of Pascal shouting in his cabin. Then the light came on behind me and Gina called my name.

There came a pattering on the deck above my head. Rain. The wind had got up too and *Spindrift* was rolling, a docile enough motion, not enough to drag the anchor.

'Jack!' Gina called again, urgently. 'It's only thunder. It's only a storm.'

The rain pattered harder, more insistently, sounding like a truck tipping a load of gravel. I turned towards Gina and she caught her breath, her eyes widening in fear.

'Don't . . . don't look at me like that, darling,' she said, her voice uneven. 'What is it?'

It was only then that I realised I was holding a gun – the .38 Police Special, always under the edge of the mattress at night. The safety was off and the hammer cocked. I shivered, but not with cold. How close had I come to pulling the trigger?

Recovering rapidly now, I rendered the weapon safe and sat on the edge of the bed, my back to Gina. My heartbeat was slowing and the sweat was already cooling on my skin. Pascal had fallen quiet as the noise receded.

'I didn't mean to frighten you,' I said. 'I must have been dreaming.'

Her arms went around me and she leaned against my back. 'It's all right, darling. It was just that you looked so . . . murderous. As if you were going to kill somebody. It was a bit terrifying.'

I twisted around, held her tight. 'You need never be frightened of me, love. You're the last person I would harm. I love you.'

'I love you.' We lay down and she snuggled up to me as another drumroll barrelled across the sky. It was but a pale imitation of its predecessor. I reached out and switched off the light.

Gina went to sleep almost at once. I lay awake, staring into nothingness and listening to the rain. Occasionally a flash of lightning illuminated the cabin, throwing the fixtures into vivid relief.

I was remembering. Remembering my dream. It had been shattered by the thunderclap, but it was with me still, in wide-screen, three-dimensional Technicolour, the images sharp and clear. I had dreamed about us – about me and Gina.

I was as I am, down to the last detail. But Gina . . . Gina was dead.

Worse than that . . . far, far worse: I dreamed *I* had killed her.

By morning the storm had passed on, leaving no trace other than a choppy sea that slap-slapped against *Spindrift*'s hull. Not surprisingly I overslept and it was long after nine when I separated the body beautiful from the mattress. All that remained of Gina's presence was an impression on the pillow and on the sheet.

Sheepishly, I pressed my hand on the place where she had lain. I could smell her perfume and I breathed it in as hungrily as any cocaine-snorter. God, I *had* got it bad.

I greeted Jean-Pierre in the galley, came upon Pascal fishing from the cockpit with the new rod Gina and I had bought for him in Geneva.

'*Bien dormi*, Jack?' he asked.

'Not so good. The storm woke me up. You too, I believe.'

'*Oui*.'

I peered over the side. Nothing swam in the keep net. 'How's the rod?'

Fantastique, it seemed. The fish just weren't biting. Too obtuse to recognize a tasty morsel dangling under their idiotic gaping mouths.

'Seen Gina?' I asked, squatting beside him. She obviously wasn't on board.

'I nearly landed a little mackerel just now,' Pascal said, still lost in his angler's world, single-minded like most children.

I cleared my throat ostentatiously.

'Sorry, Jack,' he said as my enquiry filtered into his busy brain. His grin was, as ever, ingenuous. 'I was thinking about . . . '

'The one that got away.' I didn't handle the translation very well, but he got the drift. 'I was asking if you'd seen Gina this morning.'

'*Mais oui*. She went ashore – look, there's the dinghy.' The inflatable was on the beach and a small girl and a toddler of unclassifiable sex were playing by it, building sand-castles. A woman in a faded pink dressing-gown, their mother presumably, was the only other person in sight. I recognised them as components of the large family on the sloop moored next to us.

I was still pondering Gina's departure when she came into view through the trees. She was wearing a striped shift and carrying a bag from *Spindrift*'s inventory. The snouts of several *baguettes* protruded from it. Relief washed over me like a line of breakers. Coming after my disturbing dream, her disappearance had troubled me.

'I went to fetch some bread,' she called unnecessarily across the water. The two tots on the beach broke off from their construction work to stare at her.

I took up a position on the cockpit surround ready to help her aboard. She rowed the inflatable back with flowing, powerful strokes that fairly shot her across the fifty or so metres of water. I was impressed.

'Why didn't you wake me?' I said as she came nimbly over the side, accepting my proffered hand. 'I'd have come with you.'

She deposited a kiss on my nose. It tickled. 'You had a bad night and you were sleeping so soundly I didn't like disturbing you. Aren't I considerate?'

'You're magnificent,' I countered, and earned a

long, loving look that brought me out in goose pimples.

Breakfast of bread, butter, jam, and lashings of freshly-percolated coffee was a high-spirited affair during which we planned our day. Jean-Pierre wanted to work on the bow pulpit which had been buckled in the Cap Ferrat storm. Pascal intended to hire a bike and simply 'explore'. Gina and I would do the tourist rounds: a stroll around the town, then, after a restaurant lunch, wander over to the western side of the island where I would assemble a composite picture of Tillou's villa and its environs.

We took Pascal with us into town. I hired a bike for him and we saw him off on his travels, with a picnic lunch of bread, goat's-milk cheese, tomatoes and fruit stuffed in the panniers.

'A nice boy,' Gina remarked as his bare brown back was absorbed into the general swarm of humanity. 'Jean-Pierre must be proud of him.'

'And how.' I didn't mean to sound grudging, but some nuance must have given me away for Gina glanced sharply at me, clearly surprised.

'You're envious of Jean-Pierre? Because of Pascal?'

I didn't answer and she took that as confirmation.

'Maybe we'll be able to do something about that,' she said with endearing coyness. 'If you're really sure you want to.'

I felt choked. There was a burning sensation behind my eyes and right then I would have given all I owned to be able to turn the clock back fifteen years. To wash the bloodstains from my hands and start afresh.

Castles in Spain. The past would forever remain past. Immutable and unforgiving. I must do what I could to atone for it by creating a worthwhile and selfless future. Was it possible? Or would the patina of death cling to me as long as I lived?

I tried to suppress this morbid train of thought and dragged Gina off to the Hotel de la Poste where, under riotous flowering creepers, we drank black coffee, mine well-laced with *eau-de-vie* in the hope of chasing away the blues.

I was keeping us both amused with a long-drawn-out tale about a monk who succumbed to the temptations of the flesh, when a woman sat down at the table beside ours. I noticed she had very dark, very straight hair and was probably aged about forty. Beyond that she made no impact.

Having wound up the story, I requested more coffee and went in search of a loo. When I re-emerged, the coffee had arrived, and so had the dark-haired piece who was now installed at our table and prattling away in French to a rather unresponsive Gina.

Gina saw me coming and flashed me that ravishing smile of hers that never failed to rock me back on my heels.

'This lady lives on the island,' she explained, in response to the politely enquiring expression I had hoisted into place.

'*Enchanté, madame,*' I said formally, resuming my seat.

'So . . . you are both English,' she said. She had one of those mouths that naturally curve upwards at the corners in a ready-made smile. Her looks were dramatic, with twin waterfalls of black hair descending from a ruler-straight central parting. She had good skin, if on the sallow side, and was only lightly made-up. Hard to tell sitting down, but I got the impression she was slight of stature. In ages not so far past I wouldn't have kicked her out of bed.

'We're on holiday,' I said. 'It's a beautiful place.'

Madame agreed. 'Have you visited the Plage de Notre Dame yet? Or the Fort de la Répentance? Or the vignoble?'

Laughing, I raised a restraining hand. 'Not this trip, madame; we only arrived last night. However, we've both been here before, separately, so we know most of the beauty spots.'

'*Ah, bon*. Then you will be able to enjoy your stay all the more. Personally, I have always found that at least two visits to a particular place of interest are necessary if one is to appreciate all its virtues. Do you not agree, madame . . . er . . . ?' She was inviting Gina to introduce herself, but Gina had gone into an introspective huddle and if she heard at all, she gave no sign of it.

'Mademoiselle Gregg,' I said, jumping into the breach. I glared at Gina. 'I'm afraid she is not herself today.'

'I understand. And you, monsieur . . . you are . . . ?'

'Henley,' I said, not without trepidation. Giving my real name to a complete stranger in the heart of Tillou country went against the grain. In front of Gina, though, I could hardly do otherwise.

'I am Madame Sabourin.'

'You were born here on the island?' I asked, to keep the conversation moving.

Madame Sabourin chuckled mellifluously. 'No, Mr Henley, I was born in Paris. I live there still. Like you, I am on holiday.'

We both raised our coffee cups and I succeeded in delivering a gentle kick to Gina under the table. An involuntary 'Oh' escaped her and she shied like a nervous horse.

'Wakey, wakey, darling,' I said with forced geniality. What on earth had got into the girl? 'Can't go to sleep here, you know.'

Madame Sabourin had not appeared to notice Gina's odd behaviour. 'How long will you be staying on the island?' she enquired of me.

'We're leaving tonight,' Gina blurted, before I could reply. I gaped at her. We hadn't actually talked about it, though I needed two, possibly three days, to carry out my reconnaissance. I had not, of course, gone into this with Gina.

'Where did you get that idea, love?' I said, stifling my rising irritation.

Gina was suitably nonplussed. 'Oh . . . er . . . I thought we were only staying just for the day. I was hoping to do some shopping in Toulon, darling, I *did* tell you.' She put on a reproachful pout which, if it amplified her loveliness, did nothing to preserve my sang-froid.

'I'd like to stay on a couple of days,' I said in mild protest. It wasn't her fault I reminded myself. How was she to know I was planning an assassination?

A group of mostly blond teenagers, unisexually attired in T-shirts, jeans, and sneakers, came wandering in off the street, jabbering away in some Scandinavian lingo. They were shown to a table on the far side of the terrace where they struggled to order in such incomprehensible French that the waitress switched to English to expedite the process.

Perhaps sensing that a change of subject was called for, Madame Sabourin said, 'I'm actually staying at my father's house. He's resident here.'

'How interesting.' I drained my coffee. 'We really must be off, Madame Savourin. It seems we have less time than I thought.'

'Before you go,' and she started rummaging in her handbag, 'we're having a barbecue tomorrow evening at the house. As well as French, there will be some German people, some Italians, a Spanish family . . . but no English. Would you like to come? Represent your country?' She slapped a notepad with a tooled leather cover on the table. 'Please say yes.' She smiled winsomely from me to Gina and back to me again.

Gina made an apologetic face. 'You're very kind, but we couldn't possibly.'

'Yes, we could,' I cut in, finally losing patience. 'I think it's exceptionally generous of Madame Sabourin to invite us.'

Madame Sabourin was scribbling away on her notepad. 'Here's the address. It's at the western end of the island, by the Souterrain des Pirates.' She ripped the page out and passed it to me. 'Do you know it?'

I nodded abstractedly. I was deciphering her bold script, a jumble of loops and whorls. Villa du Langoustier, Plage du Muso, she had written.

It was an address instantly and shockingly familiar and it revealed Madame Sabourin, sitting there so cool and serene with her ever-smiling mouth, in her true colours.

As Tillou's daughter.

Chapter Eleven

A bare-breasted girl was rowing a wooden tender across the bay towards a white, two-masted catamaran. At every stroke of the oars her breasts quivered and jerked – a voyeur's delight. I felt a reaction inside my swimming trunks and looked down at Gina, dozing on her tummy in the sand beside me. The narrow triangle of her bikini pants plunged lasciviously into the furrow of her behind, leaving the cheeks exposed. From the waist down she might as well have been naked. The uprising became more insistent. If it weren't for the several hundred other sunworshippers occupying the same stretch of beach . . .

It was nearly six, but still scorchingly hot. After lunch at a small restaurant we had cycled across to the lighthouse on the south side of the island, returning to town by a tortuous route that enabled me to get the lie of the land. Gina had been penitent over the business with Madame Sabourin.

'I didn't mean to be rude,' she had said as we walked our bikes along the cliff top. 'You may find this hard to believe but I was actually jealous of that woman.'

I did find it hard to believe. 'Jealous? How so?'

'Oh, I know that you didn't lead her on, but women just seem to be attracted to you and you can't help sort of playing up to them, if you know what I mean. Like a peacock displaying its tail fan.'

'If I do, I'm not conscious of it.' An almost-truth.

'I'm sure you aren't. It's probably just force of habit and I don't believe for a minute you're genuinely attracted to her; I'm not used to it, that's all.' She had taken my hand in both of hers, pressed it to her lips. 'I couldn't bear to share you, not even just a little bit. I've become all possessive, you see. When we're married I'll never dare let you out of my sight.'

'We'll even go to the john together.'

She tut-tutted in affected reproof. 'You have a tendency to bring everything down to basics, I've noticed.'

'That's what life's all about, my love – basics. Being born, eating, drinking, sleeping, screwing, dying. Rich and poor; kings, queens, and peasants like you and me: their – our – lives are all interwoven with the same basic patterns, the same basic needs. The rest is all superficial, icing on the cake. In the end we're all equal – unless you swallow all that religious hype about the kingdom of heaven.'

Huh. Henley the great philosopher. What was I trying to do? Salve my conscience? Whitewash a career in killing? If so, to whom? Surely not to a God I didn't believe existed. It was too late for that. Thou shalt not kill; so ran the sixth commandment, and you couldn't get much more unequivocal than that. Having violated God's so-called law many times, I could scarcely expect absolution even if I spent the rest of my allotted span in a monastery.

Which I wasn't about to do.

I watched a mainland-bound, tourist-packed ferry scooting past the nearby promontory, her bows leaping the waves, a line of pure white foam flashing the length of her hull. My mind shifted to Madame Sabourin and her invitation, wrestling with the dilemma of whether to go, or not to go.

Not to go had much in its favour. Unfortunately, it would leave unfinished the task I had come here to perform. I smeared Ambré Solaire on my legs, gazing thoughtfully out to sea. Do like you used to do when setting up a hit, I commanded myself. Plan for disaster; assume the worst. Assume the meeting with Madame Sabourin was a set-up. Ditto the invitation. Which meant that Tillou was aware I was on the island and must have been aware of it before we 'bumped into' his daughter. What he couldn't be sure of was the purpose of my visit. It might well be motiveless, merely part of a holiday itinerary.

Unless he didn't believe in coincidences either.

Anyway, instant flight as an option, was out. Tillou would never sit by while I cruised off into the golden sunset.

Supposing . . . just supposing I went to the barbecue, sticking my neck in the noose Tillou had prepared for me. I still held two aces: Dauphin, my cuckoo in the nest was one, and I made a mental note to phone him shortly. My other ace was that Tillou didn't know I had seen through his ploy with Madame Sabourin. That I would be on the alert.

Taking the supposing a stage further: how likely was it that Tillou would be receptive to a trade-off? The identity of his real enemy, Dauphin, in return for a cease-fire. Such a betrayal would be an out-and-out contravention of professional ethics – even hit men have a code of conduct – and if it ever got out I would be finished for good in the assassination game. But, being retired, I could afford to abandon my principles. To secure my future with Gina I would have committed far deadlier sins.

Alternatively, should Tillou prove intractable, I would revert to my original plan. It was a do-or-die situation.

What about the danger to Gina? To leave her behind would perhaps be more prudent. Yet she was almost as much a target as I. If Tillou were to succeed in snatching her I may as well stick a gun barrel in my mouth and save him the trouble. On balance, I preferred to keep her in sight.

What a God-almighty mess! However you looked at it, my only chance lay in a confrontation with Tillou, therefore his barbecue, with its protective screen of hopefully respectable guests, was an opportunity not to be missed.

A guy called Hobson had the same wide range of choices.

Dauphin's laconic '*Oui*' came half-way through the opening bleep.

'Smith,' I said. I could be laconic too.

'Ah . . . Mr Smith. You have not been entirely truthful with me.'

'You don't say?'

'You are on the island, are you not? On Porquerolles.'

'Okay, Smart Aleck. I don't have to tell you everything. Do you want the job done or not?'

A pause. 'Can it still be done? Tillou also knows you are there.'

'It can be done. Possibly as soon as tomorrow night. I've been invited to a barbecue at the villa, but I suppose you know that too.'

'Yes, I know, Mr Smith.' Another pause. 'Or would

you prefer to be called Mr Henley from now on?'

So my real name had percolated through already, courtesy of Madame Sabourin. After this business was over and done with, I might have to do something about Mr Dauphin.

'Will you be there, at the barbecue?' I said, ignoring the question.

'I? No, alas.'

'Then who will be who matters?'

'The bodyguard arrangements will be unaffected. The guests will be mostly professional people: lawyers, bankers, industrialists, one or two from the entertainment profession. Hardly anyone from inside the organization.'

I fed my last one-franc piece into the slot. 'Anything else I need to know? That was my last coin.'

'Nothing of importance,' he said, then, 'Oh, yes. There is one minor matter. Probably it can easily be explained. It was only brought to my attention last night, after you called.' The warning disc was blinking, cut-off was imminent.

'Yes . . . quickly!'

'It seems that Madame Tillou . . .' Dauphin's voice became an unbroken, electronic bleat, predictably cut off in mid-sentence.

Mildly exasperated, I hooked up the receiver. I had no more money on my person and didn't fancy trudging back to *Spindrift*, then back into town again. Whatever Tillou's wife had to do with anything, she was unlikely to influence my plans. A 'minor matter', Dauphin had said. Okay, so let it keep until tomorrow.

The day of the barbecue was a Sunday. It dawned cloudy with a light drizzle, but this cleared up after breakfast. Gina and I took advantage of the drop in temperature for a knockabout on the tennis courts at the Terrain de Sports.

Gina looked pretty spectacular in her whites, the short pleated skirt setting off her long, tanned legs. She played an embarrassingly good game, too. My squash technique, calling for nimble-footedness more than speed, did not adapt well to the larger court, and she won two straight sets before I cried quits.

'I'll get my revenge on the squash court,' I growled as we sank cold beers at the sports-centre bar.

Her eyes twinkled. 'We'll see.'

So far as any of my days since meeting Gina could be so described, it was a carefree one. We were together every minute and in the afternoon went for a ramble around the island. I had shelved my reconnaissance of the Tillou property. If there was to be a reckoning at the barbecue any photos I took wouldn't be ready soon enough to be of use.

In the course of our wanderings we happened on a lonely spot on the rugged south shore. It overlooked a tranquil lagoon where broken-toothed slabs of rock, black and smooth as gun-metal, were washed by crystal seas, and made a perfect love-nest. At once Gina was naked in my embrace and my hands roaming in soft, moist valleys and over gentle undulations, experimenting with new and intoxicating delights. Desire was instantaneous and all-consuming.

When I entered her she became as if possessed, thrusting against me with such violence that we slid backwards on the sparse grass in a series of jerks. She punctuated each thrust with a whimpering cry and her breasts danced under my chest, the nipples touching my bare flesh, exciting me beyond reason.

When we came, we came simultaneously, a

foaming, head-on collision, like two opposing currents meeting up and flinging froth and spray into the air.

Afterwards we lay there, sapped, and I marvelled that, notwithstanding all the years of debauchery, I could still be overwhelmed by the love act. That it could lift me to such soaring heights as I had never attained, never believed existed.

'I can't believe this is happening.' Gina unknowingly expressed my own feelings. 'I . . . I can't believe it can be this good. It's too much.' She jacked herself up on one elbow. 'It makes me afraid of losing it . . . of losing you.'

'Shush,' I said and kissed her. 'Nobody's going to lose anything. You're always so full of doom and disaster. Enjoy what we have, while we have it. Don't start checking off the days like a condemned prisoner in a cell. Just live . . . just enjoy . . . just love me and let me love you.'

She hugged me tightly then, nuzzling against my chest.

Around us the shadows closed in. Below, the sea washed over the rocks, a muted, soporific whisper. And above, seabirds wheeled, uttering little barking cries not unlike the yap of a small dog. Nature, pure and untainted.

It would have been no hardship to linger on in that spot and the temptation was great. But duty called and I remained first and last a professional. My determination to beard the lion in his den was undiminished.

Our return trek to *Spindrift* was conducted mostly in contented silence, with the occasional halt to kiss or merely embrace. To enjoy the close contact, the moulding together. To listen to the sound of our breathing, feel the pulse beat within our bodies. In such simple yet complex ways does love weave its tendrils, binding two people together eventually as one. Which is how it was with us.

It was Pascal who rowed out from *Spindrift* to collect us from the now-deserted beach. Jean-Pierre was out 'shopping'. Not, I suspected, for groceries.

Privacy is hard to come by on a thirty-four foot boat and I needed some on two counts. When Jean-Pierre rolled up not long after, I button-holed him in the cockpit while Gina was below decks and with the aid of our map of the island made certain contingency plans for a tactical withdrawal. He took it all in his stride, his questions concerned only with the mechanics of the operation.

'So, if you have not returned by 06.00 hours tomorrow I am to sail around the Petit Langoustier,' he tapped the islet off the western tip of Porqurolles, 'and moor here, at Port-Fay.'

Port-Fay was a horseshoe bay forming a natural harbour near to but out of sight of Tillou's villa at the Plage du Muso. It was as close as I dared bring *Spindrift* to the villa.

'If I don't show up until after you've moved, it's likely we'll have to leave very quickly.'

'*D'accord.*' Jean-Pierre was still engrossed in the map.

'Very, *very* quickly,' I said slowly and with emphasis. 'I want you to book Pascal into an hotel for the night.'

His eyes came off the map, sighted on me. 'If you advise it.'

'I do, Jean-Pierre. Strongly.'

My line of retreat secured, I nipped down into the master cabin while Gina was in the shower and satisfied my other need – firepower. The cream checked sports jacket I had chosen to wear with my dark blue slacks was fairly loose fitting and more than adequately absorbed the bulge of the .38 in the small-of-the-back clip-on holster. I also took a fistful of spare shells, distributing them about my various pockets. It was while I was slipping on my shoes that I remembered I hadn't yet phoned Dauphin. I swore succintly and was on my way out of the cabin when a much better idea struck me. I would phone from Tillou's. Let him pay for the call! I almost laughed out loud at the audacity of it.

Presently Gina came up on deck and paraded for my inspection. In a simple cream dress with a plunge V-neck and a swirling knee-length skirt, she was stunningly lovely. She was wearing flat-heeled sandals, which was sensible of her; we had to go ashore in the inflatable and then faced a twenty-minute walk to the villa.

'I'll change into my heels when we make our grand entrance,' she said, fluffing out her not-quite-dry hair.

'If you're ready then, we'll get off,' I said. I was equipped with flashlight, for dusk was well-advanced and it would be dark before we got there. Outside the town, none of the island's thoroughfares was lit.

Ferried by Pascal, we made it ashore without getting out feet wet. It turned out to be a pleasant stroll along the winding traffic-less road to the villa, the crickets creaking away in the bushes, the occasional bat flicking past. It wasn't quite dark but we couldn't have managed without the flashlight. And we still had to come back.

I hoped.

Just before ten we passed under the greenery-laden stone archway that was the only landward means of access to Fortress Tillou. The only access, that is, short of climbing the high, steel-netting fence that lurked behind a double line of cypresses, and was probably infested with alarms – not to mention electrified: I had spotted the spaced porcelain insulators along the top strand of wire. Nasty.

Most of the other guests had arrived ahead of us – by sea to judge from the several big outboard launches tied up at the well-lit private jetty. They were milling about on the terrace that was easily as big as a tennis court and lit up brighter than Soho on a Saturday night. At the end of the terrace was a trapezium-shaped swimming pool in which a group of people were splashing about and making a lot of noise.

Looming over the festivities was the villa. A cube with an acutely-angled roof, the high apex fusing with the darkness above the illuminated area. An extravaganza of climbing roses in full bloom covered most of the side wall facing us and there was an integral first-floor balcony running along the front of the building. Otherwise it had about as much character as a box of chocolates. I had frankly expected something more grandiose, more individualistic. Maybe crime wasn't paying so well these days.

Going forward into the light we encountered the whiff of barbecued steaks. The barbecue, coming into view now around a clump of laurel bushes, was an enormous stone-built affair with a tiled roof around a squat, central chimney. Three chefs in traditional tall headgear toiled over the grill, and a fourth chef was operating a giant bellows; at every downward stroke sparks shot from the glowing charcoal and burst out of the chimney like a roman candle going off. Music played in the background, a vague murmur, almost swamped by the non-stop swell of conversation generated by fifty-plus sets of vocal chords.

We reached the edge of the terrace before we were espied. A man, middle-aged but dressed younger in cords and T-shirt, separated from the throng and strode purposefully over.

'You must be the English persons,' he said in Gallic-accented English. 'I am Yves Sabourin – Jeanne, my wife, invites you.'

We went through the usual preliminaries. His English was so halting I switched to French. 'We don't know anyone, I'm afraid,' I said. 'Apart from your wife, that is.'

'Don't worry, don't worry,' he said soothingly. 'I will introduce you. Come and have a drink.' In his native tongue he spoke so rapidly I had my work cut out following him. I wondered what a dish like Jeanne Sabourin saw in him: he was balding, wore pebble-lensed glasses, and was generally as personable as a witch-doctor's mask – although if all the propaganda about bald men is true, his principal attributes wouldn't be on display.

Our hands sprouted drinks, champagne in deep, slender glasses, and we met a lot of people in a short space of time. Only a small percentage of the faces stuck and an even smaller percentage of names. We renewed our acquaintance with Madame Sabourin, petite and theatrically effusive in a flame-coloured dress that was more space than material. Then there was Prost: a smooth, dangerous-looking character, about my height but a bit younger; his handshake would come in useful for cracking coconuts. We also met Sabourin's daughter: eighteen, nineteen maybe, and thin as a walking stick. Spiky, black, punk hair, yet feminine with it and very pretty. She inspected me with an uninhibited frankness that was an open invitation. Gina picked up the vibes and snuffed them out with her full weight on my toe. We moved on, me limping, Gina smiling sweetly.

'Which one of those was our host?' I said afterwards to Sabourin. I wasn't supposed to know Tillou, therefore a natural enquiry.

'The *patron* is indoors at present. He is not a well man. But do not worry, you will see him later.' He slapped me on the back, buddy-buddy fashion. 'He especially wants to meet *you*, Mr 'Enley.'

I bet he did.

'Is that right?' I pretended to be flattered. 'But he doesn't know me – us.'

'My wife has told him of you.' Sabourin put his head close to mine as though about to impart some juicy item of gossip. 'The *patron* has a great admiration for the English as a race.'

'Really?' I murmured.

'There's someone else you should meet,' he said, persevering in his role as surrogate host. He beckoned to a thick-necked bull of a guy, incongruously overdressed in a white tuxedo.

Gina had been waylaid by a man who was the double of the burly French actor, Philip Noiret; now she rejoined us just as the tuxedoed gorilla swaggered up.

'May I present Fernand Jourd'hui.' Sabourin eased the newcomer into our circle. Polite noises were exchanged. Jourd'hui slurped from a bulbous glass containing a colourless liquid and appraised Gina's modest but comely cleavage.

'And what do you do, Mr Jourd'hui?' I asked. 'Are you in business with Mr Sabourin?'

Jourd'hui wasn't listening. His nose was all but wedged down Gina's swooping neckline. Fidgeting with embarrassment, she had drawn the material together, pinching it between finger and thumb. All wrong, my love – that makes it more, not less, interesting.

Torn between amusement and outrage, I nevertheless left Gina to fend for herself. I was loath to be dragged into a brawl with a drunk – and Jourd'hui plainly was drunk: when a waiter arrived with a tray of brimming champagne glasses he lunged wildly at it, lost his balance, and had to grab Gina for support. The waiter, lips stiff with reproof, placed a glass in his hand.

Sabourin and I chatted on, fencing with words, each trying to trip up the other. At some point in this farcial dialogue, I turned to Gina for an opinion and found only an empty space. Likewise Jourd'hui. Ominous. I scanned the bobbing, jawing heads in my immediate vicinity. No almost-blondes. Well, if she had sneaked off for a surreptitious necking session with that over-developed baboon, I was the worst judge of character since Neville Chamberlain got suckered by Adolf. I was partly reassured almost immediately, when Joud'hui's thick-necked profile reeled into my field of view. He was alone and tossed me a loose grin around the rim of his glass.

'Gina seems to have gone missing,' I remarked to Sabourin who cut short a yawn to glance around.

'I don't suppose she's far away,' he said reasonably.

A safe enough assumption. If this had been just a harmless evening out I would have thought no more of it. As it was, I had to track her down and fast.

For Sabourin's benefit I shrugged expressively,

dismissing it, and knocked back what remained of my bubbly.

'Point me towards the lavatory, will you?' I said.

He looked dubious. Letting me roam around unchaperoned wasn't part of his edict. He offered to escort me – an offer I politely declined – and finally insisted on taking me as far as the patio door. 'Through the alcove, then first left, first right.'

I set off across the brown-tiled floor of a vast dining-room. Sabourin's directions led me into an internal corridor with several doors and a curved staircase. Here the noise of the festivities was subdued, no more than a remote buzz. The house itself was as quiet as a funeral parlour. I tried a couple of doors: kitchen, laundry-room. A third door was wide open, as if in invitation, projecting a strip of yellow light on to the corridor floor and wall.

I went cautiously in. It was a study-cum-library: a pleasant room, cool and with a restful atmosphere. The furniture was heavy and dark without being sombre. Book-laden shelves lined two walls; the other two contained an imposing traditional *cheminée* and more patio doors; this was the rear of the house: external floodlighting showed a small terrace and a lawn that looked in dire need of a watering.

Underfoot was polished block, laid in a chevron pattern of alternating light and dark wood. As I ventured further in, I picked out a Picasso in the space to the left of the *cheminée;* around it a handful of recognisably French impressionists. My eyes alighted on the big, solid desk parked at forty-five degrees to the patio doors, and travelled thence to the telephone that sat on a corner of it. It was one of those imitation antiques, all brass and marble. Ring Dauphin: I was across the room almost as quick as the thought.

I never made it. A female voice said '*Salut*' from the doorway, and whirled me round so fast I nearly fell over my own feet.

'I'm Hélène. Remember me?'

Sabourin's daughter. The girl with the walking-stick shape and the punk hair-do. And the sex appeal that was as subtle as a red light in the Reeperbahn.

'*Salut*,' I returned guardedly.

She closed the door and startled me by turning the key in the lock. Oh-oh. I had run into girls like this before. Silly, shallow rich men's daughters with minds that only functioned at crotch level. Not that they didn't have their uses.

She had a small, vamp mouth, etched in ruby-red lipstick and her smile had all the come-hither you could wish for plus a few extra volts. Added to which she did all the coming-hither herself; she planted her long, skinny legs on their long, skinny heels in front of me, and made a gesture with her pelvis that removed any remaining doubt as to her ambitions.

'You are the most handsome man I have ever met,' she said. She had good teeth. Straight and very white.

'You're not so bad yourself.'

She was wearing a black mini-dress of a velvety consistency. But not for long. That is to say she took it off, or rather she sort of shrugged her shoulders and it fell in a heap around her ankles, one of which was encircled by a thin gold chain. Underneath the discarded dress she wore a skimpy suspender belt and white stockings. Oh, and a necklace that could have passed for an Olympic medal. That was all.

I had two clear alternatives and, though it was contrary to my nature, I chose the negative one: I told her to hop it, only I used stronger language. And just in case she felt inclined to persevere I threw in a couple of insults that even the thickest-skinned of street-walkers might have taken amiss.

I thought she was going to slap me. She went white and the rouge on her cheeks stood out like clowns' make-up. Her legs were no longer apart and inviting – the show was over. Sigh.

'You . . . you . . .' She eventually hit on an appropriate French epithet to use on me and I digested it with a polite nod. Back on went the dress and she marched out, stiff-backed and stiff-legged, leaving me stiff-pricked and trying to recollect when I had last been so iron-willed. I couldn't.

Hélène had obligingly slammed the door shut on her way out and it was a credit to the builder that the house stood the shock. I was over to the phone in a jiffy.

Dauphin sounded edgy. Probably I did too.

'Make it quick,' I snapped. 'I'm phoning from the villa.'

A disbelieving gasp. 'You're crazy! Someone might be listening in.'

'No, they're not. They're all outside having a ball.' Except Tillou. If he was eavesdropping on us the damage was already done. Might as well press on.

'What's the latest? You said something last night about Madame Tillou. There isn't any Madame Tillou any more; he's a widower.'

Exasperation crackled along the line. 'Don't be so stupid. What I can't understand is what you hope to achieve by associating with her. Are you playing some kind of double game? Is *she*?'

I looked blankly into the mouthpiece. 'Talk sense, Dauphin. I haven't associated with Tillou's wife – she's dead! Sabourin told me.'

'This conversation is ridiculous!' Dauphin exploded. 'You know who I mean – Fabrice's widow. Georgina. According to my information, you've been keeping company with her for days. Is my information incorrect?'

I have to confess that, even spelled out in plain language, it didn't register. My brain rejected the implications.

'Explain yourself,' I said with a snarl. 'I've spent some time with a girl called Georgina, yes, but what has she got to do with Tillou – father or son?'

'*Merde alors, quel idiot!*' I visualised him smacking the flat of his hand on his forehead. An emotional race, the French. 'Georgina, the girl you have been seeing, is the widow of Fabrice Tillou, the man you killed in Munich. Is that clear enough for you? Don't tell me you didn't know?'

By the door was a grandfather clock with an octagonal face and intricate Roman numerals. The tick-tock of its mechanism was suddenly very loud, though I had scarcely noticed it before. My own breathing too, became audible, rasping inside my head. Sounds. I tried to shut them out. To concentrate. To *think*. I couldn't think. Inside me pain was blooming and it wasn't just ordinary pain. It was a knife shoved between my ribs and twisted round and round and round. It was a tearing apart. It was disintegration.

'Smith? Smith?' The quacking voice ruptured my cerebral paralysis. 'Are you there, Smith?'

'Yes,' I said and it was a dry whisper. 'Yes, I'm here.'

'Why have you been seeing her?' Dauphin demanded, like a petulant child. 'Don't you realise she's spying on you, reporting back to Tillou, keeping him informed? How do you think he found out you were on the island?'

Shut up. For God's sake, *shut up*!

I was sweating. This couldn't be happening. Pinch yourself and you'll wake up.

There was nothing more to be said. Nothing more to hear. It was finished. All of it. *I* was finished.

I put the phone down and Gina walked in.

Chapter Twelve

She halted there on the threshold, her lips parted in consternation. Lissome. Lovely.

My she-Judas.

'Jack?' she said uncertainly.

'You're his wife . . . his widow. Fabrice Tillou.' It didn't sould like me speaking, more like a zombie.

Her jaw sagged and she staggered slightly. 'Who . . . who told you?' At least she didn't try to bluster.

'It's true then,' I said needlessly. What a blind infatuated fool I'd been!

She closed the door softly. 'I love you. That's also true.'

I dismissed that with a flap of the hand. 'How can you talk of love? You're nothing but a stinking spy.'

'Listen to me.' She came to me, pale and so damnably, damnably lovely that an unwanted lump formed in my throat. 'It's not the way it seems, I swear.' Her eyes were moist, tears only a blink away.

'Don't explain, Gina.' I felt curiously detached. I still half-wondered if I were dreaming.

'But you must let me explain.' She too was calm, the tears still held at bay. It was I – I who couldn't meet her gaze. I who wanted to run and hide, just as I had all those years ago when Marion died. To lose myself out there in the dark. Forever.

'No, Gina,' I said, refusing to look at her, afraid of

weakening. Afraid that if I let her speak she would seduce me into forgiving and forgetting. And that would be almost as intolerable as her betrayal.

'But you must!' Agitation bursting through like water through a breached dam. She held my arms, willing me to acknowledge her. 'You don't know the full story. It wasn't what *I* wanted. It was him . . . Fabrice's father . . . he . . . he . . .' She broke, succumbing to a torrent of tears, her body against mine, soft and helpless. My arms stayed by my sides. Sympathy was out. Compassion was out. I was ice: hard, cold, pure.

'Darling.' An anguished groan. 'I love you. I *love* you.'

Then the door was thrown back and two men came in: Prost and Jourd'hui. Jourd'hui wasn't drunk any more, if in fact he ever had been.

Behind them came a man in a wheelchair, and he needed no introduction.

Tillou bore little resemblance to the image in the fuzzy, out-of-date photograph supplied by Dauphin. The present-day Tillou was a shrivelled leprechaun of a man, almost delicate, with fine, aristocratic features and the most brilliant blue eyes, unusual in that the whites showed all around the irises. He had a thatch of yellowish-grey hair, thick and dense and somehow dead-looking, like grass in need of watering. His nose was an eagle's beak, his mouth rosy-lipped and pursed. It was the sort of mouth that would be at home sucking a thumb.

At his age – rising seventy-two – and given his poor state of health, some physical attrition was to be expected. But I was taken aback by the ravaged, crumbling contours of his face, the skin drooping underneath his eyes and along his jawline like drapes; also by the hands that were like mechanical claws grafted on to the arms of the wheelchair; but most of all by the voice, a sinister, breathless hiss that seemed to come from some remote external source.

'It gives me great pleasure to meet you at last, Mr Henley,' the voice said. The pursed lips actually smiled. 'Your arrival here is long overdue.'

The right claw moved, operating a diminutive joystick set in the chair arm. The contraption glided forward, Prost and Jourd'hui gliding with it, covering the flanks as it were. A third member of the team, tall, slim, young, and clad in tight blue jeans, slid around the doorpost into the room.

Tillou braked to a standstill. He was studying me earnestly, the ruined physiognomy alight with malice and glee; it blazed like a hallowe'en mask. His disciples, in contrast, were impassive: Prost flexed his knees, unconsciously caricaturing an English bobby, while Jourd'hui flicked imaginary specks of dust off his lapel. Blue Jeans rested against the door, arms folded. No guns had been produced as yet.

'Bernard.' It was Gina who broke the silence. 'Bernard, let him go . . . please.' She went down on one knee beside the wheelchair. Tillou was outwardly unmoved. He had eyes only for me.

'Leave us, Georgina,' he said tonelessly.

'No – I'm staying.'

'Leave us.' The tone hardened. 'Please.'

'I'm staying!' she said hotly. 'If you want to get rid of me you'll have to carry me out.'

Tillou's lips set hard. Still he continued to stare at me as if fascinated. It was mutual.

'You don't have much to say, Mr Henley.' He paid no further attention to Gina and she got up slowly, flung a defiant stare at the heavy mob, and came to stand beside me. I was acutely conscious of her nearness, her perfume, the warmth of her . . . I banished a million racking memories. She was nothing to me now. Nothing.

'Aren't you curious to know what all this is about?' When Tillou spoke, only his lower mandible moved; in poor light it would be easy to mistake him for a ventriloquist's doll. 'If you were an innocent man, you would think our behaviour very strange, would you not?'

'The world's full of strange people.'

Tillou gave me a sly look. 'Are you armed, Mr Henley?'

That was my undoubted cue for a Billy the Kid fast draw. Except that friend Blue Jeans was even faster. A long-barrelled revolver materialised in his hand and I stared into its uncompromising muzzle – as black and forbidding as the entrance to Mont Blanc tunnel.

'You killed my son, Mr Henley,' Tillou said, a flat statement.

'Yes. Why do you think I'm here?' I bent towards him, bringing my fact to within a foot of his. In close-up he was like a character from a horror comic. 'Why do you think I came to the island in the first place if not to see you? Christ, man, I've been wise to you for months.'

This patently displeased him. The hallowe'en mask frowned, adding to the grooves and trenches. 'How can this be?'

'You used cut-price spies.'

He grunted, snapped mechanical fingers at Prost who came and frisked me thoroughly. He sneered when he found the .38. I sneered back, outwardly unabashed.

'Did you also know about Georgina?' Tillou said,

rotating the wheelchair on its axis as he spoke, and detouring round me to get to the desk.

I looked at Gina and couldn't help hurting. 'No, I didn't. She was a juicy mantrap, I'll admit, but she didn't influence my plans at all. As a plant, she was a failure. I've enjoyed screwing her though.'

Gina flinched, drawing away, her face flaccid with shock. Distress came flowing out of her in almost tangible waves. I felt no remorse: the bitch deserved it and more.

Tillou ignored the slight on his daughter-in-law. 'So if Georgina didn't tell you, how . . . ?' He was behind the desk now. He tapped a bony forefinger on his lips, regarded me thoughtfully.

'Sources.'

'Sources,' he repeated, hissing like escaping gas. 'What sources?'

'Have you asked yourself who wanted to kill your son? Or did you think it was personal between me and him?'

'Yes, to answer your first question. And no, to answer your second. I assume you are going to tell me who hired you.'

'In return for my life?' I raised a cynical eyebrow. 'I came here tonight to propose a deal.'

Tillou smiled and this prompted smiles all round; Prost, Jourd'hui, Blue Jeans, all smiling. I wished I was in on the joke. I had a feeling it was at my expense.

'You are not in a position to bargain.' Hook-like fingers drummed on the desk top. 'The information can be extracted.'

'My safe passage for the name you want.'

Prost jingled coins in his pocket – or maybe he had steel balls. He was growing restive, constantly shifting his stance. Couldn't wait to be turned loose on me.

'Let me deal with him, *patron*,' he said, almost wheedling. 'Five minutes and he'll sell out his own mother.' He sounded confident. He convinced me.

'You see, Mr Henley,' Tillou said with an apologetic spread of hands. 'Why should I bargain with you? Léon here could make a mummy talk.'

Prost grinned delightedly, an ear-to-ear split. 'Do you remember that Corsican, *patron*? The one we stuffed into the furnace feet first.'

Distaste twisted Tillou's features. Evidently a man of some sensitivity.

'He talked before the skin on his feet had even begun to scorch.' Prost was addressing me now. 'But we carried on anyway, just for the hell of it; we fed him in a centimetre at a time. It took nearly an hour to get as far as his bollocks.' Gina shuddered beside me; I felt slightly sick. 'Which was about when he croaked.'

'Must you recall the incident in such detail, Léon?' Tillou reproved mildly. 'We don't want to frighten Mr Henley.' He eyed me speculatively. 'I'll make you an offer: give me the name, now – right away, and I promise you a quick, clean death.'

My laugh was a seal-like bark. 'This isn't a fairy-story, Tillou. People don't make deals like that, except in the movies. Sure, you can put this ape to work on me and cause me a lot of pain, and if I die before I talk – what then? You'll never know who wanted your son dead, will you?'

'Please don't hurt him, Bernard,' Gina said, before Tillou could reply.

He looked at her with a show of irritation, the electric-blue optics filmed over, appearing sightless. 'I understand Georgina has formed an attachment to you, Mr Henley. You would not expect me to approve: it shows remarkable disloyalty on her part, not to mention lack of taste.' That was rich, coming from him. 'However,' he went on, the smile shining through again, 'I am rather fond of her and I am prepared to overlook her wayward behaviour. Regrettably, whatever pain it might cause her, I cannot make similar concessions for you.'

'Bernard, please . . . it's all in the past . . .' Gina pleaded hard for me. I didn't want her to – especially I didn't want to be in *her* debt. But it bought a few precious seconds, while I considered Tillou's Freudian slip: so he was fond of his daughter-in-law, was he? Fond enough to baulk at harming her? It was a possible soft spot and I had to exploit it because, short of suicidal heroics, there was nothing else to exploit.

Gina was still pleading for me when I swung her round, pulling her up tight against me, one arm twisted savagely up her back so that she cried out. My right hand I curled around the back of her neck, cupping her jaw; a sideways wrench would snap her neck like a dead twig. It was an unarmed combat technique I had learned during my stint in the army.

She squirmed, trying to break free. 'Jack . . . let me go. Don't do this.'

'Shut up, bitch,' I snarled, my mouth up against her ear. 'Unless you want a broken neck.'

'Let her go, Mr Henley,' Tillou said, unperturbed as ever. 'Whatever you do, you can't possibly get away.'

Blue Jeans's gun was still covering me. Prost and Jourd'hui were looking towards Tillou for guidance.

'Don't shoot while Georgina is in danger,' he ordered. The glare he directed at me was straight from Siberia.

'The first wrong move and she gets a broken neck.' I injected a mean note into my voice. Gina struggled some more, yelped when I put pressure on her arm.

'Keep still, Gina. I've no choice.'

Blue Jeans advanced, holding me unwaveringly in his gun-sights. In appearance he was closer to a college boy than a villain, but there was nothing juvenile about his handling of that long-barrelled revolver.

'Hold it there, sonny boy,' I warned, tightening my hold on Gina. She was no longer struggling; her body was relaxed, moulded against mine. Again, I was aware of the smell of her, a heady drug in my nostrils. I put it from me in silent fury, despising my own weakness.

Tillou flicked a finger at Blue Jeans who halted reluctantly.

'Now,' I said, maintaining the hard-boiled facade. 'My gun, or you lose a daughter-in-law – and don't think I wouldn't do it. I've had plenty of practise at this kind of thing, as I'm sure you know.'

For emphasis I gave Gina's arm an extra twist.

'No . . . aah!' Her body writhed.

Tillou, to give him his due, showed genuine concern.

'Very well, very well. You've made your point, Henley.' I didn't rate a 'mister' any more.

'Let us take him, *patron*,' Jourd'hui urged. He was doing a sort of lateral shuffle, working around behind me. I stepped back, dragging Gina with me, hugging her tighter than I ever did in bed.

'Don't be stupid – I'm not playing games!'

Tillou snapped out, '*Personne ne bouge!*' and Jourd'hui froze, chafing palpably.

'The gun – quick!' I gave a threatening twitch of the hand that held Gina's jaw. 'Give it to Gina.'

Everyone's attention, including mine, was on Tillou. All the advantages still lay with him. My roughness with Gina had been all bluff and he only had to call it.

'Jack . . . my arm,' Gina whimpered.

'Shut up,' I said, and my voice resembled gears grating.

Then Tillou said resignedly, 'Give him his gun.'

I experienced a passing flare of triumph; passing, because even as he uttered the words he conveyed an unspoken message to Prost. It was no more than a contraction of the eyebrows and I nearly missed it. It clearly nullified the spoken command.

I took the only course open to me: I moved first and fast. I flung Gina at Blue Jeans, the most immediate threat, and went for Prost with my head down. He was quicker on the draw than on his feet; a gun appeared from the depths of his jacket and if he'd been a shade more nimble he would have stepped aside, leaving me to plough through some very solid pieces of furniture. As it was I connected with him at about waist level and he deflated like a burst paper-bag, crashing to the floor.

In the background all was commotion. Jourd'hui or Blue Jeans shouting, 'Get away from him, Léon!'; Tillou's hoarse, 'Don't kill him! Don't kill him!' and through it all Gina giving a fair imitation of a police siren.

Prost made no contribution. His skull had come into contact with the floor and it sounded like a sledgehammer driving a stake into the ground. I was glad it wasn't my head. His condition wasn't improved when I fell across his stomach.

As I got up on my hands and knees, slightly winded, a shot ripped through the general din and I swear it parted my hair laterally. I heard a grunt of pain and glanced up: Jourd'hui was also on his knees, eyes turned up, pistol dangling from a limp wrist, a tomato splash on the washday white shirt-front. Then he toppled, in slow motion, like a felled tree.

'Blanc!' Tillou's voice came from the rear, a raucous screech. *'Lachez-la!'*

Let her go! Some hopes. Gina was coiled around Blanc-alias-Blue Jeans like a boa-constrictor.

Now to get me a gun. Prost's, the obvious choice, had last been sighted going into orbit. I didn't even attempt a search, dived instead into his pockets and right away struck gold, or more properly, blued steel in the shape of my faithful .38.

Another shot, bringing plaster down to patter like snowflakes on the coffee table. I executed a barrel roll which brought me up against the front of a settee. I assumed a crouch, my fingers curling lovingly around grip and trigger, my thumb crunching back the hammer. Highly satisfying sensations: it was a kind of homecoming.

My prime target was Blanc. Problem was, he and Gina were tangled together and bullets tend to be indiscriminate once they've left the muzzle. So I went for Tillou who was gabbling into the phone, summoning reinforcements.

The little swine must have been stronger than he looked because he tipped himself and that heavy motorised chariot over on its side with a crash that made the floor tremble. The phone went with him, dinging and donging merrily. My two rapid shots passed mortifyingly overhead by at least a foot.

I wavered. The base of the wheelchair was presented to me, a crisscross of struts and mechanisms that might or might not stop a bullet. I didn't put it to the test; a thunderous banging on the door caused a change in priorities.

'Que se passe-t-il?' a loud male voice demanded.

'Rien,' I shouted back.

Eliminating Tillou now took second place to a speedy exit. First I had to deal with Blanc who had forced Gina back to the wall and was poised to restructure her face with that big, ugly revolver. A belt with the .38 nipped in the bud such ungentlemanly conduct and nearly took his ear off. He subsided in a graceful slither, like flowing oil.

I grabbed Gina by the wrist. 'Come on. It's not healthy here – for either of us.'

The banging had ceased. In its place, a great deal of shouting and coming and going from the corridor. We went out via the patio doors on the small floodlit terrace.

'This way,' Gina said as I hesitated. I had forgotten – as a member of the family she would know the layout. We ran past a lily-covered pond and across the parched lawn but were still under the floodlights when a jubilant *'Le voila!'* shattered my hopes of a smooth, well co-ordinated retreat.

I snap-shotted towards the house. Glass shattered, but nobody shot back. Into the darkness we thankfully plunged and instantly I tripped over something, a hosepipe, I think it was, and measured my length among the flower beds. I didn't lose my hold on the gun, which was fortunate because at that moment they set the dogs on me – well, dog singular. But there was about as much similarity between this particular hound and your average canine as between Goliath and Tom Thumb.

It was a black-and-white spotted monstrosity, easily bigger than a Shetland pony. Across the turf it pounded, straight and true, the floodlights playing across its flanks, highlighting the quiver of skin over muscle and sinew, accentuating the effortless, elastic flow. Its head was square with a blunt nose and its lips were drawn back over a grid of teeth from which flecks of saliva streamed.

Gina screamed a command but the dog didn't even break its stride. I was up on one shaky knee, the .38 lined up, when that thing steamrollered into me and prostrated me in the flowers once again, pinning me beneath a hundred pounds of muscle and bone. The dog – if it *was* a dog, I was beginning to have doubts – and I thrashed about in an embrace, a parody of two lovers in full-blooded copulation. It snarled continuously, an unearthly crepitating slobber right by my ear. And God, was it strong! It made me feel puny. Panic swept over me in a debilitating wave, draining my strength. Saliva dripped from its jaws onto my cheek and its hot breath was a cloying aura about my face. I hugged its head to mine, neutralizing those awful gnashing jaws. My gun offered the only hope, but it was crushed against my ribs by the dog's weight. If I fired I was more likely to shoot myself.

For the second time that night Gina came to my rescue – by yanking on the hound's spindly apology for a tail, engendering a howl fit to raise the whole island. It pulled free from my grip to aim a vicious snap at her which she narrowly avoided. This released my trapped arm which I promptly pulled free, just as the square head came swinging ponderously back, lower jaw hanging, those awesome fangs glistening in the great, dark cavern of its mouth.

I fired upwards, once, twice, at the brute's chest. The range was, of course, point blank: both bullets pierced the chest wall and, being nickel-jacketed, carried on to emerge at the vertebrae in miniature eruptions of flesh and gore, some of which fell back to earth, some of which fell on me. Even with four holes in its body the beast didn't collapse there and then: it began to sway from side to side, setting up a macabre moaning, like a spirit in torment. I wriggled out from under and was back on my feet, dazed, staggering, but still battleworthy, when it crumpled up, air escaping from its gaping, still slavering jaws in a long, hollow sigh. RIP, thou good and faithful servant.

Gina tugged at my sleeve. A gun cracked, no louder than a popping exhaust, and something zinged past my nose. More to deter than to injure, I pumped my remaining shot at the group of warily advancing figures, bunched up together on the lawn. One of them went down, clutching his stomach. The group scattered then, firing arbitrarily, and the night became full of a deadly twittering. They couldn't see us but we were lucky to escape unhurt. As their guns emptied, the shooting dried up, and we used the lull to put some distance between us and the house. We came across a path that Gina felt sure led down to the beach and hot-footed along it as best we could in the Stygian conditions. Too late a torch beam came probing for us; by then we were a good two hundred yards from the floodlit area and shielded by a lot of thick shrubbery.

The sea came into view, black like sludge under the moonless sky. Now we were treading sand, every footfall a gritty scrunch. Gina kicked off her high heels.

'Be careful,' she cautioned. 'There are rocks just ahead.' It was lighter here by the sea and I could make out her features. She looked calm, as if battling with a monster hound, being shot at and pursued, were all in a day's work. She had guts all right.

Bent double and groping with outstretched hands, we made it over the rocks and struck out inland, the blackness sucking us in again, unseen bushes and thorns whipping us as we stumbled along. Eventually, scratched and bruised, we came back to the shore at a tiny, sheltered cove.

'Should we stay here or move on?' Gina asked me in a whisper.

'Better stay here,' I said. 'Crashing around in the bushes will just make it easier for them to find us. As well as inviting a broken ankle. We'll wait until first light.'

She didn't dissent and we flopped down between a pair of lumpy rocks, to sit, close yet not quite touching, staring out across the water. Still on the alert for sounds of pursuit, happily in vain. It was a reprieve, a stay of punishment. They weren't finished with me yet – nor I with them.

As the danger receded, Gina stirred restlessly once or twice, then suddenly blurted out, 'I'm sorry. I'm sorry . . . but I'm glad as well. We would never have met if I hadn't done it.'

The things I wanted to say were stuck like a fishbone in my gullet. In the end, I grudgingly mumbled, 'Thanks for the help back there.' Then, relenting further, 'I wouldn't have made it without you.'

An impatient rustle beside me. She wanted the air cleared between us, not platitudes.

'So tell me about it,' I said, after another longish hiatus.

She bent forward so that her hair hung down between her knees. Her shoulders fluttered: she was crying inside, a deep intravenous weeping, and I wished I could comfort her, reassure her. She needed it, even deserved it, but I had no compassion to draw on. I was still reeling from the concussive shock of betrayal.

When she finally lifted her head and spoke again, her voice carried no tremor.

'I'll only tell you if you really want to hear it,' she said with a sniff. 'If you've already made up your mind, if you've already judged me, I can see no point in going over the whole rotten mess. Much as I love you, Jack, I'm not going to let you put me in the dock.'

Between the lines she was telling me she had a lot of pride. I was half-ashamed. The wound wasn't healed, but she was making me think again, making me want to understand; even, if it were possible, to forgive.

'Tell me.' I put as much sympatico as I could into the words. Hoping that from the telling would come an understanding.

She wiped her cheek with the back of her hand. The tears hadn't all been inside. 'I met Fabrice, my husband . . . the man they say you killed . . . when I was eighteen. I told you that, didn't I?'

I grunted.

'I was silly, immature, and a virgin, and he swept me off my feet with his good looks and his . . . *élan*. I knew nothing of his criminal background, nothing about his parents. We got married against both our parents' wishes, though his didn't oppose it quite so strongly as mine who simply felt I was too young, and much too immature. I was too. But Fabrice was so glamorous and such fun – you can't imagine. We honeymooned in Thailand and his parents bought us a sumptuous villa near Marseilles. We lived high: entertained every other day, hob-nobbed wth the cream of Marseilles society, travelled just about everywhere, private yacht, private plane, expensive cars. Oh, we had a *fine* time. It was several years before I found out how they really made their money. I'd thought it all came from the nightclubs and casinos they owned – still do own; I didn't realise these were just a front for the drug smuggling, the prostitution, and the rest. When, eventually, the odd whisper began to filter through to my giddy brain I was shocked. But Fabrice was such a persuasive charmer he convinced me that what he was doing wasn't so bad. That he was just supplying a service, meeting a demand.' She tilted her face towards the sky and there were damp patches on her cheeks.

'So help me, I shrugged it aside. I was still madly in love with him and I was estranged from my own family by then; they refused to have Fabrice in their home. Maybe they knew about him but didn't want to tell me – who knows? The upshot of their hostility was that I was drawn closer to Fabrice's family. His parents – his mother was still alive then – came to accept me as their own daughter almost, and . . . and I actually grew very fond of them. In my preoccupation with *la dolce vita*, you know, I shoved the unsavoury stuff into the background. Nothing must touch my fairy-tale existence.'

She broke off, still gazing skywards where stars sparkled in clusters. It was a balmy night, the wind a light zephyr rustling the trees and bushes behind us. Crickets sawed away non-stop.

'What went wrong?' I hazarded. Call it intuition, but I was sure that weeds had sprouted in her rosy garden.

'Wrong? How did you know?'

'I guessed,' I said. 'Go on.'

'All right. You ask what went wrong: I got

pregnant, that's what went wrong.' Shades of bitterness.

'You didn't want a baby, huh?'

'What? Oh, you fool . . . you've no idea how much I wanted it. I . . . I was unbelievably happy. Fabrice was just as thrilled; he became even more doting.' Her voice cracked. She took a long, shuddering breath. 'Then, at five months, I miscarried. Nobody's fault except my own. Playing tennis, like an idiot. I'd taken it easy – or so I thought. Anyway, there it was; my dream shattered.'

'Did it have to be the end of the world? How old were you? Why didn't you try for another?'

'I was twenty-five and we didn't try for another because I'd become sterile – or so I was told. Some complication with my Fallopian tubes, the doctor explained it all to me, but . . .' A hand, dismissive, brushed against my knee. 'To me it was all high-flown Hippocratic cant. I suppose I could have learned to live with it, given time. It was Fabrice who really took it hard. No babies equalled no sons and heirs to the Tillou Empire. He went off me immediately and totally: I scarcely recognized him as the attentive, loving man I'd married. He was still polite, still considerate, but it was only superficial, for appearances' sake. We continued to live together in the same house. We even *slept* together when he came home, which wasn't always. Now and again, when he was in between mistresses, he condescended to . . . to make love to me.' She stopped talking abruptly and I guessed she was reliving those moments when, in the knowledge of her husband's infidelity with who-knows-what brothel flotsam, she gave her body to him, let him use her as a convenience.

I wasn't sorry I'd killed him.

She let out a sigh that came from deep within. 'Incredibly, pathetically, I still loved the swine. For nearly four years we lived together like that, pretending to ourselves and the outside world, and right up until his . . . his death I loved him.' Her head turned towards me. 'And do you know, Jack, I was never unfaithful to him. Not once – not . . . bloody . . . once.' She punctuated the words by banging her clenched fists on her updrawn knees. 'That's what I meant when I said to you in Geneva about wallowing in pity for myself and contempt for all things male. You remember, don't you?'

'Oh, yes.' I remembered too much – that was the trouble. I remembered all the loving words and all the loving deeds and asked myself how many of them, if not all, had been false. How many of the scenes had been pre-ordained. How much of the dialogue written and rehearsed in advance?

'How did the family treat you? After the miscarriage, I mean.

'They were fine. Wonderful, even. Fabrice's mother died the same year – a brain tumour – and for Fabrice that just piled misery on top of misery; they were very close. But Bernard and Fabrice's sister, Jeanne, couldn't have been more supportive. Of course, Fabrice didn't let on to them how he felt: like the cold, calculating pig he became – or maybe that had been his true nature all along – he pretended everything was as good as ever and that he didn't mind a bit that we couldn't have children.' She gave a snort. 'He was quite an actor, my husband. Quite an actor. The irony is, I wasn't sterile after all, not permanently. I had some tests done earlier this year and it seems I'm okay now. What do you think of that for a sick joke?'

'Life is one big sick joke. God's been getting even with the human race ever since he created it.'

I linked fingers behind my neck and leaned against the rock. I loved Gina, yet hated her deception. Neither emotion was controllable. I hated all the more because I loved so much. I had given my all: soul, spirit, every damned bit of me had gone into the pot. My commitment had been absolute, and now my torment was absolute. Even Marion's death had not hit me so badly.

'Jack . . . did you really kill Fabrice?' The question was inevitable, I supposed. This was confession time.

'Ouch,' I said, then gruffly, 'Yes, I killed him.'

'I hoped you didn't, that it was all a mistake.' She sounded unhappy, fighting a private battle no less bloody than mine. 'I hoped you really were a retired spy after all. Not that it makes any difference now. To how I feel. My marriage died long ago, even though my feelings lived on. It could even be . . .' she laughed shakily, without mirth, 'it could be said you were sent by divine intervention to rescue me from my miserable state.'

'Like Rapunzel in the tower.'

'Yes, something like that.' She gave a tiny chuckle.

'You know I've killed other men,' I said. My brutal frankness was intentional. 'A lot of men. For money.' Bring out all the dirty washing. Get it over with.

'Ten years ago I would have been horrified if someone had said that to me. Being married to Fabrice and hearing about things I thought only existed in fiction, I've become inured to . . . to crime and violence.'

Sad that, I couldn't help thinking.

'If I'd learned about the goings-on in the Tillou organization all at once,' she went on, 'I might well have left Fabrice. As it was, I only found out in dribs and drabs, which gave me time to absorb and adapt, so that eventually each new discovery ceased to shock me. I became blasé about it all.' She laid a hand on my leg, just above the knee. 'Did you know they actually *sell* young French girls to Arab sheikhs and such-like?'

'White slavery, you mean?'

She nodded. 'And I even accepted *that*. Can you imagine?' There was self-disgust in her voice. 'So you see, compared with the things I've condoned in the name of love, what you've done doesn't seem so much worse. I've tried to convince myself the people you . . . you know . . . well, that they deserved it. That they were criminals themselves. Like . . . Fabrice.'

'Believe it or not, from Day One I honestly only ever accepted contracts on known criminals. I needed some kind of standard, I guess. Not that I'm seeking absolution – no need to let me off the hook. I'm retired now, in any case. It's history. I can't put the clock back.'

Her hand moved restlessly on my thigh. 'I know you can't. It's like you yourself said: our life together began when we met. Anyway, I can't even plead ignorance. Though I kept hoping it wasn't true I knew all about you before I met you. Before . . . before I fell in love with you.'

'So that much is true?'

'That I love you?' She seemed startled by the implication. 'Do you doubt it?'

'I did. For a little while. Now . . .' I hesitated.

'Now?'

'I . . . I'm not sure. Was our first meeting accidental – at the Grand Hotel de Paris? No, no, of course it wasn't.' Blind I had been, gullible I was not.

'When Fabrice was killed, Bernard went off his

head with grief. Only son and all that. I looked after him, which also helped me: kept my own blues at bay. When he started to think rationally again, he set about tracking you down. It took the best part of four months; I was never told the details, but I understand the lead came via someone in Germany. Bernard planted one of his trusted generals in an apartment near you, a man called Schnurrpfeil. He was supposed to check you out, to make certain that you really were the man they were looking for. They were very thorough, you see: Bernard didn't want to make a mistake. I don't know how Schnurrpfeil set about it, but he came up with enough evidence to satisfy Bernard.'

'He posed as an ex-SS officer; gave a big sob story. It was a ruse to get me to confess my own sins. Like the game kids play: you show me yours, and I'll show you mine. The philosophy was sound enough. It almost worked; correction – it did work. It must have because Schnurrpfeil gave me the thumbs-down to Tillou.'

'He's a clever man. And he really is ex-SS; a war criminal.' She made a sound, implying distaste. 'He gives me the creeps.'

'After Schnurrpfeil reported back – what then?'

'Then Bernard thought of using me. As bait.'

'Bait,' I repeated expressionlessly. Apt.

'Mmm. I was to seduce you into the spider's web. To get you to come here, to Porquerolles. Isn't that a laugh? You came of your own volition! And I actually ended up trying to dissuade you. I couldn't be too insistent, otherwise you would have been suspicious; but I *did* try to get you to change your plans and go to Toulon instead.'

That was true enough. She had made a protest of sorts.

'Originally, when Bernard asked me to do the bait thing, I refused. But . . . well, he's very persuasive. He bullied and cajoled and ranted about obligations and family honour, and generally used every subterfuge under the sun. When that didn't work he resorted to threats. I was frightened and so . . . I agreed. I became part of the team that had you under observation and I was supposed to enter your life at a propitious moment. Bernard was confident you would fall for me.'

'He's a good psychologist,' I said sourly.

Not far away an engine sputtered and fired, unmistakeably an outboard. A search getting under way? Or merely guests embarking for the mainland? I slid the .38 out of its holster, fished around in my jacket for spare cartridges. I found five, thumbed them into the cylinder.

A second engine crackled, and a third. Throttles opened and a boat came flicking around the headland, moving fast, almost skimming the water. It headed out across the channel, away from the island, and I realised I had been holding my breath; I let it out noisily.

Gina noticed. 'Yes, I thought it must be them, too.'

Two more outboards emerged, pale skittering shapes, seeming to aquaplane, and the combined snarl of the three engines burst across the millpond waters, amplified in the pre-dawn stillness. While it lasted, we didn't speak.

Then, picking up the threads of Gina's story, I said, 'As I recall, you turned me down when I proposed dinner, that day I drove you to Monaco. Was that because you changed your mind about helping Tillou?'

'I would like to be able to say yes. But it was simply

part of the master plan; to keep you dangling. "Play hard to get," Bernard said. "Don't let him have it all his own way." So I played hard to get. Rather, I *over*played – you went away after that, on your Mediterranean cruise, as I now know. At the time it was as if you'd gone for good. Bernard was furious.'

'Must have been a worry.' I couldn't keep the dryness out.

'Not to me: I was relieved. Then you came back. Bernard had stationed someone in Monaco and your return was reported. I was despatched post-haste to the Hotel de Paris, which is where you saw me and dragged me away from my breakfast. I wasn't overjoyed, I must say: I'd been glad to wash my hands of the whole dirty business. I tried to discourage you, yet I was . . . drawn to you, in spite of myself. In spite of your having apparently killed Fabrice, though at that time I wasn't convinced you'd done it. I didn't think you were capable of killing someone – and that's meant to be a compliment.

'My conscience gave me a bad time at first. But because of how things had been between Fabrice and myself I didn't feel entirely disloyal. He'd been disloyal to me many times over when we were married. I thought I was about due for a new and better deal.'

'I'll say.'

In the east the sky was lightening, indigo giving way to slate blue above the tree tops. It was after four o'clock I discovered to my surprise. I was instantly uneasy. Daylight spelled danger. We must be ready to move as soon as there was light enough to see by.

'I almost killed you myself, you know,' Gina said, her voice subdued. 'On the boat, on *Spindrift*.'

'What are you talking about?'

'When Pascal fell overboard and you dived in after

him. I was going to let you drown. That's why I . . . I stayed out of sight when you were trying to get back on board. I heard you calling: I thought as long as I couldn't see you, as long as I didn't have to watch you drown, I could do it – leave you there.'

It all came back to me now. Splashing about in those frenzied seas, and calling, calling, wondering where she was. Why she didn't come. Now I knew.

'But you weakened,' I said and even managed a grin. 'You repented your sin before you committed it. You didn't leave me there, did you?'

She shook her head and the sweeping, almost-blonde tresses shook too, catching the pale blush of the as-yet-invisible sunrise. 'When I looked over the side and saw you, I couldn't let you die. Especially as you'd been so brave.' She laughed softly. 'That sounds corny, doesn't it? But you *were* brave. And in a way, even though I'd been ready to abandon you only minutes before, I was proud of you.'

'Some Mata Hari you were,' I said. 'And talk about mixed-up!'

'You're so right. That was me: mixed-up; ambivalent. On the one hand I wanted you dead, on the other . . .'

'Why did you come to Geneva? The real reason, I mean.'

'Reasons,' she said, emphasising the plural. 'Bernard wanted me to; I resisted at first, then I discovered I wanted to go anyway. Not for revenge, his or mine. I just wanted to see you again. It shook me when I faced up to it. Maybe I was already in love with you by then, but wouldn't admit it. Even without the Fabrice thing, I was still anti-male; that much of what I told you was true.'

An early-rising seabird drifted across the empty

vault of the dawn sky on rigid pinions, describing circles at random. Every so often it emitted a squawk, a desolate lament. My sentiments exactly, chum.

I lobbed a large pebble aimlessly into the water. 'When did you become certain of your . . . feelings for me?'

'The very moment I saw you again outside your apartment. I was still fighting it inside, but it was a rearguard action. After we'd made love, I just accepted it. It was a sort of re-birth for me, having lived a lie with Fabrice for so long.'

A re-birth. Funny how we had both, for quite different reasons and quite independently of each other, viewed our relationship in that light.

'But you still sicked a couple of Tillou's thugs onto me, that night at the P'tit Vegas. *And* you let him know we were on Porquerolles. Not very loving behaviour.'

'I didn't, darling.' She grabbed my hand, squeezing it. 'Not that business at the club. They must have followed us – me. I knew nothing about them, I swear.'

'Okay, but that still doesn't explain why you told Tillou we were on the island. You phoned him, that first morning when you went to buy the bread, I suppose.'

'That's right. But not to *inform* on you. My God, please don't think that.' She made a helpless gesture. 'I loved you. I couldn't have purposely done anything to bring harm to you. No, I did it to persuade him to leave you alone, to call off his vendetta. You see, I was certain he already knew we were here; he has spies everywhere. Half the island's population is probably in his pocket one way or another. You might have been able to hide yourself but you couldn't hide the boat. I thought . . . I thought I might be able to reason with him.' She paused. 'I told him how I felt about you.'

'And?' I prompted when she didn't continue.

'He hung up on me.'

That figured. 'What did you expect?'

'I'm not sure.' She scuffed her bare heels in the sand. 'I thought anything was better than just *waiting* for Bernard to pounce.'

She had meant well. What could I say?

'And Madame Sabourin? Was she part of the set-up too?'

'Well, she was obviously sent to make contact after my telephone call to Bernard. But I had no hand in that. She came to sit beside me while you were in the loo and warned me to act naturally when you returned, and to treat her like a stranger. I was too frightened to argue. She also brought a message from Bernard: he wanted you to come to the barbecue but simply to talk to you; to find out who had employed you to kill Fabrice. Through Jeanne he gave his word it wasn't a trap. I wanted to believe him, yet I didn't trust him. When she invited us to the barbecue I did my best to discourage you: you remember, I said we were leaving that day. I pretended I wanted to do some shopping in Toulon. Without giving away my identity, I couldn't warn you off. I just had to hope Bernard was genuine in wanting simply to talk to you. I thought that with all those respectable people there . . .' She fiddled with the hem of her dress. 'I should have told her to go to hell. I should have told all of them!'

'If it's any consolation, even without you, I'd intended to visit the island. You needn't reproach yourself. Without your help I'd never have escaped.

And, incidentally, I'm sorry I had to hurt you back there . . . I mean, I wasn't quite myself.'

Her eyes filled with tenderness. 'I understand that. I'm glad you did what you did. It was the only way – for both of us.'

Her generosity made me feel humble. 'I wouldn't have harmed you – *really* harmed you, that is. I was pretty het up, sure; I even hated you a bit, but that was mostly hurt pride. I wouldn't have . . .'

'Killed me? I know. I know.'

I kissed her, a nominal meeting of the lips. Neither of us yet ready for real passion.

'I was beginning to think you were a moody girl, you know,' I said, holding her. 'You were so touchy at times.'

'Full of doom and gloom, you called it. Now you'll understand why, though it wasn't only that I was frightened of Bernard and what he might do to you. You see, we had a detailed dossier on you; we were fully acquainted with your . . . appetite for women. I used to wonder if I was just another fling. In spite of all you said about loving me, I had doubts whether you were serious.'

'O ye of little faith. And now?'

'Now? Yes, now I am finally convinced.' She touched my cheek. 'What about us, Jack? Where do we go from here?'

'Well, where *do* we go?' I retorted lightly.

She stared at me, round-eyed.

'If you mean, do we still have a future,' I said, 'the answer, as far as I'm concerned, is . . . yes, we do. Nothing has really changed, when all's said and done.' I placed an arm around her shoulders; her skin was clammy. 'I'm hooked, love. I'm a junky. I need my daily fix of Gina Gregg, Gina Tillou, or whoever she is, and I'm not interested in kicking the habit. You're a virus in my blood.'

'You don't know, you can't possibly, possibly know how happy it makes me to hear that.' She snuggled up to my shirt-front with a murmur of contentment. 'I do love you so, Jack.'

'And I you.'

I lay back against the rock, still embracing her. The stars were gone; sunrise wasn't far off. Soon we would have to leave. But not just yet. Not for an hour or so.

Tiredness settled on me, light and gentle as mist. I surrendered to it.

Chapter Thirteen

The sun was high when I awakened – roused by the pulsations of a helicopter prowling along the foreshore: a bright yellow job with an all-perspex cabin like a goldfish bowl and torpedo-shaped floats. As I watched, only semi-awake, it dropped down behind the old fort at the western tip of the island and was gone from sight.

'That's Bernard's,' Gina announced, yawning and rubbing sleep from her eyes. With her hair all tousled and her make-up mostly worn away, she looked like a teenage urchin. There were superficial scratches on her forehead, cheeks, and arms, inflicted during our safari through the undergrowth. I was similarly scarred: though my arms were protected by my jacket, the backs of my hands had suffered. Speaking of jackets, that particular garment was a write-off. The considerable quantities of canine blood and goo deposited on it had dried to form a rust-coloured map. That made two suits and a jacket Tillou owed me; not that I was ever likely to collect.

I stood up, stretched, checked my watch. It was 10.20. I had overslept by a wide margin; I was stiff as a seized engine and my mouth tasted like the bottom of a primeval swamp.

The helicopter was a rude surprise. I had forgotten its existence. I was chastened; high time I stopped underestimating Tillou. High time I got smart. I totted up my assets: me, a .38 with five shells, and a boat. Not much to pit against Tillou's private army with its helicopter and all.

'Here's what we do,' I said, and it was instant improvisation. 'I have to meet up with Jean-Pierre in that bay . . . I've forgotten its name . . . by the Pointe Grand Langoustier.'

'Port-Fay.'

'Right. Now, whatever happens, I don't want you hurt and that means we have to separate.'

Now she was standing too. 'Whatever we do, we do together.'

'Be sensible, love. Tillou isn't after you. He's not pleased with you, but he's not out for your blood. If you stick with me though, sooner or later, you could cop a bullet. You can see that, can't you?'

Her silence was answer enough.

'You're to go into town and take a boat to the mainland.' I pulled a handful of hundred-franc notes from my wallet, wrapped her fingers round them.

'I can't just run away. Desert you.'

'You can and you must.' I struggled to unclip the key to the apartment from my key-ring, cursing when a fingernail ripped. 'For us.'

Her eyebrows rose. 'For *us*?'

'Yes, you silly girl. What future will we have together if you get killed?' I gripped her shoulders, shook her, 'What use will all your support and loyalty be if you're dead?'

Again she was silent.

I gave her the key, sucked at the split fingernail. 'Okay,' I said roughly. 'This is how we'll play it: I'll take off and meet up with Jean-Pierre. You get off the island, take a train or fly to Geneva. Go to the apartment and just *sit tight*.'

She clung to me. 'Sit tight while you're being hunted down? How can you ask it of me?'

I blew my stack. 'Christ, Gina! Haven't you done enough damage already – even if it was well-intentioned? Don't make things worse than they are.'

She recoiled as if I had slapped her, eyes bright with pain. It was on the tip of my tongue to apologise, then I thought better of it. Angry, she was less likely to press me to relent.

'I should be there by Sunday.' Four days hence. 'If you need money there's about a thousand Swiss francs in the wall safe behind the Manet painting. It's a combination safe.' I reeled off the numbers, made her repeat them twice.

'I'll say *au revoir*, then.' I stuffed the .38 in the belt holster.

'Good luck.' The kiss she planted on my cheek was cool.

'Give me half-an-hour to get well clear before you go.' I gave her a parting hug, ran lightly up the short slope leading from the beach. At the top, I pivoted round. She was watching me and her features were etched with lines of strain.

'Be there when I arrive,' I called. 'I love you.'

The impact of those three words was immediate: like switching on a light in a darkened room. She blew me a kiss and her smile was dazzling as the sun.

'Take care, darling.'

I gave her a last, cheerful salute before setting off at a lope with dry mouth and thudding heart.

Initially my progress was rapid.

The Ile de Porquerolles is networked with narrow, tunnel-like footpaths, primarily for tourist use. I headed more or less south, taking my bearings from the sun, augmented by occasional glimpses of the sea that was blue as blue could ever be. Once I caught sight of the rooftop of Tillou's house; there was no bustle of activity from that quarter as far as I could tell. Maybe they'd given up, or more likely they were out combing the island for me.

My environment, pretty though it was, made little impression on me beyond a few kaleidoscopic flashes: an ancient stone bridge over a dried-up watercourse, brim-full of dead leaves; stepping over a rotting, fungus-covered tree trunk; labouring up a series of natural steps in a rocky hillside. As long as I kept to the footpaths I was relatively safe. Even from above I would be invisible. The primitive but wide thoroughfares posed the greatest danger; I crossed several, but apart from a family of cyclists, I saw no one.

As I came to the crest of a hill, the small, close-packed trees thinned out in favour of equally dense, waist-high shrubs – tough and wiry, with a treacherous scree underfoot. I was able to see right across to the peninsula that curved protectively round the Port-Fay cove. And – God bless Jean-Pierre – there was *Spindrift*, anchored just inside the clawing rocks that acted as a breakwater. She looked like a million dollars. A figure, impossible to identify at this distance, was bent over the bow pulpit.

I blundered on down the far side of the hill, fighting the scrub, sliding on the loose shale, and soon came to the brink of the low cliffs that edged the bay. The prospect was picturesque: a wide, sandy beach, sprinkled with holidaymakers and assaulted by foaming rollers. The sea within the bay was a deep ultramarine, changing dramatically out beyond the rocky spit, becoming choppy and mottled with white.

Spindrift was bucking slightly, the short white-tipped combers breaking against her bow. Wind about force four, I estimated: superb conditions for sailing.

I followed the line of the cliffs, avoiding the Hotel Langoustier, whose red-tiled roof was a splash in the profusion of green, and opted for the shortest, most direct route to *Spindrift*'s anchorage. This required me to forsake the shrubbery and take to the beach. I stripped off my bloodstained jacket and shirt and parted with my holster, making a bundle of them and stuffing them down a crack in the rocks; the gun went in my pocket. Now I would just about pass muster as a rather scruffy tourist.

On the beach I attracted less attention than a taxicab in Piccadilly Circus. The only second glance came from a lithe blonde, reclining alone on a beach mat, and I'd like to think her interest was strictly physical. I wished I could reciprocate. I settled for a murmured '*Bonjour, mademoiselle,*' which had her raising her pink-framed sunglasses for a more searching appraisal. In case she was missing something.

My affectedly casual stroll carried me to the far side of the bay in the space of a few minutes. I was within hailing distance of *Spindrift* by then, but there was no longer anyone on deck for me to hail. It was coming up to mid-day so Jean-Pierre might be preparing lunch. A hunger pang surfaced; I hadn't eaten since lunchtime yesterday.

It was beginning to look as if I might make it, when that blasted helicopter came chop-chop-chopping along, overflying the ruined fort atop the peninsula and bee-lining for *Spindrift*.

I ducked down in a cleft between some rocks. Watched it chatter off over the bay, silhouetted briefly against the sun's glare. If they had spotted me or recognized *Spindrift*, they weren't letting on.

I got moving again, tried a yell or two as I hopped from rock to rock. 'Ahoy, Jean-Pierre!' But it was not until I was so close that the smell of cooking wafted across the intervening water, that I got a response: Pascal burst out of the companionway with the velocity of a champagne cork.

'Jack!' he shouted gleefully, windmilling his arms.

I stiffened in dismay. What was Pascal doing on board when he was supposed to be safely ensconced in an hotel? What was Jean-Pierre thinking of?

I windmilled back, suppressing my fears. Then Jean-Pierre came up on deck, imparted an economic nod of acknowledgement and set about lowering the inflatable. I kept ear and eye cocked for the chopper while he rowed across for me.

His handclasp was perfunctory. No questions were asked; my appearance must have told its own story. On board *Spindrift*, we secured the inflatable and I sent him to start the motor.

Pascal, after his usual effervescent welcome, rushed off to raise the anchor. I flopped exhausted on the cockpit seat and the .38 slid out of my pocket, falling into the cockpit-well with a clatter. I left it there.

'How come Pascal's still aboard?' I demanded, angrily – an anger born out of fear for the boy. Tillou's mob were unlikely to make distinctions between adult and child if it came to a gun battle.

Jean-Pierre juggled with the throttle, getting the tickover to his liking before replying. 'The hotels were all full on the island. I telephoned several in Giens and in Hyères, but they were also full. It is the height of the season . . .' He shrugged. 'What else could I do?'

Abandon me, you stupid bugger, that's what. Though I was glad he hadn't.

I squeezed his shoulder. 'Thanks for being here, Jean-Pierre. But now we've got to get the hell out.'

'I know.' He looked me up and down. 'The *soirée* was not so pleasant, *hein*?'

'Too much excitement for an old man like me.'

A halloo from Pascal: the anchor was up. The wind was already nudging the bows to starboard, towards the open sea. Jean-Pierre took up a stance behind the wheel, applied throttle, and *Spindrift* came obediently round into the wind, south-by-south-west.

'Where is Gina?' he asked, a parental eye on Pascal who was scrambling back along the cabin roof.

'She's safe.' Wondering, even as I spoke, if that were true. 'She should be on her way back to the mainland by now.'

He studied me, nakedly curious. 'Do you want to tell me what is happening? Perhaps I can help – perhaps not. I am willing to try.'

'You're doing all you can. Maybe when it's all over. But to be fair to you, and especially to Pascal, I should tell you that someone wants me dead and he happens to be a big wheel in the underworld with a swarm of thugs at his disposal – *armed* thugs. They won't make special concessions for you and Pascal: do you understand what I'm saying?'

He understood well enough. His expression was sober as he glanced at Pascal, now sitting next to me, hugging his knees and unconcerned by the talk of armed thugs.

'I am worried for Pascal, not for myself.'

'That goes double for me. We must make for the mainland.'

'Toulon?'

'No,' I said with emphasis. 'This man – this *chef de*

gang – has spies everywhere. Put me ashore in a cove near Hyères-Place – that'll be safer.'

'Are we going ashore?' Pascal asked. 'I need to buy some fishing hooks.'

Prosaic Pascal. Jean-Pierre and I grinned at each other over his dark head.

'So,' Jean-Pierre said. 'Hyères-Plage. Via the Petite-Passe?' The Petite-Passe was the smaller of the two channels into Hyères bay.

'I think not. We'd have to pass the *chef*'s house and they know the boat. Better to go the long way round, through the Grande-Passe.'

Jean-Pierre grunted assent and rotated the wheel, bringing us round on to a south-easterly course. The wind was now on our starboard beam and blowing steadily.

'We could put some canvas on her,' I mused aloud, listening to the strum of the rigging.

'Leave it to me.' Jean-Pierre inclined his head towards the companionway. 'Would you like some pizza? We were preparing lunch when you arrived.'

'I'll get it!' Pascal cried, jumping down into the well and thence through the open hatch. The clatter of plates rose from the saloon.

Running beam on to the seas, *Spindrift* was rolling a bit. The waves were more vicious than they looked and fairly banged against the hull, even slopping over the gunwale occasionally. I was getting wet, but since all I had on was a pair of ruined trousers, I was inclined to be philosophical about it.

Summoned by Pascal, I went below. He and I dined together on pizza and salad, with a coarse *vin de pays* to wash it down, his diluted with water as always. While we ate, Jean-Pierre engaged the autohelm and raised the mainsail. Presently the engine died. The crackle of canvas took over, the deck canting as *Spindrift* responded to the power of the wind, like an animal freed from a cage.

I showered, changed into shorts and T-shirt, and toddled back on deck to watch the pale cliffs of Porquerolles recede; wise sailor that he was, Jean-Pierre was steering away from the island, opening up sea room to leeward. Though benign weather conditions were forecast, he always planned for the worst.

We were fairly ripping along, even with only the mainsail set, the wind freshening as we cleared the southern tip of the island. We were not the only sailing vessel out that afternoon: the seascape was speckled with white, shark-fin shapes, darting back and forth in apparent disorder. Powerboats were out in force too, from tiny outboards to stately cruisers.

A red-hulled launch away off our port quarter stood out from the rest. It was bow on to us and throwing up a geyser of spray on either side, closing with us rapidly.

Jean-Pierre followed my gaze sternwards. 'What is it?'

'Maybe nothing.'

The glasses brought the launch up close and it was a spectacular sight, hurdling the waves, the hull sometimes coming completely clear of the water. A Starcraft 22 – fibre-glass construction, inboard motor, American-built. Capable of twenty knots or faster. I concentrated on the crew: four or five in number and all male. All strangers to me. Or were they? A burly figure in a sleeveless black T-shirt: Prost? Or just my over-active imagination.

'Jack?' I detected a note of anxiety in Jean-Pierre's voice.

'I can't tell.' I lowered the glasses. The launch was less than a mile away; say three or four minutes to come alongside. If those guys were sent by Tillou we were in big trouble. I cast around for the nearest vessel: two yachts to the east, sailing in tandem, were nearer than the launch, only they were going away from us. Not a hope of catching them up.

'More sail?' Jean-Pierre suggested.

'Too late. In any case they'd still catch us.'

I focused on the launch again and my stomach lurched. It was Prost all right. To be back in action so soon after that skull-crunching fall, he was either solid bone from the neck up or a robot.

There was a tug on my arm. A solemn-faced Pascal held out my gun.

'Thank you, Pascal,' I said, matching his solemnity.

I went down on my haunches, facing him. 'Now listen, Pascal: some men – bad men – are chasing me. They won't harm you or your father, not if they can help it; but if they shoot at us, which is likely, you may be hit accidentally. So I want you to go below, lie down on your bunk, and stay there until either I or your father tell you it's safe to come out. Got it?'

He nodded trustingly. No sign of fear; he was too young to know the ruthlessness and the degeneracy of man. Too young to comprehend the finality of death.

He looked towards Jean-Pierre. 'Papa? Are you coming down too?'

Jean-Pierre's grim visage softened. 'No, Pascal. I must stay and help Jack.'

'You don't have to . . .' I began, but his barked '*Je reste!*' forestalled my objection.

The launch was no more than a quarter of a mile behind, battering through the waves, the sleek V of its prow glistening with spray. They were travelling too fast for the conditions, pitching badly in the longer troughs. They might even yet hit a freak wave and bury their bow or capsize.

Wishful thinking wouldn't make it happen.

I propelled Pascal down the companionway and went after him. When I rejoined Jean-Pierre, complete with box of .38 cartridges, Prost and company had been reinforced – by one yellow helicopter. It swooped in astern, a persistent glass-eyed bug we couldn't swat away.

With so many other boats on all sides, presumably crewed by solid, law-abiding citizens, it was hard to believe they would actually attack us. Actually fire on us. Unless nothing mattered to Tillou any more, except his revenge.

The chopper's speed bled off and it took up station to port. A man leaned out, armed with a megaphone.

'Ahoy, *Spindrift*,' came the metallic yelp. 'Heave to or we sink you.'

Sink us! God, they didn't pussyfoot around! And what with – torpedoes?

I stuck up a rude middle finger, French equivalent of the famous Anglo-Saxon salute.

'You have one minute,' the megaphone blared. 'One minute. There will be no second warning.'

I raised the gun, using both hands, and let them have six rounds rapid. They made a fast, straight-up getaway; for all the effect my shots had I might as well have been throwing pebbles.

A squall would have come in handy. I cranked my head round all points of the compass, hoping for signs of one; the sky had never been bluer. So, no meteorological assistance. We were on our own.

The sixty-second period of grace was just long enough for me to cram six more bullets into the .38.

'Keep your head down,' I cautioned Jean-Pierre, as our ultimatum ran out. 'War is about to be declared.'

He was tense and grave, but managed a ghost of a grin.

The launch was to starboard, on a converging course. I expected them to try and board us like pirates of old, grappling irons, cutlasses between their teeth, and so on. But I had it all wrong.

There was no further warning. The helicopter's nose dipped and it flew straight for us, floats skimming the wavetops. A head and torso protruded from the side opening of the cabin. Beads of orange sparkled around it, like firecrackers, and holes began to appear in the mainsail and chunks of fibre glass whizzed past my ear: they were using a machine-gun! Now its stutter reached me over the clamour of the engine.

I returned the fire ineffectually, crouching behind the cabin for protection. Jean-Pierre had already dropped below the gunwale, still holding the rim of the wheel. His face was as white as the mainsail, fear and rage all mixed up together.

The machine-gun had fallen silent. The chopper's engine note rose as it zoom-climbed over *Spindrift*'s mast, whirling away to port. The lull was likely to be brief. I reloaded the .38 fast – so fast I spilled half the shells in the cockpit-well.

Jean-Pierre set the autohelm, crawled towards the cabin hatch. 'Pascal!' he called out, his voice off-key. 'Are you all right?'

'Oui, papa,' came the tremulous response.

I ventured a peek at the launch. No change there, still maintaining a watching brief, like vultures waiting to dine off a corpse. Then back came the chopper, full tilt. Now that I was listening for it I detected the rattle of the machine-gun at once. It sounded so distant, so puny, that I was unprepared for the veritable blizzard of bullets that ripped into the hull and cabin. Over the helicopter's stammer, the gunfire, and the splintering of fibre-glass, I heard a wailing cry: fear, pain, it was hard to tell, but it came from inside the cabin and it had a stricken Jean-Pierre snaking along the cockpit floor and through the hatch in a quicksilver slither.

Let the boy be all right, I pleaded to a God I had long denied. Don't let him be hurt. Or worse.

I raged uselessly. Tears flowed, lava-hot, and I didn't attempt to stem them.

'You bastards!' I screamed, feeding more shells into the gun. My nose was running; I wiped it with the back of my hand, smearing snot and tears across my cheek.

'Jean-Pierre!' I bellowed, ducking down to hatch level. 'Is Pascal all right?'

No answer. The only sound now was new – an ominous gurgle. We were taking in water. *Spindrift* must have been holed below the waterline in the last attack.

'Start the pumps, Jean-Pierre!' I would have done it myself, but the chopper was commencing another run and I was going to hit them hard this time, even if it cost me my life.

I scrambled up on the cabin roof, adopted a classic legs-apart, gun-at-arms-length pose. It made me a juicy target, but when that machine-gun opened up, the shots went nowhere near me; they were still out to take me alive. To shoot the boat from under me and trawl me out of the water.

And if innocent people died in the process, that was just too bad.

The helicopter was less than a hundred yards away, the orange sparks still dancing a lethal, demented jig, when I opened fire. I placed my shots meticulously, aiming for the pilot. I actually saw the second one strike the perspex bowl, starring but not shattering it. My third shot was way-off, but not because my aim was lousy: the helicopter wobbled – perhaps the pilot had flinched from my shots – and it lost a foot of height it couldn't spare just as it passed over a modest wave. The front end of the floats kissed the water and were flipped over: it was as instant, as effortless, as undramatic as that. Rotors flailing, the machine performed a complete somersault, the slender tail slicing through *Spindrift*'s sail, through the boom, and through the cabin roof which, by then, I had vacated, propelled by reflex into the cockpit. I landed in a sprawl, lost the gun, and made painful contact with the steering control. Behind me, flames erupted.

I got to my feet, staggering, shaking the fog from my brain. The helicopter – what was left of it – was a blazing tangle of metal, a column of oily smoke spewing upwards from it, staining the sky's rich backcloth. Someone was screaming, a high, thin ululation.

'Jean-Pierre!' It was supposed to be a shout; it came out as a croak. 'Jean-Pierre! Pascal!'

The screaming stopped, cut off in full flow. I moved forward in what I thought was the direction of the companionway, though I couldn't be sure: everything was enveloped in black smoke and *Spindrift* was a smashed-up shambles. She was also settling by the bow.

The helicopter's fuel tank went up, sounding exactly like a gasp of breath amplified a thousand times. Scorching-hot air slammed into me and it was my turn to do somersaults. I went over the gunwale, limbs gyrating like a broken doll, entering the water feet first and going under so quickly I had no chance to inflate my lungs. Fortunately, having entered at a shallow angle, I came up immediately, coughing up seawater, my legs instinctively pedalling.

I was off *Spindrift*'s port beam, on the opposite side to the launch and therefore hidden from it. It was only a temporary refuge: *Spindrift*, a dismasted wreck with the helicopter wreckage embedded amidships, was well and truly ablaze, her foredeck already awash. Her life could be measured in minutes.

I tried not to dwell on Jean-Pierre and Pascal. They were dead – nobody could have survived that holocaust. They were dead and I was as much to blame as if I had been flying that chopper, firing that machine-gun myself. Sicker at heart than I had ever been, I trod water, staying alive.

Wishing I was dead.

The survival instinct goes deep. To shrink from death is natural, no matter how deep one's despair, how abject one's misery. And yet my burden of guilt was so oppressive that I would gladly have sacrificed myself to bring Jean-Pierre and Pascal back to life. It was a profitless line of thought.

So I carried on treading. Considered what to do.

Spindrift was foundering. Most of what remained above sea level was helicopter wreckage. The fire continued to burn, but only feebly, steam mingling with the tower of smoke that still spiralled skywards. Through the smokescreen I glimpsed the red hull of the launch. Decided I ought to be elsewhere and, taking a deep breath, crash-dived, going deep, aiming for an invisible point somewhere beyond *Spindrift*'s stern on the premise that Prost would expect me to swim *away* from the launch. Always assuming they weren't as devious as me.

I was an accomplished underwater swimmer and could stay down for up to two minutes at a pinch. This I did, and as I swam, I had a fishes' eye view of *Spindrift*'s final plunge: she sank in a leisurely, even graceful manner, descending through that slightly milky-blue world, the magnifying effect of the water making her appear closer than she really was. The helicopter tail broke loose, tumbling off the cabin roof and, being metal, sank faster than the boat, dragging with it the broken mast and boom. No bodies floated free of the hull and I was thankful for that small mercy.

She disappeared from sight, fading into the opaque depths, a spectral object, shattered but her former glory not entirely extinguished. It had not been an ignoble demise. She would make a fitting resting place for my friends.

I swam wretchedly on, setting a punishing pace. Swamping my remorse in a physical self-chastisement. When, at last, I was forced to the surface, rising from the depths like a Polaris missile, the launch was nowhere to be seen. I couldn't believe it, couldn't believe they had given up so easily. And they hadn't: a wave lifted me and another conveniently parted and there was that red hull cruising through some debris, the green-brown hump of the island behind them. They would presume me dead, killed in the explosion. Not at all in accordance with Tillou's wishes. Shame.

I stayed on the surface, swimming more slowly now, conserving my strength. I didn't stop until, aeons later and still going strong, I ran into a solid object and knocked myself out.

*   *   *

'*M'sieu.*' The voice rattled around inside my skull like a marble in a tin can. '*M'sieu!*' More insistent now.

I wished the voice would go away. It made my head hurt.

'*M'sieu!*' There it went again.

Then memory exploded with the impact of a motorway pile-up. I sat up quickly. Too quickly. My head protested, dragging an involuntary groan from my lips.

A circle of anxious faces blotted out the sky. Two men, two women; all elderly, grey hair proliferating. Nobody amongst them I knew.

'You swam right into us,' one of the men said wonderingly. He was tall and bony and sported a dark blue baseball cap. 'You hit your head on our hull.'

'I was pretending to be a torpedo.' I squinted up at him. 'So you picked me up?'

'You'd have drowned if we hadn't,' he said with a chuckle. 'You were unconscious.'

'Well . . . thanks.' I made an effort to rise. Failed dismally.

'Here.' The man with the baseball cap offered me a glass. I sniffed at it. Cognac – what else on a French boat? I downed the lot – and he hadn't been stingy – in a single swallow.

'I had an . . . an accident,' I said. How much had they seen? 'A helicopter . . .'

'We saw it.' This from one of the women. 'What happened?'

I thought fast. 'Hard to say exactly. I was out sailing – alone. The helicopter pilot must have either been drunk or crazy in the head. He kept flying over my boat very low; then he collided with the mast and *pouf*!' I pantomimed an explosion with my hands.

'Some people in a red launch searched the area for a long time afterwards. I'm surprised they didn't see you.'

I, too, was surprised. Not to mention relieved.

'You are English?' The second woman asked.

'Dutch.' From the point of view of accent, most French can't tell the two nationalities apart.

'Monique, my wife.' the man with the cap indicated the second woman. 'Monique thought . . .' He looked uncomfortable and scratched his chin where a couple of days' growth of bristle sprouted.

'What?' I said benignly, and gave a friendly grin to encourage him.

'It sounds silly, but she thought she heard, well, shooting.'

My incredulity brought a flood of relief to their creased faces. 'Shooting?' I said. 'You mean . . . shooting as in guns?'

Four heads jerked up and down. They reminded me of a music hall act.

'You must be mistaken.' I forced a grin. 'Shooting, eh? I think it must have been part of the engine noise.'

They seemed collectively satisfied that the shooting had been the product of Monique's imagination; even Monique herself didn't press the point.

With some assistance from my rescuers, I managed to stand upright. I was now able to look about me properly: the boat was a cabin cruiser, rather long in the tooth, and with a large stern cockpit. Designed for fishing. Rust stains and cracking paintwork abounded. She was hove to, her engine ticking over, and rolling as powerboats tend to do in all but the most tranquil seas.

'Would you like some dry clothes?' someone asked.

'No thanks. Mine will dry soon enough in this heat.'

'The accident must be reported,' Baseball Cap said officiously. Righteous little prick. 'Unfortunately we have no transmitter.' Hooray.

I agreed the accident *must* be reported and without delay. Which was why I would be *so* grateful if they would run me ashore where I would inform the local police. My virtuous tone met with approval and to seal their conviction I asked them to write down their names and addresses on a slip of paper in case the police wanted to contact them for statements. That would also make it unnecessary for them to accompany me to the police; no sense in disrupting their holiday if it could be avoided. What a thoughtful young man, you could see them thinking. Baseball Cap positively beamed at me.

'We'll get going right away,' he announced.

'Splendid,' I returned his beam and hoped I wasn't overdoing it. 'Head for the mainland though, will you? This will be a bit beyond the Porquerolles police.'

'You're right. How about Hyères-Plage? That's the nearest harbour.'

Hyères-Plage, a small holiday resort on the mainland proper, suited me fine.

'I must say you've been really marvellous. I haven't even thanked you for saving my life.'

This smarm went down like sludge on a slide. They helped me below to a bunk where I remained until we entered harbour.

They dropped me at the main landing stage and I waved and thanked them on their way. And tore the list of names and addresses into confetti to scatter in their wake.

Since I had no cash, my first objective was a bank. My credit card wallet was still in my button-down back pocket and one of those little scraps of plastic would surely serve to magic up the price of a train ticket to Marseilles – that fairy-tale city where all wishes, especially the illegal variety, can be made to come true.

Chapter Fourteen

Darkness, and the swish-slurp of sea against shore.

Standing on the shale beach that bordered Tillou's property on the Ile de Porquerolles and staring up the short incline towards the tea-chest of a house, I recalled another time and another place. Specifically, November last, on the banks of the Ammersee near Munich. Where this damned business had really begun. A routine, relatively straightforward contract which had degenerated into a nightmare of persecution, resulting in the death of a good and faithful friend and his son whom I loved almost as much as if he were my own.

I had spent a day and a night in Marseilles – hot, smelly, noisy, bustling Marseilles. Stayed at a squalid no-questions-asked hotel near the Old Port, and killed the first evening in my room, surrounded by peeling wallpaper and a smell that might have been rotting fish but wasn't, with a bottle for company. It was many years since I had been on a solo binge and while the effects lasted, they anaesthetized guilt, sorrow, rage, and all the emotions that were tossing and turning inside me like washing in a tumble-dryer. I expected to pay for my over-indulgence next morning and I did.

By mid-afternoon though, full of aspirin and hairs of the dog, I was kitted out in new clothes, and a

French Identity Card and Driving Licence in the name of Jules Leroy.

The decision to go to Marseilles had not been a random one: it was the home of my regular supplier of false documentation. Working ultra-fast and ultra-ultra-expensive, Thierry Mazé had produced the necessary inside two hours. Equally important, in recognition of our long-standing trading relationship, he not only extended me credit for his handiwork, but, against my IOU, advanced me ten thousand francs.

Armed with my 'papers', I hired a car from Hertz. Paid for two days in advance, in cash, qualifying for a wide smile from the pretty receptionist. Poodled down the six-lane Avenue de Prado to the main shopping-centre, where I made a number of purchases: some innocuous, like a dinky unbreakable torch, a canoe paddle, a capacious hold-all; others less so: Mazé had recommended an illegal arms merchant operating circumspectly out of shabby basement premises behind the Musée de la Marine, and, at prices well above manufacturers' recommended, I became the strictly temporary owner of a small arsenal. Its principal component was an Ithaca 'Stakeout' twelve-bore riot gun, fitted with a sling. Designed mainly for police work, it has a pump-action eight-round magazine and a pistol-type hand grip instead of a wooden stock. Compact, utterly murderous: as nasty a killing machine as ever devised by man.

I also acquired a Ruger Redhawk revolver, .41 magnum calibre with a five-and-a-half inch barrel – stopping power and accuracy in one hefty package – plus a quantity of ammunition for both guns, a cartridge belt, and a Horshoe fast-draw shoulder rig.

The complete Action Man kit for anyone with ambitions to take on an Armoured Division single-handed.

Down the road from the arms dealer's troglodytic premises was a grubby telephone kiosk. It stank of sweat and piss inside, but miraculously the phone worked. With the door wedged open I dialled my apartment in Geneva. No response. It was by then over thirty hours since Gina and I had parted. If she had gone by plane, she ought to have been there. Or she might have arrived but be out shopping, or having a meal. Or she might have gone by train.

Or . . . or . . . or . . .

At about 11 p.m. that day, I left Marseilles, took the autoroute to Toulon, and got to the Giens peninsula, across the water from the island, at two in the morning. Leaving the car in a lay-by just outside the town of Giens, I proceeded to the harbour on foot. Within minutes I had selected suitable water-borne transportation: a tough-looking inflatable equipped with a hefty Johnson outboard. No key, but that wouldn't cause much inconvenience; short-circuiting ignition systems was another of my more dubious talents. I lowered the hold-all on to the wooden main thwart, lowered self after it. Paused to listen. Nothing stirred. Only water tapping against assorted hulls. Owners asleep or absent.

I had one nasty moment when, as I unhitched the mooring line, a light came on in a lean greyhound of a yacht berthed at the neighbouring jetty. Raised voices carried clearly across the water. Of all the times to have a tiff!

Under cover of a rising storm of vituperation I paddled the inflatable clear of its berth and got the hell away before the rest of the marina woke up. The slanging faded into the night and once out of earshot I rested briefly from my labours.

I didn't start the outboard until I was well beyond the headland of the peninsula. Here, I had to risk using my dinky torch: I held it between my teeth while I re-arranged the ignition wiring. The motor fired as soon as I brought the two bare leads into contact and ran freely on minimal choke. A twist of the throttle grip and we went away like a racing hydroplane.

My arrival off the Ile de Porquerolles had been timed to coincide with first light, when the faint glow from the east would take the edge off the darkness, helping to guide me in to a safe landing place on that rock-infested shore. Navigation was simplified by the beacon perched on La Jaune Garde, an islet to the west of Porquerolles. I kept it to starboard, taking a fix from it and another islet lying close in to the shore, just down from Tillou's beach.

Coming ashore at the Plage du Muso's northern end, I dragged the inflatable clear of the water – not easy to do quietly on shale. Around my black-clad person, I distributed the tools of my trade: torch in pocket, jemmy in belt, shoulder-holster where shoulder-holsters usually go and pulled extra-tight so it didn't swing. The cartridge belt with its forty pockets pre-filled, went around my waist, and the Ithaca riot gun where it would do most good – in my hands.

I had no anaesthetic on hand now. Nothing at all to distract me, to dull the pain of the loss of my friends. All I had was a cold, calculating fury, driving me on to finish this damned business. It wasn't just revenge, though it could have been. It wasn't money either, though I had a contract of sorts. No, all I wanted was to be allowed to live in peace and love in peace. Even if by rights and by all that is fair and just, I didn't deserve to.

There was light enough to grope along by if you didn't crib at the odd stubbed toe or barked shin. I suffered these minor hurts with stiff upper lip and in due course came under the shadow of the house, a black slab made even blacker by the patio lights that had been left on.

As it turned out, I didn't need the jemmy. All ground-floor and basement windows were either shuttered or had vertical bars set in the recess. Upstairs they were more lax; height tends to induce a feeling of security, usually misplaced; some windows had their shutters open and neither of two smaller windows was barred. I singled out what was, to judge from the adjacent pipework, either bathroom or loo, and shinned up a handily-located drainpipe, the riot gun slung across my back. Weighed down with hardware and thirty-eight years, it was no mean accomplishment. I was helped by the pipe's wall fixings which were nicely spaced to serve as footrests. Even so, the climb left me huffing and puffing like the big bad wolf who blew the pigs' houses down.

The window was made to open French-style, that is, inwards. In full expectation that it would be securely latched I gave it a gentle push; I nearly fell off the drainpipe in surprise when it swung open, presenting a dark rectangle. I took a firm hold of the sill and swung the top half of my body towards it, still hanging onto the pipe with my right hand and my legs. The pipe creaked under the unaccustomed lateral stresses; I pretended not to hear it. Now I had both hands on the sill and was able to abandon my foothold. I went in over the sill and, gravity taking over, made an inelegant landing – in a bath.

The clatter of the riot gun on enamel was loud as gunfire in that still house. I crouched in the tub, hand on the Ruger, a pneumatic drill hammering away inside my chest. In the distance a dog was yapping, a sustained bleep like signals from a satellite. The Tillou household slumbered on. Unhearing and unheeding.

Reassured, I clambered gingerly out of the bath onto a tiled floor. Snapped the torch on and off, taking in the geography of the room, then tiptoed past bidet and wash-basin to the door.

The next phase in the operation was crucial. The first floor of Tillou's house was virgin territory to me. I listened, every sense tuned to a fine pitch. Silence still ruled. I moistened lips that were as dry as dead leaves, twisted the door knob, pulled, and stood aside, flat against the wall. Listened again. Not so much as a dripping tap broke the absolute stillness.

My every move seemed clumsy and uncoordinated as I felt my way along the wall of what I supposed was a landing or gallery. I came to an alcove, only it wasn't an alcove but a short passage, a dead end. I was tempted to use the torch again, but to do so would have destroyed my night vision, so I shuffled on and eventually came up against some banisters, ornately carved from the feel of them. At last I had something solid to guide me to the stairs. Thence to the ground floor. And so to the study. To lie in wait there for Tillou. My plan was as embryonic as that. I was counting on the element of surprise combined with superior firepower to see me safely through.

My descent to the ground floor was brilliantly executed, though I do say so myself. Stairs, even in new houses, have a tendency to creak. By keeping to the sides, hugging the rail, I avoided this pitfall; a phantom couldn't have done it with less disturbance.

It was like emerging from a fog into brilliant sunshine. The layout of the ground floor had lodged in my subconscious the night of the barbecue, the result of years of housebreaking practice. At the foot of the stairs I turned right, crossed a narrow corridow, and bingo! flattened my nose on the study door.

It was a heavy door, but it swung freely on its hinges. I drew the Ruger, a precautionary measure. Cooking it produced a metallic double click that made my nerves jangle like wedding bells.

I eased the door shut behind me. Leaned against it, exhaling pent-up breath.

That was when the lights came on.

I blinked, momentarily dazzled, and if they'd been smart they would have wasted me then. It was probably the Ruger that made them hesitate: cocked, ready to go off, and pointing, quite by chance, at him. At Tillou.

Huddled up in his Rolls-Royce wheelchair, a dried-up homunculus, pie-crust skin drawn tight over crumbling, shrunken frame. And standing beside his master, a faithful hound, *Sturmführer* Carl Schnurrpfeil. A revolver of uncertain make and calibre held loosely but confidently in his pudgy hand.

'Good morning, Mr Henley,' Schnurrpfeil said. He fought with a smirk and lost. 'We've been expecting you.'

'So nice to see you again,' Tillou said. He was toting iron too: a dainty automatic, Walther or Mauser. Firing a round no bigger than an orange pip. But even an orange pip makes its presence felt when it runs into you at 600 mph.

'Put the gun down,' Schnurrpfeil said coolly. His was as steady as if it had been grafted on to the end of his arm.

I grinned. 'You first.'

Tillou shifted restlessly.

'How did you know I was coming?' I asked, to keep the conversation going.

'We have men posted in the grounds.' Schnurrpfeil's smirk returned. 'We have been expecting you, you know. That is why we brought her back here – to make sure you came.'

'Brought her back?'

'Enough of this!' Tillou snapped. He pressed a button on an intercom next to the phone.

'*Oui, patron?*' The acknowledgement was immediate.

'Prost? *On l'a attrapé. Venez . . .*'

The rest was lost in the blast of the Ruger; a magnum cartridge makes a heck of a din. Two shots, both for Schnurrpfeil, smashing into his chest and hurling him to the floor. He squeezed the trigger of his own gun as he toppled, but it was no more than a muscular reflex. The bullet buried itself in the floor.

That left just me and Tillou, and in speaking to Prost his vigilance had lapsed, the titchy little gun drooping, no longer covering me. Considering his age and physical handicaps though, he put up a good show. He banged off at me, upsetting my aim, driving me down behind the settee. I turned, as a bullet plucked at the upholstery, inches from my nose, and got off two quick ones at his head, the only part of him I could see properly. His face disintegrated into a pizza of blood and shattered bone as he rocked back in the wheelchair. The little automatic fell with a metallic rattle.

Elation surged through me. The bastard was dead!

I had done what I came to do. Mission accomplished. Enemy destroyed.

I was in the act of rising, the smoking Ruger still extended, when the door was flung open. I fired, blindly, defensively, at the human outline in the lighted oblong of the doorway, a spontaneous reaction to a dimly-seen threat. Even at that, my aim was true. For once, alas, too true.

My victim was a woman in a red and cream kimono-style robe. Like Schnurrpfeil she took both bullets in the chest and spun round, arms thrown outwards, falling heavily against the bookshelves and taking a row of leather-bound volumes to the floor with her.

She came to rest face-up, in an attitude of crucifixion, and what my appalled eyes had registered in the very instant of firing was confirmed: the woman I had shot, almost certainly fatally, was Gina.

On feet that were weighted with lead I ran to her, knelt beside her, watched the colour wipe from her face, even the full wide lips becoming pale and bloodless.

She was dying. People aren't made to take that kind of punishment. I couldn't bear to look at the wounds; at the back, where the bullets had exited, it would be much worse.

Her eyes flickered open; those eyes, green with their lazy lids, that normally sparkled with vitality, now dulled as death drew its veil across them.

'Jack?' Her pallor was ghastly – grey-green under a sheen of perspiration. 'Jack . . . I . . . thought it . . . was you.'

'What are you doing here?' Fatuously, it was all I could think of to say. 'You're supposed to be in Geneva.'

God, let her be in Geneva! Let this be a nightmare!

A scarlet pearl oozed from the corner of her mouth, that same mouth I had tasted so often and with such desire.

'They . . . caught . . . me. I . . .' She broke off with a groan of such agony I felt as if my own guts were being ripped out.

'Don't talk. Don't talk.'

She pawed feebly at me. 'Hold . . . me . . . darling.'

A long sigh escaped her and her body seemed to deflate. Her eyelids slowly lowered with the finality of a curtain ringing down on the last act of a play. A convulsive shudder ran through her frame, her limbs went slack, her head lolling sideways, mouth slightly open. The trickle of blood slowed.

I didn't need a degree in medicine to diagnose death. Gina was as dead as dead could be.

I straightened up, kicked out savagely at one of the books that Gina had dragged off the shelf and was lying beside her. It shot across the room, pages fluttering.

I felt nothing. I was numb. I gazed down at Gina for what might have been seconds or might equally have been a quarter of an hour. Drinking in every facet of her beauty, the almost-blonde hair in a cascade about her head, the exquisitely sculptured features that mere words could never do justice to – just a mask now, without the sparkle of those green eyes; the figure, rapier slim, yes, but unquestionably, excitingly female.

And now she was no more. Taken from me by my own hand. Exactly as my dream prophesied. A victim of the skill, the lightning responses of which I was so proud. How puerile these attributes looked now.

Running feet in the corridor brought home to me

my still precarious situation. That old survival instinct was still functioning. I put away the empty Ruger and had the as-yet unblooded riot gun off my shoulder and targeted on the doorway in an easy, flowing movement.

The feet were no longer running. Through the still-open door came the mutter of voices. Impelled by nine-parts blind fury to one-part commonsense I ran to the door, soundless in my sneakers, and burst out into the corridor.

They were roughly where I expected them to be; Prost and two underlings, in a huddle only feet away from the doorway and all armed. From the hip I blasted off a single shot, missing by design to cleave the air only inches above their heads. The cartridge pulverised the green *crepi* wall-covering and flung great shards of it along the corridor to patter on the floorboards. Immobilised, initially by the suddenness of my attack, now, after the warning shot, by fright, the three were swift to capitulate; only a man with no nerves – or no brains – outfaces a shotgun. Pistols crashed to the floor. Hands rose shakily.

'Don't shoot, 'Enley,' Prost quavered. His eyes were glazed with fear.

Smoke hung suspended in wreaths above them and the tang of cordite stung my nostrils; it was as quiet as a dentist's waiting-room.

'Kick the ironmongery over here,' I said at last, waggling the riot gun menacingly.

The three pistols slid across. An interesting assortment: Prost's was a Colt Commander, the cut-down version of the famous 1911 model; his sidekicks were more modestly equipped with a Colt snub-barrelled revolver and a hammerless automatic, probably a Heckler & Koch P7. The details registered by instinct.

As I shoved this weaponry behind me with my toe, Prost's name was called from the general direction of the kitchen.

'Answer,' I ordered and Prost dredged up a croaky '*Oui?*' Then to me, 'It's Blanc. He has two men with him.'

'What's going on?' Blanc demanded loudly.

'This is Henley,' I called back. 'It's finished, Blanc. Tillou and Schnurrpfeil are dead. Prost is here and I have a gun on him.'

A muffled expletive. Whispers, degenerating into dispute. Blanc again, '*Merde! Non!*'

'Give up, Blanc. I've no quarrel with you.'

'The *patron* is dead? Truly?'

'Come and look; he's in the study. Him and Schnurrpfeil.' My thoughts drifted to the other body lying there in the study and tears welled hotly. I blinked them back, raging inside at my weakness.

'We are not afraid of you, 'Enley. We are three against one.'

'Tell my shotgun that. Do you know what a solid cartridge does to a man?'

Evidently he did. More cursings and more whisperings, terminating in a sharp '*Allons-y! Foutons le camp!*' Another way of saying 'Let's fuck off!'

Then the sounds of hasty departure: feet on the move, a door crashing back, voices fading.

Silence. But silence is easy to fake.

'They've gone,' Prost volunteered.

'You say.' If they hadn't, if it was just a ploy, there wasn't a lot I could do about it.

A floorboard creaked upstairs and I was so wound up I nearly squeezed the trigger.

'Who's up there?' I demanded of Prost.

'Monsieur and Madame Sabourin, their daughter . . . and Sabrier.'

'Sabrier?'

'Our . . .' Prost faltered. 'Our new boss, I suppose. Now that Monsieur Tillou is dead.'

The new *patron*. That made Sabrier Dauphin, and therefore a potential ally. 'Fetch him,' I ordered Prost. 'Fetch them all. But stay in sight unless you want an enlarged arsehole. You two – face down on the floor!'

I backed against the wall. From there I had an unobstructed view of the whole landing and most of the doors leading off.

Prost sidled towards the stairs as if reluctant to present his back to me, and went up at a run. He beat a tattoo on the first three doors in turn, identifying himself with '*Ici* Prost. *Déscendez*.' Monsieur and Madame Sabourin came meekly enough; he fully dressed but for his shoes, she in a white towelling robe and curlers, pale and trembling. Daughter Hélène, next door, was quite the opposite: indignant and brash, sporting black leather pants and a black shirt. Her icy glare swept over me like a searchlight, her nose at maximum elevation. One-handedly I checked her and her parents for weapons.

That left just Sabrier. He was slow to answer Prost's summons. Repeated assurances from Prost, prompted by me, finally enticed him out, a blue pyjamad figure. It was Dauphin all right. Hair tousled, chin shaded with overnight growth, a travesty of the spruce and dapper image I carried in my mind. Mister Big himself. Long live the king in the blue jarmies. I giggled and they all gaped at me as if I'd sprouted antlers. In that instant I wanted to kill Sabrier-Dauphin even more than I had wanted to kill Tillou. Without him, without his imperial ambitions and his resentment of Tillou's son, none of this would have happened. His was the responsibility: for Tillou's vendetta against me; for the deaths of Jean-Pierre and Pascal; above all, for Gina.

My finger had tightened on the trigger. I itched to turn the gun on him.

Then reason seeped into my madness, diluting it, lacing it with expediency and pragmatism. Wiping the red mist from my vision. To get clear of the island I might need his cooperation. In return . . . in return I could cancel his debt. Waive my fee. A million dollars in return for a period of grace. It was either that or kill him. And not just him; if he went, the rest would have to go too. Wholesale slaughter, in other words. Mass murder.

I wasn't capable of it. Surely.

Was I?

I felt old and worn out. I hadn't slept for eighteen hours and it was telling on me.

'Mr Sabrier, I presume,' I said to the man I knew as Dauphin. 'Come on down, Mr Sabrier. You too, Prost.'

They descended the stairs side by side, slowly and warily. Sabrier was wearing backless slippers that flip-flopped as he walked. He looked faintly ludicrous and he was aware of it.

Prost took his place in the line-up and Sabrier was set to join him when I beckoned him over.

'Is there a cellar under here?'

'Of course. Where else would they keep the wine?'

How silly of me. This was France.

I addressed my captive audience. 'All right. Now listen to me. You're going to be locked in the cellar. That's the worst that can happen to you . . . provided you don't do anything rash, such as trying to escape.'

Hélène spat at me. Literally spat. Thank God her aim was lousy.

'Lead on, Mr Sabrier,' I said, ignoring her. 'The rest of you follow in single file, hands on heads.' Hélène naturally declined on both counts until I walloped her backside with the gun barrel. The look she gave me was neat venom.

The cellar was reached via the kitchen: through a recessed door, and down narrow stone steps.

'Where's the key?' I asked Sabrier from the top of the steps, as he hauled on the heavy cellar door.

'In the lock.' He pointed. So it was.

'Lock them in, then come up here; *with* the key.'

Hélène was last in line. As the others filed submissively into the cellar, she hung back. I prodded her with the gun.

'Get on down there.'

She pivoted round with the grace and co-ordination of a ballerina and came at me, fangs bared, claws unsheathed, and a thin-bladed sticker in her fist. Intentions clearly hostile.

My unpreparedness was absolute. The riot gun was pointing down the steps and therefore awkwardly placed for fending her off. She hit me in a sprawling leap, sank the knife into my shoulder, below the bone. I let out a yelp that was more shock than suffering. Then we were rolling on the tiles and she was punching and scratching, her spiky hair filling my mouth. I brought my knee up between her legs, knee-cap driving into her crotch with a force that jarred my whole body; what it did to her can only be imagined. Her eyes bulged, her mouth opened to scream but compromised with a gurgle. I pushed her aside and, struggling to rise, lashed out at Prost who had aspirations of joining the party. He dropped as if hit by a runaway bus. The blunt snout of the riot gun swung to threaten Sabourin and the two goons, coming up behind Prost in a tight bunch. Sabourin managed a strangled 'No!' before the gun crashed and hurled a solid cartridge past his ear. I pumped the slide and another round clunked into the firing-chamber.

'Right, back off,' I rasped, using the wall for support. Four inches of steel were still embedded in me and just breathing was agony. 'Get down to the cellar,' I said to the petrified Sabourin. 'And take these two.' Prost was unconscious; a thin trickle of blood, dark like treacle, wormed from his hairline and across his forehead. Hélène was writhing beside him, whimpering and moaning alternately, nursing her groin. Something had busted down there. I was sorry for her, but she'd had it coming. Fortunes of war.

Temporarily on my ownsome, my immediate concern was the knife in my shoulder. It had to come out. It would hurt like crazy, but it was hurting anyway. So I braced my back against a cupboard, gritted my teeth, and gave it a sharp tug. Easy, really. Only I nearly fainted as it slid out of my flesh, dragging on the lips of the wound. Blood spurted, was soaked up by my T-shirt. Stop the bleeding, my brain commanded, and by some miracle the other parts of me obeyed.

A hand towel served as a pad. I was trying to position it inside my T-shirt when Sabrier reappeared.

'Help me fix this.' I covered him with the Ruger while he found some surgical tape and secured a makeshift dressing.

'The gun is not necessary,' he remarked as he worked on me. 'You and I are on the same side.'

I gave a sardonic grunt. 'Where's the key?'

He handed it over: a heavy, strictly functional

hunk of metal with a plastic tag on which was written *Cave*.

A thought struck me. 'The servants. Are they in the basement? They must have heard the shooting.'

'Don't worry, 'Enley. Two of them live in town. They are not due until seven o'clock. As for the other – old Thomas – there you are indeed fortunate. He went to the mainland yesterday to spend some time with his family and will not be back until the weekend.' Sabrier finger-combed his hair, a series of quick, jerky strokes. 'Tillou and Schnurrpfeil – they are dead, yes?'

Boss and chief rival both eliminated. This was a great day for him.

'They're dead. So is . . . so is Gina.'

'Ah.' He peered at me and comprehension came gradually like sunrise. '*Aaah*.' Much deeper. 'Now it is clear. She is, was, important to you. But how . . . ?'

'Never mind how! It's none of your business.' I reined in my temper, made an effort to speak evenly. 'I'm leaving. This minute.'

He made with the shoulders, French-style. 'So . . . leave.'

'I need time to get clear away. I need forty-eight hours.'

'You think I will inform the police?' A mocking smile.

I had the riot gun barrel wedged under his chin so fast the smile stayed in place for several seconds afterwards, becoming fixed as I gouged into his bristles.

'Don't patronize me, mother-fucker. I'd as soon blast your head off your shoulders as do a deal with you. But I need your help.'

'M-my help?'

'I'll explain in a minute. First the deal: cover up for

me and don't squeal to the *flics*, and I'll forget about my fee.'

That appealed to the right instincts. 'Leave it to me, *mon ami*.' Suddenly we were *amis*. The way to Sabrier's heart was through his pocket, all right. 'I will conceal all evidence. Nothing will incriminate you.'

'You needn't worry about evidence: there won't be any.'

His narrow brow creased. '*Comment*?'

Instead of enlightening him, I said, 'Find me some petrol or paraffin.' Which, I suppose, was an explanation in itself.

He goggled. 'You are going to burn the house?'

'Just find it. Move!'

He scuttled off and I sagged against the kitchen sink, mentally and physically sapped. My shoulder throbbed, but compared with the other, inner pain, it was a pin-prick.

Gina, Gina, Gina. How could I have done such a thing? Was it divine punishment? Had God guided my hand? I shook my head to clear it of such pious claptrap. Stop passing the buck; *you* killed Gina and you're stuck with it. For as long as you live.

The kitchen shutters were not properly closed and through the gap the sky was lightening. The dawn chorus, hitherto unnoticed, was gaining momentum. I had planned to be away from here before daybreak. Where had Sabrier got to?

A light footfall in the corridor. I didn't even have the energy or the will to defend myself, so if it was Blanc . . .

Sabrier entered, carrying a five-litre plastic container. I smelled petrol. 'Here you are. Petrol. It was in the garage.'

I didn't speak.

'Why are you going to burn the house?'

'I like fires.'

In fact the fire was for Gina; her cremation. My farewell gift. The house just happened to be there. I wasn't leaving her for others to maul, to cut up, to eviscerate. A shudder wracked my body. I pressed the tips of my fingers against my temples and they came away slick with sweat.

'What is it, 'Enley?' Sabrier took a step forward. I waved him away.

'Give me the petrol.'

From down in the cellar came a banging. 'Hey! You up there. Let us out.'

'Glad you reminded me,' I said softly and tossed the key to Sabrier. 'As soon as I start the fire, release them. If anyone comes after me I'll hold you personally responsible. Likewise if you sick the law onto me. I'll come looking for you, Sabrier – just like I came looking for Tillou.'

He lost colour, but his voice was steady as he replied. 'You worry needlessly, 'Enley. We have a bargain. I am very happy with my side of it.' He stuck out a hand. 'Start your fire. I will deal with everything else.'

I took the proffered hand, twisted a grin at him, and went. To the study to sit on the floor by Gina. I stroked her cheek. Was it my imagination, or was she already growing cold? I wanted somehow to convey to her my regret, my grief, and above all my love. But there was no spark. She was just a collection of dead organs. I was but a step removed myself: dead in all respects but the physical.

I unscrewed the cap of the container, twitched my nostrils at the sickly-sweet fumes that rose from within. Half of the five litres I splashed around the study, over furniture, curtains, and rugs; around, but not on, Gina. The other half I doled out among adjacent ground-floor rooms. Returning to the study I bumped into Dauphin, but he just nodded and smiled distantly.

On Tillou's desk was a heavy table-lighter that had the feel of gold. As I flicked it experimentally my gaze alighted on its late owner, slumped in the wheelchair, held there by the high sides. The shattered features seemed to jeer at me. With reason. Although technically I was the victor and he the vanquished, I had lost much more than I had gained.

Never was a victory more Pyrrhic than mine.

Lighter in hand, I went to Gina, drawn by invisible strings. I knelt, bent over her, pressing my lips to hers. Wishing her alive. Wretchedly. Uselessly.

I touched the lighter to the petrol-doused settee. A wall of flame instantly bloomed, singeing my eyebrows, and I retreated in haste. Out through the patio doors, across the terrace at a trot. No backward glance. The fire crackled and spluttered, already taking hold.

There was light enough to avoid obstacles, and following the route Gina and I had taken during our escape two nights ago (was it *really* only two?) I came quickly to the beach. The inflatable was where I had left it, the empty hold-all lying in the bottom. The relief I felt proved all too premature.

The first shot, a whip-crack from the bushes on my right, went wide, zinging off a rock. The second smacked into my right thigh and the impact was just enough to tip me over; I never realised sand was so unyielding. A triumphant Apache whoop and out of the shrubbery leapt Blanc, flourishing a machine pistol, a demoniacal puppet-figure in the glare of the mounting flames. As a souvenir of our last encounter, he had a bandaged ear, but his trigger finger was healthy enough. He opened up, firing as he ran at me. Belly-down on the beach, in the semi-darkness, I made a poor target and his bullets went everywhere except where he intended them; light automatic weapons have a tendency to climb. The short curved magazine emptied in about two seconds. And that was just too bad for him.

Now came my turn. I fired, once only, transforming his head into a bloody, featureless stump. He kept coming on though, a headless chicken, crossing the narrow strip of sand in a drunken totter to finally pitch into the water, raising a splash like a depth charge going off.

I got up on my knees: that was as much as I could manage for the moment. I was swaying like a poplar in a hurricane. Blanc floated face down by the inflatable. Dead with a capital D. He too, had had it coming. My stomach churned and vomit bubbled geyser-hot in my gullet and gushed out over the sand at the water's edge. I spat weakly, wiped goo from my chin, sweat from my eyes. Again it came, a foul-tasting eruption, sucking me dry, leaving me gasping and sobbing. Then a third attack, less gut-wrenching: bile, bitter and caustic, was all that remained. It drooled from my slack lips, dripped down my clothing. If Blanc's chums were out there waiting for an opportunity – here it was. I was theirs for the taking.

Behind me the roar of the flames intensified as something caved in with a crash. Incandescent reflections danced and shivered on the water; darkness had been banished by a fiery arcade, a ruby-red aura that shimmered and pulsated. I heard, or imagined I heard, shouting.

My leg was paining me now. Yet even in my battered, weakened state, the professionalism, the self-discipline, continued to function. I lurched over to the inflatable, hoping it wasn't full of the bullets that had been meant for me, and sort of toppled in. Dumped riot gun, shoulder rig, jemmy, the lot, into the hold-all. Nobody shot at me. Blanc had been alone after all.

The outboard fired at first go. I steered out of the bay, a shade unsteadily, then piled on the revs, skating across a blood-tinted sea. Flames leaped and roared on my left, but were soon behind me and I was in open water, aiming for the just discernible shoreline across the channel. Willing it nearer.

The sea, dark now and silken, that most capricious of elements, unrolled beneath me in a blur. It would leave no trace of my passing. It would also hide the evidence of my crimes. The sea was my accomplice.

About a mile offshore I heaved the hold-all over the side. I had left it partly unzipped to prevent an air pocket from forming inside and it sank readily, with only a solitary burp of protest. Moving about brought twinges from my thigh. I knelt and lowered my jeans, examined the wound as best I could in the poor light. It was hardly more than a graze. The skin around it was tender to the touch, but it wouldn't slow me down and that was all that really mattered.

I pressed on at speed between the ragged islets of Grand Ribaud, presently coming ashore in a narrow, V-shaped cove, the surf swirling about my craft like lather and nudging it up onto a steep pebbled beach.

Ordinarily I would have sunk the inflatable offshore, to further cover up my tracks. However, it now seemed a rather superfluous precaution. Whatever I did, I was finished in France.

The sun was just breaking the horizon, throwing up a saffron fan, diffusing the sky with pale light. Another, different, glow drew my eye, on the island. A twinkle, no more than that. Orange shot with red. I whispered a last goodbye to Gina and turned away.

I scrambled to the top of the overlapping rocks that enclosed the cove and set off, favouring my injured leg and coddling my perforated shoulder, across a flat grassy terrain towards the Giens highway.

Chapter Fifteen

I was clear of the area before the sirens started to wail and back in Marseilles for lunch.

My shoulder was stiff and sore by then, and medical attention a must. Thierry Mazé proved his worth all over again by drumming up a struck-off quack who, for a consultation fee that would have represented a week's income to legally-accredited members of his profession, performed the necessary services and left me strapped and smarting.

Collecting the Jag from Monaco came next. Unwise though it was to prolong my stay in France, I was not about to abandon that expensive piece of machinery so I booked on an Air Inter flight to Nice. I remained fairly confident that Sabrier would keep his side of the bargain and this was borne out up to a point by a late-afternoon TV newsflash which I caught over coffee in a waterfront bar: in reverential tones the newscaster announced a multiple murder – ten bodies had been discovered at a house on the Ile de Proquerolles, nine of them burned beyond recognition. A Toulon-based gang was suspected. Stay tuned for further developments. The bar erupted into an excited babble – stupefaction, horror, disbelief; to each his own reaction.

Mine was a mixture of all three. By my reckoning, there should have been three bodies in the house, plus Blanc. Which meant that Sabrier had left the Sabourins, Prost, and the other bodyguards to burn to death in the cellar. Eliminating all witnesses and rivals and no need to dirty his hands or his sensibilities. All he'd had to do was . . . walk out. A gloriously classic crime of omission. Not only that: technically all those deaths were now laid at *my* door. I stopped feeling so confident about Sabrier and tossed a coin on the table and went to catch my flight.

At Marseilles-Marignane airport my papers were perfunctorily checked, the first sign of abnormal police activity, though by and large internal flights would probably be exempt from close scrutiny. My false identity card raised no flickers. At the other end, Nice, nothing.

From Nice by helicopter to the heliport at Fontvieille, a residential suburb of Monaco built on reclaimed land, and thence by taxi through tourist-clogged streets to the port.

At the Bar du Port, Victor welcomed me effusively and sold me a stiff Pernod. No messages. I relieved him of the keys to the Jag and went to fetch the car from the lock-up garage on Avenue John Kennedy, where it reposed during my longer absences. My bona-fide papers, hidden in the front passenger-seat squab, were undisturbed. I was now obliged to revert to my true identity to conform to the car ownership documents. Additionally, my Swiss resident status and British passport ensured more respectful treatment from the police – in theory. I shredded the bogus papers and sprinkled them over a drain in the gutter. Goodbye Jules Leroy.

Then back on the road, the well-trodden path via Nice, Castellane, Digne – a bitter-sweet reminder of the day I met Gina. Driving fast, too fast. On roads that teemed with holiday traffic and swaying, overloaded Italian trailer vehicles, I averaged 100 kph. Madness.

North of Digne, in the village of Lajaire, I growled past a solitary jacket-less gendarme in debate with a man in a blood-spattered butcher's apron outside the *La Poste* building. Further on, as I accelerated out of a bend, I met a blue gendarmerie van going the other way. The two kepi-ed occupants eyed me balefully, frowning at my speed. These were my only sightings of the forces of law and order.

I drove through the night, halting only twice: once to refuel car and stomach, once for a short nap. Grenoble, hushed and lifeless at three in the morning, came and went. Then into the last lap, all autoroute, whipping the Jag up to 200 kph and more, exhilarating in the sensation of speed, the cool night air buffeting me through the open window.

At last, the frontier, the illuminated *Douanes* sign welcoming me like an old friend. On the far side, Geneva. Had Gina been waiting for me, asleep in my – our – bed, as she should have been, it would have been a true homecoming. But Gina was no more. And that special loving she had introduced into my loveless existence was also no more.

No more . . . no more . . . The words mocked me.

There are no French customs for vehicles entering Switzerland at the Thonex checkpoint. Decelerating for the Swiss border-post, I crossed the invisible line and entered my adopted country: I had made it! I was back in my sanctuary. Safe, for a while at least.

'*Bonjour, monsieur.*' The Swiss customs officer in his drab sludge-coloured outfit bent down to peer inside the car, bright suspicious eyes roving. At this hour of the day they would be short of trade. 'Are you carrying any goods?'

I shook my head.

'Your identity papers, please.'

I offered my Swiss residence permit and my UK passport, and he went off through a door marked POLICE in the long, low building at the roadside. A second officer stayed with me. He was young and therefore not yet de-humanised, and we chatted about this and that until the first officer reappeared, on the heels of a blue-uniformed policeman. They approached. The policeman was still adjusting his peaked cap but managed a curt nod, followed by a request to accompany him.

I stiffened inwardly. 'Is there some problem?' I asked, smiling a fixed, meaningless smile.

'A matter of . . . identification.'

Bullshit, was my private response to that. I got out just the same. I really had no alternative except to put my foot down and trust to the Jag's acceleration to extricate me. Without papers I wouldn't travel far.

Inside the office it was warm, uncomfortably so. At a desk against the wall a young, shirt-sleeved police officer was pecking painfully at a computer keyboard. He was engrossed in his labours and didn't look up.

A seat and coffee were offered. I declined the seat – I'd been sitting for most of the night – but accepted the coffee. The customs man went out of the office through a swing door; I glimpsed a stark, white-walled corridor before the door flapped shut. The police officer remained, rocking slightly on his heels, hands clasped behind his back. We ignored each other.

The customs man returned with two steaming plastic cups, depositing them with haste on the corner of the nearest desk, licking spilt coffee from scalded fingers. The policeman at the keyboard glanced up and laughed unsympathetically.

'That machine makes hot coffee,' he observed.

The other swore good-naturedly at him and handed me a cup. It *was* hot; I left it to simmer on a shelf behind me.

'What's this all about?' I said, with a show of part-bafflement, part-vexation.

'We are waiting for a telephone call, *monsieur*,' the police officer said, his smile flashing on and off like an Aldis lamp. 'Just a routine enquiry. Nothing to worry about.'

Sez him.

I tasted the coffee. It was drinkable in an emergency. This wasn't an emergency—not yet. The clock on the wall said 3.27. Antemeridian. It was a hell of a time of day to be cooling one's heels in a nick. The minute-hand edged onward in staccato jerks. I fumed. I fretted. I held my tongue – with difficulty. The hands had travelled round to 3.50 when, preceeded by a gust of self-importance, in breezed Inspector Klaus Diethard Wittwitz, scourge of the Geneva underworld. In train, naturally, was Sergeant Dumas, aglow as ever with brotherly love and goodwill to mankind.

'So you have returned to us, Mr Henley,' Wittwitz said in his impeccable English. His smile was broad and his teeth boosted to maximum candlepower.

I shrugged. 'Why shouldn't I? I live here – remember?'

He turned to the policeman. 'Have you searched him?'

'Er . . .'

'*Quel idiot!*' A gun sprang into Wittwitz's hand faster than a conjuring trick. Dumas was a fraction slower, but then his gun was bigger. 'Do it now!'

The policeman, sizzling with resentment, ambled over. '*Vous permettez, monsieur?*'

I reached for the sky in classic Western-fashion. The frisking was proficient but unproductive: I wasn't carrying so much as a nail file.

The policeman stepped back. 'Nothing, *monsieur l'inspecteur*.'

'This is a very dangerous man,' Wittwitz said sternly, as if lecturing a refractory child. 'You should not be so lax.' Back to me. 'Now then, Mr Henley. If you would be so kind as to come with me; I have a car waiting outside.'

'Before we leave,' I said, 'I'd like to know what's going on. I'd also like to call my lawyer.' At four in the morning? Jules would love me.

'You will not need a lawyer, Mr Henley. Not where you're going. As for what is . . . er . . . going on . . .' He stroked his elongated chin reflectively. The gun watched me. I'd looked down a lot of gun barrels lately; I was getting fed up with it. 'Shall we just say it's a continuation of the unresolved matter we discussed during our last meeting? In fact, one might almost say we are bringing it to a satisfactory resolution.'

What new evidence had come to light, I wondered? Jules had assured me I couldn't be extradited without incontestable proof. And even then the procedure would be lengthy and subject to appeal. So what, if anything, lay behind this Gestapo-style arrest?

'Shall we go?' Wittwitz reversed away from the door. Dumas came alongside me, took my arm. I shook him off, gave him a blistering glare that dented his case-hardened exterior about as much as would pissing on armour plate.

We went: Dumas, me, Wittwitz. The police officer bade us a courteous goodnight. Nice guy.

My car had been moved and now stood in a rank of more modest conveyances at the end of the building. A white Opel with police markings and uniformed officers in the front seats was waiting, engine running, exhaust dribbling blue smoke. As we moved towards it, a beat-up, German-registered motor bike, groaning under two beefy riders and enough camping gear for a troop of boy scouts, pulled away from the checkpoint. They pop-popped past us, faces swivelling enquiringly.

Then I was sliding along the back seat of the Opel, Dumas nudging from the rear; Wittwitz entered from the other side. I felt the clasp of cold steel around my right wrist: handcuffs. The snap of the ratchet had a chilling finality about it.

'Am I under arrest then, Inspector?' I asked, watching Dumas attach the other cuff to his own wrist.

Wittwitz snuggled up to me. He didn't have any choice – the back seat was a tight squeeze for three big 'uns.

He took his time about replying. Then he said, 'You are in custody. Let's leave it at that, Mr Henley.' He leaned forward. 'The airport, Sergeant.'

The airport!

The car accelerated smoothly away down the dual-carriageway, through the suburbs of Chêne-Bourg towards the city. I was frantically feeding data into my personal computer: two facts to consider and interpret. One: Wittwitz was still pursuing the Munich killing; two, I was going for a plane ride. Conclusion: extradition. But without the formalities of a formal application through the courts. Thus *illegal* extradition. Not that pointing out as much to Wittwitz would cause the minutest deviation from our arrow-straight course, let alone a U-turn. He would be a sight more *au fait* with Swiss law than I was. In any case, Wittwitz was not the instigator, merely the instrument. While the rank of Inspector in the Swiss police force is a shade more exalted than the same rank in Britain, it is still in the lower half of the police hierarchy and, unless Wittwitz was gambling with his career out of spite or financial gain, the operation had been authorized at the highest level.

I looked sideways past Dumas's lumpy profile, at the buildings flitting past, bathed in the pale orange of the street lights. We were fairly rocketing along the empty road. Dawn was still an hour ahead and Geneva, wisely, was not yet up and about. The traffic lights were with us – green, nothing but green. A privilege only the police seem to enjoy. On either side now it was all multi-storey blocks and trees: trees are everywhere in Genava.

Then we hit a red light and came shuddering down from 120 kph to zero in the space of fifty yards and who cared how much tyre tread got left behind on the road? The Swiss tax-payer could afford it.

A city refuse truck lurched out of a turning, grinding across the intersection in low gear. Rue de Malagnou, I read off the corner of a block of flats. One of the main thoroughfares into the city from the east. Not all that far from my apartment – any right turn along here would do. Funny how nostalgic you can get about a place you never really cared for when it seems likely you'll never see it again. Flashes of the recent past appeared, to trouble me, like images projected on a screen: the few, all-too-short days when

Gina, by her very presence, had transformed my apartment from a collection of rooms into a real home. The images were infinitely painful. The most painful of all was only twenty-four hours old.

The lake, black and glossy like ink, opened out on our right as we sped across Pont du Mont Blanc to the north side of the city. It was a dry night – morning, I mean; no rain, except on me. I had my own private depression.

An Aéroport direction sign glowed from an overhead gantry. We rumbled through the cobbled Place des 27 Canons and down into the underpass beneath the railway, then out into the long straight of Rue de la Servette. The airport beacon was in sight, suffusing the night with an alternating white and green corona. Not far now. And precious little prospect for a miraculous escape; I wasn't Houdini and the handcuffs weren't made for slipping out of. Even if they were that still left me in a four-to-one minority. Lousy arithmetic. Forget it, forget it. Apathy and weariness were weaving their insidious spells. Notions of escape faded into ethereal oblivion.

Up ahead a line of illuminated lettering crawled over the rooftops: AEROPORT GENEVA-COINTRIN; then one after another, the sodium lights along the road to the airfreight terminal appeared. At the T-junction, where the road joins the RN1 autoroute to Lausanne, we went left and slowed. Wittwitz was on the edge of his seat again, directing the driver in an undertone.

We swung into the Route de l'Aéroport, but left it almost immediately, taking a narrow road, hemmed in by high concrete walls.

'You just took a wrong turn,' I said facetiously. 'The air terminal's back there.' I jerked my thumb backwards at the lit-up area, receding behind us.

All I got for my whimsy was an elbow in the ribs from Dumas which jolted my wounded shoulder. I gritted my teeth and pictured him spit-roasted over a slow fire.

The walled road led directly onto a part of the airport apron. It was overshadowed by the blank end-wall of a flat-roofed, windowless building – probably the freight terminal. An assortment of aeronautical hardware was standing around, doing nothing, and I guessed we were in a maintenance area. Just a kilometre away lay the French border; a five-minute jog, say. I was in no rush to cross it though. Right now, France was as hot as Switzerland.

The uniformed policeman in the front passenger seat got out. So did Wittwitz, then Dumas, who, as he wriggled his bulky frame out of the car, wrenched my arm so badly that the knife wound reopened. Warm blood trickled behind the dressing.

'Take it easy,' I protested. Predictably he ignored my plea. I seethed quietly and stuck close to him to prevent further damage.

Then I saw the helicopter and stopped thinking about how I'd love to stake Dumas out on an ant-hill.

It was parked between two single-engined aircraft and the main rotor over the cabin was revolving lazily. The fuselage was white and egg-shaped, with a single black stripe running the length of the tail rotor boom, and it had skis instead of wheels. Apart from the row of registration letters along the lower fuselage, it was undistinguished by any markings.

Wittwitz and Dumas frog-marched me towards it. We were perhaps thirty yards away when a man jumped down from the open cabin door, and called a monosyllabic greeting. The turbulence from the rotor flipping past overhead tossed his hair about and, though there was ample clearance, he ducked and came forward at a crouch. A second man, plump and wearing a trilby, stepped down from the helicopter, but stayed by the door, arms folded, face in shadow.

'*Wie geht's?*' Wittwitz said as the stranger came up. Hands were shaken. Not mine though; I was beyond the hand-shaking pale. The stranger gave me a flinty appraisal and spoke to Wittwitz in quickfire German of which I understood less than one word in ten. Wittwitz answered in the same lingo and got a grunt from the stranger. He was about my age, as far as I could tell in the indifferent lighting, and clad in a grey suit, quite well-cut. Fair hair, thinning on top; thin, stretched features.

'So you are the famous Mr Henley,' he said in halting but grammatical English. 'My name is Vogel. *Bundestaatpolizei*.'

A kraut cop. As I suspected. The bastards were actually going to airlift me to Deutschland. It wasn't a prospect I relished.

'This is illegal,' I said to Wittwitz, without much hope.

'I suggest you complain to the authorities when you arrive in Germany.'

Such humour.

'It's illegal,' I repeated.

Wittwitz remained unmoved. 'So is murder, Mr Henley.'

'You've got the wrong man.'

The Kraut, Vogel, snapped handcuffs on my right wrist and stood aside while Dumas removed his. I was glad to be shot of *him* anyway.

Wittwitz gave me a pitying look. 'Do not waste your protestations on me.'

'Condemned without a trial, eh?' I said through stiff lips. 'You can't do this, Wittwitz. Switzerland is supposed to be a democracy. Christ, man, I've lived here for seven fucking years. I pay my taxes. I've got rights!' I was shouting.

'Mr Henley,' Vogel said, and he was as calm as I was agitated. 'You gave up your rights when you killed in my country. When we prove you are . . . are . . .' he appealed to Wittwitz for help, '*Schuldig. Wie heisst man in Englisch*?'

'Guilty.'

'Yes. When we prove you are guilty, it will do no good to speak of rights.'

Another brief exchange in German between Wittwitz and Vogel, a spate of '*Auf wiedersehens*', and I was towed away to the helicopter, where Vogel's team-mate hooked a second set of cuffs on me.

We sat behind the pilot on a segmented passenger seat, a three-in-one job with head-rests. Vogel fastened my seat-belt. Considerate of him.

The pilot, youngish with blond cropped hair, half-turned his head.

'*Heben Sie ab*,' Vogel ordered.

The pilot spoke into his mouthpiece, got the go-ahead there too, and proceeded to wind up the rotors. Through the glass-bubble nose of the cabin Wittwitz and Dumas looked as if they were in a wind tunnel, their clothes flung against their bodies, their hair tossing crazily.

Our ascent was fast and steep and left my stomach on the runway. Voices crackled through the R/T set – just general radio traffic. The sky was clear and growing light in the east. Three mornings running now I had seen dawn break. It's a lovely and often dramatic sight, but I'd willingly have exchanged it for a decent night's sleep in my own bed.

Wittwitz and Dumas were gnome-ish figures on the tarmac, several hundred feet below. I wouldn't miss them at all. The helicopter slanted across the sky, flying parallel to the northern shore of Lac Léman, and they were lost from sight. Geneva, a swarm of twinkling lights fused into a lustrous mass at the centre, fell away and now, as we picked up speed, and the noise and vibration escalated in roughly equal amounts, there was only the empty spread of the lake and, beyond it, Switzerland, just bumps and bulges, vague, amorphous. Beyond Switzerland lay my future; a future as vague and amorphous as the landscape. And guaranteed unrosy.

Chapter Sixteen

We flew to Munich and I thus came full circle.

To Munich, but not to the grim, fortress-like *Polizeiamt* – Police Headquarters – in Karlstrasse. Instead we landed on a football pitch, some kilometres from the city centre, and were whisked by a black Mercedes with black tinted windows along a ruler-straight dual carriageway, thence through an industrialised suburb to a house at the very end of a tree-lined cul-de-sac. A typically modern-traditional model-railway-set building, five storeys high, steep orange-tiled roof, beige stucco walls pock-marked with small square windows divided into four panes of equal size. Harmonising perfectly with its neighbours; it would rate no more than a casual glance, if that.

My room was on the top floor. Hot, airless. A cranked strip of ceiling where the slope of the roof encroached on it. Bars on the inside of the window; narrow, prison-issue bed; table with a laminated top that was peeling away at the edges; two upright chairs that looked ready to fall apart if you so much as flashed your backside at them. On the linoleum floor, a rectangle of pink carpet with a burn hole in the middle.

Comfort and character rating: zero.

Leading off, behind a sliding door, a toilet with

washbasin. I visited it and pissed long and loud into cracked and stained ceramic. Flushed it noisily, drowning the doom-knell of a nearby church clock. Ever noticed how solemn and funereal German church bells sound? Apposite, considering my circumstances.

Too tired even to agonize over the turn of events I flopped on the bed, fully dressed, shoes and all, and the lights went out all over me.

When I awakened, it was not because I had slept my fill but on account of some inconsiderate person shaking my shoulder. As I came to, he quit shaking and stepped back from the bed in haste – the haste of vigilance, not panic. A tallish, completely bald man in a pale grey suit with a maroon handkerchief stuffed carelessly – or arranged carefully – in his top pocket, and a matching slim tie.

'Schmidt,' he said by way of introduction. His top lip had a kind of built-in sneer, lifting lop-sidedly when he spoke, and he lisped ever so slightly. And he really was bald – I've seen more hairs on an egg.

'Hello, Schmidt,' I said quickly, vocal chords still furred with sleep. My watch showed twelve o'clock and the sunlight swarming into the room made it noon. I had slept for just two hours. I felt used-up, wrung-out. Dirty too; I hadn't washed since . . . since I couldn't remember when. My chin, when massaged, sounded like a saw cutting wood. And my wounds were sore and throbbing.

I wanted to ask for a drink, but my tongue was stuck to the roof of my mouth.

'Would you like a drink?' Schmidt enquired, mind-reading to perfection. His English was as smooth and natural as my German was almost non-existent.

I nodded and he fetched water in a tooth-glass. I

never realised water was such amazingly drinkable stuff. Resolved to try it more often. The thought raised a hollow internal laugh; water would very likely form part of my daily diet from now on.

'Come.' Schmidt reversed to the door. Not once did his incisive blue eyes leave me. Under his armpit, the line of his well-cut jacket swelled revealingly; his right armpit, which made him left-handed. These days police usually wore their hardware in the small of the back where it was less obvious; Schmidt was either ultra-individualistic or high enough in the law enforcement strata to play by his own rules. The latter, was my bet.

'Come,' he said again. 'There is a person downstairs who wishes to see you.' He flung open the door and barked a command at two hunky plain-clothes men lounging there. Guns were displayed, and not the kind you keep under your armpit either: these were mean-looking Ingram Model 10 machine-pistols, fitted with sound suppressors, a watered-down silencer that doesn't inhibit muzzle velocity. More than anything else, they impressed upon me the deadly seriousness of my predicament.

The four of us descended by a succession of right-angled staircases to the first floor where I was shown into a room at the back of the house, facing out over a large and unkempt garden with a cluster of young, thickly-foliaged conifers at the bottom and a double row of the same species along either side. An effective natural screen.

Schmidt had left me standing-at-ease in the centre of the room which contained only a long oval table encircled by matching chairs. The walls were painted insipid green. I dwelled uninterestedly on the view beyond the garden, of a factory – a grey shoe-box building topped by a pair of tall metal chimneys that vented thin plumes of smoke, the only cicatrice on the picture-postcard spread of blue. My thoughts were on another plane, with Gina, when the tattoo of high heels on wood ruptured them.

'Mr Henley.' Schmidt's voice was quietly authoritative.

I revolved slowly through one hundred and eighty degrees, my gaze passing over Schmidt, then Vogel, coming to rest on the woman: a woman last seen comatose at Schloss Thomashoff many, many centuries ago. A ghost of my forsworn past, risen from the dead to condemn me.

She was dressed in a lightweight cream costume that had clearly cost a mint, and her shoes and handbag toned precisely. The hat too, a flat-brimmed hidalgo style, tilted jauntily. The whole ensemble shouted money. She was quite a looker: much, much better without the bullet-hole in her throat.

Under my scrutiny, she first paled then reddened. Neither of us spoke.

'You know each other, I think,' Schmidt said.

'Do we?' Maintaining my innocent stance to the last. Going down with flags fluttering from the masthead, guns booming a final defiant salvo – that was me.

'Frau Thomashoff?' Schmidt said and his voice was a confident purr. '*Kennen Sie oder nicht diesen Mann?*'

Do you know this man or not? Even my German was capable of unravelling that sentence.

Her eyes were blue-grey, widely spaced, below blue-tinted eyelids, the only make-up she wore other than a subtle shading along the cheekbone. She looked younger than I remembered; maybe it was the absence of cosmetics. She would be what . . . thirty-four, thirty-five?

As we stared at each other, a spark leapt across the gap, a telepathic link-up that brought a hot flush to my body and fomented a wild surge of hope.

'Frau Thomashoff?' Schmidt was tapping his foot ostentatiously. Vogel, shrewder perhaps, glanced from the woman to me in puzzlement.

Then, ever so, ever so slowly, almost imperceptibly, she shook her head.

'*Was meint das*?' Schmidt fired at her, perplexed.

Another shake, firmer, more vehement.

'This is not the man,' she said in English, each word pronounced clearly without even the tiniest tremor. 'This is not the man,' she repeated more forcibly. A second spark fizzled between us, then she turned and walked to the door, letting herself out.

One of the Ingram-wielding sentries thrust an enquiring head through the door as Frau Thomashoff clip-clopped past him. Vogel telegraphed a resigned gesture. Schmidt was oblivious; he was giving a fair imitation of a pressure cooker on the boil. Any moment now he would go off pop.

I was no less mind-blown: I had accepted as inevitable my identification by Frau Thomashoff and the consequences thereof. Now . . . now my thoughts were a crawling, writhing snake-pit. Why had she let me off the hook? *Why*? Never mind debating the point, more pragmatic counsel interposed – just be grateful. Accept the gift.

The same head was back at the door. '*Sie ist gegangen.*'

Schmidt was cooling to a gentle simmer. '*Scheisse,*' he said without emotion. '*Doppel-scheisse.*' He glinted at me. 'She is lying. I know it. You know it. If only I knew *why*.'

He pounded fist into palm over and over again,

then stormed out, still pounding away, leaving Vogel to escort me back to my eyrie.

During the day I was fed and watered and provided with the means of removing my facial fungus. Also a handful of tatty paperbacks and, most welcome of all, a two-days old *Daily Telegraph*. At my request, a doctor came to change the dressings on my wounds, no questions asked. Though it still hurt to move my arm, both wounds were healing fast and cleanly.

Next morning, as I was polishing off my third cup of breakfast coffee, Schmidt came in and crashed down on the spare chair, heavily and to the accompaniment of ominous splinterings. He pitched into me without so much as a '*Guten Morgen*'.

'There is something that puzzles me . . .'

'Me too,' I interrupted. 'Like what am I doing here? Like who the hell are you? Not the police, that's for sure.'

'Never mind who I am; I have all the authority I need under German law. Just tell me this – why did you shoot Mrs Thomashoff with a different gun from the one you used on the Frenchman? He was wearing an empty shoulder-holster. Did you kill him with his own gun?'

'All this talk of guns! You're crazy.'

The lip sneered. 'Which movement are you with, Henley? Hey? The Red Army Faction?' He proceeded to reel off seven or eight meaningless titles and sets of initials.

I acted dumb. Not that I needed to act.

'*Action Directe*, then. Or FP-25. Or what about the CCC?'

I stared at him uncomprehendingly.

'The Greens?' he said finally with a hint of desperation.

'If you're asking am I a terrorist – the answer is don't be so bloody stupid.'

His face clouded over. 'Careful, Henley, careful. I could easily get nasty with you . . .'

'. . . But you won't,' I finished for him. 'Face up to it, Schmidt: you've dropped a clanger. Made a mistake. I'm no terrorist, never have been, never likely to be. Furthermore, you heard your star witness – she didn't recognise me.'

'She was lying,' he said slowly and departed without another word.

I didn't see him again for two days: two monotonous, dragging, solitary-confined days. Time for reflection, so when I wasn't sleeping, reading, or moping, I reflected . . . no, I grieved. Over Gina. Over all those deaths. Over thirty-eight wasted, self-destructive years.

I was much changed. Bordering on unrecognizable. Even to save my own skin I doubted I was capable any longer of dispensing death. I'd had my fill and more. Since I couldn't actually go back, make myself virgin pure again, I would have to compromise; make do with the retirement I had once coveted and latterly come to despise. Climb right out of the cesspool. A lot of shit would still cling to me, but in time . . .

If Gina had lived I would have done it for her. Why not do it for her memory? Make a bad debt come good. I owed her that much. I owed her infinitely more.

Stargazing. That's all these exalted declarations would amount to, unless I succeeded in prising Schmidt's grip from my short hairs.

* * *

On my fifth morning in custody Schmidt delivered my breakfast in person. A hard-boiled egg, various meats and salamis cut thin, coarse-grained brown bread, also cut thin. I wasn't hungry, but I managed the egg and a couple of circles of salami while Schmidt stood with hands clasped behind his back, a plain pink folder tucked under his arm, gazing out at skies that contained more cloud than of late.

When I had clearly eaten my fill, he came and sat across from me. The chair bore up manfully.

'Do you find Frau Thomashoff attractive?' was his initial – and bewildering – ranging shot.

'Frau Who? Oh, you mean the lady who doesn't know me from Adam.'

The pink folder was in his hand; in a fit of pique he lashed me across the face with it. I jumped up, sending my chair spinning, instinctively preparing to meet violence with violence. But there was a gun between us and I was on the wrong side of it. My temper plummeted from boiling point to deep freeze while Schmidt was flipping the safety catch to 'fire'.

'Come on, Henley.' He was ready to let me have it; his finger was up tight against the trigger. All he wanted was an excuse and I would be meat on the mortuary slab. 'What are you waiting for, Henley? Come on. Save us the cost of keeping you in prison for the rest of your life.'

I would have loved to have had a go at him, but self-immolation wasn't written in my tea-leaves. I backed off.

As the heat went out of the atmosphere, he covered up his undoubted over-reaction with the nearest I ever saw him come to a grin. He waggled the gun in semi-apology and slid it back behind his lapel.

'Sit down,' he said, and I fetched the upended chair

and did like the man said. 'We have talked again to Frau Thomashoff. She now confirms you are the man who shot her.'

The big bluff. I didn't believe him for a second.

'So you may as well confess,' he said stolidly. 'It may help lighten your sentence in court if you are co-operative.'

The sun had been skulking; now it came out and stabbed a sword of light through the window. Schmidt's bald head glowed like a light bulb.

I let my disbelief hang out.

'It is possible you will be sent to an open prison,' he battled on. 'The conditions there are . . . are . . .' He scowled. 'Well?'

'Confront me with Frau Thomashoff again. Let me hear it from her.'

'You . . . filth!' The table jumped under his balled fist. 'You think you are so smart! We know all we need to know about you!' Suddenly he calmed. 'Unfortunately, what we can prove is another matter. If you were not an *Ausländer* . . . if you were a German, we would very quickly make you confess. Very *very* quickly.' He got to his feet slowly and tiredly, like Atlas carrying the weight of the whole world on his shoulders. Though he was probably a year or two younger than me, right now he could have passed for fifty.

'In one hour from now you will be released.' He was very erect, looking straight ahead. 'Where do you wish to be taken?'

I blinked at him, too stunned to reply.

'Where do you wish to go? Geneva?' His eyes lowered, focused on me.

'I . . . nowhere,' I gasped. 'Just . . . just open the door and . . . I'll walk away.'

Fast.

'Very well. Please be ready in one hour.'

I was ready there and then, but spent the hour as fruitfully as I could, making myself presentable – not easy in a shirt that hasn't seen the inside of a washing-machine in six days. At the appointed time I was taken downstairs by a member of my guard detail. No machine-pistol in attendance. I was officially a law-abiding citizen again.

Schmidt and Vogel stood in the entrance hall. Vogel returned my wallet and other personal belongings. No receipt to sign; this wasn't a police station. The front door was open. Sunlight streamed in, symbolising freedom.

'Before I leave,' I said to Schmidt, 'there's something I'd like to know.'

'Yes?' His manner was frigid, unresponsive.

'Who, or what, are you exactly?'

A bleakness came over him. 'One day, Henley . . . one day I think you will find out. I think we shall meet again, you and I. *Sie sind Dreck*!' Spittle flew. '*Scum!* And scum always rises to the surface. Next time, when you rise to the surface, I shall be there to welcome you.'

I was too exhilarated to take offence. 'Not this scum, Schmidt. No rising for me. On the other hand, should you happen to cross my path without your army of goons to back you up, I might . . . just might . . . be tempted.'

The corner of his mouth lifted, exposing his teeth. We had perfect mutual understanding. I winked back, conveyed a nod to Vogel, and strolled out into the warm morning air, and its sweetness was nectar on my tongue. Behind me the door shut. I had a feeling that if I were to return to the house tomorrow

I would find no Schmidt, no Vogel, no goons; no trace in fact of their ever having occupied the place. Nor indeed that *I* had spent the best part of a week up on the fifth floor.

It was a spooky, disturbing feeling.

In the shade of a spindly sycamore tree on the pavement was a woman. Standing very still and taut, hands interlocked before her. Gone the prim and proper cream suit; in its place a frothy white dress, neckline plunging towards soaring hem, the twain not quite meeting.

She smiled, shyly to begin with, then easily, boldly. A smile of invitation.

I strode down the short paved path and joined her under the tree.

'Frau Thomashoff,' I said and executed a stiff little Prussian bow. 'What a pleasure.'

The smile softened. 'Mr Henley,' she acknowledged with a certain dignity. 'I hope you are well.'

'Very, thank you.' So formal.

'Quite near here is the Englischer Garten. Let us walk there. We have much to talk about.'

'*Zu befehl, gnädige Frau.*' I said, dredging up a line from an old war movie.

She chuckled, a delicious babbling-brook sound. 'You and I must get to know each other,' she said as we moved out from under the tree. She took my arm. 'Tonight we shall dine and drink champagne at the best restaurant in town – the Käfer-Schänke; you know it? In Schumanstrasse.'

'Only by repute.'

'You will be the handsomest man there, I am quite sure of it.'

'And you, *gnädige Frau*, will be the loveliest lady in all of Munich.'

'How gallant!'

'And afterwards?' I said. 'After the meal?'

We hurried across a busy road. Just ahead was a bridge over a canal.

'We go that way, over the bridge. The gardens are on the other side.' Then, demurely, 'Afterwards? Afterwards I will take you to my home. Since I divorced my husband I am living permanently by München. I have this small house by the Ammersee – a lake to the west of the city.' Her eyes found mine and a galaxy of promises twinkled. 'But why do I tell you this? You have been there before, surely you remember . . . ?'

THE END

Aspire Publishing

1 UNIT

No. T.002

SAVE 10 Units

and exchange them for any **1** Aspire book of your choice

SAVE 20 Units

and exchange them for any **3** Aspire books of your choice

THIS OFFER IS VALID INDEFINITELY

Redeemable at any stockist of Aspire books or by post to:

Aspire Publishing
16 Connaught Street, LONDON W2 2AF

For the name of your nearest stockist telephone, fax or write to:

Aspire Publishing
Voucher Redemption Dept.
8 Betony Rise
EXETER EX2 5RR
Tel: 01392 25 25 16
Fax: 01392 25 25 17

ASPIRE
1 UNIT
No. T.002

Aspire Books are available from bookshops, supermarkets, department and multiple stores throughout the UK, or can be ordered from the following address:

Aspire Publishing
Mail Order Department
8 Betony Rise
EXETER EX2 5RR

Please add £0.50 PER ORDER for postage and packing irrespective of quantity.